William Quintard Ketchum

The Life and Work of the Most Reverend John Medley, D.D.

First Bishop of Fredericton and Metropolitan of Canada

William Quintard Ketchum

The Life and Work of the Most Reverend John Medley, D.D.
First Bishop of Fredericton and Metropolitan of Canada

ISBN/EAN: 9783337187279

Printed in Europe, USA, Canada, Australia, Japan

Cover: Foto ©Raphael Reischuk / pixelio.de

More available books at **www.hansebooks.com**

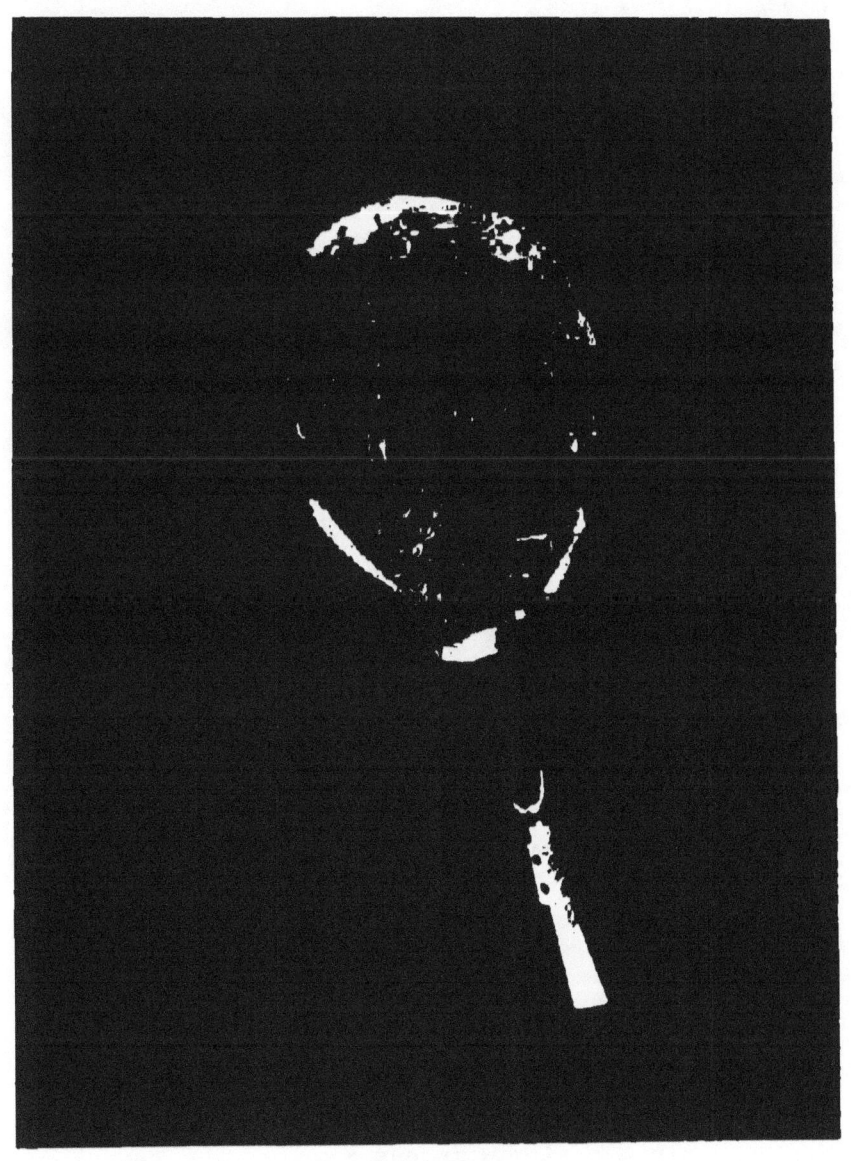

THE LATE THE MOST REVEREND JOHN MEDLEY, D. D.,
LORD BISHOP OF FREDERICTON AND METROPOLITAN OF CANADA.

THE LIFE AND WORK

OF THE

Most Reverend John Medley, D. D.

First Bishop of Fredericton and Metropolitan of Canada.

.

---- ✠ ----

BY

WILLIAM QUINTARD KETCHUM, D. D.

Rector of Saint Andrews, N. B.,

AND

Honorary Canon of the Cathedral, Fredericton.

---- ✠ ----

SAINT JOHN, N. B.
J. & A. McMillan, Printers, Publishers, Etc.
1893.

PREFACE.

The writer has ventured upon this work at the suggestion of many whose opinions and wishes are greatly valued. The brief history of the Church in earlier years will, it is believed, be of interest. By very many throughout the Anglican Communion the name of John Medley, the first Bishop of Fredericton, is well known, and held in high regard. His life and work are worthy of enduring record. •

The writer had the opportunity, in his early years, of personal knowledge of much to which he has referred in those pages. He was a Divinity Student at the time of the Bishop's arrival in the Diocese, and was the first Deacon he ordained. For fourteen years, with rare exceptions, he was associated almost daily with the Bishop. As Secretary of the Diocesan Church Society, for more than forty years, he was present with him at all the meetings of that Society. In later years, in charge of a Parish at some distance from Fredericton, the writer was favoured with frequent visits.

In further justification of this undertaking, the following extract of a letter is subjoined. It was written shortly before that attack of illness from the effects of which the Bishop did not recover: "I cannot let your letter pass without a few words of thanks and of hearty return of most affectionate regard. Your home has always been to me a resting place in all the troubles and cares which of necessity fall on the head of the Bishop of the Diocese, and I know not when I have been more entirely able to shake off those cares than when under your hospitable roof, and in those happy services we have enjoyed together. . . . I feel fully assured of your firm affection. . . . . I need not ask your prayers and those of all your household. They are mine, I know, before I ask them."

The writer desires to express his great obligations for much assistance in his work, and for the use of documents by which he has been enabled to exhibit the life and character of the Bishop, as far as possible, in his own words.

He is especially indebted to the Rev. W. O. Raymond, M. A., Rector of St. Mary's, St. John, for the use of old S. P. G. reports, and other works which supplied important information, as well as for valuable assistance in other ways.

THE RECTORY,
St. Andrews, N. B., Canada,
May 25th, 1893.

CONTENTS.

(13)

CHAPTER IX.

CHAPTER X.

CHAPTER XI.

CHAPTER XII.

CHAPTER XIII.

CHAPTER XIV.

CHAPTER XV.

CHAPTER XVI.

CHAPTER XVII.

CHAPTER I

NATIVE AND FRENCH POPULATION — ARRIVAL OF THE LOYALISTS.

THE origin of the Church of England in New Brunswick is peculiar In almost every instance, elsewhere, the establishment of the Church has been the result of the work of missionaries in places where previously there was little knowledge of the truth. So it was in this Province before the time of the American Revolution. The inhabitants in the interior of the country were native Indians. Religious instruction was afforded them by Roman Catholic missionaries. Theirs must have been an arduous, self-denying work, and worthy of high regard. At intervals along the coast, and on portions of the river banks, were French settlers, who shared with the natives in the ministrations of the French priests. After the conquest of Quebec, and the final triumph of the British arms in the prolonged contest waged with France in America, a few English settlements were established on the St. John and Miramichi rivers, at Passamaquoddy, and in the County of Westmorland. The great majority of the new-comers were of Puritan stock, and strongly antagonistic to the Church of England. With the exceptions referred to, the whole Province at the time of which we speak, was for the most part, an unbroken forest.

All at once a great change came over the scene. That sad, unhappy war, between Great Britain and the Colonies, was at an end. Separation and independence were secured. Among those who contended to the last on the Royalist side were those who were members of the Church of England, resident in New York, Connecticut, and the adjoining states

B

of New England. Their position was necessarily a trying one. They could not endure subjection to the recently established republican government, and they were objects of aversion to the majority now in the ascendancy. The downfall of the monarchy seemed to imply the downfall of the Church.[1] Excepting in the City of New York, and in a few other favoured places, the ministrations of the Church of England ceased. In some places they were forbidden by the civil authority. Among the Loyalist minority were many of considerable means and culture, who, previous to the war, had occupied prominent positions in their several localities.

It must have been a trying wrench to leave their homes, in many instances so dear, for new, untried regions. This, those loyal to their Church and King felt must be done, at all hazards. In their migration we are somewhat reminded of what poets told, ages ago, of early settlements on the coasts of the Mediterranean. There was, however, one great difference. In the latter case, everything was attractive to the exiles in the way of climate and many other advantages. The Loyalists left comfortable homes, and a more favourable climate, for that of New Brunswick, with its long, stern winters, its native Indians, its unbroken forests. Aid, indeed, was generously and promptly afforded by the British Government. Means of transport were pro-

---

[1] How little did those hardy, devoted men know of the future of the Church which they considered was "finished" in the United States! There it is now passed from "darkness to dawn." Merging in fuller light, the American Church is to-day the most important branch of the Anglican Communion outside the British Isles. There is no Diocese in the Dominion of Canada to compare with that of Connecticut, from whence a large portion of the Loyalists came. It has its churches, schools, hospitals, and church homes, with over one hundred and fifty clergy. A church recently destroyed by fire in the Parish of Stamford, whence one of the earliest missionaries in New Brunswick came, has lately been rebuilt at a cost of about $200,000. Surrounding the church are grand buildings for schools, a church home, and hospital.

vided for those who wished to seek new homes. On the 18th May, 1783, the first band of exiles, numbering three thousand souls, landed near the mouth of the River St. John, where is now the flourishing commercial city of that name. The father of the present writer was one of those exiles. He was at the age of thirteen. In after years he would tell of that landing on the shore, of the brushwood extending to the water's edge, and of the encampment on the banks of the harbour. In the same year vessels continued to arrive throughout the summer, and a considerable party of disbanded soldiers were added to the colonists.

At the time we speak of New Brunswick formed a part of the Province of Nova Scotia. Careful and minute arrangements were made by the government for the comfort of the new settlers. Farming utensils, seed, and other necessaries were liberally provided. To each family tracts of land were granted from three hundred to six hundred acres. Over and above two thousand acres in every township were allotted toward the support of a clergyman, and one thousand acres for the maintenance of a Church school. A small minority of the refugees were non-conformists. Several clergymen of the Church of England accompanied the new settlers. At that time there does not appear to have been a minister of any other communion. Soon after, by the kind and bounteous aid of the Society for the Propagation of the Gospel, Loyalist clergymen from the new Republic arrived. To that Society many of the most important missions in the colonies, now independent, owed their maintenance. The seed, thus cast upon the waters, was plainly seen after many days. It can be traced out to-day. It was now felt that grants from the Society should be transferred to those in greatest need and to loyal subjects of the Crown. By this means men well trained and well fitted for most trying work were provided with

partial means of support. Among the number were gradu-
ates from King's College—now Columbia—New York.
They had received ordination in England. The names of
many of these devoted men are remembered with reverence
and deep regard. Opportunity has not been often found
to minister to congregations like those which met together
in those trying times. The very line they had taken, their
loyalty so fully proved, the trials they were called to undergo,
their cheerful endurance, marked them as men of no ordinary character.

It is hard to imagine greater difficulties than those which
beset the work of the clergy at the period of that early
settlement. Though in most instances roads were wanting,
and there were only paths through the primeval forest, the
most distant residents were not neglected. Ere long, as the
country prospered, additional missionaries were provided for
by the Society in England. Churches were built and schools
established. In many respects there was much wanting,
which churchmen of our modern days look for and provide.
But, best of all, sound teaching in the principles of the
Church was uniformly afforded. The young, both in the
schools and in their homes, were well trained in the teaching of the catechism and prayer book. Whenever public
services were performed there was a large attendance of
devout worshippers.

The following interesting account has been kindly furnished by the Honorable Mr. Justice Hanington, respecting
one of the few pre-Loyalist settlers who was a churchman:

The first English settler at Shediac was Wm. Hanington, Esq.,
of London, England, who came there early in 1775 in company
with a friend, a Mr. Roberts, who only remained a short time, and
then returned to Europe. Mr. Hanington had purchased from the
representatives of Governor Williams a tract of about five thousand
acres of land, thinking it lay near Halifax, but on his arrival found

it was at "Chediak." There were then no other settlers but a few
families of French Acadians about that harbour. The feeling
against their then recent conquerors was strong, and, in consequence, Mr. Hanington was subject to many privations incident to
the early settlement of the country. Mr. Hanington for some years,
so far as English neighbours went, was alone, but quite early in the
present century, having afforded every encouragement to good
neighbours, several families were added to the neighbourhood ; and
as soon as two or three could be gathered together he began and
maintained, till the advent of a clergyman to the parish, morning
prayers and evening services each Sunday. This good work, as the
families increased, was very successful, and has borne good fruit in
creating and fostering a strong Church feeling in the village. As
early as 1810 works of the S. P. C. K. were kept and circulated as
part of the Church work at Shediac, and these books may yet be
found doing missionary work for the Church. The rector of Sackville, the late Rev. Mr. Milner, occasionally visited Shediac, which
was then within his charge, and administered the sacraments and
ordinances as often as he could. In about the year 1824, chiefly
through the liberality of the S. P. G., and of Mr. Hanington, the
present church was erected in the parish, and the Rev. Mr. Arnold
took charge there until about 1831, when he was succeeded by the
Rev. Mr. Black, after whose removal to Sackville in 1836 the late
Dr. Jarvis was inducted and remained rector there until his death
in 1881. Shediac was visited by the Lord Bishop of Nova
Scotia about 1823, it being a part of his Diocese. He came there
in one of H. M. warships, and also then visited Prince Edward
Island. The parish was again visited and confirmations held by
the Bishop of Nova Scotia down to about 1843, and since the year
1845 it has been under the pastoral charge of our late Lord Bishop
Medley, whose constant visitations have done so much to maintain
a good Church feeling there.

CHAPTER II

NEW BRUNSWICK SET APART FROM NOVA SCOTIA — AN ARCHDEACONRY.

MEANWHILE, the Province of New Brunswick was set apart from that of Nova Scotia. A separate legislature was assigned, and a governor appointed as a representative of the Crown.[1] As with the clergy, many of the laity were men of culture, and well fitted for the office of legislators. Of such men were the officials of the first separately established rule in New Brunswick composed. They were, without exception, members of the Church of England. Hence it came about that, in addition to original grants from the Crown, considerable portions of land were assigned for the maintenance of the Church. Provision was made for grammar schools in the several counties, under the control of the rector and local Church authorities. By the interest and exertion of Sir Howard Douglas, the lieutenant governor at the time referred to, King's College was established at Fredericton. A handsome building was erected; it was endowed with six thousand acres of land and about £2,000 a year from the provincial revenues. The management was vested in a council of members of the Church of England, with power to confer degrees.

[1] The Royal instructions to Governor Carleton of August 18th, 1784, minutely describe the steps to be taken in the organization of the new Province. Section 70 reads thus: " You shall take especial care that God Almighty " be devoutly and duly served throughout your government, the Book of " Common Prayer as by law established read each Sunday and holy day, and " the blessed sacrament administered according to the rites of the Church of " England."

The year 1787 formed a marked era in the history of the Colonial Church. The Rev. Charles Inglis, D. D., was consecrated Bishop of Nova Scotia, that Diocese then including what is now the Diocese of Fredericton. His son, the Right Reverend John Inglis, was consecrated Bishop in 1825. In the following year he visited New Brunswick and confirmed one thousand seven hundred and twenty persons. Many of these were advanced in years, who, in their youthful days, had left their early homes. On that occasion the Bishop consecrated no less than nineteen churches. In the year 1832 the Bishop visited the north and eastern shores. He travelled eight hundred miles and confirmed in seven different places. A third visitation in 1835 occupied two months, when eight hundred persons were confirmed.[1] "Every toil," the Bishop writes, "was lightened by a well encouraged hope that, through the blessing of God, this portion of the gospel vineyard is in a state of progress and improvement. . . . The missionaries are labouring faithfully through many difficulties, under which they are supported by a confiding trust in Him, whose they are and whom they serve. They are exemplary in their life and conversation. . . . In all my communications with them, which have been constant and intimate, I have found them respectful and affectionate, and it has been a delightful task to share their labours and their prayers."

New Brunswick, in the year 1825, was set apart as an Archdeaconry, under the Rev. George Best, who was also the first president of King's College. "He was a man," it is said, "full of gentleness and genuine unaffected piety." Owing to failing health he returned soon after to England, and in the year 1829, he was succeeded by Archdeacon Coster. It was a great misfortune to the Church that Archdeacon Coster, from physical inability, was unable to perform

[1] Annals of the Colonial Church, by E. Hawkins.

all the arduous duties pertaining to his charge. He was a graduate of Cambridge, an accomplished scholar and well read theologian, courteous and gentle in his manners, with that calm dignity appertaining to his holy office and high position. Bodily infirmities, in some degree, hindered the effect which his sermons and addresses, from their singular efficacy, would otherwise have produced. Although naturally reserved, those who knew him most intimately, were drawn to him by his sympathy and kindness of heart.

A great change had now come about alike with regard to the body politic and the Church. The first members of the legislature had grown old — many had passed away. In few instances did their descendants inherit their decided principles. The young men of the country, with many also who had come from elsewhere, claimed the right to prominent political positions. They sought for a change, by which the whole government of the country was to be left more fully to the popular voice. At length this movement was successful. The day of exclusive privileges was at an end. Henceforth legislation was no more in favour of the Church. It soon became in some instances hostile. That connection which existed, or was supposed to exist, with the body politic as a part of the Established Church of England, ceased. In the colonies with established governments all communions of Christians were declared to be on a like footing.

Before long the position of the Church of England in the Province, with reference to the college, grammar, and parish schools, was entirely changed. Personal influence was now all that was left to the Church in the education of the young, so far as that education was provided from the provincial revenue.

A few years had wrought still greater changes in the position of the Church itself. The tide of emigration from the old country now set in. Thereby the population of the country began rapidly to increase. The Roman Catholic element became prominent, and the ranks of others not in communion with the Church of England were also strengthened by the arrival of the immigrants.

In the small towns, which opened up as the country advanced, there were various bodies of non-conformists. In many instances they rivalled, or exceeded, the Church in the number of their adherents and of their sacred buildings. They had learned one great secret of success — self-reliance. From the paucity of the Church's missions, especially in the country places, and in new and distant settlements, there arose estrangement on the part of those whose forefathers were churchmen. Nothing like neglect to bring about such a feeling. Those who, from neglect and lack of sympathy for themselves or their children, are alienated from the Church become, in time, the most opposed to her teaching, and the most difficult to win back. By-and-bye it will be found that schism, with all its incalculable evils and its frightful hindrances to the extension of the Redeemer's kingdom, will be laid to the charge of many too ready to condemn others. Moreover, it is to be remembered that all along there was a body of men strongly opposed to the Church of England, though at the time comparatively few in number, who came over with the Loyalists from the United States. Their feelings seem to have been deeply infused and intensified in their descendants. Among the ministers of the dissenting bodies were men of zeal and great activity — just the kind of men the Church stood in want of, had they only been in her communion. Too much and too long the members of the Church depended upon exclusive privileges, and upon aid from England.

At the time when the Church in New Brunswick needed united strength and earnest zeal her members became

divided among themselves. The Loyalist clergy, with
those added in earlier years to their number, belonged, for
the most part, to the High Church school. A different
teaching was set on foot in one of the most important places
in the Province. The City of St. John had rapidly advanced
in wealth and influence. It was the one commercial centre.
The rector of this parish—a man of marked ability and
personal attraction—was the leader of the Evangelical
section. He gained the strong attachment of many of the
most influential people in the country. Then came on, in
many instances, bitter controversy and estrangement—sad
hindrances to the work of the Church—distrust regarding
her teaching, and vast advantage to those opposed to her
ways.

Nor, apart from all this, was the Church, at this time,
alive to her real position; nor were the public services
hearty or attractive. By many it seemed as if "vital piety"
were rightly claimed under ministrations outside the communion of the Church, or by those who, within her pale,
failed to conform in many ways to her teaching. It would
be a grievous wrong to disallow the earnestness of many a
hard-worked missionary and many a devoted layman who
were a blessing to the Church at the time to which we now
allude. They bore forth good seed. Afterwards, "others
entered into their labours." Still the Church buildings and
the Church services were alike of a dull and dreary sort.
New churches were built, but more after the plan of the
meeting-house. In the public services there were no responses,—that all-important part of divine worship fell to
the lot of the clerk. This was so as late as the year 1843
in the parish church at Fredericton. The writer can well
remember attending the services there as a student at the
college. There were present the representative of the
Queen, government officials, the officers and soldiers of a

regiment, with a large congregation, including the first
people of the capital city; and he—the writer—was only
one of three who knelt,[1] and he scarcely ventured to raise
his voice with that of the aged clerk in the responses.

It is most interesting to notice the beginning of a great
change—it may well be called a great revival—even in so
insignificant a portion of the world. At the time those
publications were being issued from Oxford, which wrought
such mighty results, the Archdeacon of New Brunswick
was engaged in a course of lectures to the divinity students
on the peculiar position of the Church and her positive dog-
matic teaching. This was far from a popular course; the
tide was all the other way; soon it was to be on the turn.
Above the sound of the moving waters the voice of the.
Church—the voice of her great head—was heard, calling
on all the members of His body to contend for the faith
once for all delivered. By the mighty power of the Spirit
of truth that "sound has gone out into all lands, and the
words to the ends of the world."

[1] This refers to *men* only.

CHAPTER III.

ARCHDEACON COSTER—ORIGIN OF THE DIOCESAN CHURCH SOCIETY.

UP to the time to which we now refer (A. D. 1843), the clergy in the Province were almost wholly dependent upon the grants made by the Society for the Propagation of the Gospel. There was not one exception. At least thirty clergymen were in this way provided for, with a generous provision for their widows. This required a large expenditure on the part of the Society. Comparatively little was contributed in the several parishes. Now it was properly and plainly intimated that the payment of these stipends, with the provision before alluded to, could not be continued as vacancies occurred. Even a reduced amount could not be relied upon for a lengthened term of years. Other and more pressing claims from almost all parts of the world must be regarded. Never can the Church in this Province fail in deep gratitude for all that long-continued aid, which has not wholly ceased at this present time. Nor should we forget to notice the vast benefit derived from generous gifts from the Society for Promoting Christian Knowledge. There is scarcely a Church in the Province which has not been assisted by a generous grant. Who can tell the benefits afforded by the publications of that Society, in so many cases freely granted for Sunday school and parish libraries?

The time now had come when the Colonial Church must be called on for self-support. On this point there had been sad neglect. Other Christian bodies, without endowment or external aid, were making their way in every direction,

(28)

in many instances leaving the Church behind in unawak-
ened zeal.   Meanwhile grants of land, formerly made by
the government, had increased in value in the way of endowment.   All this was deeply pondered over by Archdeacon Coster.   It formed the subject of correspondence
with the Bishop of the Diocese, and with the Society in
England.   The Archdeacon felt that it was beyond his
power to alter the course of things very much in his own
day.   He would do his utmost for those who were to come
after.   At a general meeting of the clergy at Fredericton,
on the 8th September, 1836, and following days, under the
presidency of the Archdeacon, resolutions were adopted for
the establishment of a Church Society, and a draft of its
constitution and objects agreed to.   It may here be mentioned that the constitution and objects of the Society
remain with little change at the present day.   "Such was
the *first* systematic attempt made in a British colony for the
more full and efficient support of its own Church.   A main
design of it was to unite the laity in hearty co-operation
with the clergy under the superintendence of the Bishop."[1]
   At this time (A. D. 1836) there were in the Archdeaconry
of New Brunswick eighty parishes, twenty-eight clergymen,
and forty-three churches or chapels.   More than two-thirds
of the whole number of parishes were without a resident
clergyman.   As a most interesting note in the history of the
Church in New Brunswick, we subjoin the following extract
from the address of the Archdeacon at the first meeting of
the Diocesan Church Society, which was henceforth to become " The Diocese in Action ":

   The importance of the occasion on which we have met can hardly
be over-rated.   We are about to enter upon business which must
very materially affect the fortunes of our Church.   I pray God that

[1] Annals of the Colonial Church, by Ernest Hawkins.

it may affect them in a way which will make this day an epoch in its history, from which we may date the commencement of a happy and glorious improvement.

We are forming what, I trust, will prove a great and powerful combination among ourselves. But combinations may prove beneficial, ineffective, or mischievous, according to the manner in which they are conducted, and the objects to which they are directed. It is the wish of us all that *this* combination should produce nothing but good. We must therefore all do our best to give it the right direction and place it under proper management; and I am persuaded that you will listen with patience to a few observations from one who has given much consideration to the subject, and feels himself deeply responsible for the part he has taken in the formation of this Society.

I need not say how cordially I approve of the plan which has been adopted — how anxious I am that the design should be successful. I firmly believe, that some such combination among the members of the Church can no longer be dispensed with. And were there much more risk than there is of an undesirable result, I should still be inclined to make the experiment. Still I would proceed with the greatest caution and recommend caution to you.

The published constitution of the Church Society will now be submitted to you for ratification and confirmation, with any amendments that may be deemed necessary. It will be borne in mind that a society like this in all respects has not, so far as I am aware, existed hitherto in our Church, either in England or in the Colonies, under the sanction of ecclesiastical authority. It behoves us, therefore, to be cautious in our proceedings; and we need not be surprised if some apprehension should be felt, lest, in our zeal "to be doing," we should attempt things which may be inconsistent with the rules and customs of our venerable establishment. It is not enough to say that we know of no such design being entertained in any quarter. I am persuaded you will agree with me that we should try to make it impossible even to suspect us of such a design. Without this, we cannot expect that the Bishop will give to our undertaking his sanction and support.

"Nothing without the Bishop" has ever been the rule and motto of the Church Catholic ; and we must take especial care that there be no deviation from it in this instance. Thus far we are honoured with his Lordship's sanction and approbation, the continuance of which we must be heedful to deserve.

No good churchman, I am sure, would wish that this Society would be an irresponsible body ; or would choose to belong to it, if it should assume that character. Our institution must harmonize with the established societies of the Church, not only in having the same objects, but also in being subject to the same control, if we would have it become a bond of union among churchmen, and not an instrument of confusion and disorder.

You see how they manage just such matters in the United States — how carefully they cherish and maintain the principle I am now recommending to you, and how they have prospered in the observance of it.

What we want in the Province is clearly this — something that will powerfully stir up the people of every class, to take that interest in the maintenance and prosperity of the Church which heretofore has not, by every one's acknowledgement, been manifested, as it must be now and hereafter, if we would have it even remain what it is, and induce them to co-operate zealously with the clergy in promoting the objects for which it was instituted and ordained. For this purpose the plan of our Society has been made as popular as possible. But none of those who have assisted in the framing and proposing of it, are men "given to change." None of them would consent to lay a rough and violent hand upon any part of the time-honoured fabric, however desirous they may be to improve it, wherever improvement is practicable and requisite.

To engage the laity in the work is what they ardently desire ; and they trust their brethren will be willing to enter into their counsel and co-operate with them, with temperate earnestness, and with a disposition to submit to those checks of which the experience of ages has demonstrated the need and the use. They wish to act with vigour, and the popular character of the Society sufficiently provides for *that*. But they also desire, that every disposition to weakness

should be powerfully restrained ; and with this view, they recommend that the Bishop should always have power to stop its proceedings, when it appears to be venturing upon dangerous ground. . .

What amount of means of doing good is likely to be placed at
the disposal of this Society, is yet unknown. Be it, however, large
or small, we have to provide for its being carefully and judiciously
managed and expended. Of course it is only the actual expense of
missionary visits that the Society can think of paying at the outset.
But everyone, I should think, will be of the opinion, that we should
endeavour to provide for as many such visits as the funds appropriated to that object will permit. It is desirable that a plan should
be laid down, to be submitted to the Bishop, upon which such visits
shall be conducted.

But here, as you all must see, a difficulty of no small magnitude
presents itself. The extent of country requiring to be visited is
frightfully great ; and where are the men to whom the work can be
committed ? The number of clergymen already employed is not
much more than adequate to the duties, in which they are actually
engaged, and from which they cannot be released without the consent both of the Bishop and of their parishioners. And from
whence such an increase of the present number, as will enable the
Society to do much for the neglected districts, is to be looked for,
who can tell ? Some means, however, must be devised ; and we
must not despair, by God's help, of accomplishing this most desirable end.   .   .   .   .

My Reverend Brethren — You who assisted in the formation of
this plan — you, I feel assured, have not seen cause to change your
mind with regard to it. I would to God that some of our body,
who were absent from that meeting, had manifested an equally
favourable disposition. I had flattered myself that, for once, all the
churchmen of the Province might have been united — that in this
cause there was absolutely nothing to which any churchman could
seriously object. Though I know not the grounds of the opposition,
I understand that opposition has been made, and with such effect
that, for the present, we must act without the concurrence of our
brethren in that part of the Province which is able to afford us the

most powerful aid.   The reasons by which they have been induced
to withhold their concurrence to such a design will, I trust, be communicated; and if, by any allowable alteration of our scheme, we
should find ourselves able to obviate their objections, no doubt we
shall be sufficiently inclined to do so.   Should they, however, prove
such as to forbid the hope of an accommodation — what then shall
we do?   Shall we be discouraged and deterred from the prosecution
of our design?   God forbid! unless we be first convinced that
our design is not what we all thought it — that this Society is not
calculated, if well supported, to render those services to religion
and to the Church, to whose altar we are consecrated and devoted,
which we fondly expected — which I still confidently expect from
it.   I am quite willing, however; nay, I desire, that the opposition
it may anywhere have encountered should have the effect of making us extremely cautious in every step we take, so that the result
of our endeavour at this meeting may, by God's help, be to win
over to our cause many who have hitherto been deterred from adopting it, by convincing them that at least we are thoroughly desirous
to do what is right and good.

My Brethren of the Laity — Permit me to address a few words
also to you.   The cause, my friends, is surely yours, fully as much
as it is ours.   You are all as much interested in its success as are
your clergy, and the success we hope and pray for can only be
obtained through your active and zealous concurrence.   And think
you that if, on any account, this design should fail, you will not
share with your clergy the shame — the intolerable shame — with
which the defeat will cover them, after the plan has been thus published to the world, and you have been thus earnestly called upon
for aid, for God's sake and charity's and your religion's?   I feel it
strongly, my brethren, and I tell you plainly, that if such a design
as this cannot find among you such support as it requires and
deserves, our Provincial Church will be a laughing stock to those
who love her not, and an object of compassion to all who do — none
will or can respect her.   Then indeed shall I begin to despair of a
final triumph over the difficulties of the times, and regret that
Providence had not cast my lot among another people.   My station

C

in this Church will become a matter of humiliation to me, since on account of it my portion of the shame will be the greater.

But think not that I wrong those who are here present by sup-posing for a moment that, so far as in them lies, such disgrace will be permitted to befall us. The commencement which has been made promises a very different result, and I shall not quickly cease to rely upon the promise being amply realized. Before this sun goes down, I trust there will have been among us such a display of zeal and unanimity in this great business, as will effectually remove all apprehension from every mind of a failure being even possible.

It was under these circumstances that the Diocesan Church Society originated. Much that through neglect the Church had lost, it has been the means of recovering, and the Society has become the main-stay of the missionary work in the Diocese. For over fifty years the Society has gone on gaining confidence and support. The foresight and sound judgment of its originators have left little to change in its constitution and rules. For a while, unfortu-nately, a strong section of the Church, especially in the city of St. John, held aloof. Still, year by year, the interest in the movement gained ground. Leading churchmen, in many instances, gave generous yearly offerings, and large bequests at their death. The Society now, from its con-siderable endowments and yearly income, can, in some degree, supply what is wanting by reason of the withdrawal of a part of the S. P. G. grant to the Diocese. It has called out, from the several parishes, more regular and substantial support for the clergy and a deeper interest in the extension of the ministrations of the Church in neglected districts.

CHAPTER IV

Death of Archdeacon Coster — His Character — His Brothers.

THE death of Archdeacon Coster occurred in February, 1859. In a Fredericton local paper it is said: "His death has aroused the sympathies of every creed and of every class in the community. . . . He was kind and courteous in his manner, liberal to a proverb in his works of charity, a clergyman of superior talents and unquestioned piety."

The late Archdeacon was a native of Berkshire, England. He was born in 1794. He took his degree of B. A. at Cambridge in 1816. In the year 1819 he was ordained by the Bishop of London. His first parochial charge was in Bermuda, where he filled a post of great importance. In 1825 he was appointed Archdeacon of Newfoundland; on the death of Archdeacon Best, he was, in 1830, appointed to fill his place as Archdeacon of New Brunswick.

The following is an extract from a letter by one of the late Archdeacon's daughters, Mrs. Edward B. Chandler:

My father was a gentleman of the old school. At Cambridge he took a high degree in classics and mathematics. As a churchman he was far in advance of the time. He was the first to introduce anything like strict adherence to the rules of the prayer book with reference to more frequent celebration of the holy communion, the offertory, holy days, and services in the week, and many other things now so common in the Church in America.

I can only tell what I know of my father in his social and home life. This he made happy by his many charming gifts of mind and manners, added to his holy and self-denying life. He was a

(35)

terrible sufferer from asthma. Still he would not give up any service or duty, if it were possible for him to leave his bed. No one ever heard a word of complaint or saw him otherwise than patient, gentle and cheerful. . . . His father had been possessed of independent means. Subsequently the family met with great losses. This obliged strict economy, in order to give *more* than "the tenth of all," which my father said was the very least to be offered to the " Giver of all."

Any in need of advice or sympathy found ready admittance at the rectory. The poor made daily visits. There was always a welcome for the clergy. Although his heart was in his Master's work, his social qualities were charming. His refinement and keen sense of humour, with his gentle kindness, made him a most delightful companion to his family and friends. . . . When he was well enough he would join in the music, of which he was so fond, and he trained his whole family in Church music, and fitted one of his daughters to play the organ in the Church. In his garden he took great pleasure, and was interested in every tree and flower. But the hours happiest to the whole family were in the evening readings, with which nothing but unexpected duty interfered. . . His reading was perfect. The best plays of Shakespeare he knew by heart. No one enjoyed more the fun and wit of Dickens and Thackeray, or felt more deeply their beauty and pathos. . . . If ever a family had cause to give thanks to God for a father, we can do so for his holy life and blessed death.

The following note, written by the Bishop, is taken from the Annals of the Diocese:

January 8th, 1859. The venerable Archdeacon Coster departed this life after a short illness of barely one week. He presented the candidates for ordination on the 19th December at the Cathedral, and received the Lord's supper on the festival of St. John. After that, he never took part in any public services.

He was an accurate scholar and took especial pains in the examination of schools. His sermons were distinguished for conciseness and purity of style with considerable force of expression. In private life his courtesy of manner, and kindliness to the poor, were most noticeable, and whenever his frequent infirmities permitted, he was most punctual in the discharge of his public duties. . . . In many ways his loss will be much felt.

He was one of the chief founders and zealous promoters of the Diocesan Church Society, and always subscribed liberally to its funds.

For many years two brothers of the late Archdeacon filled important posts in the Diocese. Rev. Frederick Coster was a man of marked ability, a sound and well read theologian, and an accomplished musician. He was a keen controversialist, and was ready to adopt changes and improvements which at the time were not favourably regarded by many. He took the foremost part, with his brother, in the organization of the Diocesan Church Society, and was for many years its very efficient secretary. For his services in this and in many other ways the Church in New Brunswick owes a debt of gratitude to the Rev. Frederick Coster.

There was another brother, Rev. N. Allen Coster. For many years he was stationed in an important district in Newfoundland, where he endured many hardships in his Master's service. Rev. Allen Coster was successively rector of two important parishes in this Diocese. In common with his brother he held what were thought at the time advanced views with regard to the position and teaching of the Church. Thereby he met often with great opposition. As a preacher he was singularly impressive. Before his death he had lived down the opposition of previous years and had gained the respect and esteem of his people.

CHAPTER V

EARNEST DESIRE FOR A BISHOP—THE COLONIAL BISHOPRIC
FUND—DIOCESE OF FREDERICTON ENDOWED.

VIDENTLY, as we have seen, the Church in New
Brunswick was being aroused to a sense of her position and obligations. Still there was a great want
—the want of a Bishop, the need of Episcopal supervision
and control. This had long been keenly felt by prominent
churchmen. We find the following editorial note in the St.
John *Courier*, March 20th, 1824:

By London papers, we observe with satisfaction that two Bishops
have been appointed to Sees in the West Indies. We would have
been happy to learn that a like measure had been pursued with
reference to New Brunswick, which for nearly twenty years has not
been visited by a Bishop.

We presume not to say where the neglect originates, but we shall
be happy to hear that an application has been made to the proper
authorities for a separation of the Ecclesiastical establishment of
this Province from Nova Scotia, and we pray that a Bishop may
be sent to us.

From a letter in a subsequent number of the same paper
we subjoin the following extracts:

. . . It had long been a matter of astonishment that the
interests of the Church in this quarter could have been so long
neglected before the appointment of the present Bishop of Nova
Scotia (Bishop Stanser) took place. We then confidently expected
to reap the benefit of his ministrations. From the effect of a serious illness, this worthy prelate, soon after his consecration, was
obliged to return to England, where he will most probably end his
days. . . . .

The tedious and expensive journey to Quebec, which candidates
for the ministry are compelled to undertake to receive Holy Orders,
is one of the many inconveniences which might be mentioned.

With reference to the above communication, the editor of the *Courier* remarks:

With our correspondent, we sincerely regret the cause that keeps the Bishop from his charge, and we also deeply lament its effects; but it is not alone because an individual occasionally suffers the inconvenience of travelling to Quebec for ordination, it is also because every member of the Church (clerical as well as laity) is affected by the absence of their spiritual head. It must be a melancholy reflection to every one reared in the Church, and feeling for her interest, to think that from such a cause as the above, the sacred rite of confirmation should be virtually abolished in this Province. This pure Apostolic institution, which elsewhere is the indispensably necessary step for admission to holy communion, is dispensed with, not from choice, it is true, but from sad necessity. It is therefore a matter of congratulation to all true sons of the Church that there is a prospect of their hopes being realized. If a Bishop is to be appointed for New Brunswick, with such powers in Nova Scotia during the absence of its Bishop, he ought to reside in this Province. We say this, having understood that it was very probable the Bishop of New Brunswick, if one should be appointed, would reside in Nova Scotia. If such be the case, a more proper time than the present cannot be for the Clergy, the Vestries, and all the members of the Church of England in the Province, to unite with one accord in petitioning His Most Gracious Majesty to appoint a resident Bishop to this his loyal colony of New Brunswick.[1]

---

[1] The resignation of Bishop Stanser a few months later, and the consecration of Bishop John Inglis, caused the movement in favor of a division in the Diocese to remain in abeyance.

It would appear from the foregoing extracts that Bishop Charles Inglis failed to visit New Brunswick during the last eleven years of his episcopate, probably on account of age and infirmities.

In his first charge to his clergy (delivered at Halifax, August, 1829; at Bermuda, May, 1830; and at Fredericton, August, 1830), Bishop John Inglis says many of the remote portions of his Diocese had never been visited by a Bishop. "More than sixty churches, scattered over an immense space, were unconsecrated, and nearly 7,000 persons were waiting for confirmation."

It is of the deepest interest, to mark the origin of that movement which effected so deeply the whole Colonial Church—the establishment of the Colonial Bishopric Fund. Surely it was a noble scheme, calling for large gifts and generous offerings. We can see in it the answer to those prayers and heartfelt longings, to which we have referred.

The S. P. G. report, 1840, says:

In a printed letter, addressed by the Bishop of London to the Archbishop of Canterbury, his Lordship proposed the following plan:

1. That a fund should be formed by voluntary contributions for the endowment of Bishoprics in the Colonies and distant dependencies of the British Crown.

2. That the fund should be held in trust, and administered by the Archbishop and Bishops of the English Church.

3. That, as a general principle, grants should be made for the endowment of Bishoprics, to meet a certain proportion of the whole amount required for such endowment, raised in the colonies themselves.

4. That the money set apart from the fund for the endowment of a Bishopric, should be laid out at the earliest opportunity, in the purchase of land within the colony.

5. That contributions may be made specifically for the endowment of particular Bishoprics.

This proposition was received with the liveliest satisfaction, both by the Society for the Propagation of the Gospel, and by the Society for Promoting Christian Knowledge. The sums of £5,000 and of £10,000 were voted by these institutions respectively, for the purpose of laying the foundation of the proposed fund, and the Christian public will rejoice to hear that the immediate establishment of Episcopal Sees in New Brunswick and New Zealand may be confidently expected.

The following statement is found in the report of the S. P. G. for the year 1841 :

The most striking feature in the occurrences of the past year, as they respect the progress of Christianity abroad, is the formation of a fund for the endowment of additional Bishoprics in the colonies.

At a meeting of the Archbishops and Bishops the plan above given was cordially agreed upon. We find New Brunswick named as the third on the list of the new Dioceses proposed. Among the officers of the Association, the name of W. E. Gladstone is given as one of the treasurers. The following minute was adopted at the meeting concerning the establishment of new Colonial Dioceses :

For the attainment of these most desired objects, a sum of money will be required, large as to its actual amount, but small when compared with the means which this country possesses, by the bounty of Divine Providence, for advancing the glory of God and the welfare of mankind. Under a deep feeling of the sacredness and importance of this great work, and in the hope that Almighty God would graciously dispose the hearts of his servants to a corresponding measure of liberality, we earnestly commend it to the good will, the assistance and the prayers of all the members of the Church.

In a letter to the S. P. G. from the Bishop of Nova Scotia (1842), published in the report for 1843, he writes :

. . . My anxiety for the accomplishment of the benevolent intention of erecting a new See in New Brunswick increases with my growing consciousness that more labour is required than any individual can perform. It is also increased by a conviction that the circumstances of the times are peculiarly calculated to insure, by the Divine blessing, the full benefit of such creation. . . .
The greatest encouragement is offered for perseverance in all those exertions which may be necessary for the accomplishment of so important and happy a work.

Sir William Colebrooke, the Governor at that time, officially reported that " a difficulty is experienced in obtaining clergymen for several parishes, in which the Church congregations have, in consequence, been dispersed."

From the S. P. G. report for 1843, above alluded to, we quote the following extract, taken from the minutes passed at a subsequent meeting of the Archbishops and Bishops:

The important colony of New Brunswick, equal in extent to one-half of England, and rapidly increasing in population, has been too long without a resident Chief Pastor. The time, however, seems at length to have arrived for the supply of this deficiency, so long felt and acknowledged. As a proof of the interest excited in New Brunswick, it may be stated that the Governor, Sir William Colebrooke, has officially expressed his opinion in favour of such a measure. The Chief Justice,' the Solicitor General,' and other leading persons in the colony, are exerting themselves to raise a fund towards the endowment.

The sum at that time raised in New Brunswick amounted to £2,150 — more was expected. The minute continues:

Having taken these matters into our serious consideration, and looking at the great importance and urgency of the case, we have determined to appropriate a large portion of the fund at our disposal, namely, the sum of £20,000, toward the endowment of a Bishopric in New Brunswick.

We must not conclude this statement of our proceedings and plans without expressing our thankfulness to Almighty God for the success He has been graciously pleased thus far to vouchsafe to this first systematic endeavour to impart the full blessings of the Church to the colonies of this great Empire, and beseeching Him to dispose the hearts of His people to carry on to its full completion a work undertaken for the furtherance of His glory in the extension of the kingdom of His ever Blessed Son.

---

¹ Honorable Ward Chipman.   ² Honorable George Frederick Street.

CHAPTER VI

Rev. John Medley, D. D., Consecrated the First Bishop
of Fredericton — His Boyhood — Scholar and Student
— Presentation on leaving England, and Farewell
Addresses — Early Years of his Ministry.

THE matter concerning the endowment was now satis-
factorily arranged. No time was lost by the proper
authorities in the nomination to what was henceforth to be known as the See of Fredericton. The appointment of the Rev. John Medley was confirmed by the
crown, and letters patent to that effect were issued.

Bishop Medley was the son of Mr. George Medley, of
Grosvenor Place, London, and was born December 19th,
1804. Mrs. Medley writes as follows with reference to his
early years:

A life of the Bishop would be incomplete without some mention
of his mother, whose careful training he always spoke of with affection and gratitude.

His father died whilst he was very young, and on her devolved
the bringing up of their only child. She was a woman of great
decision of character, high principles, benevolent, devout, and a firm
disciplinarian. She devoted him to the ministry from his birth, and
all her training tended that way. "John," she would say, "you
cannot do, or have everything you want like other boys; you are to
be a clergyman!" This was always kept before his mind, and influenced his whole life. His earliest recollection was of "preaching
the Revelation," from an upturned chair, with his pinafore turned
back to front as a surplice.

His daily lessons were from the Bible, and to this he attributed
his great knowledge of its contents. He knew the Psalter faultlessly,
and in later life, in any temporary indisposition, never needed a book
given to him when the daily portions were read. He knew the
style of the different writers in both the Old Testament and the New

(43)

so well, that he could at once tell where a text was taken from, and turn to it with ease. In his mother's Bible (1769) are these entries: "John, born December 19, 1804." "John began to learn the Psalms April 3, 1808." Then follows a list of eight Psalms, and the dates when they were learnt, ending with "John can say the 119th Psalm, aged six years." At four years he could say the 1st and the 23rd Psalms, but the effort of memory needed to learn the 176 verses of the longest Psalm in the Psalter, at the early age of six years, is indeed remarkable.

On one occasion he unfortunately fell asleep in Church during the sermon, and slipping from the little bracket, where he was perched in the high pew, struck his forehead against the sharp corner of his mother's footstool, and naturally whimpered a little. His mother took no notice, but on their return home, he was well whipped for disturbing the service, and never remembered transgressing in like manner again. He was sent early to school, as she felt he needed the companionship of other boys. The Bishop had many amusing stories to relate of school-boy life at Bristol, Bewdley and Chobham.

The following extracts from his mother's Journal will show how constantly she kept his preparation for the ministry before his mind and her own, and how untiringly she prayed for a blessing on each act of his life:

1810 — April 27. John began Latin (aged six years) with Mr. Biddulph, a private tutor.

1812 — July 12. John first went to Rev. J. Sawyer's school.

1813 — Brown, a soldier of the East Middlesex Militia, came to teach John his exercises.

1814 — March 10. John began Greek (aged ten).

1815 — July 28. Dear John went to school in Bristol.

1816 — John began Hebrew (aged twelve).

1818 — Our beloved John confirmed (aged fourteen) at Chertsey, by the Bishop of Lincoln, June 28. "Confirm him, O Lord, in Thy ways, for Thy Name's sake."

1822 — Received a letter from dear John with his decision about going to Oxford.

November 14—My beloved John went to Oxford to enter at Wadham College. "O God, give him grace to devote all that he is and has to Thy service."

1823—April 10. My dear John left for Oxford, his first term (aged nineteen). "O Lord, be Thou with him to bless him, and make him a blessing to others."

1825—December 19. My beloved John is of age this day—twenty-one years. "Help him, O Lord, to devote his life to Thy honour and glory."

December 25—Received a present this day from my dear John of £100. "Grant, O Lord, that what he layeth out it may be paid him again, and Thy blessing added to it."

After his confirmation, and when about fourteen years of age, he began work as a Sunday School Teacher, a thoughtful, reserved, and earnest-minded boy. He also began about this time to write sermons, and submitted his *first* to his mother with the following note:

"*My Very Dear Mother:*

"I have sent this attempt to you, hoping you would not wholly despise this first essay towards making a little sermon.[1] But may the Lord grant that at some time hence I may be able to compose what may really be styled *sermons*. Give my kindest love to dear aunt, and accept the same yourself.

"I remain,

"Your dutiful and affectionate son,

"J. MEDLEY.

"P. S.—I have considered myself in a church preaching to very rustic auditors."

[1] This is doubtless the sermon of which the Bishop's son, Rev. John Medley, writes: "I have a sermon by my father, written when he was a boy fourteen years old. The text is Isaiah xxviii., 16: "Behold I lay in Zion," etc.; and this note is added at the end: "Written on the 20th September, 1818."

In persuading those he is addressing to come to the Lord, he makes a quotation (I do not know from whom): "If you wait till you are better, you will never come at all."

The tie between mother and son seemed to strengthen as years passed on, and her prayers were unceasingly offered in his behalf. In 1828, when he received Holy Orders, the following written prayer is found pinned in her book of devotions:

A PRAYER FOR JOHN MEDLEY AS A MINISTER.

O Almighty God, who hast (I trust) given him the will, grant him also the power to perform the same; accomplish the work Thou hast begun in him, endow him with a double portion of Thy Spirit, and clothe him with power from on high. Increase his love for souls. Impress his mind deeply and constantly with a sense of the solemn account he must one day render to Thee of his stewardship. Enable him faithfully to exercise the gifts bestowed upon him. Lift up his hands whenever they hang down, and strengthen his feeble knees. Help him to be in Thy hands as clay in the hand of the potter, willing to be fashioned, ruled and employed by Thy godly wisdom, in the manner and in the service Thou thinkest proper. May he ever feel he is nothing in himself; may his eyes be ever directed to Thee, in whom the fatherless find mercy. Thou art a faithful God, remember and fulfil that promise to him, " I will put my fear into their heart, that thou shalt not depart from Me." Enable him at all times to depend on Thee, believing Thou never failest those who trust in Thee. Hear me, Heavenly Father, for Jesus Christ's sake. Amen.

At Wadham College, Oxford, the Bishop graduated with honors in 1826.[1] He was ordained deacon in 1828, and in the year following advanced to the priesthood. For three years he was curate of Southleigh, Devonshire. From 1831 to 1838 he was incumbent of St. John's, Truro. From that time, to his nomination to the Bishopric, he was vicar of St. Thomas, Exeter, and prebendary of Exeter Cathedral. As a parish priest, he is said to have been most efficient,

---

[1] In the hall of Wadham College, Oxford, there is a life size oil painting of the Bishop in his robes.

zealous and untiring. In a letter recently published by one of his successors, the present vicar of St. Thomas, it is said:

In material things also the late Bishop has left his mark broad and deep upon his old charge. Not only was the chancel of St. Thomas adorned and beautified by his taste and liberality, but St. Andrews, Exwick, was erected through his zeal and munificence, and the pretty chapel at Oldridge, enlarged and almost entirely rebuilt.

Speaking of the early years of the Bishop's ministry, a clergyman in this Diocese writes:

From the University, the transition was wide to the retired fishing village of Beer, just on the border of the Devonshire coast. But the young curate brought that sturdy individuality and genial face, which New Brunswick knows so well, to bear upon the descendants of smugglers and wreckers; and "Parson Medley" is still talked about by some of the village grandsires, as they watch the matchless prospect across Seaton Bay.

In Devonshire, he found the very characteristics which suited him, the simplicity, humour, force, and a certain almost Caledonian clannishness of country folk, helped by a local accent, which, once heard, is ever loved, and never forgotten. So, after a sojourn in Cornwall, it is no wonder that he returned to take the rectory of St. Thomas, in Exeter, the ever-faithful city, where he laboured until his call across the Atlantic, there to spend the strength and maturity of his life.

To those who only know the new world, it is hard to describe the beauties of an old world city like Exeter; the Cathedral, solid and almost lowly in its unassuming strength and beauty; the old wood-carved houses in the High street; the Guild Hall, where Charles I. was welcomed by the burgesses in the course of his daring western march in 1644 to intercept Essex; the market day, when the quiet streets are filled with the country farmers, and re-echo with the cheerful Devonshire tones until the evening, when by each devious and hilly road, return the belated visitor, after a jovial

dinner at the "ordinary," the day not having been entirely passed
in total abstinence, but whose safety is well ensured by the steady
progress of the "old mare," ambling along the well-known road,
the reins hanging loose on her neck, and the driver usually fast
asleep.

What a change to New Brunswick, as it was in 1845! This,
only those can measure who know our Province as it then was.
For one coming from the old-fashioned life of Devonshire, and the
cultivated society of Coleridges and Bullers, there was a wide chasm
to pass in order to understand the state of affairs of those days.

The Rev. Henry Budd Morris, of Bairdsville, Victoria
County, N. B., writes as follows:

My grandfather, Rev. Richard Budd, was rector of Ruan Lani-
shorne, in Cornwall, in the same rural deanery with Truro (that of
Powder), and was intimate with Bishop Medley when he was at
Truro. I enclose some reminiscences of him sent by my uncle, Rev.
Theodore Budd, Vicar of E. Dereham, Norfolk.

My mother sends the following note:

Rev. S. T. Trist, Vicar of Veryan Trist, was, at that time, Rural
Dean, and he persuaded Mr. Medley to write a paper on Episcopacy.
This was read at the meeting of the Chapter, and was so excellent
that it was printed by request, and Mr. Trist playfully said: "If
you ever are made a Bishop, remember it was my doing."

Reminiscences by Rev. Theodore Budd:

When I was at school at Truro, I had a class in Mr. Medley's
Sunday School. One Sunday there was a total eclipse of the sun,
probably 1835 — in the afternoon. Mr. Medley got appliances to
explain the subject to the elder boys in his garden, and in the evening preached on the words: "Sun, stand thou still upon Gibeon, and
thou moon in the valley of Ajalon."

The living of Crediton fell vacant. The parishioners had the
appointment; Mr. Medley was a candidate and went up to preach
a sermon. He stood at the head of the list. The supporters of
Mr. Hill, next on the list, would not give way to the supporters of

Mr. Medley, and so the living passed to number three on the list, and Mr. Medley returned to St. John's Chapel of Ease at Truro, much to the gratification of his congregation, where he remained till he removed to St. Thomas, Exeter.

While at St. Johns, Truro, Mr. Medley held a class of Sunday School Teachers in his drawing room every Sunday morning at nine o'clock, explaining the Collect for the day, and giving us an extemporaneous prayer.

The monument erected the other side of the street to the memory of the Brothers Lardner, explorers of North Africa, fell down, but the work of Mr. Medley fell not, for it grew and multiplied, and still lives in many hearts of the West.

One day I was returning home from college, accompanied by a sweet young lady on a visit to us; on our reaching the station at Exeter, whom should we see emerging from the same train but Dr. Medley, just consecrated to the Bishopric of Fredericton, holding a tolerably heavy oak box—the communion plate for his new Diocese, or Cathedral; so he put it down at our feet saying: "There, you stand by that till I come again."

The Bishop was twice married—first to Christiana, daughter of John Bacon, Esq., Jun. (a son of the eminent sculptor), whose effigy, "wrought by the hand of her father," adorns the chancel of St. Thomas; and, secondly, to Margaret, a younger daughter of the late Mrs. Hudson, of Crossmead, in the parish of St. Thomas, Exeter. By his first marriage his lordship had five sons and two daughters, of whom there still survive — the Rev. John Bacon Medley, M. A., Oxon, till lately rector of Orchardleigh with Lullington, Somerset; Captain Spencer Medley, R. N.; and the Rev. Edward S. Medley, B. A., vicar of Hopton, Great Yarmouth. Another of his lordship's sons who entered Holy Orders, but died some three years ago, was the Rev. Canon Charles S. Medley, M. A., well known in New Brunswick for many years as the esteemed rector of Sussex and Studholm, and secretary of the Diocesan Synod.

D

His future high attainments show the Bishop must have continued a diligent student. He came into note as an accomplished scholar at a marked period—when the greatest minds of the present century were beginning to employ their powers in a movement which was to exercise such a vast influence in the future work of the Anglican Communion. With these great men, Dr. Medley was in many ways a coworker. He was the intimate friend of John Keble.

In the preface to the translation of the Homilies of St. Chrysostom, it is said: "For the translation, the editors are indebted to the Rev. John Medley, M. A., of Wadham College, Vicar of St. Thomas, in the city of Exeter, and also to Rev. H. K. Cornish, late fellow of Exeter College. The indices are almost entirely the result of Mr. Medley's valuable assistance."

On the 4th day of May, 1845, Rev. John Medley, the first Bishop of Fredericton, was consecrated at the Chapel of Lambeth Palace, London.

A public meeting was held at Exeter on the 13th May, to present the Bishop with a testimonial on the eve of his departure for his Diocese. The meeting was largely attended. A local paper of that day states: "We have seldom seen a more respectable or influential assemblage on any public occasion. Among those present were all the clergy of the city and its neighbourhood, and a number of country gentlemen. On the platform were displayed the valuable gifts presented for the use of the Cathedral."

The Lord Bishop of Exeter was in the chair. Among the addresses was one from the Right Rev. Bishop Coleridge, who spoke as follows:

My Lord Bishop,—It is a subject to me of peculiar gratification that I have been selected to present to your Lordship, in the presence of our revered Diocesan, and of this numerous assembly of your friends—and in their names—a parting token of esteem and

regard.   Other modes might have been chosen for the expression of
our feelings, but there is none, I am assured, more in unison with
your own than that, so wholly detached from all private considerations, which has been adopted.   Called, as you have happily been,
to preside over a distant portion of the Lord's vineyard, it will be
a primary object of your solicitude, not only under the Divine
blessing, to feed the flock committed to your charge with the wholesome doctrine of the Gospel, and duly to administer the discipline
of the English Church, but to exhibit also, before the eyes of your
people — to their hearts and to their understandings — the scriptural
ritual of that Church, in all the fullness and impressiveness of a
faithful outward observance.   For this end, you have judged
rightly, my Lord, in proposing to erect, with as little delay as possible, after your arrival in your Diocese, an adequate and becoming
edifice for the public worship of God — worthy, I might hesitate so
to speak, even of the costliest achievements of architectural science,
yet worthy, in some sense — in all humility, be it spoken — of that
Being, who, though He dwelleth not in temples made with hands,
ever deserveth the best from us.   Built, as you are desirous it should
be, after an ancient model, of singular beauty, and cathedral ap-
propriateness; and of dimensions sufficient, not only for the ordinary
services of the Church, but for administering the more solemn rites
of confirmation and ordination, and for accommodating those larger
assemblages, which, as in the cathedral of this Diocese, will, we trust,
be annually brought together in yours, with the same gratifying
results, at the pressing call of Christian charity.   Your friends, my
Lord, entirely concur with your lordship, in the desirableness and
importance of this undertaking; they deem it a privilege to be permitted to contribute towards it — they confidently anticipate, that
the colony of New Brunswick will heartily respond to your wishes;
and whilst they deeply regret on their own personal account, your
approaching separation from them — a separation, however, which,
from the shortness of the distance, and the facility of communication,
precludes not the hope of your revisiting, from time to time, your
native land — they have deputed me to assure your lordship that you
will carry away with you from your native shores, their most fervent
wishes and prayers for the success of your spiritual labours; and to

express the hope, that the pecuniary contribution which they now
offer for your acceptance, will be an encouragement to you to go
forth the more cheerfully, on your high and holy mission, and prove
a nucleus, around which the future contributions of the colony will
abundantly gather, and be received by you as a mark, however inadequate, of the very great and affectionate respect in which you
are held among us, and of the lively interest, with which, though
absent in the flesh, yet present in the spirit, we shall watch your
movements, "joying," in the words of the apostle of the gentiles —
"and beholding your order, and the steadfastness of your faith in
Christ." I will not trespass, my lord, further on your feelings;
but as one who has trodden, with whatever step, the same field
of labour before you, and has largely tasted, through God's un-
merited mercy, of the consolations, which, amid difficulties, privations, and dangers, are ever springing up to gladden the path of
ministerial duty, I may claim the especial privilege — with a full
heart, and in much hope — to commend you and yours, to the
Father of mercies, and God of all consolation, in and through
Christ Jesus our Lord. — [The Right Rev. Prelate then placed a
cheque for £1,500 in the hand of the Lord Bishop of Exeter and
resumed his seat.]

The Lord Bishop of Exeter then arose, and addressed the Lord
Bishop of Fredericton nearly as follows: In spite of the apprehension that I may weaken the effect of that most touching address
which you have just heard, I cannot permit myself to be made the
channel of conveying to you this interesting testimonial, without
expressing my own special sentiments on this occasion. In you I
have had one of the most valuable and exemplary of my clergy.
To me, therefore, and to my Diocese — to this city especially — this
day, though it is a day of thankfulness, is not one of unmixed
gratification. We regret that you are about to leave us; but we are
thankful that you are called to a larger and nobler field of labour;
and we humbly hope that the God who has called you to it, will
give you strength and grace to work for Him there, as you have
worked for Him here. And let me express one sentiment — the
only thing, as it appears to me, wanting, in what has been said so
well by my right rev. brother on my left — let me express one senti-

ment, which he, probably, was restrained by his modesty from uttering. We cannot adequately rejoice to see — that, while colonies are led forth to the distant possessions of this country — while missionaries go there to instruct them — they are no longer to go, without being blessed with the superintendence of that high officer of the church, whom Christ Himself has appointed, to be over her in His name. . . . May it be long, my lord, before we may have occasion to thank you for the services which you have rendered. May it please God to give you such health and strength, as will permit you to spend, and to be spent, in the field to which He calls you ; and though we look forward with joy and hope, to the gratification of occasionally meeting you, may we always see you as about to return again, to the Church over which you have been called to preside. — [His Lordship handed the cheque to the Bishop of Fredericton.]

On an occasion of such deep interest, it seems fitting to subjoin the reply of the Bishop in full:

The Lord Bishop of Fredericton rose and said, — My Lord Bishop of Exeter, Bishop Coleridge, and dear and valued friends — so many of whom I meet on this occasion, with very mingled feelings — feelings indeed of a very painful character — for one cannot separate one's self, with whatever hope one goes forth, from friends so loved and valued as mine have been to me, without pain — though I trust that feelings of faith and hope do triumph and will triumph over those feelings, which would swallow up the rest — I hope I may say, without any want of humility, that I feel that God has called me to this post. The circumstances under which it was offered to me — the circumstances which preceded it — with all that followed and accompanied it — have been of such a character as to leave no doubt upon my own mind that it is God's calling; and how untrue and unfaithful a servant of the Church should I have been, if, having this conviction, I had not obeyed the call. Bishop Coleridge, and you, my Lord Bishop, were quite right, when you said that a present made in this particular form was much more congenial to my feelings than it would have been in any other. It would, indeed, have been most painful to my feelings — most unmixedly painful — if any other form had been adopted — if any of those personal testimonials, which are now so common and so cheap, had been presented to a Bishop of the English Church, going out to perform a spiritual duty, in an important Diocese. I should have felt that our own tone had been lowered by it — that we had gone back from the spirit of the Gospel to the spirit of the world — that we had exchanged good gold for wretched dross — and had sacrificed high and solemn considerations in order to gratify a momentary feeling of vanity. In accepting this valuable tribute, I do it as the servant of the Church — as your trustee, for the fulfilment of a high and holy trust. I accept it as a proof that you believe the doctrines of the Church — that you love the principles of the Church — that you are prepared to live and die in the service of the Church — and that whatever difference of opinion there may be, upon some points, between different individuals among you — you are in the main agreed — a body of sincere, and faithful, and conscientious churchmen. Upon no other condition could I consent to accept your gift; but I do accept it, because I believe I have interpreted rightly, the feelings with which it is presented, and it will be, I assure you, a matter of great gratification to me, if I find that it is received in the colony of New Brunswick with that cordial welcome, which I have reason to believe awaits it. As a proof that I have ground for this hope, I may mention one fact; a gentleman connected with my own family, who is a missionary in New Brunswick, had sent home to his friends in England to solicit contributions towards the restoration of his own Church, which was falling into decay ; but no sooner did he hear that a Cathedral was to be erected at Fredericton, than he wrote to me to request that no such collection should be made, but that his friends should contribute in lieu of it to the Cathedral fund. I am happy to be able to say, on behalf of the gentleman who manifested this strong interest in our work, that those valued friends of his, who had intended to contribute towards his Church, gave their contribution still, but they did not on that account, withhold their aid from our own Cathedral. The occasion on which we are met, is doubly pleasant to us all, inasmuch as it evinces a growing power of expansion in our beloved Church — it shows that the time has come, when God will lengthen her cords and strengthen her stakes—and it shows that, whatever divisions may arise among us—and no man can lament them more than I do— there is, in the Church herself, that growing power, which proves her to be sound at heart, and which could not be manifested if there were not soundness of heart.   We all know that coldness, in a person who is about to die, begins at the extremities, and where we find that the extremities are warm, we hope that the heart, and all the vital organs, continue to perform their functions.   So also, when we find the Church sending forth her missionaries to the distant colonies of the empire, and her clergy and her bishops supporting them, we may feel assured that God is giving His blessing, and that, somehow or other, all will come right at last.   I am sure that in going forth to a distant colony, that unless we do go forth in the spirit of hope, we°may as well not go at all.   With what advantage should I go forth, as the missionary of the Church, to a distant land if I were in despair of the Church at home?   What use would it be for me to attempt to carry out the liturgy of the Church among the colonists of New Brunswick—to express an affectionate zeal for their welfare—to multiply churches and clergymen among them— and to exhibit to them there the Church in all its fullness, if I felt all the time that the Church at home was going to decay.   But I have no such feeling.   I am confident that the more we exert ourselves to give to those who are at a distance, the Church in all its fullness, and in all its efficiency, the more surely shall we find it return, in blessings upon ourselves.   I will now take the liberty of stating to you, what is the actual position of the Diocese of New Brunswick; and in doing so, I shall pass no censure on any.   I must, however, remind those who hear me, that the state of things there is totally dissimilar from anything that we find in England. The government, from whatever cause—for I know not, and will not stay to inquire—are acting, in the colonies, rather upon the numerical principle—giving assistance to various denominations of Christians, but scarcely recognising the Church as an established church, and only allowing her to take her own position, as she may be able by her own exertions to attain it.   Whether this is right or wrong, I will not stop to discuss.   It is sufficient that the fact is so, and we should be very foolish indeed, if we did not consider it in all

its bearings and effects, before considering what we ought to do for
the colonies, with a view to the relief of their spiritual destitution.
Its disadvantages of course are obvious, and I need not, therefore,
dwell upon them, but let us look for a moment at the other side;
and let us consider in what way a Bishop of the Colonial Church is
affected by such a state of things.   It leads him then, not to look to
his connection with the state, so much as to the spiritual power and
authority given him by the Lord Jesus.   It leads him to look far
above men, or the smiles of princes, for support; it strengthens the tie
that binds him to his flock; and it makes him feel that, in proportion
as he can unite the richest and the poorest of that flock in one brother-
hood with himself, in that proportion will his Church flourish, and,
let princes smile or frown, he will still be enabled to carry out the
Gospel of Christ, in all its fullness and Apostolic purity, and to
make Jerusalem a praise and a glory in the earth.   No person will
understand, that, in the remarks which I have made, I intend to
cast censure, either on the state or on individuals; but we cannot
shut our eyes to the plain fact, and we cannot help seeing — when
no distinction whatever is made between truth and error — and
when it is openly professed that the state cannot have a conscience —
that the Church must rely more and more on its own resources —
and we must tell the people of England that they must come forward yet more zealously to support that Church which depends, in a
great measure, on their exertions.   There are in the colony of New
Brunswick eighty-seven parishes; when this division took place I am
not able to inform you, but the number is quite clear.   For these
eighty-seven parishes there are thirty clergymen, and forty-seven
churches.   A single clergyman has often the charge of two or three
churches, separated by great distances from each other — and it
occasionally happens that one clergyman has charge of a district
of one hundred and twenty miles in extent.   Many parishes are
left without the ordinances of religion, ministered in such a
way, as we, of the Church of England, believe to be the right
way, and to be most conducive to the purity and spread of the
Gospel.   I only mention this that you may see what is necessary
to be done, and I trust, if God's blessing shall attend me, I may
yet live to see the day when the same result shall follow, which

gladdened the heart of my right rev. friend, Bishop Coleridge, in his own Diocese of Barbadoes — when the clergy of New Brunswick shall be doubled — trebled they ought to be at once, to secure even an approach to efficient pastoral superintendence in that important sphere of labour. Bishop Coleridge, allow me to thank you, in the name of the Diocese of New Brunswick, as well as in my own, for that most touching and affectionate appeal which you have made on our behalf, and for the warmness and kindness which you have shown towards me, on this, and on many other occasions. That kindness will not be forgotten by me, and I shall always rejoice to recollect the time, when I met you in this place, with one, whom but lately I was accustomed to look up to, as my spiritual father in Christ, and from your hand receive this valuable testimony of affection and respect. One word more as to the wants of the Colony of New Brunswick — and first we want Men — we want men who will go forth to minister as the servants of the living God — we don't want the refuse of England for the Diocese of New Brunswick — we don't want men to be sent out there because they can't be employed at home — we want the best blood of England, in order to show what England can do. Therefore — if you send out clergymen from this country to gladden my heart — send out men who have a due appreciation of the work in which they are to engage — men with missionary hearts, and missionary spirits — men who are anxious for their own eternal salvation, and are therefore desirous to communicate the blessing of salvation to others — send not men to me whom the Bishop of Exeter would refuse — let no father place their children in the Church, in the belief that anything will do for a distant land. Such men as these we do not want; but we want holy men of God — men of earnestness and pious zeal — of reflection, of consideration, of judgment — better men if possible than you have need of at home. At the same time, allow me to observe, if you do send men out to New Brunswick, let them be earnestly attached to the communion to which they belong — men anxious to carry out all the injunctions of the Church, and ready to yield due obedience to her rulers — let them be men possessed, in every respect, of the spirit of the gospel. Then shall I hail their approach with joy — shall receive them with brotherly affection, and my only delight shall be to minister to them by every means in my power. We must have men. It is impossible that a population, comprehending at present 150,000 souls, and constantly increasing by emigration, can be rightly ministered to without a great increase of labourers — I had hoped to have taken out persons from England with me — alas! only one, at present accompanies me — I had hoped that there was more of the missionary spirit — I will only appeal to you, and through you to those who shall hear my words, though they do not listen to my voice, to recollect how great is the reward laid up for such as possess the missionary spirit and the pastor's heart, and who think it a joy and an honour to embark in their master's cause. I will only remind you that though absent in the body we may still be present in the spirit; that in that Cathedral which we shall build, the same strains will be sung as we have been wont to listen to here, with so much delight — that those who worship there will use the same liturgy — will have the same Church to embrace them — the same Spirit to animate them, and the same God to love, to bless, and to reward them. I have now to thank you, my lord, for all that kindness which you have shown me during my stay in your lordship's Diocese; for, at your hands, I have never received anything but kindness, which I know I have too little merited. I thank also, all those who, with the utmost zeal and affection, and Christian feeling, have contributed on this occasion. I have received many testimonies, on this occasion, of a very pleasing character; children have contributed to this blessed work, and have thought it an honour and a comfort to be permitted to do so. I am surrounded by many memorials, which will come before me often hereafter; and whenever the Holy Sacrament shall be administered in the Cathedral Church of Fredericton, I shall bear before me, and have engraven in my heart, the names of those who, with so much Christian zeal, have contributed towards the erection and decoration of the building. I shall feel that, though far distant, nothing really separates us, and that, as I am one with you, in that true Christian affection, which, I hope, nothing in this world can shake, so I trust I shall be one with you hereafter, in another and a better world. In taking leave of those kind friends who are with me here to-day, I cannot but recollect that human life is short, and uncertain, and that, chequered as my life has been, with sickness and with sorrow, I may be taking leave of you for the last time. But whether it be so or not—whether I ever re-visit the shores of England or not—I shall never forget this day—I shall remember it with thankfulness to God—and shall pray to Him for a blessing on your lordship's labours—for a blessing on the laity and clergy here present—and I shall never cease to hope that your prayers may accompany me on my voyage to a distant land, and that when I arrive there, I may still have the happiness of knowing, that I continue to enjoy the prayers of those of whom I now take leave, with so much affection and respect, blessing you in the name of the Lord.

Before proceeding to speak of Bishop Medley's arrival in New Brunswick, a few words may be added to what has already been related regarding the circumstances under which he was appointed first Bishop of the new Diocese.[1]

The years immediately preceding the Bishop's appointment to the See of Fredericton were marked by unusual domestic sorrow and trial.

In 1839, his second son, Thomas Fisher, died. In 1841, his young and beautiful wife faded away from his side in consumption, leaving six children, one an infant of a year old.

In 1843, his eldest daughter, Emma, who had taken charge of the house and family, was suddenly snatched away by scarlet fever; a most severe blow to him, as she had shown quite a womanly power of managing the household and a devoted care of her father. His mother then broke up her own house and went to the Vicarage to take charge of the family, but in the autumn of the following year (September, 1844) she was killed in a carriage accident by his side. She had not been in an open carriage for some years, but wishing to see a church in the Parish, at the hamlet of Oldridge, which she had assisted her son to restore, she determined to take the drive of about six miles.

---

[1] For the particulars here given, the writer is again indebted to Mrs. Medley.

In returning, the horses ran away down a steep, newly-stoned hill, and near the bottom the double seated carriage broke in two, and all were thrown out. The Bishop was badly cut, bruised and stunned; his mother was instantly killed. When consciousness returned, he asked for her, the doctor answered "she is in no pain," and he did not inquire further. His left arm was so seriously injured that the doctor decided it must come off, but the Bishop was so opposed to this, that other means were tried, and in time circulation was restored and it became useful, though it always remained weak.

Shortly afterwards the letter of the Archbishop of Canterbury, offering him the Bishopric, arrived, and in all probability this was the first real intimation he received respecting his appointment to the See of Fredericton.

The position was entirely unsought; indeed it is said the Bishop never knew the names of those who first recommended him to the Archbishop as a suitable man for the post he was destined to fill with so much ability.

None can do otherwise than admire the brave, manly way in which he entered upon the duties of what was well known to be an arduous and difficult position. In addition to the responsibilities of his office, there was thrown upon his shoulders the care of a large motherless family of young children. He was still suffering physically from the effects of the terrible accident, destined to leave a permanent mark on his form and features, and above all, there was the sad bereavement sustained in the tragic death of a mother so greatly revered and so tenderly loved. Yet in the face of what would have crushed one with less faith and courage the Bishop bravely came out to New Brunswick, loyally identifying himself with his Diocese from the very first, and forming the mental resolve years afterwards reaffirmed in the presence of a vast assembly in the mother land, "the

Lord do so to me, and more also if aught but death part thee and me."

The Archbishop's letter just referred to is as follows :

ADDINGTON HEAD, CROYDON,
October 31st, 1844.

REVEREND SIR,—It has been determined to separate the Province of New Brunswick from the Bishopric of Nova Scotia, of which it now forms part, and to erect it into an independent Bishopric.

It is most desirable that this important station should be filled by a clergyman well qualified by learning and ability, by temper and judgment, by piety and soundness of doctrine, to discharge its arduous duties.

I have been informed by competent judges that you possess these qualifications in no ordinary degree, and their report has been fully confirmed by the answer of the Bishop of Exeter to my inquiries. I therefore request your permission to mention your name to Lord Stanley as Bishop.

The office is not to be coveted on account of its emoluments. The income will be about nine hundred a year, or perhaps a little more; but the style of living in the country is not expensive. That which will recommend it to you will be the consideration of the benefit which the Church and the cause of religion in general will derive from the superintendence of a zealous and judicious Bishop, which in the present state of the colony is much needed. There are indeed few situations in which a good man could be more useful.

If you have any doubts, you will, of course, take time for deliberation. I have only to request that, in case you should decline the proposal, you will consider this communication as confidential.

I remain, Reverend Sir,
Your humble and obedient servant,
Rev. John Medley.   W. CANTUAR.

After due deliberation, a favourable reply was returned to the Archbishop's letter, and "Mr. Prebendary Medley" at the same time informed his own Diocesan, the famous

"Henry of Exeter," of his decision, from whom the following gratifying letter was received in reply:

BISHOPSTONE, 26th November, 1844.

MY DEAR SIR,—I receive your communication with very mixed
feelings.   Personally, and as Bishop of this Diocese, I deeply
lament the loss which both myself and the Diocese are about to
sustain.   As a Bishop of the whole Church, I rejoice in the prospect of so important a post as the See of New Brunswick being
filled by such a man.

It will give me much pleasure to receive you here, if you can
spare to me time for a visit before you leave England.   If not here,
I hope I shall see you in Exeter.   Wherever you may be, accept
my warmest assurances of my *brotherly* feelings towards you.

Yours, my dear sir,
Very faithfully,

Rev. Prebendary Medley.   H. EXETER.

As has been already stated, the Rev. John Medley was
consecrated at Lambeth, May 4th, of the following year.
The Bishops taking part in the consecration, in addition to
the Archbishop of Canterbury, were the Bishops of London,
Lincoln, Rochester, Hereford and Lichfield.

CHAPTER VII

THE BISHOP'S ARRIVAL AT FREDERICTON—CHANGE FROM
FORMER LIFE—FEELINGS OF DISTRUST MANIFESTED—
LAYING OF THE FOUNDATION STONE OF THE CATHEDRAL.

THE present writer has a vivid recollection of the lovely
evening—the eve of St. Barnabas—when the arrival of the Bishop took place at Fredericton. The
steamboat wharf was crowded by a large number of churchmen in joyous expectation. The Governor, Sir William
Colebrooke, was the first to greet the Bishop as he landed
from the steamer. He was accompanied by his chaplain;
five of his children, with their governess, and servants.
"I take the opportunity," the Bishop writes to the S. P. G.,
"to inform you of my arrival here, and it will gratify you
to learn, as it has me to witness, the cordial manner in
which I have been met by the members of the Church, and
also by others estranged from her communion. On St.
Barnabas' Day I took possession of the Cathedral Church,
and my patent[1] was read by my chaplain. After I had
preached I assisted at the holy communion. There were
one hundred and fifty communicants, among them some
coloured people, who had walked six miles to be present."

From what has already been written, the peculiar difficulties ready to meet the Bishop in his work may readily
be anticipated. The change from Exeter Cathedral and
intercourse with such as Keble and his associates, and the
society of men of deep learning, in whose work the Bishop

[1] This document has since been declared nugatory in Colonies vested with
local authority. All difficulty, however, in this instance has been set at rest
by readily adopted enactments on the part of the Provincial Legislature in
all necessary points.

(63)

was fitted to take a prominent part, to what met him at
every hand in the new Diocese, must have been great indeed. At the time of the Bishop's arrival there was not
one Church in the Diocese which, at the present day, would
be considered as properly arranged. Already we have
spoken of the dulness and lack of responses in the services on the part of the people. The Parish Church at
Fredericton — the pro-Cathedral — had lately been enlarged.
It was well kept, and in good repair. It had its galleries
and square pews. There was no chancel. The altar stood
in a narrow space between the reading desk and the pulpit.
In most instances, throughout the Diocese, the holy communion was celebrated quarterly. As we mentioned before,
the good Archdeacon Coster was doing all he could in the
way of improvements; but there was a bitter and strong
feeling against what were termed *innovations*. Among these
were classed, at the time referred to, more frequent celebrations, the offertory, the prayer for the Church-militant, and
the disuse of the black gown. Church music was little
understood or attended to. In some instances objections
were made to chanting the canticles. The so-called hymns
in use consisted of a very slim selection from the " metrical
version of the Psalms, by Tate & Brady." All this must
have been deeply felt by the Bishop, with his love for earnest,
reverent services, and frequent communion ; with his excellent taste in Church music and architecture, and his earnest
wish and longing to have everything of the best and the
most fitting in the house of God.

At the present day, we can scarcely understand the sharp
line of separation existing, say, forty years ago, between
that section of the Church with which the Bishop was in
sympathy, and that represented by the Evangelical school.
The blessed change, which has since come over every candid,
thoughtful mind, was, at the time we speak of, wholly

wanting.   It seemed to be supposed that real vital religion
could not exist in connection with High Church views.   The
principles which ruled the Bishop's mind were soon well
known.   There was no attempt to disguise them.   By the
Evangelical party he was regarded with distrust, which
was felt the more, as accounts came of terrible secessions to
the Church of Rome, on the part of the most prominent of
those concerned in the Oxford movement.   All this was
diligently set forth in the public press, and in much public
teaching.   It had its weight in many parishes, and with
many minds.   For a while they watched rather than yielded
to the Bishop's teaching.   He found it hard, in many instances, to bring about the most desirable and harmless
changes in the mode of conducting divine service.   Such
changes were often earnestly desired by the clergy, but
opposed by the congregations.   Any proposed alteration was
called the " entering wedge," " the step by step system."

As an illustration of this feeling, one incident may be
mentioned.   The Bishop had laid the foundation stone of
his Cathedral.   On his first visit to England, warm friends
had given him generous aid.   At the time of his return, one
of the clearest-headed statesmen was Governor of the
Province.   Afterwards he was Governor General of Canada.
He was a personal friend of the Bishop, a man of deep
learning, devoutly attentive to his religious duties, and well
acquainted with all the controversies and movements which,
at the time, were exciting such interest in the Church.
When he was told of the Bishop's return, and the success
of his mission in behalf of the Cathedral, with a characteristic
shrug of his shoulders, he said: *Timeo Danaos et dona ferentes!*
If thus it was in the case of a sound and apparently unpre-
judiced mind, can we wonder at the feeling exhibited, and
often strongly expressed, by those less capable of forming a
correct judgment ?   We shall see, by-and-bye, how all this,

E

which, with "the care of all the churches," must have been hard to bear, was patiently endured; how opposition was lived down by a constant, unswerving setting forth of the truth, combined with kind consideration for those of different opinions, and the quiet influence of a life of self-denial and beneficence.

In the autumn after his arrival in the Diocese, the Bishop made preparations for the erection of the Cathedral. He writes in his first letter to the S. P. G., before referred to:

I met on the Monday following (*i. e.* his installation) a body of the inhabitants, laid before them my plans for a Cathedral, and they responded by promising £4,500 in five years. Colonel Shore has kindly offered two and a half acres of land, and a lady the stone. There appears much anxiety on this matter, and never have I witnessed greater earnestness and zeal, or a disposition more kind towards myself. There is a willingness to defer, in points of situation, entirely to me.

Opposition, based upon the feelings of distrust before alluded to, had yet to be encountered.

The following account of the laying of the foundation stone of the Cathedral is taken from an English publication : [1]

In ancient times the cathedrals of old England, which are still the glory and ornaments of that country, and are now more visited and admired than ever, were built by the Bishops of the respective Sees, assisted by the multitude of the faithful, who rejoiced to pour their offerings into the treasury of God. In faith the work was begun ; the builders died and left their work unfinished, but others took it up, and by God's help brought it to an end. But the Colonies of England, though everywhere dispersed, knew no such glory ; and for a long season the gathering in of the "unrighteous mammon" seemed to be the sole end of colonization. At length the note of preparation is heard, and in more than one colony God's servants "think upon the stones" of His Church, and "it pitieth them

---

[1] The Church in the Colonies, S. P. G., second edition.

THE CATHEDRAL, FREDERICTON, N.

to see her in the dust." New Brunswick is one of the first colonies in which the foundation stone has been actually laid : an event the more remarkable, when we reflect, that no such work has been begun since the Norman Conquest, that is for the last seven hundred years; a work in which the goodness of God is manifestly made known towards us.

As many persons are interested in the success of this undertaking, the following account may not be unacceptable :

On Wednesday, the 15th of October, 1845, pursuant to a notice signed by the Lord Bishop, a procession was formed at the Province Hall, a short time before three o'clock in the afternoon, and the whole body proceeded to the ground in the following order :

The Band of the 33rd Regiment of Foot.
The Officers of the Regiment.
His Excellency the Lieutenant Governor in Military Uniform.
The Members of the Legislative Council.
His Honor the Chief Justice, the Master of the Rolls.
Mr. Justice Carter, Mr. Justice Parker.
Members of the House of Assembly and Members of the Bar.
The Lord Bishop, bearing his Pastoral Staff.
The Archdeacon, the Bishop's Chaplain,
And nineteen other Clergy in their Robes.
Inhabitants of Fredericton and other parts of the Province.

A large multitude accompanied the procession on either side, and when it reached the ground every place was occupied, the number of spectators being probably between two and three thousand.

The Bishop, presenting His Excellency with a silver trowel (the gift of Mr. Spahnn, of Fredericton), requested him to lay the foundation stone of the new Cathedral, and, previous to the ceremony, offered up the following prayer :

"O Lord, mighty and glorious, who fillest all things with Thy presence, and canst not be contained within the bounds of heaven and earth, much less within these narrow walls, yet dost vouchsafe to accept the poor endeavours of Thy humble servants allotting special place for Thy worship ; we humbly beseech Thee to accept this day's service of separating this place from worldly uses, and marking it out to be hereafter wholly dedicated to Thy glorious name. Accept, O Lord, the offering of this spot at the hands of those who have faithfully given it unto Thee. Prosper the work, and those who build in it. Make it Thy holy dwelling place for evermore. Let it be hereafter consecrated and made wholly Thine by the ministry of Thine appointed pastor. Here may prayers, supplications, intercessions, and giving of thanks be made for all men : here may Thy sacred word be read, preached, heard, and blessed. And be present with us, O Lord, at this time, and with all who shall hereafter minister or worship in this place ; and consecrate us unto an holy temple unto Thyself, dwelling in our hearts by faith, and thoroughly cleansing us from all worldly and carnal affections, that we may be devoutly given to serve Thee in all good works. Thus may we ever continue in the mystical body of Thy blessed Son our Lord ; and united in the bonds of a true faith, a lively hope, and a never-failing charity, may we, after this short life ended, enter with joy Thy everlasting kingdom, and be built up as pillars in the temple of our God, to go no more out for evermore. Amen."

The prayer ended, the stone was raised, and His Excellency proceeded to deposit the bottle containing a few coins, with an inscription written on parchment, in a cavity of the large block of granite selected for the foundation stone. The following is a copy of the inscription :

In Honorem Dei Opt: Max:
Patris, Filii, et Spiritus Sancti,
Ecclesiæ hujus Cathedralis
Fundamenta jecit
GULIELMUS G. M. COLEBROOKE, Eques Hanovensis,
Provinciæ Nova-Brunsvicensis, pro hac vice Legatus,
Res divinas peragente JOANNE MEDLEY,
Episcopo Frederico-politano.
Anno Episcopatus Primo.
Idibus Octob: MDCCCXLV.

The stone having been lowered with the accustomed formalities, His Excellency proceeded to address those present as follows:

"*My Lord Bishop, Reverend Gentlemen, and Gentlemen:*

"Called by your indulgence, and at the special request of you, my lord, our respected and esteemed Diocesan, to take a prominent part in the laying of the foundation stone of this Cathedral about to be erected, I cannot but regard it as an occasion for solemn thankfulness that I should thus be associated.

"To any one who has beheld the noble structures, which by the piety of our ancestors have been raised to the honour of God in our Mother Country, I can appeal for an acknowledgment of those feelings which their contemplation awakens. I have ever considered that the elevation of our Gothic spires — contrasted as they are in this respect with the temples of heathen antiquity — are calculated to inspire those lofty and sublime emotions which are the peculiar attributes of our Christian faith.

"To our worthy Bishop, gentlemen, we are indebted for the pains he has taken in obtaining for us a fine model for the edifice we are about to raise, and which, I may be permitted devoutly to anticipate, will long endure after we have passed away, though not, as I hope, to be obliterated from the pious remembrances of those who may succeed us and witness its completion.

"There is something at once solemn, impressive, and consoling in the reflection, amidst the perishing elements around us, and the cares and vicissitudes of our brief existence, that we are contributing to rear a solid and imposing structure, to be dedicated to the worship of that Being Who has ever existed, and will ever exist, and 'Whose service is perfect freedom;' and as Englishmen we must feel grateful, that it has pleased Him to put it into the hearts of our fellow-countrymen at home to assist our slender resources in such an undertaking.

"Till this hour, and for more than forty years, we may consider that we have been wanderers in the wilderness, though not, as I trust, without the Ark being with us in our wanderings, which is henceforth to find a habitation and a resting place.

"It is pleasing also to reflect that — as in the erection of the first temple, and in the more memorable foundation of the Christian Church—the period chosen for our solemn dedication is one of universal peace.   Our country, in the full career of her high and honourable destiny, respected among the nations of the world for her piety and for her charity, as she has been in the day of trial, with the blessing of God, in her martial achievements.

"It has been said that the sun never rises nor sets upon English-men; and wherever it shines upon them, whether in the temperate or the torrid zone, by sea or by land, may they never forget the hand that has hitherto conducted them through perils; or, that they are engaged in the service of Him who has promised to those who faithfully serve Him, to be with and sustain them always, and to build His temple in their hearts.

"It has been my lot to visit many regions where Englishmen have lived and died, far remote from the sepulchres of their country; and from the sense of desolation to which the impression has often given rise, it is to me an especial consolation to witness in the latter part of my life, the growing expansion in the east and in the west of our ancient and venerable Church, destined, as I believe, by the Providence which watches over us, and sanctifies our labours, to sustain her part in the spread of the gospel, the herald of ' peace on earth, and good will towards men.'

"The occasion may not inappropriately suggest to our minds the words of the Prophet:

"' Behold, I lay in Zion for a foundation a stone, a tried stone, a precious corner-stone, a sure foundation.

"' Judgment also will I lay to the line, and righteousness to the plummet.' "—*Isa. xxviii.* 16, 17.

The Lord Bishop then spoke to the following effect:

"*Sir William Colebrooke, and Gentlemen:*

"It affords me the highest gratification to hear from your Excellency sentiments to which every Christian heart must respond, and to find myself, on this eventful day, surrounded by the judges and law officers of the Province, by members of the Legislative Council and House of Assembly, and by men high in station in the Province, and distinguished for their talents, who have, with a unanimity worthy of the occasion, come forward to support this great undertaking. The building a Cathedral in this Province may in some sense be called a national work : for whatever reflects the genius,. the piety, and the glory of England, adds lustre to the nation from which the original idea is derived. It is in many other respects important ; not only as a national type of the unity of the Church, but as a consecration to God on the part of man of all these gifts which God has been pleased to vouchsafe to him. For when do we glorify God so much as when we consider nothing to be properly our own, when we look upon all as His, lent to us for our use, but to be given back to Him, the great and glorious Giver, and employed in His peculiar worship and service. Thus whatever our gifts be, whether they be gold and silver, whether they be wood or stone, whether they be skill in carving, force and eloquence in utterance, sweetness in music, taste in decoration, all are well used and employed in the material expression of our inward thanks and praise, of our love and devotion to His glorious Name.

"A Cathedral Church is also the common home of all ; for as it is the mother of all the churches in the Diocese, so every one has a right to resort to it without payment, without that exclusive property in seats, alike forbidden in scripture, and unsanctioned by the custom of the purest ages of the Church. And I joyfully anticipate the day, whether I live to see it or no, when the full importance of this great principle will be felt, that all men are sinful creatures, desirous to abase themselves in God's sight, and that, therefore, none should be excluded for want of money, and that there should be no distinction, but between those who serve the people and those who are served by them. And possibly many who do not yet enjoy the full blessing and privileges of our Church may yet feel inclined occasionally to enter a building so founded and built up.

"I am well aware that to the foundation of a Cathedral in this Province some persons may object that the money might be better expended than in what appears to them to be a lavish and wasteful expenditure, and needless display of ornament on the house of God: I for one, fearlessly appeal to the laity of this country, and plainly ask them, whether the foundation of a Cathedral is not accompanied by a simultaneous movement on the part of the Church, to extend and improve her missions, and to diffuse the glad tidings of the gospel to the remotest corners of the Province, and whether there be not an anxiety on the part of the founders of the Cathedral to promote the welfare of the poorest Church, and of the most uneducated and needy settlers?

"But let us join issue with such objectors on the footing of scripture; let us ask them, whether they recollect that on a single building, ninety feet long by thirty wide, every part of which was built by express direction from the Almighty, vouchsafed in writing, no less a sum than three or four millions of our money was expended?

"And if under any dispensation whatever, Almighty God would never have sanctioned anything morally wrong, why should we object to what has the direct sanction of the Old Testament, and is no where forbidden in the New? And when this so much praised plainness is carried out into the houses of the objectors themselves, when, in proportion to their increased means, men cease to ornament and fill with splendid furniture their own 'ceiled houses,' it will be time to let God's house lie waste, and to strip it of the ornaments which a grateful heart may bestow upon it. Such parts, however, of every such building are probably better bestowed as gifts than taken from the general fund appropriated for the fabric.

"Having disposed, as it seems to me, of this objection, it remains that I endeavour to impress upon this large assembly the duty of united and zealous co-operation. This Cathedral Church will best be built by our adopting the excellent Cornish motto, ' *One and all;*' by our reflecting that if we have little, 'we should do our diligence to give of that little;' but if we have ample means, an abundant contribution will alone ensure its acceptance from the Almighty.

"Would to God, indeed, that every one who hears me this day could have worshipped within the walls of one of our glorious cathedrals in Old England! Then I am sure I should not need to urge on you this duty, but your own zeal would outrun my desires. Recollect that, though built in Fredericton, it belongs to the Province; the design was conceived, and the first contributions were

raised in the Mother Country, and it would, indeed, be a disgrace to
New Brunswick if the efforts of Englishmen were not seconded here.
But I believe they will be seconded. The attendance here of so
many from all parts of the Province, the zeal of all classes and condition of men, the kind and generous feelings already exhibited,
put it beyond a doubt, that if we be only true to ourselves and to
God, and do not suffer ourselves to be disheartened by the cry of
the desponding, the work will be done; and we, by God's grace,
shall live, some of us, to see the topmost stone erected, and it will be
a joy to some of the children whom I see around me to say, when
they reach old age, My parents helped to rear the stones of that
Cathedral Church, and my children's children will rise up and call
the builders blessed.

"I have now only once more to return you all my sincere thanks
for your kindness in attending, for your active support, and likewise
to the officers and band of the 33rd Regiment, who have so cheerfully
rendered their assistance on this solemn occasion."

"Let us conclude, as we began, with prayer."

When his lordship had concluded his address, he proceeded to
use the following prayer:

"O God, who hast built Thy Church on the foundation of the
Apostles and Prophets, Jesus Christ Himself being the Chief Corner
Stone; we give Thee humble thanks that Thou hast called us to the
clear knowledge and light of Thy gospel, in Thy most blessed Son,
by the Holy Spirit.

"We bless Thee that Thou hast at this time given us the opportunity to lay the foundation of this house of God. May it be raised
in due season to be a most Holy Temple unto Thee—'where our
prayers may ascend up before Thee as incense, and the lifting up of
our hands as the evening sacrifice.'

"Finally, we give Thee most high praise and hearty thanks for
all Thy servants departed this life in Thy faith and fear. Patri-
archs, Prophets, Apostles, Martyrs, and all others, whom Thou hast
delivered from the miseries of this wretched world, from the body
of death and all temptation, and who have committed their souls

into Thy holy hands, as into sure consolation and rest: whose
examples teach us to follow.

"Grant, we beseech Thee, that we, with them, may fully receive
Thy promises, and be made perfect altogether, and being set on Thy
right hand in the place where there is neither weeping, sorrow, nor
heaviness, may hear those most sweet and comfortable words—
'Come to Me, ye blessed of My Father, possess the kingdom prepared for you from the beginning of the world.'"

The 100th Psalm was then sung by the assembled multitude, the
band taking the instrumental part, after which the Lord Bishop
gave the blessing, and the procession moved back to the Province
Hall and dispersed.

The proposed Cathedral was to be the first built in the
Colonies. None as yet had been erected by the Church in
the United States. Nothing could, under all the circumstances, have carried such a project into effect at that time,
save the Bishop's unequalled zeal and determination. The
required expenditure was large. The sum subscribed by the
people in Fredericton was only a very small proportion. It
did not grow to be a popular movement. The feelings
aroused by the addresses and appeals of the Bishop were
not lasting, excepting with the few. A leading non-con-
formist, looking at the progress of the work when rising
slowly from the foundation, was heard to say: "So we went
towards Rome."

CHAPTER VIII

St. Anne's Chapel—Laying Foundation Stone—Consecration of Chapel—Bishop's Sermon.

IN the meanwhile the Bishop built the beautiful Church
then known as St. Anne's Chapel, in the upper part of
Fredericton.

On the 30th May, 1846, the foundation stone was laid by
the Hon. John S. Saunders, who had presented the land for
the site. There was a large assembly present, including His
Excellency Sir William Colebrooke and the principal inhabitants of the city.

Mr. Saunders addressed the meeting in the following
words:

Much as I feel gratified by your lordship's kindness in requesting me to assist in laying the foundation stone of your lordship's
Chapel of St. Anne, I can assure you it affords me a far deeper feeling of satisfaction to have had it in my power to remove the difficulty you experienced in obtaining a lot, by presenting you with the
ground on which it is to be erected, and to have aided in the accomplishment of so desirable an object.

The extension of Church accommodation thus afforded will be
an invaluable benefit to the increasing population of this part of the
city, and as we are assured that the sittings are to be free, it must,
to every pious mind, be a cause of devout thankfulness to the
Almighty, to know that the poor of our community will no longer
be excluded from the right of attending the services of the Church
and of partaking of all its holy ordinances.

The name of St. Anne, by which the place was designated when
the present site of Fredericton was an Indian encampment, and the
earliest settlers first erected their rude huts, and prepared to clear
their way into the dense forests which surrounded them, cannot fail
to give rise to recollections of deep interest at a time when we are

(75)

called to aid our revered Bishop in laying the foundation of a
second Church in this city. . . . .

While assisting in this solemn ceremony, I trust I may be excused
for reverting to a subject so near to our hearts — the fulfilment of
that sacred pledge made to his lordship on our part — to rear to
the Almighty — to His honour and glory that hallowed edifice,
the Cathedral of this Diocese, an object from which none other
can divert our hopes and wishes. . . . .

We fervently trust your lordship will be long spared to us, to
rejoice in all the blessed results to flow from your labours. . . .
And when the rich and poor are mingled in one common dust, even
a fuller reward will, we trust, await the Apostolic labours of him
who has so munificently contributed to these sacred objects, and that
there will be then found many a stray member who has been
gathered into the fold, to rise to the glories of the life eternal.

In the newspaper of the day it is said that his lordship
made a most impressive reply, and concluded by thanking
those present for their countenance to his undertaking.

This Church, though of comparatively small dimensions,
is of stone, with a gable for three bells, and is perfect in its
way. The cost of the erection came, it was said, largely
from the Bishop's private means. It was afterwards made
over to the parochial authorities as the Parish Church, thus
leaving the Cathedral solely under the Bishop's control.
Here, till the completion of his Cathedral, the Bishop had
daily service, frequent celebrations, improved Church music,
and earnest hearty services.

St. Anne's Chapel was consecrated on the 18th March,
1847. On this occasion the Bishop preached from Zechariah
xi. 7: "And I will feed the flock of slaughter, O poor of
the flock. And I took unto me two staves; the one I
called Beauty, and the other I called Bands; and I fed the
flock."

In the course of a most impressive sermon the Bishop
evidently alludes to some prevalent objections. "If," he

says, " there be no necessary connection between external beauty and spiritual religion, is there any closer connection between spiritual religion and external deformity? . . . The point for consideration is, whether the giving to holy things and to holy places the honour that belongs to them, is not more likely to promote a religious frame of mind than the withholding such honour. That there is danger in external forms there is no doubt; there is danger in every act of a Christian's life; danger in alms, lest we give them ostentatiously; danger in worship, lest we pray pharisaically; or lest we slumber over the prayers, and go to sleep over the sermon. In all we say, or do, or think, there is danger; for our adversary, the devil, ever seeks to turn our food into poison. Holiness is not ensured by the observance of external rites, but is it ensured by their neglect? Are they who despise the Church of God, and lay out all their substance in the decorations of their own houses, of necessity the most holy? We all admit that we are in imminent danger of substituting outward acts for inward piety, and of neglecting the interior holiness of our souls. But this may be done everywhere, and no more belongs to a church adorned and comely, than to one which is less worthy of the name. The evil lies not in the building, but in the heart of man.

" The objection is sometimes repeated in other words. God, it is said, looks to the heart, at the heart only. Cannot God be worshipped in a plain, simple edifice, with four plain walls, seeing ' the Most High dwelleth not in temples made with hands?' To which we reply, ' Undoubtedly He may.' The Apostles worshipped in an upper room, because they were poor and had no other place of worship. St. Paul knelt down on the sea-shore and prayed. . . . God can be worshipped, and acceptably worshipped, without a house of prayer, if we have none to offer; in a plain house

if we cannot provide a better; but let us be well assured
that God is not the more spiritually worshipped, when our
meanness refuses to offer Him the best we have, though the
very best is unworthy of His Majesty. For, when the Most
High directed men to build Him an house, He gave directions to build it in so costly a manner that the most gorgeous
of our edifices is perfect simplicity in comparison.

"'The staff' implies authority, direction, support, and comfort. This comfort we find in the sacred words in the Book of
Common Prayer, a book so scriptural that it is full of scripture, and built upon it; so Catholic that nothing therein is
found contrary to the decrees of the Apostolic—nay, the
Universal Church—men's private fancies only being excluded; so comprehensive that every man finds his wants
represented or his petitions anticipated; so varied that we
may reap pleasure from it every time we wish; so full and
frequent in its offices of prayer that, let a man be as devout
as he will, he will find his devotion cannot soar to a higher
pitch, if it be sober, rational, and Christian; and withal, so
elevated that it leads us above the narrow views and petty
prejudices of party into the calm and holy atmosphere of
heaven. . . . While others turn aside to drink of other
waters on the right hand and on the left, I desire no higher
honour, blessing or happiness for myself or my children
than to drink of the well of English undefiled, and to uphold
in very poor measure 'the staff' of Beauty and the staff' of
Bands,' as set forth in the Book of Common Prayer.

" Of the building in which we are now assembled for the
first time, it becomes me to say no more than this—that it
is a very simple, humble, and unworthy effort to glorify
God, and to give access to His worship to all who choose
to avail themselves of His ordinances, especially the poor.
And as in the building of it, it is my duty not to look for
human praise, so it is equally incumbent on me to give no

heed to the rash and groundless censures of those who say 'Our lips are our own, we are they that ought to speak, who is Lord over us?' To the erection of this building scarcely any one has been asked to contribute. Your contributions of a larger kind are reserved for a higher edifice, in the erection of which a great number of the inhabitants of this place have pledged themselves to support me. From you, particularly, I claim this support, as your Bishop; as your friend; as one who has no interest at heart but yours; as one who, whatever may be his personal failings and defects, desires to benefit you, your city, and the people of this Province.

In this place may many a sluggish soul be quickened, many a wanderer recalled, many a consistent Christian be edified, many a mourner wipe away his tears. Here may 'the Son of Righteousness arise with healing in His wings,' and grace and love and peace be multiplied!"

CHAPTER IX

FIRST VISITATION OF THE DIOCESE—NOTES OF VISITATION TOUR IN 1846.

ALTHOUGH, as is plainly seen, the Bishop's mind was earnestly set upon the erection of the Cathedral, there was no neglect of other arduous duties pertaining to his office. Not long after his arrival in the Diocese he had visited every parish and mission. There were no railways in those days. The means of reaching his destinations by steamers were very limited. Trying, beyond measure, must have been many of his frequent and extensive journeys.

The following notes, taken from the "Annals of the Diocese," are of interest as giving an account of the Bishop's first official work :

1845. On Monday, July 28th, the Bishop consecrated the church of St. Thomas, in Stanley, the service being compiled from writings of Bishop Andrews, Bishop Wilson and Bishop Patrick. The holy communion was administered. A burial ground was also consecrated, not far from the church, on the hill.

August 4th. The Bishop left Fredericton, accompanied by his Chaplain (the Rev. R. King), on his primary visitation. He confirmed at St. Andrews, twenty-one ; at Campobello, nine ; at Grand Manan, twenty-eight; at St. Stephen, six ; at St. David, two; at St. George, twenty-five; at Portland, St. John, seventy-eight; at Trinity, St. John, sixty-eight; total, two hundred and thirty-eight.

At Grand Manan, the Bishop held his first ordination, when the Rev. James Neales, missionary on the Island, and the Rev. Thomas McGhee, were admitted to the holy order of the priesthood, after due examination.

(80)

At St. Andrews, on his return, the Bishop consecrated a piece of ground for a new burial ground.

From St. John the Bishop proceeded to Norton, where he confirmed forty-two; at Hampton, thirty-six; at Upham, fifty-four; at Sussex Vale, thirty-four; at Studholm, nineteen; total, one hundred and eighty-five.

The Bishop also visited the churches of Upper and Lower Loch Lomond, accompanied by the Rev. W. Gray, and preached in them; and also visited the village of Quaco, where he was desirous to establish a new mission. He preached there and baptized five children.

At Upham, the Bishop confirmed fifty-four and made provisional arrangements for a settled missionary.

The Bishop proceeded from Studholm to Springfield, where he confirmed fifty, and made arrangements for a weekly offertory; at Kingston, sixty-four; total, one hundred and fourteen.

On the 28th August, he returned to Fredericton and made arrangements for the excavation of the ground granted for the site of the Cathedral.

On Monday, September 1st, the Bishop proceeded to Woodstock. He was met at Eel River by the Rev. Lee Street, who accompanied him the next day to Tobique.

On Wednesday, the 6th, the Bishop consecrated the church at Tobique, by the name of the Holy Trinity, administered the holy communion, and confirmed three persons.

He then proceeded to Grand Falls, and on Thursday, held divine service in the large room of the principal inn, there being no church. He confirmed seven and baptized three. Several persons had come sixty-five miles to be present. After service the Bishop selected a spot for a church, to which the people undertook to subscribe £100, since increased to £168. The Roman Catholic landlord offered £5 and refused to take any remuneration for the Bishop's entertainment.

On Thursday night the Bishop arrived at Tobique. On Friday he confirmed at River de Chute church, nineteen, and returned to Woodstock, having held divine service at an inn on the road, where no clergyman had held service for three years.

F

On Saturday the Bishop confirmed at Richmond, fifteen; on Sunday, at Woodstock, twenty-three; at Jacksontown, ten; and endeavored to remove the objections of some of the people to the offertory.

At Prince William church, the Bishop confirmed seven, and consecrated a burial ground at Dumfries.

On Thursday he returned to Fredericton, having held service in a school-room at Long's.

During the Bishop's visitation he licensed three lay readers, Mr. George Street, Mr. Thomas Turner, and Mr. Charles Bliss. He also held a meeting of the Church Society and inhabitants at St. John, when arrangements were made for a union with the Society, and some new regulations were agreed to.

The Bishop likewise, at the request of some of the inhabitants of Lubeck and Eastport (in the State of Maine), held divine service at both these places, when he was staying at Campobello. He also licensed Mr. Bartholomew to a lay readership for the Island of Campobello.

1845. St. Matthew's Day, September 21st, the Bishop held his second ordination in Fredericton Cathedral, when the Rev. E. J. Roberts was ordained priest, and the Rev. W. Ketchum, deacon. Mr. Roberts then accepted the mission of Kingsclear, and Mr. Ketchum was appointed curate of Fredericton.

Michaelmas Day, a confirmation in the Cathedral, when one hundred and six were confirmed, eighteen of whom were from Kingsclear. The holy communion was administered. Total confirmed, seven hundred and twenty-seven.

On Tuesday, October 29th, the Bishop confirmed twelve persons at the church at Oak Point; on Wednesday, ten persons at Westfield; and baptized at the former place two children by immersion.

On Thursday he consecrated the church at Long Reach, in the Parish of Kingston (the seats being made free).

On Sunday, November 2nd, he consecrated the church of the Ascension in Norton, the seats being all free; and on Wednesday, St. Paul's chapel, Portland, was consecrated. On Friday, November 7th, forty-five persons were confirmed at Gagetown.

October 15th, by the divine blessing, the foundation stone of the Cathedral was laid.

On the 16th July, 1846, the Bishop consecrated the chapel of St. John Baptist, at Chamcook, St. Andrews, the seats being all free.

Returning to Fredericton — at Carleton, St. John, he received into the Church a convert from the Church of Rome. (The form of reconciliation is given in full in the Annals.)

Summary for 1846 — Travelled two thousand eight hundred and fifty-nine, miles; ordained five deacons and two priests; confirmed five hundred and four; consecrated two churches.

A similar summary is given at the close of each succeeding year. After that for 1849, the Bishop adds these words: " Travelled two thousand three hundred and ten miles; preached and addressed the people about sixty times, besides the ordinary sermons of the year. All praise be to God!" We find this ascription appended at the close of each year.

From the Bishop's report to the Society for the Propagation of the Gospel are taken the following notes of the visitation tour of 1846 :-

On June 25th, I left Fredericton at an early hour, and reached St. Andrews (about seventy-five miles) in the evening. I remained in the neighbourhood for a few weeks (being kindly received by Dr. Alley) in order to visit the neighbouring parishes and missions. Whilst there I consecrated the little chapel at Chamcook, three miles from the town, which has been built by the exertions of the missionary, the subscriptions of the inhabitants and others, and the liberal aid of Mr. and Mrs. Wilson, who reside on the spot, and take a lively interest in all that concerns the Church in that neighbourhood. The building is of stone, and the seats are all free. The holy communion was administered, as is my invariable custom on such occasions. The chapel is beautifully situated on a piece of ground beneath a high wooded hill, overlooking one of the numerous creeks with which that part of the country abounds. The people were very orderly and attentive. Service is performed once every Sunday, in the morning, and at a more distant station in the afternoon.

July 18th, I left St. Andrews for St. Stephen in the steamboat which plies up the River St. Croix, and the next day I preached, administered the holy communion to (I think) between fifty and sixty persons, and confirmed one, a confirmation having been held there the preceding year. In the afternoon I preached again at St. James, seven miles distant, and visited a sick person.

The next Sunday, the 26th, I preached at St. David's church in the morning, and late in the afternoon at St. Patrick's, which is fifteen miles distant, part of the way through an unusually bad road. Generally speaking, the roads in the Province are better than the English country cross-roads, and some of them are equal to any turnpike roads in England.

Both St. David's and St. Patrick's churches are beautifully situated on hills, the former overlooking a wooded island, surrounded by the Rivers St. Croix and Didueguash; the latter on a high wooded knoll, with a most picturesque prospect. The people at St. Patrick were very desirous of having a missionary to themselves, and they require it as much as any persons in the Province. Their settlement is nearly twenty miles from any town, and is large and increasing. They were not prepared to do much for the support of a clergyman, so that I was compelled to depart without accomplishing the object of my visitation to them. As, however, they attended the church in great numbers, some having come twelve miles, I hope that matters may be arranged.

The whole of this mission, including six churches, and being more than thirty miles in length, is at present under the care of one missionary, Dr. S. Thomson. Since his return from England, himself and his curate, the Rev. H. Tippet, undertake to serve five churches every Sunday, each taking three full services. St. Patrick's has only been served once a month. The Dissenters in this mission are very numerous, and owing to its contiguity to the United States borders, and the multitude of conflicting sects, the difficulty of keeping steady congregations is very great. Added to which, in the remote country districts, it is difficult to sustain a good Sunday

School, and the ordinary religious teaching in the Province is lamentably deficient. There is also a great want of good books.

Whilst I was staying at St. Andrews, I attended a treat annually given to the Sunday School children connected with the Church, of whom about one hundred were present. It was conducted much after the English manner (except that none of the parents were present), and seemed to give the greatest satisfaction. During my visit to this place, I had the gratification of receiving a letter from a gentleman in England, reminding me that about thirty years ago, I had taught him and others in a Sunday School, and acknowledging the obligation he felt for such instruction. I need hardly say that I had entirely forgotten the circumstance. I only mention it, to show how ready we should all be to do the smallest act of love to our fellow-Christians, and how certain we may be that "the seed cast upon the waters," shall not be suffered to lie wholly waste.

On Monday, July 27th, I left St. Patrick for Pennfield, a parish in charge of the Rev. Samuel Thomson, an old missionary of the Society, and confirmed twenty-five persons, one of them an old man of seventy, who had once before presented himself for confirmation, but had been prevented from receiving it by an accident. I proceeded on my journey that night, and the next day confirmed fifteen young persons at Musquash, an old mission revived. I also administered the holy communion.

When I first arrived in the Province I found the church in this parish deserted, and no missionary visits paid there. The settlement is large and flourishing. I am happy to say that good has arisen from the revival of the mission. The Rev. Thomas Robertson, ordained by me, having been educated in Windsor College, Nova Scotia, was very kindly received by the people. Appreciating his activity and diligence, they speedily commenced and completed a parsonage house; and two additional churches, one within three miles of St. John, and one in an opposite direction, several miles distant, at a settlement called Dipper Harbour, have been commenced, and the former is nearly ready for consecration. The people have also liberally subscribed toward his maintenance. He receives only £25 a year from the Society, the rest is made up by the people and the Church Society of the Province. Thus a district of twenty-two miles in length is brought within the teaching and privileges of the Church of England.

From Musquash I proceeded to St. John, where I was met by several of the clergy, who accompanied me the next day to Carleton, the mission of the Rev. F. Coster, where I held an evening confirmation for the convenience of the poorer classes, baptized after the second lesson two adults, confirmed forty-six persons, and received into our communion a convert from the Church of Rome, who was recommended to me as a sincere and intelligent person. I can safely say that no efforts were made to proselytize, and that a considerable sacrifice on her part was made in joining our branch of the Church Catholic. She appeared fully to understand the points on which we agree with the Church of Rome, as well as those on which we differ, and as far as I could discover, showed no unchristian bitterness of feeling.

The next day I returned to Fredericton, and again, on August 4th, I set out on my visitation of the north and eastern part of the Province. Having travelled thirty-eight miles, chiefly through the woods, I reached Boiestown, where I was met by the Rev. S. Bacon and the Rev. J. Hudson, the travelling missionary of a large district, in length ninety miles. There being no church in the place, I held an evening service in the school-house, and preached.

The next day we set out at seven for Ludlow, fourteen miles, where I consecrated a burial ground; and, as the heat of the day was very great, was obliged to ride in my robes in a common wagon to the place where confirmation was to be held. This was nothing more than an open barn, where, however, a congregation had assembled, and before a rough table thirteen persons, several of them of mature age, knelt down with great apparent devotion to receive the solemn blessing of the Church of God. I addressed them afterwards at some length, and took occasion to point out to them the advantages of a more settled and orderly place of worship. Their poverty has hitherto been their hindrance to the execution of my wish. They presented me with an address signed by, I think, one hundred and thirteen persons, couched in earnest, affectionate language, expressive of their sense of the value of Church ordinances.   At present, however, Mr. Hudson is only able to devote to them one Sunday in a month.   No place, I confess, struck me as more lonely than this, or more needing the care of one who would rather leave the ninety and nine than lose one stray sheep in the wilderness.

From this place, we journeyed on thirty miles to Blackville, and reached it at half-past five, and soon had a full congregation in a very neat little church.   I there confirmed twenty-nine young persons ; addressed them on the usual topics ; replied to an address presented to me, and consecrated the burial ground.   After service, we repaired to the inn, where I had some conversation with the members of the flock.   We then proceeded fifteen miles further, and needed no cradle to rock us to sleep.

Next morning, at eleven, we had service in an unfinished church, furnished with a spacious chancel, and an open roof, by the exertions of Mr. Hudson, and the liberality of his friends and neighbours.   The church was quite full, though the morning was stormy, a large party having come to meet me from Miramichi.   I preached to them from Acts ii. 42.   I did not hold a confirmation, as Mr. Hudson wished that his church should first be completed.

In the afternoon, in company with some esteemed members of Mr. Bacon's flock, we reached Miramichi.   Having received, on Saturday, a visit from the Church corporation, on Sunday I confirmed eighty-one persons in St. Paul's church, and addressed them from the pulpit, on various topics connected with their growth in grace.   The congregation was very full and attentive.   In the evening I preached again to an overflowing congregation (among whom were many dissenters) on the text : " If any man speak, let him speak as the oracles of God."

The next day Mr. Bacon accompanied me to Bathurst, forty-seven miles.   The day following I confirmed thirty-two persons, and addressed them especially on the practical duties of a holy life.   After church, a gentleman of the Scotch Kirk, named Ferguson, very politely offered me the use of his carriage, and accompanied me in it all around the beautiful harbour of Bathurst, pointing out the most agreeable views. He also showed me his farm, which is one of the best in this part of the country. On the same day I received an address from the vestry, which was couched in kind and respectful terms.

The next day we drove in company with the newly appointed missionary, Mr. Disbrow, to New Bandon, an interesting settlement of North-country Irish, many of them strongly attached to the Church. The little building was crowded to excess, though it was the harvest season. I confirmed sixteen, and administered the Lord's supper to fifty, including ourselves. I was much struck with the simplicity and earnestness of these people; and their devotion at the communion was remarkable. They expressed an earnest wish to see me soon again.

The next day, Thursday, we set out for Dalhousie, the most northerly part of my tour, distant fifty-four miles. Thither we were conveyed by the kindness of Mr. J. Cunard and other gentlemen (as indeed, all the way from Boiestown), free of expense. The road led through several fine settlements (many of them French), along the bank of the Bay of Chaleur, a magnificent sheet of water, one hundred and twenty miles long, by from twenty to thirty miles wide, with the mountainous coast of Gaspé and Bonaventure in Lower Canada on the other side. The weather was fine, and the whole ride most exhilarating; the road, moreover, one of the best in the Province. Dalhousie, from its distance, had not been visited by any Bishop, except on one previous occasion by the Bishop of Quebec, and had scarcely ever been visited by a clergyman of our Church. There were formerly many members of our communion there, most of whom, however, have left us, and have joined the Presbyterians, who are the prevailing body. The few remaining Churchmen received me cordially, and we were hospitably entertained at the house of Mr. Barbarie, one of the members for the County. The next day I went to see Campbellton, a flourishing village, near to which is a church glebe; and went on eight miles further to view the enchanting scenery with which this neighbourhood abounds. The Restigouche, which flows into the interior one hundred and fifty miles, is, at its mouth, three miles wide, and for twenty miles has a width of from three to five miles, with hills of from one thousand to one thousand two hundred feet, wooded to the very top, rising from its banks. The farmers here are of industrious and active habits, many of them Highlanders.

In the evening, after travelling forty-eight miles, we had a service in the court house, there being no church, and I confirmed six persons and administered the Lord's supper to ten, one of whom had had no opportunity of receiving it from a clergyman of our Church for seventeen years. Nothing but necessity would, of course, induce me to perform this most holy rite in such places; but we must hope that he who requireth " mercy, and not sacrifice," will accept what was the only available means for comforting and sustaining the hearts of his destitute and scattered flock. The next day, before I left them, they placed in my hands a guarantee for £50 a year, for two years certain, towards the support of a clergyman, in case I could send them one, which I fully intended to do immediately; but unfortunately on my return home, the illness of the esteemed and laborious missionary at Portland, the Rev. W. Harrison, demanded the assistance of the young clergyman on whose service I had reckoned.

Our brethren in England can hardly understand the desolation of spirit that must be felt by those who have been induced, by a desire of bettering their worldly circumstances, to plunge into the wilderness and find themselves reduced to the sad alternative of forsaking the communion of their fathers for a less perfect faith, or of seeing their children grow up unbaptized, uncared for, and even unburied by a pastor of their own Church. How rapidly, under such circumstances, do good impressions fade away, and the heart becomes thoroughly worldly and thoroughly callous! For good books there are few or none, except such as the settler had brought out with him. There is no association of the frequent summons to a common house of prayer; the unwearied offices of mercy; the soothing, tranquilizing, yet awakening, services of the Church. Money! get money!—is the only sound that vibrates in his ears all the year round; and for my part I know not whether the polluting worship of idols is much worse than this cold, selfish, deadening atheism, which freezes up the heart against all the holier and more vivid impressions. As to anything like a knowledge of the truths of the Creed, that of course is out of the question. It is well if the settler escapes the gross profligacy, and still baser cunning and fraud, which are ever found where " the strong man armed keepeth his palace and his goods are in peace." It is observable, also, that where some good impressions remain, the mind, irritated by a sense of neglect, easily resigns itself to the objections which are commonly made by different parties against our Church. It is felt not to be a reality; it loses all power over the minds of men ; it lives only in written documents, and persons who are themselves conscious of not living up to their knowledge of duty, attempt to justify themselves in their neglect by retaliating on the Church, and by broadly asserting that her services are inconsistent or delusive. Thus, when the missionary goes into the wilderness expecting to find himself received with open arms, and the Church welcomed as their mother and their guide, he finds a rapid under-current of suspicion, jealousy and division —a feeling that the people are to be placed under some hateful, undefinable restraint which they have never known, and would be glad to shake off. Simplicity, unhappily, is not the characteristic of our North American mind ; every man's wits are keen and trenchant, and this increases the difficulties of the spiritual labourer ; not to speak of that awful effect of our interminable divisions, the lurking doubt that steals through many a mind, that as all cannot be equally true, all *may* be equally false.

One circumstance has often struck me in passing through the country, as a mournful evidence of its spiritual destitution. One finds separate and lonely graves scattered about on farms, or by the roadside, without any mark of Christian, or even common sepulture. The communion of saints is not found even in our last resting place ; nor is there any visible sign that " the spirit of a man goeth upward, and the spirit of a beast goeth downward to the earth." Men and beasts are mingled together ; our brethren are committed to the earth without any token of Christian fellowship or a future resurrection. O that God would give our English churchmen grace, instead of " biting and devouring one another," to fight against the common foe of all ; to remember how vast a field is open to their exertions, and that there is still room to occupy it ; that He would give us grace to humble ourselves before Him with weeping and mourning over wealth unseasonably wasted and talents thrown away ; that He may yet have mercy upon us, and save us !

But I must return to my sphere of duty. From Dalhousie we returned to Bathurst, where I preached once on the Sunday, and in conjunction with Mr. Bacon administered the holy communion. Mr. Bacon addressed the congregation in the evening.

The next morning we left Bathurst at an early hour, and reached Chatham at two, where I spent five hours in endeavouring to compose some differences between some members of the flock. The next day we set out for Baie des Vents, a remote country settlement on the coast, where I confirmed twenty-three persons, who were very devout in their behaviour. This is on the whole, I think, one of the most church-like edifices in the country ; the Bishop of Nova Scotia having already mentioned it with approbation, it is not necessary for me to say more than that, though plain in its exterior, and of wood, the internal arrangements are good, and the effect reverent and devotional ; and this seemed to me the natural result on the minds of the people. I observed also that means were taken to prevent the entrance of dogs, which are most commonly brought with their masters, and which are a profane and intolerable nuisance in our country churches.

Having returned once more to Chatham, we set out for Richibucto, thirty-six miles. On my way thither I was met by Mr. Desbrisay, who kindly took me into his carriage and drove me the rest of the way. A few miles from this place we were met by His Honor, the Speaker of the House of Assembly, the High Sheriff, the Rev. Mr. DeWolfe, the clergyman, and several other gentlemen, who escorted us into Richibucto. Most comfortable apartments were provided for us at the truly English inn, without any expense to ourselves. Soon after my arrival, I attended a Wednesday evening service, and preached. The next day I confirmed nine young people, and addressed them and the whole congregation at some length. An aged and afflicted female came to thank me with tears in her eyes. In the evening we met several members of the Church at the Speaker's house.

The next day we drove before breakfast to the hospitable abode of Messrs. Chilton and Holderness, whose kindness and respectful attention I shall not easily forget. The yards of the vessels at their wharf were hung with flags as we rowed to the shore. Mr. Holderness accompanied me to Welford with Mr. Desbrisay, Mr. Bacon and Mr. DeWolfe. We were warmly and hospitably received by Mr. Ford, one of the principal residents; and at the little church we found an attentive congregation, and I confirmed thirteen persons. They were earnest to have a resident clergyman, being twenty-three miles from Richibucto, and having service only every alternate Sunday. They promised to contribute liberally to his maintenance, and I undertook to bring their case before the Church Society.

The next day, Mr. Bacon having returned to take his duty, Mr. Chilton kindly drove me part of the way to Shediac, and I was met on the road by Dr. Jarvis, the Society's missionary at Shediac. With him I spent the two following days. On Sunday I confirmed thirty-two at Shediac church, and eight at Cocaigne in the afternoon, returning after service. I was gratified, the next day, with the inspection of the school in connection with the Madras Board on Dr. Bell's system. The orderly behaviour of the children, and their knowledge both of scripture and the prayer book, reflected the highest credit on their teachers, and was very encouraging. I scarcely put a question which they could not answer.

On Monday I proceeded, in company with Mr. Black, the Society's missionary at Dorchester and Sackville, to his residence at the latter place, and having arranged the times of confirmation on my return, I went on with the Rev. Mr. Townshend, of Amherst, Nova Scotia, to Westmorland, a very important parish, of which Mr. Townshend had the charge until I made it a separate mission, as the Society has been informed. I found a very crowded congregation at the church, administered the rite of confirmation to nine (the smallness of the number being accounted for by the fact of there being no regular missionary in charge since Mr. Arnold's departure), and baptized three adults. A very sensible and well written address having been presented to me, we adjourned to the house of Mr. Buckerfield, an English gentleman, who, with several others in the parish, is very anxious for the welfare of the Church. We then proceeded to view the glebe and glebe-house lately erected, though not yet complete, and had much conversation with Mr. Etter, a liberal benefactor to the Church in that neighbourhood. All seemed most anxious to do their utmost towards the redemption of the glebe and towards securing the services of a resident pastor. In this parish are two churches, one at Baie Verte, twelve miles distant from that at Westmorland, with a considerable population. The whole Parish of Botsford is contiguous, being without church or clergyman, so that the Church people are sadly destitute of the means of grace. A missionary here is indispensable, and two would find ample employment.

Having visited Bay Verte and arranged with the people some matters relative to the finishing of their church, I returned to Mr. Black's at Sackville. The next day I confirmed nine in the morning, and fifteen in the afternoon at Dorchester, addressing the congregations at both places, and replying to addresses presented to me. In the afternoon we had a very full and attentive congregation, with delightful congregational singing, led by the clergyman, who acted as organist. I dined and slept at the hospitable mansion of the Hon. E. B. Chandler.

The next day, Dr. Jarvis and the Rev. W. Scovil, who had come to meet me from Norton (upwards of seventy miles), accompanied me to the Bend of Petitcodiac, a place of great resort for persons connected with the lumber trade. The only place in the village suitable for public worship was a chapel open to Christians of all denominations, whither we went; and I administered confirmation to three persons of mature age, and preached afterwards. After service we talked over the practicability of building a church. A site was offered, and it was reported that, if a clergyman could be procured, the church would soon follow. Finally the sum of £51 was subscribed towards a clergyman's maintenance. This place, which is likely to be the centre of mercantile resort, is in

Dr. Jarvis' mission, though it is fifteen miles from his residence. A missionary stationed here would be of great use, and with two assistants, Dr. Jarvis writes me word, "there would be work for us all " in the six parishes, of which his mission is composed. Having left the Bend, and having a Sunday to spare, I determined on a missionary expedition into the new county of Albert, in which there never has been any clergyman of our Church resident. It is a large and flourishing district, possessing large tracts of what is called intervale land, or as we should say in England, low meadow land. These tracts, when in the neighbourhood of water, yield almost inexhaustible crops. We set off on Saturday morning, and made our way through twenty-five miles of chiefly bad road to Hillsborough, where we put up. Our inquiries were not very encouraging, for we could meet with no Church people; and on asking where we could hold service, we were told that there were two meetings, and "we might suit ourselves with either of them." Having arranged for a service at Hillsborough the next day, we arrived about three o'clock in the afternoon at Hopewell, where we found that the person to whom we had been recommended was not strictly a Churchman, and lived eight miles further. The only person who could give us any information was a Baptist preacher, who most obligingly offered to do all he could, showed us where we could put up our horses, and assisted me and Mr. Scovil in taking them out of the carriage, remarking that our Lord had said : " He that is greatest among you, let him be your servant." These worthy people then offered us refreshment, and procured us horses (our own being too fatigued to go further) for the rest of the journey. Our host, to whom we had been recommended, was out when we arrived, but on his return he welcomed us heartily, and sent out a man on horseback to announce my·coming, and my errand.

Next morning (Sunday), though the notice was so short, the whole country was in motion, some on horseback, some in wagons, many on foot. Having robed at a cottage hard by, we proceeded to a chapel, where three hundred people had assembled, scarcely any of whom had ever seen a Bishop, nor had ever heard the Church Service. They behaved with great decorum, and we sang the Old

Hundredth Psalm. I preached from the text: "Whose fan is in his hand, and he will thoroughly purge his floor." I never had a more attentive auditory. A few very zealous Churchmen were there, who, aided by others not Churchmen, subscribed £50 towards a missionary, who would no doubt find an opening for his labours, and might do extensive good. We returned to our friend's house, who gave us some dinner, fed our horses, and wished us God speed on our way.

In the afternoon we just escaped in the rear of a most terrific thunder storm, and I held service again, where I feel sure the sound of our liturgy was heard for the first time. I preached from, "Behold! He cometh with clouds," etc. Though the evening was wet, it was necessary that we should get into the high road again that night; so we again returned twenty-five miles, and having travelled forty in all, were very glad to retire to rest.

The next day we proceeded on a smooth and easy road to Sussex Vale, the residence of the Rev. H. N. Arnold, one of the Society's missionaries. Mr. Arnold accompanied us the following morning to a place called English Settlement, where a church is building, in which, though unfinished, I held service, and was pleased to find several of my countrymen from Plymouth, Taunton and the West of England. They rejoiced to hear of the prospect of a missionary among them, and one of them zealously undertook to be responsible for the completion of the little church, and said the clergyman should never want a home whilst he lived. This worthy man also expressed his intention of giving land for glebe.

Having been kindly welcomed and hospitably entertained by these settlers in the wilderness, we proceeded on our way to Grand Lake, the mission of the Rev. A. Wood. Our road was very bad and very tedious, and we were from half-past three till near ten accomplishing a journey of twenty-three or twenty-four miles, the last part of it in the dark. Heartily glad were we, after numberless turnings, to find ourselves within sight of the lake. This is a noble sheet of water, thirty miles long, and in one place nine miles wide, in most three or four. Mr. Wood attends to a district about thirty miles in length, chiefly on the shores of the lake.

The next day we visited Young's Cove, where a new church is in the course of erection, and called on some worthy members of the Church.

The day following I crossed the lake in Mr. Wood's boat, in company with himself and Mr. Scovil, and we proceeded thirteen miles further in Mr. Earle's wagon to Newcastle, where Major Yeaman, a liberal contributor to the Church, received us hospitably. The next morning I held service in an upper room in his house — the new church, which has been chiefly built by him, being unfinished and full of shavings. About sixty assembled for prayer and hearing the word, an opportunity seldom, alas! granted. Along this side of the lake there are settlers for forty miles, and some, though not many, members of our Church. There is also a parsonage, and there are two churches, but no clergymen. All I could undertake for the present was that Mr. Wood and Mr. Stirling, two of the Society's missionaries, should each visit once a quarter, giving them a service once in six weeks. Alas! how meagre and unsatisfactory a performance of duty; yet it was all the case admitted of. The lake is often dangerous to cross, which renders the difficulty greater than it otherwise would be, and the roads are very bad.

On Sunday, September 6th, I held service at Mr. Wood's lower church. The congregation was larger than the Church would hold, and I confirmed thirty-five and addressed them. In the afternoon I crossed the lake and held service at Canning, on the other side, when I preached from Romans, 7th chapter, the latter part.

Having slept at a comfortable inn, about two miles above the church, I left it for Maugerville, where I found my family waiting to accompany me to Fredericton, and reached my own home, through divine mercy, in good health, without any accident or serious illness, having travelled nine hundred and thirty-nine miles, and in all since January 1st, 1846, two thousand five hundred and fifty-seven miles, for which all praise be to God.

Those who read the foregoing account will, no doubt, be struck with the small number of young people confirmed in each place. This may be accounted for, in part, by the prevailing custom that each single parish should present its own flock to the Bishop.

Though the social character of the ordinance is thereby diminished, its devotional effect is increased. I do not recollect to have seen a single instance of that levity, which is so common in English churches, where vast numbers are brought together from the surrounding parishes. With us the young people come with their parents, and sit with them, the congregation taking a deep interest in the holy rite; and when service is ended, they return quietly to their homes. This appears to me to compensate abundantly for the want of numbers. Still, it must be confessed that one reason of the small number of young persons who are confirmed is the prevalence of other bodies of Christians on the eastern shore of New Brunswick, particularly of Roman Catholics and Presbyterians; although wherever an active, useful clergyman is placed, our Church not only holds her ground, but more than holds her ground, and I think we may reckon on a steady increase in such places.

But the Society will judge of the destitution that prevails, when I tell them that after filling up twelve vacancies I could find immediate and full employment for twenty additional clergymen without diminishing the labours of any one at present in Holy Orders. Unhappily I have at present neither the means nor the men; but it will easily be seen that when one clergyman attempts to discharge the duties of three, four and even six parishes, it must be done imperfectly and unsatisfactorily; schools cannot be superintended, the sick and the whole cannot be properly visited; and after hurrying from place to place on the Lord's day, the result is exhaustion of mind and body, without a due effect on the minds of the flock.

One of the great difficulties we have to contend with is that of bringing home to the mass of professed members of our communion the duty of exerting themselves for the increase of Missions. A few give liberally to all good objects, and these few give again and again; but there are numbers, and these not the least wealthy, who seem entirely blind to their own responsibility, and indifferent to everything but making money and enjoying the good things of this life. Such is not the case (I am bound to admit) among Dissenters and Roman Catholics; and from all I can learn they do far more towards the maintenance of their ministers than we do;

G

and had they been as supine as the members of the Church of England, many of them must, long before this, have become extinct.

The same feeling induces many persons to put their names to a subscription list, for the maintenance of a clergyman, which they have either not the means or not the inclination to act upon; and it is notorious, that no subscriptions are worse paid than those which are promised to the clergy. Some system must, I think, be devised, by which the clergy may be saved the difficulties under which they labour from this source, wherever they depend on the voluntary contribution of their parishioners. Among instances of a better feeling I am happy to notice Maugerville, where the people raised £200 towards the rebuilding of the parsonage house, besides nearly £400 raised in Fredericton on the same occasion; and Woodstock, where more than £200 has been contributed this last year for various Church purposes, the effect of which is that there are now five services on the Sunday in different parts of the Parish, the Rector and his Curate each travelling from twenty-five to thirty miles.

To arrive at a sound conclusion respecting the whole effect of our Church in the Province is a very difficult matter, but I am in great hopes that we are advancing rather than going backwards. Still I confess our state morally and spiritually seems to me to resemble the church of Laodicea much more than that of Smyrna and Philadelphia: "The deceitfulness of riches and the lusts of other things enter in and choke the Word," and many, if they could have their heart's wish, would have a new preacher every month, who should send them all away satisfied with themselves. It is our place, however, to labour to be what we advise others to be, to see in their faults only a type of our own, and to trust that when God has brought us to confess our sins, "He will be faithful and just to forgive us our sins and to cleanse us from all unrighteousness."

In conclusion, I must thank God for the kind and cordial reception I met with in my visitation tour from all classes of persons, both within and without the Church; and will add my earnest prayers, in which I trust every member of the Society will join, that I and all my fellow-labourers may be found more diligent and faithful, and may see the fruit of our toil.

October 29th, 1846.   J. FREDERICTON.

CHAPTER X

Report to S. P. G.—Extracts from Primary Charge—
Visit to England in 1848—Visitation of Clergy in
1850—Address of the Clergy and Bishop's Reply—
Appointment of Rural Deans.

ROM the first, the Bishop identified himself with his
Diocese. He made no complaint of the difficulties
by which he was beset. No doubt he felt most
keenly the opposition and distrust he met; though with
regard to it all, he held his peace, and took no notice of the
attacks often made in the public press. He had taken up
his work, and that work was for the Blessed Master whom
he loved. At times he must have sadly yearned for so
much that was dear to his heart in his early home. There
he had the warmest friends—men of high position and
culture. And yet it was on the occasion of his last visit to
England he said, on his departure, "The happiest part of my
visit will be, when I set my foot on the steamer for my
return." He once said, "I would not exchange my own
Diocese for any that could be offered me in England."

Here it may not be out of place to notice what the Bishop
wrote at the time of his arrival as to the climate of New
Brunswick.

"Beyond all question," he says, "it is a finer climate
than that of England. It is undoubtedly hotter and colder.
But neither the heat nor cold are so trying as they would be
in England. . . . I do not hesitate to say that the chilly,
starving feeling of cold and wet together is almost unknown
here. Our sunshine in winter is at least three to one compared with England; the bright sun giving a cheerful look
to the snowy landscape. . . . The roads of general

(99)

communication from town to town are very good; in the
unsettled places they are what roads in woods and bye-places
in England are, very bad; but, if men's hearts could be
mended as fast as their roads, no one could complain
of New Brunswick."

In writing to the S. P. G. in 1847, the Bishop states that
already the number of the clergy had been increased from
twenty-nine to thirty-three. Referring to the need of additional clergymen, and the state of the people in the
neglected districts, he says: "It is surely our fault more
than theirs that so many stray from the fold and are lost to
the Great Shepherd altogether."

In the course of his two first visitations, the Bishop confirmed upwards of six hundred candidates, and was struck,
he said, "with their serious and devout demeanour."

The first visitation of the clergy took place at the pro-
Cathedral—the parish church at Fredericton — on the 24th
of August, 1847. From the charge of the Bishop delivered
on that occasion the following extracts are taken:

Our great business seems to me to be, to teach men not to study
controversy, but to study holiness; to manifest their Christianity
and their Churchmanship, not by hollow sounding words, but by
solid and fruitful actions; and to confute or convince their real or
supposed antagonists by a more virtuous and practical kind of
religion, and by a humbler walk with God.

.   .   .   .

And if the remembrance of sins of omission weighed heavily on
the dying moments of the profoundly learned, diligent, and heavenly-
minded Archbishop Ussher, how painfully sensible ought we to be
of our faults in this particular! Which of us can say that the
theory of our Church in regard to pastoral duties has been, to the
full, exemplified in our own practice? Where is the clergyman so
deplorably ignorant, or so intolerably vain, as to imagine that his
own life or labours are a perfect copy of the exhortation to Priests
in the Ordination Service? How sad it is to reflect that some souls

may have been led astray into heresy or schism, whom a kind word from us might have stayed; some blinded spirits have passed into eternity, whose blood may be required at our hands! How often have we been content with the ordinary routine of Sunday duty! How often has the ingratitude or churlishness of man paralyzed our exertions, and we have "persuaded men, and not God!" How often has the worldly spirit, which we deplore or censure in our flocks, crept in upon ourselves, and rendered all our discourses unimpressive and nugatory! We "watch for men's souls." "It will be work enough," says the holy Bishop Wilson, "for every man to give account of himself; but to stand charged, and be accountable for many others, who can think of it without trembling?" We can indeed easily preceive the evils which abound among our flocks; and we wonder that they listen to our discourses, and continue unimproved. But may not a counterpart of their sins be sometimes detected in ourselves? Do we not read and expound the Holy Scriptures to others without that stamp of reverend piety, that indubitable seal of holiness which impresses where it cannot persuade? If men saw in our order universally an entire self-denial, a fervent and unshrinking zeal, a thorough love for the ordinances and discipline of our Church, and a perfect union of mind and action, could they remain so worldly, so self-indulgent, so disunited as they are? If all the bishops and clergy of our Church were "perfectly joined together in the same mind and in the same judgment," and if that mind were "the mind of Christ," we should have more hearts with us, and our adversaries would have less power. The disorderly spirits among the multitude appeal to similar passions raging among ourselves; and while we creep and grovel on earth, we fail to "point to heaven, and lead the way."

Our reformation then must begin at home. To cure our flocks of schism we must heal our own disorders. We must banish that frightful party spirit, that minute exclusiveness, which refuses the hand of fellowship to those who have signed the same articles, own the same creeds, and are built on the same foundation with ourselves. The odious cries of High-Churchman and Low-Churchman, with other more offensive names, must not be heard in our mouths, lest our own weapons be turned against ourselves. We should take our tone of doctrine and practice, not from low interested writers, but, next to the pure fountain of Scripture, from the manly expositions of the master-spirits of the English Church. There must be about ourselves that genuine heartiness, that honest simplicity which no man can mistake, and which will persuade more forcibly than the most elegant diction, the most impressive delivery. . . It may sound strange in your ears, yet I feel it necessary to say it, be not ashamed to be *real men;* to state distinctly, though with sobriety and respect for others, your acknowledged convictions, and to set your seal to what you believe to be true; and let *mendax infamia* do its worst.

No man, indeed, gains much, even in the opinion of the world, from a cowardly shrinking from the cross, which the profession and practices of the gospel impose. Though he may not be attacked with public and open slander, he will be met with the wink of contemptuous reproach, as one well known to be sailing in the same boat, only to be a little more sly.

Remember that if public characters are public property, much more should public accusers be public characters, or rather real characters. Shun, therefore, as a moral contamination, the ignominy of anonymous censure; nay, it might be better generally to avoid the risk of anonymous defence. For you may sometimes wound when you only mean to uphold.

.   .   .   .

But to return to our own practical duties. The first to which I desire especially to call your attention, is that of public prayer. I have observed with regret that the churches in this Diocese are seldom open during the week for prayer. Now, without wishing to press upon you duties which you might feel unequal to perform, it appears to me that there are few places in the Diocese (none where any number of parishioners reside) in which prayers on the Litany days at least, and in many cases oftener, might not conveniently and most profitably be made.

The state of the Church and of the world demands more frequent intercession. The very life of the Church hangs upon it. Our people require it, and would in many instances be refreshed and comforted by it. The objection that few would attend is met at once by the fact that our Lord's promise is given not to the many but to the few : that the all-seeing presence of God should be our great inducement and reward : and that the prayers of two or three would not continue without a blessing. Not to say that others would probably by degrees be found to add to the "little flock;" and, if I must name a more humiliating reason, that we are almost the only body of Christians in the Province whose churches are shut up from one Lord's day to another. Let me hope that those who have for some time past continued this good practice will soon be no longer the exceptions, but that the rule will generally be observed among us. No idle distinctions of party can be a reason for the omission of prayer and intercession. A custom enjoined in Scripture, sanctioned by our Saviour, followed by His apostles, and for which ample provision is made by our Church, requires no recommendation from me, the most unworthy of its servants.

"Preach the word," is the eternal command ; and what must be done in obedience to God ought to be done in the best possible manner. One of the great faults commonly found with sermons is, that they are dull. Preachers do not sufficiently study variety and copiousness of information. They "bring" not "forth out of their treasures things new and old." Either they dwell on single points of doctrine in every sermon, in almost the self-same words, or confine themselves to the same round of moral duties, or preach about nothing but the Church, or else they never mention it. If we take the Scripture for our guide in preaching, we shall find it otherwise. Continual variety is found in the Word of God. History and exhortation, precept and parable, sententious proverbs, simple narratives, holy and comforting doctrines, supported by weighty arguments, and followed by practical exhortations, are interspersed in rapid succession in its sacred pages. I would advise my younger brethren not to confine themselves to single trite texts, divided into three regular parts, with the same kind of conclusion for all. It is useful often to expound a longer passage of scripture, as, for instance, a Parable, a Psalm, or one of the Gospels or Epistles of the day ; and by following in the wake of the Church throughout the year, we are sure to obtain a variety of useful and interesting subjects. Thus the lives of the Saints, the sayings of our Saviour, the Christian application of the Jewish Psalms, the principal events in our Lord's life, the prophecies of His first, the signs of His second advent, the doctrines and duties contained in the Creed and the Commandments, Prayer and the Sacraments, the nature, constitution, and progress of the Church, will all in their turn furnish matter for instruction. *Decies repetita placebit.*

The style of preaching is, in its degree, of as much importance as the matter. My meaning on this head cannot be so well expressed as in the words of Archbishop Secker. "The concern of a parish minister," says the Archbishop, "is, to make the lowest of his congregation apprehend the doctrine of salvation by repentance, faith and obedience, and to labour, that, when they know the way of life, they may walk in it. Smooth discourses, composed partly in fine words which they do not understand, partly in flowing sentences which they cannot follow to the end, leave them as ignorant and unreformed as ever, and lull them into a fatal security. Your expressions may be very common, without being low; yet employ the lowest, provided they are not ridiculous, rather than not be understood. Let your sentences and the parts of them be short where you can. Avoid rusticity and grossness in your style; yet be not too fond of smooth, and soft, and flowing language, but study to be nervous and expressive; and bear the censure of being unpolished, rather than uninfluencing."

.   .   .   .

Let us remember that, though we have truth, we have not numbers on our side in this Province: it becomes us, therefore, to be "modest and humble in our ministration," not speaking of other bodies of Christians with a bitterness which will do us no good, and the Church all possible harm; but letting them see that we respect their zeal and honour their piety, though we believe our own system to be truer and more effectual for good. Hasty anathemas and execrations upon those who cling to the faith of their parents or ancestors, are neither worthy of the Christian minister, nor serviceable to him. The anathema is a two edged sword, a weapon only to be wielded by an apostle or a council; and if the weight of ecclesiastical censure is to fall upon any, it should rather be upon the notorious profligate, drunkard, or worshipper of mammon, *within* our own body, than on, as we deem them, mistaken, but sincere and zealous persons *without* it.

. . . .

As regards ourselves, one thing seems certain, that, humanly speaking, very much more than we seem to imagine depends on the energy and truthfulness of the Churchmen of this Province, even in this generation. England may dole out to us her money, but our real strength and prosperity must come from within. If we are disposed to tamper with religion, to deal with it as if it were a system of traffic,—as if we neither realized nor believed the doctrines of our Church, nor were desirous of practising the duties which it enjoins, and only cared to find all manner of fault with everything which earnest-minded men are doing, then I see not what good can come of it. Hollow hearts and sinful lives will make a Church that is rotten at the core, and " whose breaking cometh suddenly, at an instant." Then it had been better a Bishop had never been sent out: nay, far better that those who thus deal with the Church had never been born. But if our hearts be true, and our eyes single, we shall not suffer from our present poverty; we shall grow and increase. Then it will be said of us, " I know thy works, and tribulation, and poverty, but thou art rich: fear none of those things which thou shalt suffer: be thou faithful unto death, and I will give thee a crown of life." Alas! who can look on all that is passing around us, on the unknown future, and on the fearful alternative, without fear and trembling? " O Lord, revive Thy work in the midst of the years: in wrath remember mercy."

I have now brought before you such thoughts on the duties of a Christian pastor as have appeared to me to be both necessary and profitable at this time. And though I am sensible how unworthy they are of the great subject, how inadequate even to express my own deep and growing convictions, I feel assured, and I trust that you also are persuaded, that such a course is far preferable to engaging in the mazes of interminable dispute. I am sick at heart of controversy on trifles; and on great points your minds as well as mine are, I hope, made up. I see that those who delight to agitate and inflame the public mind on disputed questions, neither grow in grace, nor benefit their fellow-creatures, and only hinder the good which others attempt to do. If there are any who affect to believe that I am not sincerely labouring to do the work of the Church of England in this Province, but that I have other designs in the back-ground, they are welcome to their opinion. I have accepted an office which nothing but a desire to work for the Church of England would have induced me to accept, and which, if it were not from the same paramount considerations of duty and affection, I would not retain one hour. But if what is done does not move men to take a more liberal and charitable view, nothing that is said will effect it. We shall soon stand before another tribunal, where it will be impossible any longer to conceal names, motives, and actions.

To you, my reverend brethren, I may speak in another manner. I claim your indulgence both on the present occasion and on all others, for inadvertencies and negligences, from which the most diligent and persevering are not wholly exempt. The same indulgence I am prepared to extend to others: but this must not be mistaken for a corrupt allowance of sin, a blind indifference to clerical misconduct. Such instances it is my bounden duty not to overlook: it is due to my office, to your own respectability, it is necessary for the maintenance of the Church in its integrity, that discipline should be enforced. A church whose pastors preach what they do not endeavour to practice, and who records on paper what she does not aim to perform, is a pretended truth, and a real lie: rejected by God, and despised by men.

In the great duty of maintaining the doctrines, and upholding the discipline of the Prayer Book, we shall all, I hope, be united: and if our union in these vital matters be sincere, the differences which in so wide a range of thought must occur, will be of lesser moment. Let us learn to act together: mutually to confer, mutually to instruct and comfort each other. Though additions have been made to our number, we are even now a small, and for the work we have to perform, an insufficient body. But our actions are not the less keenly watched, and carefully noted down. It becomes us therefore to be tolerant on matters of speculative opinion; and in action to be prompt, compact, and united. Our influence then will be felt: and even our opinions cannot safely be disregarded. Especially let us seek to win the affections, as well as to conciliate the respect of our lay brethren. They are equally with ourselves, members of Christ's body, though not placed in the same peculiar relation to our common Head, and are at all times most valuable co-operators in every work of Christian charity. To some of them no thanks that we can pay are too great for the services they have already rendered to the Church, for the cheerfulness with which they have been given, with a happy mixture of discretion and of zeal.

May a far larger number imitate their good example: and if I am not permitted to see it, may some worthier Bishop be gladdened with the sight of a numerous, exemplary, and united clergy, earnestly labouring with unwearied zeal to promote the temporal and spiritual well-being of flocks who more than recompense their pious toil by an affectionate respect, a heavenly conversation and a faith that "worketh by love."

The foregoing lengthened extracts from the Bishop's primary charge will be read and valued for their intrinsic worth. They are given here to show the sort of guidance he sought to extend to the clergy in the early days of his episcopate. From that sound Catholic teaching it will be seen he never varied.

Four of the Bishop's charges (1853-1862) were published in 1863, by the Rev. E. C. Woolcombe, Balliol College, Oxford, with interesting notes and an account of the Cathedral, Fredericton. A number of copies were sent the Bishop for the use of his clergy and friends in the Diocese. These he never distributed, assigning as a reason that he considered the preface too laudatory. The remarks of Mr. Woolcombe, from which the Bishop's natural humility shrank, were these:

I was anxious to bring, if possible, into wider circulation, in the cheapest form, the weighty teaching, at once so primitive, and so peculiarly suited to our own needs, of a Bishop, who even among the many admirable men who are guiding and governing the Church in our colonies holds a foremost place.

It would be unbecoming in me to praise these Charges; but it would be, I believe, most unnecessary also. There is a manly vigour, a firm grasp of the whole body of Truth, a courage and yet a gentleness in stating it, above all a deep, holy earnestness in every word, which is singularly winning, wonderfully refreshing.

I remember well how in troublous times, when the Church at home was suffering the loss of some of her noblest sons, our spirits were cheered once and again by the consecration of true-hearted men to the posts of chiefest danger and difficulty in the Church's warfare ; at present we are again in the midst of controversies, and I would fain call the attention of my younger brethren in the ministry, and of candidates for holy orders, to the brave and bold, but still more to the loving, fervent words, of one who is indeed a Father in God.

Bishop Medley, of Fredericton, very remarkably combines the gifts of a real theologian and a devoted pastor with practical skill in architecture and music, in a way which we supposed belonged only to the prelates of a far distant age of the Church ; but, besides, he is a noble self-sacrificing leader, where difficulties are great, and the fellow-soldiers are few. May young hearts be kindled by such an example, and may we who are older take fresh courage, when we trace the work of such a standard-bearer in our battles.

It was at the first visitation of the clergy, in 1847, that the Diocese was sub-divided into seven deaneries. Seven rural deans were chosen by the clergy, and their election was confirmed by the Bishop. Instructions for the guidance of the deans were given by the Bishop. At each triennial visitation, to the present day, the like election and confirmation has taken place. The instructions then given and recorded in the Annals of the Diocese are still in force. This arrangement has been found of benefit in many ways, and has been the means of material assistance to the Bishop in the affairs of the Diocese.

On the 17th March, 1848, the Bishop, accompanied by his family, left for England. He remained in England till September 2nd, endeavouring to procure funds for his Cathedral, candidates for holy orders, funds for a travelling missionary, and books for the Cathedral library. He succeeded partially in all these objects. Two thousand pounds were subscribed for the Cathedral, the S. P. C. K. also voted £1,000; £50 a year for five years were granted for a travelling missionary, and £300 a year additional for missionary efforts by the S. P. G. The University of Oxford gave £100 for the Cathedral library; and benevolent individuals gave the Anglo-Catholic Library, and Library of the Fathers, making in all about six hundred volumes. The Bishop also procured a small organ for St. Anne's Chapel.

In a letter on his leaving England, addressed to the secretary of the S. P. G., the Bishop says:

. . . Were our Church become reprobate, or a castaway, the blessed fruits of the spirit would not abound, love and joy would not utter their glad voices throughout our borders; we should not be enlarged everywhere, and be the heralds of mercy to the uttermost parts of the earth. I am not blind to the sad, sad tokens of our unfruitfulness, our backslidings, or national guilt, but the greatest sin of all is despair of the mercy of God.

Oh, let English churchmen pray for an increase of this true spirit among all sincere persons, though they be of different views; let them give up hard thoughts of each other and all will yet be well; let them not be so anxious to pull down what is erroneous, as to build up what is true. Love, victorious love, will win the day at last.

. . . After a three years' absence, I see more earnestness and reverence in the English Church than when I left for America, and I do not see that those who have gone out from us have improved their position or their usefulness. . . . . .

I shall return to my Diocese benefitted in many ways; personally cheered by sympathy amidst severe and unexpected trials, and assisted by men and means.

On his return to the Diocese, the Bishop proceeded at once on a long visitation tour.

The second visitation of the clergy was held at Fredericton on the Festival of St. Barnabas, 1850. At the close of the proceedings, on the morning after the delivery of the charge, the following address was presented to the Bishop:

We, the clergy of your Diocese, feel that we ought not to return to our several homes without having first tendered to your Lordship our grateful acknowledgement of the paternal kindness which has marked all your intercourse with, and proceedings towards us, during this visitation.

Having seen with admiration your unwearied labours for the promotion of the general interest of the Church throughout the Diocese, we rejoice in believing that, by the blessing of the Almighty, they have been productive of valuable fruit, and that in a time of considerable trouble and difficulty, we have been making progress in the right direction.

We shall return home cheered and animated for our holy work by the solemn services in which we have been engaged together, and shall endeavour to turn to profit the wise counsel we have received; and your Lordship may rest assured that no difference of opinion which may exist among us will be allowed to prevent us from co-operating faithfully and earnestly, one and all, with him who is set over us in the Lord, and with each other, for extending the knowledge of divine truth and the practice of righteousness among the people.

On behalf of the clergy of the Diocese of Fredericton.

GEORGE COSTER, Archdeacon.

To this address the Bishop made the following reply:

The affectionate and cordial address which you have presented to me, signed by yourself on behalf of the clergy, I receive, I need not say, with pleasure and gratitude.

I rejoice to find that my imperfect endeavours have been so far successful as to be appreciated by you; for though, next to my own salvation, the welfare of this Diocese is nearest my heart, I know that I can only be useful when I work with you, as well as preside over you in the spirit of love and in obedience to the laws of God, and to the rules of His church, and when you, in the same spirit, work with me.

The present visitation has been happily marked by general harmony, by a delightful interchange of good offices, and what is of more importance, by solemn acts of Christian communion between ourselves and our lay brethren, to whom we owe our warmest thanks for the readiness which they have manifested in entertaining us, not as strangers, but as brethren, and "in bringing us forward on our journey after a godly sort."

Let this heavenly communion go with us to our homes! If any words of mine have been of service to you, if I have been, by the help of God, able to preserve charity and good feeling towards them, who in any point differ from me, I give God thanks; being, at the same time fully conscious that your words instruct me what I ought to be, rather than what I am.

Earnestly soliciting your daily prayers, and commending you and your labours to the blessing of our Lord.

JOHN FREDERICTON.

CHAPTER XI

The Work of the Diocesan Church Society—Notes from Annals of the Diocese—Consecration of the Cathedral.

WE have already noticed that, in the organized missionary work of the Diocese, undertaken by the Diocesan Church Society, a large number of influential Churchmen stood aloof. This was in many ways a great hindrance to the progress of the Church. Soon after the Bishop's arrival an effort was made to unite all parties in the good work the Society had undertaken. This effort was crowned with success. It was found that, when men alike earnest and sincere in their desire to do what was right, met together, consulting and acting for the common good, their differences grew smaller. In promoting the interests of peace and good will, the Bishop set a noble example. Sincere and firm in his own opinions with reference to the doctrine and position of the Church of England, he was ever kind and considerate towards those who took what were called *lower* views. A consistent line of action was exhibited throughout his episcopate, both in his dealings with candidates for holy orders and in his appointments to vacant parishes or missions. No complaint was ever made of undue bias or party feeling.

Now it was this sort of thing that gave a heartier tone to the proceedings of the Diocesan Church Society, and was the beginning of that great change which, in time, came over the Church throughout the Diocese.

The work of the Society, of which the Bishop is president, is mainly carried on by a general committee, consisting of all the clergy and representatives of the laity. It having been

(112)

found desirable to apply to the legislature for a charter, there was great opposition to the passage of the act of incorporation, in consequence of a provision which gave the Bishop a veto on any changes in the constitution of the Society. The bill finally was passed by a small majority.

And here we may anticipate a little. The Society has been in operation over fifty years. Apart from the blessings conferred through its missionary work, it has done very much good through its meetings and mutual work of its members. In no one case has the Bishop ever been called upon to exercise his veto power; nor has there, during the long course of years, been any instance of a grant or vote on the part of the general or subordinate committees carried contrary to his wishes or expressed opinion.

NOTES FROM THE ANNALS OF THE DIOCESE.

1851, September 11.— The Bishop of Newfoundland (Dr. Field) arrived at Fredericton, preached twice on Sunday, 14th, and left Fredericton in company with the Bishop of Fredericton on Monday, the 15th, on his way to Boston. Thence the two Bishops proceeded to Montreal, where they were met by the Bishop of Toronto. The Bishops preached in several churches of the city. On Tuesday evening they all went to Quebec, where they were hospitably entertained by the Bishop. On Sunday the Bishop of Fredericton preached in the Cathedral for the Widows' and Orphans' Fund of the clergy.

On the Feast of St. Michael, the Bishops received the holy communion together, in the Cathedral, with many of the clergy of Quebec. On Wednesday the Bishops left for Montreal, and the Bishop of Fredericton proceeded to the United States, where he visited New York, Philadelphia, and other places. By the liberality of many friends, especially of the vestry of Trinity church, the Bishop collected upwards of £180 towards the Cathedral, which, with some other money, enabled him to order the east window. October 19th the Bishop preached twice at the Church of the Advent, for the

H

Rev. Dr. Croswell. The sermons have since been printed at the request of the vestry.

During the stay of the Bishops in Quebec, they proceeded to draw up certain resolutions, a copy of which is subjoined. They were transmitted to the Archbishop of Canterbury by the Bishop of Quebec.[1]

Summary of year ending 31st December, 1851: Churches consecrated, three; burial grounds, two; ordained priests, two; confirmed, six hundred and one; travelled three thousand eight hundred and seventy-five miles. "All praise be to God."

1852, April 1.—The Bishop left Fredericton for England with his family. At Boston he attended the services at the Church of the Advent, where Bishop Southgate is rector, and assisted in administering the holy communion. On Easter Sunday, Bishop

---

[1] These resolutions, referred to by the Bishop, formed the groundwork of the Declaration of Principles, Constitution and Canons of the Provincial Synod. The following are the concluding words:

"Lastly, while we acknowledge it to be the bounden duty of ourselves and our clergy, by God's grace assisting us, in our several stations to do the work of good evangelists, yet we desire to remember that we have most solemnly pledged ourselves to fulfil this work of our ministry according to the doctrine and discipline of the Church of England, and as faithful subjects of Her Most Gracious Majesty Queen Victoria, unto whom the chief governments of all estates of the realm, whether they be ecclesiastical or civil, in all causes doth appertain, and is not, nor ought to be, subject to any foreign jurisdiction. And we cannot forbear expressing our unfeigned thankfulness to Almighty God, that He has preserved to us, in this branch of Christ's Holy Church, the assurance of an apostolic commission for our ministerial calling, and together with it, a confession of pure and catholic truths, and the fulness of sacramental grace.

"May He graciously be pleased to direct and guide us all in the use of these precious gifts, enable us to serve Him in unity of spirit, in the bond of peace, and in righteousness of life; and finally bring us to His heavenly kingdom, through Jesus Christ our Lord."

(Signed)   G. J. QUEBEC,
JOHN TORONTO,
EDWARD NEWFOUNDLAND,
JOHN FREDERICTON,
F. MONTREAL.

Southgate addressed to him, before the congregation, an affectionate farewell, and Mr. Wainwright accompanied him to the ship.

He reached England, by God's mercy, April 27. The Bishop preached at Liverpool, Oxford, London, Winchester, and many other places, and collected nearly £1,200 for his Cathedral, but was taken seriously ill from over-exertion. At Westminster Abbey he attended the concluding Jubilee service of the S. P. G., but was unable to take any part in the services.

The Bishop received several munificent presents for the Cathedral and Diocese, a list of which is subjoined, viz.:

Eighteen hundred volumes of books for the Cathedral Library; donor, Rev. R. Podmore.

A large brass eagle, towards the cost of which £60 was given by Mr. Podmore.

A pair of candlesticks for the altar, by the same donor.

An altar cloth, by the Hon. Mr. Justice Coleridge.

An altar frontal for Easter, by Mrs. Woodcock, of Wigam.

An altar carpet, by Mrs. Shutelsworth.

Carpets for sedilia, etc.

Altar frontal, by Rev. O. Prescott.

Twenty pounds' worth of books from S. P. C. K., and various musical books by Rev. R. Podmore.

Several chalices and patens, by the same liberal donor.

Encaustic tiles, by H. Minton, Esq.

Especially three dear little boys at Hursley, nephews of Miss Young, gave silver spoons, which were all made into one paten.

The Bishop ordered eight bells for the Cathedral.

He left Exeter on the 15th August, . . . and on 6th September he reached Fredericton in safety with his family.

This year the main aisles of the Cathedral were changed into transepts.

On his return, the Bishop put in the east window, by Wailes, of Newcastle. This window was partly the gift of the members of the Church in the United States and partly the gift of the artist himself, who donated £80 towards it.

As already noted, the corner-stone of the Cathedral was laid by Sir William Colebrooke, at that time governor of the Province, on the 15th October, 1845. For some time the work proceeded slowly. Once it was thought necessary to enclose only a portion of the building, and leave the remainder to be erected at a future day. This was to the Bishop a source of great preplexity and trial. Just then, as if in special answer to prayer, the Bishop most unexpectedly received a letter from England, enclosing a large gift in aid of the Cathedral building. The name of the generous giver is unknown to this day, but the initial letters F. S. M., carved in one of the stones which support the chancel near the Bishop's seat, mark the place where the work was suspended, and where, by this timely offering, it was resumed. At length the work was finished throughout.

Since the above was written, the following most interesting incident has been kindly supplied by Mrs. Medley :

When at school at Bristol, the future Bishop very early became a Sunday school teacher, and was much loved by the boys in his class ; and one of these boys, George Hatherley, became a devoted helper when the Bishop began to build his Cathedral. Mr. Hatherley was at that time a traveller for a tea merchant in Bristol, and when he had finished his employer's business, and taken such orders as he could secure, out would come his subscription list for his old Sunday school teacher's Cathedral, for which he pleaded so eloquently and effectively, that he was able to send contributions amounting to £500 sterling.

In the Annals of the Diocese, the following mention is made of Mr. H.'s kindness by the Bishop :

1853. "Among the benefactors to the Cathedral, special mention must be made of Mr. George Hatherley, of Bristol, England, who, by unwearied personal efforts, has raised and transmitted to the Bishop the sum of £500."

Mrs. Medley gives the following details regarding the initials on the tower pier:

When the Bishop was building the Cathedral, and had completed the nave and aisles, the funds were at so low an ebb that he called the building committee together, to see if any means could be taken for getting in promised subscriptions or collecting more money. He had himself given largely, and his friends in England had been nobly generous, so he could not well appeal to them again. But the committee, lukewarm and indifferent, suggested that the part of the church already completed should be shored off and used for divine service till better times and new subscribers enabled them to resume the work. The Bishop was sorely hurt and distressed, and spent the night in anxious prayer, that he might be enabled to see his way to completing the work he had begun for the honour and glory of God.

Next day brought the English mail (which then came but once a month), and a letter in an unknown hand. Prayer was turned into thanksgiving, for when opened, it contained a cheque for £500 sterling, with these words: " To the glory of God, and for the completion of Fredericton Cathedral, F. S. M."

The Bishop felt this direct interposition of Almighty God so deeply, that he was always loth to speak of it: it seemed too sacred for ordinary mention.

He had the initials " F. S. M." cut on the next stone laid in the south-west pier of the tower arch, and the anonymous gift was so abundantly blessed that means flowed in as required, the church was completed, all debt wiped out, and in addition to all the valuable property of the Cathedral, plate, library, altar hangings, etc., etc., the Bishop left a handsome cash balance to his successor.

What an encouragement is this to make, as God prospers us, offerings to Him for His Church and her services!

The Cathedral was consecrated on the 31st August, 1853. The following account, taken from the New York *Churchman* of that date, is from the pen of the late Dr. Haight, of Trinity church, New York, who was present at the service:

For several days previously, the clergy of the Diocese, and several from the neighbouring Provinces and from the United States, had been assembling at Fredericton, so that on the morning of the consecration there were many gathered round the eminent prelate, whom God had placed over this extensive Diocese, and whose labours have been so zealous and successful.·

Of his lordship's clergy, all, with a very few exceptions, were in attendance to cheer him with their presence, to aid him by their prayers, and to assist in rendering the service in some small measure worthy of the greatness and solemnity of the occasion.   From abroad, the Right Rev. the Bishops of Quebec and Toronto, the Right Rev. Bishop Southgate, of the American Church, with several Presbyters from Nova Scotia, Canada and the United States, came, animated, as their words and deeds testified, by a spirit of true Catholic love, rejoicing in the prosperity of their brethren, and anxious to mingle their prayers and praises with those of their fellow-members of Christ's Mystical Body on this high festival.

Early in the morning the Royal standard and other national flags were unfurled from the windows of the tower, and the sweet-toned bells rang out a merry peal.   The apprehensions of unpleasant weather, with which the clouds and mist had agitated many breasts, were soon happily removed ; and, long before the hour appointed for the commencement of the service, the spacious nave and aisles were crowded to their utmost capacity.   At eleven o'clock the procession formed at the Province Hall, and moved in order to the Cathedral.   A number of boys bearing appropriate banners preceded and flanked it.   The members of the legislature present, the officers of the 76th, the members of the bench and bar, the wardens and vestrymen of the parish, the master workmen, the mayor of the city, with other inhabitants and strangers, were followed by sixty-one of the clergy in surplices, the architect, Frank Wills, Esq., the Archdeacon, and the four Bishops in their episcopal robes.   On reaching the Cathedral grounds the bishops and clergy commenced chanting the 121st Psalm to the fifth tone.

In the paper referred to, a minute description is given of the service, and the names are subjoined of those who took part in it, and it is added :

Thus closed a service which, in point of interest, solemnity and importance, has rarely been equalled. Notwithstanding the vast assemblage, which crowded every part of the building, the utmost decorum prevailed. The spirit of the occasion was evidently felt by all.

.   .   .   .

The edifice itself, which was thus solemnly consecrated to the service of the Triune God, now demands our attention. It is situated at the eastern end of Fredericton, within a short distance of the bank of the river St. John, and is the first object that strikes the eye as you approach the city from that quarter. A more desirable and beautiful site cannot be conceived. The style of the architecture is that generally denominated second pointed, or decorated, with a determination rather towards the flamboyant, than the geometrical, in the great eastern and western windows. The ground plan is cruciform with central tower and spire. The nave, including the aisles, is eighty-four by sixty-two feet, and is divided into five bays, the porch being projected from the second bay on the south side, from the west end. West of the chief doorway, in the west end, which is of small dimensions after the manner of ancient English churches, is a porch, or triple arcade, flanked by massive buttresses, and surmounted by a cornice on which is inscribed the following legend :

Deo et Ecclesiæ A. D. 1849.

Over the inside of this doorway, between its apex and the sill of the west window, in richly illuminated letters on a scroll, are inscribed the following legends :

I have waited for Thy salvation, O Lord.

The Lord of Hosts is with us.

O pray for the peace of Jerusalem.

Enter into His gates with thanksgiving and into His courts with praise.

.   .   .   .

The exterior of the Cathedral is striking, both from the cruciform nature of the plan, and from the numerous bold and massive buttresses, and the pinnacles and crosses surmounting the gables and spires. The extreme length of the building is one hundred and fifty-nine feet; breadth across transept, seventy feet; height of nave and choir roof, sixty-two feet; height of cross on west gable, seventy-one feet; height of cross on transepts, fifty-four feet; height of aisle walls, twenty feet; height of clerestory, forty-three feet; height of tower to base of spire, eighty-five feet; to apex of cross surmounting the spire, one hundred and seventy-eight feet. The building is entirely of stone excepting the spire. The stone of the body walls is from the immediate neighbourhood; the weatherings of the buttresses, string-courses, cornices, etc., are from the Bay of Fundy; all the dressings of the doorways and windows are of Caen stone, executed in England. It appears to stand the climate of New Brunswick admirably, and by its beautiful texture and light cream colour, forms an agreeable contrast to the more gloomy-toned masonry around it. We ought to have mentioned before that the piers and arches supporting the clerestory wall, and also those supporting the massive tower, are all of cut stone. The spire, as well as the roof, is covered with metal. There is an admirable chime of eight bells in the tower, the tenor bell weighing two thousand eight hundred pounds, key E flat. They were cast by the celebrated firm of Messrs. Warner, London.

The collection at the offertory, morning and evening, amounted to $1,320.25, which was, however, insufficient to pay the debt remaining on the church.[1] This, with so much else connected with the holy services of the day, caused great joy and thankfulness to the Bishop.

The following notice in the *Churchman* is from the pen of the eminent clergyman from the city of New York, before referred to :

On the following day, Thursday, the Bishop held his Triennial Visitation in the Cathedral. All the parochial clergy of the Diocese were present in the chancel, in surplices. After Morning Prayer

---

[1] Of this debt the Bishop personally assumed a large amount, which was afterwards paid in a way subsequently to be noticed.

the Bishop proceeded to deliver his Charge, after having received and confirmed the nominations of the several Rural Deans. We have not space to give an analysis of this masterly production, nor is it necessary, as it will soon be published. It was marked by his lordship's usual perspicuity, eloquence and strength—his deep Catholic feeling, and his lofty views of the responsibilities and duties of the Church of Christ, and of all its members, and especially of those "who bear the vessels of the Lord." His closing words were most solemn and touching. Every heart was melted, and we retired from the sanctuary, feeling that we had indeed heard words of wisdom and power not soon to be forgotten.

After the morning service on Friday, the bishops and clergy assembled in the library, when the following address was presented to the visiting bishops and clergy by the Bishop of Fredericton in the name and on behalf of himself and his clergy :

We, the bishop and clergy of this Diocese, now assembled in this city, having brought to a close the business on which we came together, could not think of separating without an attempt to give expression to the feeling with which we have seen the delightful solemnities of the last three days graced with the presence, and forwarded by the assistance, of three distinguished prelates —two of them belonging to our own branch of the Church Catholic, and the third a Missionary Bishop of the Sister Church in the United States—together with that of several presbyters of other Dioceses, American and Colonial.

We are grateful for the honour you have all been impelled by the best of feelings to do to a portion of the Church not long ago so small and insignificant; and shall not fail to derive hope and courage to grapple with the difficulties of our position, from the kind interest you have shown in our well-being, and from the animating words you have addressed to us.

The presence among us, on this great occasion, of such a noble band of Fathers and Brethren in the Lord, some from very distant parts of the world, has enabled us to exhibit an example of Catholic union upon which we shall never cease to look back with comfort and encouragement; and we trust this is only the first of many occasions on which similar examples of it will be exhibited on this side of the Atlantic.

We entreat, Fathers and Brethren, your prayers to the throne of grace upon our labours in the cause of Christ and His Church, which you have done so much to stimulate; and shall from our hearts pray God ever and in all things to prosper you and yours.

(Signed)   JOHN FREDERICTON,

And on behalf of the Clergy.

Fredericton, Sept. 2, 1853.

The Archdeacon then came forward and presented the following address to the Bishop of the Diocese :

To the Right Reverend JOHN, *Lord Bishop of Fredericton :*

MAY IT PLEASE YOUR LORDSHIP, — Your clergy cannot permit this, their first meeting in the permanent Cathedral of the Diocese, to separate without offering your lordship their most heartfelt congratulations on the completion of this great work, which they pray may long continue to afford your lordship, personally, all the satisfaction that you have anticipated from it, and to the worshipping people over whom you preside, all the religious advantages you have hoped and prayed for.

It is needless to assure your lordship that your clergy highly appreciate the excellent charges you have delivered to them on different occasions, and especially at this present Visitation. Their unanimous vote to request its publication is sufficient evidence of their feelings on that subject.

Your clergy would beg further to thank your lordship, and through your lordship the other munificent contributors, for the inestimable gift of the Cathedral Library, a collection of books of such varied literature as cannot fail to supply, to a considerable extent, the deficiency of their own generally limited collections.

Deeply sensible of the solemn truth, of which your lordship so feelingly reminded them in your excellent address, that, probably, they shall all never again meet in this world, they would conclude with their most fervent prayer that God may long continue your lordship's presidency over this extensive Diocese, and bless it with increasing happiness to yourself and the flock over which the Holy Ghost has made you overseer.

In the Annals of the Diocese the Bishop makes this brief entry:

1853, August 31.—The Cathedral, the corner stone of which was laid October, 1845, was consecrated this day. All praise be to God, who has enabled me, amidst many difficulties and much opposition, to finish it. May the Lord pardon all that is amiss, and make it His holy dwelling place for evermore. Amen.

Towards the close of the year, as it appeared that the Bishop would suffer a heavy pecuniary loss in the Cathedral debt, for which he was personally responsible, the Rev. C. C. Bartholomew, Mr. Hatherley, and other friends, raised most nobly £1,000 sterling for its liquidation. This paid £400 sterling due on the bells and £600 of other debt, leaving still a balance against the Bishop of £500, afterwards reduced by a benefaction of £100 from Mr. Rooke, and smaller sums from other friends, for which the Bishop tenders his grateful thanks to the donors, and above all to Him to whose goodness he owes all he has and all he hopes for in time or in eternity.

On the 19th December, 1854, there is the following note in the Annals: "On my birthday, received a letter from Mr. Hatherley, who has collected sufficient to pay off all the Cathedral debt, for which great mercy all praise be to God. Thus is the year of trouble and perplexity joyfully ended through the never-ending goodness of my God."

Beyond a question, the erection of the Cathedral, with its constant, reverent, soul-inspiring services, produced a beneficial effect on the whole Church in the Diocese. An end was brought to the building of any more unsightly edifices.

On the occasion of his early visits throughout the Diocese, the Bishop had remarked, that there was nothing externally to distinguish the sacred buildings of the Church of England from those of other bodies of Christians. It was wholly otherwise, he said, in every town and village in England. In the Diocese of Fredericton, the style of church architecture of olden days has been revolutionized, and all through the influence of the Bishop and his practical skill in architecture. At first there was some opposition. The Bishop's good taste and knowledge on the subject, were not all at once appreciated. Time soon wrought a change. For many years past, few churches in the Diocese have been planned without the Bishop's advice. In the city of St. John, Trinity church would compare well with a city church any where. So would the church of St. Paul, though built of wood. A traveller throughout the Province well knows now when he comes to a church belonging to our communion.

Following the example of the Cathedral, the system of free seats has been adopted in most instances throughout the Diocese. Each year has been noted by more frequent celebrations of the holy communion, and more frequent week-day services, and those responsive and reverent, while in many other matters of minor importance, the advice and wisdom of the Bishop have been very generally regarded.

CHAPTER XII

THE BISHOP'S TEACHING AND EXAMPLE — MARKED CHARAC-
TERISTICS — ILLUSTRATIONS — ESSAY ON " GOOD TASTE "—
CONFIRMATION TOUR IN 1857 — EXTRACTS FROM ANNALS
OF THE DIOCESE.

THE life of the Bishop was always one of unceasing
activity. In the intervals between lengthened journeyings to the distant parts of the Diocese, his attention was much given to the services and duties connected
with his Cathedral. He generally preached there twice
every Sunday, and also found time to pay a visit to his
Sunday school. All this to him was a work of love. In
his letters, he often speaks of the happy hours given up to
worship in the house of God; of the crowded attendance on
the Lord's Day, and the increasing number of communicants.

As years went on, the Bishop was better understood.
Those feelings of distrust to which we have repeatedly
alluded were passing away. People began to see that there
was no going towards Rome, no danger from Grecian gifts,
nothing to be feared either in the Cathedral services or the
teaching of the Bishop.

Very great was the influence of his preaching and addresses. Their excellence will be plainly observed in the
preceding extracts. There was something wonderfully attractive in his sermons — always something fresh — something original in the way of holy teaching and illustration,
which seemed to go straight to the heart and conscience of
the hearer. There was displayed profound learning and
knowledge of the holy scripture, and yet the language suited
the capacity almost of little children. Those who had

(125)

listened most frequently to his addresses to those confirmed, could hardly ever find a repetition of what had previously been said.

Once during the season of Lent, in the city of St. John, the Bishop gave a course of instructions on the difficulties in the Old Testament scriptures. He spoke without notes, and engaged the rapt attention of all his hearers in a large and crowded hall. "He spoke," said one, capable of judging, but who had not beforetime fully appreciated the Bishop's ways, " as one inspired." The study of the original text was with the Bishop, constant and unvarying. His Hebrew psalter — frequent companion in his journeys — had his own marginal notes on every difficult passage. His translation of the Book of Job, dedicated to his clergy, displayed accurate knowledge of the Hebrew, and close and careful study.

The example of the Bishop, as a student, had a blessed influence on many, especially among the younger clergy. With what deep reverence, with what sound, unchanging views did he look upon the word of God! It was a great privilege to hear him read the lessons. He generally read one or both at the daily services in the Cathedral. Both in reading and in preaching there was a quiet simplicity, combined with a softness and clearness of utterance, which reached the ear of the most distant in very crowded assemblies. One filling a high position in social life, who had for many years been an attendant at the Cathedral, said that she received the greatest spiritual strength by the deeply impressive manner in which the Bishop pronounced the benediction.

In imparting information in private, the Bishop had the kindest manner. He was ready to listen with attention to the opinions of others, and then he would give his own, void of all assumption. Upon any difficult passage in holy scripture his explanations were often found clearer and more satisfactory than those imparted by valued commentaries.

What was said of the late Bishop of Winchester, very fully applies to the first Bishop of Fredericton:

He was a man of great learning, and had read very widely, and yet it would not be very easy to find any one so exceedingly modest and gentle in putting forth his learning to others. It would not be easy to match him, in that sweetness of humility, which, even when he was talking to others who had no pretensions to share his very wide acquaintance with the writings of the early church, caused him to be so simple and so gentle in the assertion of his opinions, so ready to listen to what any one else had to say, so singularly deferential in his manner, and so encouraging to those younger than himself.

It was a vast advantage to students in divinity to have recourse to such an instructor, guide, and example. When at home in Fredericton, the Bishop had, once a week, a class for instruction. To candidates for holy orders he ever afforded kindly help. Many were indebted to him for the gifts of valuable works, and others received substantial assistance when it was needed. In the case of the younger clergy stationed in Fredericton, the Bishop was ready to go with them to visit the sick and suffering, and in other cases of difficulty. All through his life, till the later period when physical strength began to fail, he was ever ready with his wise and kindly ministrations to the sick and dying, and no temporal want brought to his notice was left unrelieved. When his mind was preoccupied with weighty cares and difficulties, the Bishop was, at times in these earlier years, abrupt and hasty, especially in his intercourse with those wanting in zeal and love for the Church. If, in this way, offence was given, it soon wore away, and in many instances ended in enduring friendship. Under a manner at times repelling, there was found true sterling worth—the sincere good heart. As the Bishop's teaching and character were more fully understood, people felt he was worthy of the fullest trust and confidence.

What we are speaking of may be illustrated by one marked instance. Among the opponents of the Bishop in the earlier years of his episcopate was a leading member of the bar and the legislature. He afterwards filled the highest judicial post in the Supreme Court of Canada. When·this gentleman had learned to know more of the Bishop and of his work, he came forward manfully, and, to his honour, at a meeting connected with the work of the church, said that he desired to express his regret publicly for the line of action he had previously taken. "I have discovered," he said, "that your lordship was right and I was wrong."

In Church music the Bishop took great delight. His proficiency and good taste are generally known and highly appreciated. The reader will see this point well set forth in a valued letter written by Colonel Maunsell, which appears farther on.

A Diocesan Hymnal had been compiled in 1855 by the Bishop, with the assistance of a committee of his clergy. This was a great improvement on the old metrical version of the Psalter by Tate & Brady. Soon this hymnal was found too meagre, and, at the recommendation of the Bishop, Hymns Ancient and Modern was very generally adopted. In nothing was there a greater improvement gradually brought about in the churches in the Diocese than in all that relates to public praise in the services of God's house.

In the Bishop's lengthened and frequent journeys, before the existence of railways, he came in contact with all sorts of people. They invariably treated him with the greatest respect. He would, however, often tell of many most amusing incidents, and of jokes, sometimes at his own expense; for, with all his seriousness, he had a keen sense of the ludicrous, and a peculiar delight in anything quaint or odd. This vein of humour made him charming in social life, when surrounded by his friends, and the cares of his office laid aside for awhile. He was so quick to see the humorous aspect of things or persons, and his way of speaking of them was inimitable, always taking care to keep back what would injure or hurt the feelings of others.

The Bishop was at one time on his way to England, probably on his second visit. On board the steamer was a very active, forward lady, who was seeking to obtain autographs of any distinguished passengers. After repeated solicitations she persuaded the Bishop to sign his name in her book, "John Fredericton." This was not sufficient. "I want you to say what you are." The Bishop complied with the lady's request, and wrote beneath his name, "A miserable sinner!" At one time he was waited on by a clergyman who was ready for employment in the Diocese. "To be very candid," the reverend gentleman said, "you must know, my lord, that I am a very low churchman." The Bishop replied: "I only hope you are a very humble one."

We have already noticed the Bishop's chief joy in the public service in the house of God. This was especially marked in the celebration of the Holy Eucharist. On such occasions it would seem as if his whole mind and spirit were absorbed in worship and adoration. In his constant private devotions also, "he strengthened himself in God." Nor did he pray for himself alone. We have already called attention to the prayers of his mother in her son's behalf in his early boyhood. In the notes kindly furnished by Mrs. Medley, she adds:

A prayerful mother made a prayerful son, as the following testimony from one of his clergy will show:

"Few of us know how much of our dear Bishop's work was done upon his knees. Through all his long episcopate he daily prayed

I

for every clergyman in his Diocese, remembering each one in turn before the throne of God, not by name only, but as to his own special needs and the circumstances of his individual work. As the years passed on the list became a long one, for though many went to other spheres of labour, and many, we trust, to the rest of Paradise, yet their names were neither struck off nor forgotten. Whether in other lands or in other mansions of the Heavenly Father's house, they were still commended to God's care and bless- ing, and as the task grew longer the love grew stronger to perform it. Can we doubt but that this was one secret of the almost un- bounded influence he had among his clergy. Their work was his, and while he helped it with sympathy and counsel, and by open- handed liberality, he helped it still more by his *secret prayers*."

The earnest desire of the Bishop when a boy, " that he might be able at some time to compose what might really be called sermons," was granted in full measure, as years went by, as the following testimony will show :

A warm personal friend of the Bishop's, a Canadian, had some literary business with one of the law lords of the House of Peers in London. When the interview was closing, Lord H. spoke of Fredericton, and said he was on the western circuit nearly fifty years ago, when Mr. Medley was appointed to the Diocese, and accompanied Judge Patteson to St. Thomas' to hear his farewell sermon. The church was densely crowded, and it was evident that it was no ordinary tie of love and esteem that bound the people to their pastor — every one present seemed to feel the parting as a personal sorrow. The sermon was plain, earnest, practical, but with a tenderness of appeal, a spirit-stirring earnestness that could never be forgotten. The fifty added years of a busy life had not erased the distinct impression of it from his mind.

The Bishop's friend said something of his later life, and that he was as deeply loved and revered by his Canadian as he had been by his old English friends. Lord H. at once quoted those beautiful lines —

"Upon its mother's knee, a new born child
Weeping it lay, while all around it smiled,
So live, that sinking to thy last long sleep
Thou, then, mayst smile while all around thee weep."

Bishop Medley was always the Bishop. Unconsciously you were made to feel that. But it was the office he magnified and not himself, so that you never found his manner out of place. As it has been written of another:

There was an unconsciousness of outward things, of the furniture of life, which left him freer than most men to face the individual soul that approached him, there was also a fine consistency in his originality; no tampering with the world, no trying to serve two masters. The graveness of his presence was felt by all who approached him; he seemed to be invested by a strange remoteness from the affairs of the world.

His mode of life at Bishopscote was singularly plain and unostentatious. What was largely saved from outward show and expensive living, was added to the funds for the poor or for the benefit of the Church. In this, as in so many other ways, he set a bright and needed example. Nor was there at Bishopscote any want of hospitality and kind, cheerful greeting; and marks of high culture and good taste were evident there. The words of Tennyson, of one of the great among men, might be applied to Bishop Medley in his domestic and social life:

"As the greatest only are,
In his simplicity sublime."

The following incident is given by the Rev. Charles Medley, late rector of Sussex, in his report to the S. P. G., in the year 1869:

One very stormy and bitterly cold Monday in March last, the Bishop started with me for Dutch Valley. We had to break our road through about fourteen inches of snow for nine miles, and then climb up on our hands and knees to the church, which is on a steep hill—a feat not easily accomplished, for underneath the snow was a thick crust of ice, upon which we slid down almost as fast as we crept up. However, after many struggles and efforts, we succeeded in reaching the corner of the church, when a furious gust of wind sent the Bishop and his missionary flying down the hill again, with the Bishop's robe box following. When at last we managed to get inside the church, we found four men for a congregation. On the following day I met one of my most constant attendants at church, and asked him why it was he was not present, especially when the Bishop was there. "Well, sir," he said, "it was such an awful storm, it wasn't fit for a dog to be out."

As an illustration of the Bishop's varied mode of teaching, the following extracts are given from a lecture on "Good Taste," read before the Church of England Young Men's Society, St. John, 1857 :

We are all impressed by the past in a far greater degree than we are willing to allow ; but we must remember that the past history of mankind is a treasure given us by God for our present improvement. In referring to this history, we ought to endeavour to form a cautious, charitable and discriminating judgment, and we should especially be on our guard against two errors, equally pernicious — a wholesale condemnation and a slavish imitation of past ages.

To refer to the first, our ancestors, and the ancestors of other nations, were men of like passions, beset by like temptations, and possessed of like virtues as ourselves, and in many respects neither much better nor much worse. For the political institutions or religious errors of their times they were not wholly responsible. . . . But they ought never to be judged by the standard by which we ourselves should be judged, who live in times of liberty, of which they knew nothing, and under the shade of institutions many of which did not then exist. . . . . . .

On the other hand, a servile imitation is as much to be censured, though perhaps, in the present day, not so much to be apprehended. Whatever was noble, generous or wise in the manners, morals or institutions of the past, we should study, and, as far as possible and useful, we may reproduce. . . . Mere servile imitation is characterized in our tongue by a very contemptuous, but a very forcible and significant term, *apishness*, which exactly expresses the error I am speaking of.

. . . There is another error of which I have taken note, and which good taste will always eschew. In writing controversial letters, it is astonishing how eager people are to fasten on each other the charge of falsehoods, and to hurl at each other the most vile and contemptuous epithets. Now falsehoods should never be alleged against another without the clearest evidence. All allowance should be made for the mistakes into which the most accurate are prone to fall, and no virtuous or charitable mind can feel a pleasure in the discovery that his former friend, acquaintance or neighbour, is guilty of the sin of falsehood. . . . The affixing this bad construction is a mark not only of bad taste, but of a very unscrupulous mind. The time will come when one grain of real charity will be more valued than all the clever, bitter things written or spoken; and it is one sad effect of writing to please the lower class of minds, and to humour the caprice of the hour, that such writers appear to be entirely reckless as to what they say, or whom they wound.

In our household arrangements, in our dress, in the social festivities, we shall eschew the extremes of extravagance and meanness, and look upon all things, great and small, as given us that we may discharge the duties belonging to them in the best possible manner. Especially we shall seek to lead the mind of youth from the love of all that is selfish, sensuous and degrading, and to give them opportunities of enjoying real beauty in this beautiful world. . . . and pleasures which are conducive to their physical and moral health and intellectual growth, and which leave no sting behind.

Thus, while we carefully guard the sacred deposit of truth from all adulteration, and found our religion strictly and soberly on God's most holy word, good taste will preserve that religion from sourness and self-complacency, and will make it gracious and acceptable to all who have sufficient candour to appreciate our intentions, and generally useful to the world.

As illustrating the Bishop's devotedness to his work, and also the simple, homely way in which he went in and out among his people, a few extracts are now given from the very interesting summary of a recent confirmation tour

which he read before the anniversary meeting of the Church
Society, February 11th, 1858 :

I left Fredericton on St. Barnabas' day, June 11, for St. Andrews.
On Sunday, the 14th, I confirmed twenty-nine and preached morning and evening. The congregations on both occasions were large
and attentive. Dr. Alley, who has held the rectory between thirty
and forty years, is still able, by the blessing of God, to perform
three full services on Sunday, one of them at a village three miles
distant, a duty which very few at his advanced age could perform.

June 16th, I proceeded with Dr. Alley to St. Stephen, and on the
17th confirmed eleven. It was a great satisfaction to me on this
occasion to be assisted by the Right Rev. Dr. Burgess, Bishop of
Maine, who very kindly preached to us, and gave us a most earnest
and instructive discourse, useful alike to young and old, which I
enjoyed exceedingly. He was accompanied by his valued friend
and presbyter, Rev. G. W. Durell, of Calais, who has been of signal
benefit to this Diocese. The church at St. Stephen has been greatly
improved by the addition of a new chancel, an excellent organ, a
better arrangement of the pulpit and desk, a new communion table
and chair (carved, I believe, by Mr. Durell's own hands), and by
being painted throughout. The singing also was much improved.
For many of these additions to the church, and for much of its
life and spirit, we are indebted to the zealous liberality of a young
layman, whose modesty might perhaps be pained if I mentioned his
name, but whose kindness will not be forgotten by his blessed Master.

June 18th, I proceeded to St. Davids ; confirmed nine, and
preached. There was a large and attentive congregation, though
the day was wet. The church, as a whole, is one of the best of our
country churches, and reflects great credit on the zeal of its pastor,.
Rev. J. S. Thomson.

June 19, Mr. Thomson drove me to St. Patrick, distant thirteen
miles. It was a wet and fatiguing day. I confirmed seven persons
there, and preached. Mr. Carson extended to us his usual kind
hospitality.

On the 20th I went to Campobello, to a house where hospitality
always makes a welcome, and on Sunday, 21st, confirmed five and

preached twice in St. Ann's Chapel, lately built by the exertions of
Hon. Captain Robinson, aided by the S. P. C. K., the D. C. S., the
parishioners, and a few friends.   The Rev. J. S. Williams assisted
me and accompanied me in walks to visit some sick and suffering
members of the congregation and some young and old persons.

On Saturday, the 27th, I left in the packet, accompanied by Dr.
Alley, and with some difficulty and not a few curious adventures or
misadventures, we reached the parsonage at Grand Manan after
dark, very much disposed to retire to rest.   The next day (Sunday)
I confirmed four and baptized an adult, and preached again in the
afternoon.   Mr. Carey, at my request, rode five miles to take his
usual afternoon service, but all his flock had come up the same five
miles to hear the Bishop, so that his labour was lost.   The congregation was very attentive, and I saw with pleasure many old familiar
faces and heard them join heartily in the prayers, and some of them
still more heartily in the singing.   Mr. Craig, who seems to be
elected church warden for life, was at his post as usual.   The
next day I went to Seal Cove and held services there and preached.
Thence over a very rough road to Southern Head, where I baptized
Mrs. McCaughlan and three infants, and confirmed Mr. and Mrs.
McCaughlan.   As they reside on Gannet Rock, eight miles from
shore, and perfectly inaccessible for three-fourths of the year, my
visit was timed very seasonably.   I have since sent them a little
present of books, as they have a great deal of time for reading.

Sunday, July 5th, I confirmed thirty-nine at St. George, a very
considerable number, considering that there is also a Roman
Catholic, a Baptist, and I believe a Presbyterian congregation there.
There is a good Sunday school and an excellent day school in the
place.   In the afternoon we went to Pennfield, where I confirmed
twelve.   The congregation was crowded.   It is not too much to
say of this mission, that I never visit it without fresh evidence of
the zeal and usefulness of its pastor, and I never leave it without
being strengthened and refreshed.

On Tuesday we drove to Lepreaux, and thence thirteen miles,
happily accompanied by a guide—for otherwise in crossing the tide-
harbour, we should probably have got a good wetting, or worse —

and reached Lepreaux light-house in the evening. Here Mr. Thomas hospitably received us, and the next day I confirmed ten, baptized a child, administered the Lord's Supper, and preached in the little church at Dipper Harbour, three miles distant. At Musquash the next day I confirmed six, preached and administered the Lord's Supper. The church at Musquash has been much improved, and a chancel has been built. The congregation are remarkable for their excellent way of responding, the two church wardens and their families setting them a good example in this respect. The singing also is hearty and general.

On Friday, July 17th, I went up to Hampton in the steamer, and on Sunday confirmed thirty-seven in the Parish Church, and addressed a congregation so crowded that sixty or seventy persons could not find seat room. In the afternoon I proceeded to Norton, where I confirmed eighteen and preached. The singing was excellent, and staying to practice with the choir the time passed rapidly away. I did not return till eight o'clock.

On Monday, 20th, Mr. DeVeber drove me to his parsonage at Upham. Mr. Walker accompanied us, and at his request I turned aside from the road to visit and confirm a blind woman, aged eighty-four, in her own house. She appeared very devout and very thankful for my visit. On Tuesday we went to Quaco, distant twelve miles, but from the extremely hilly nature of the road, one hill being nearly three miles long and another two miles long, it appears much further. The mission of Quaco for a long time was in a very doubtful state, and the people were very apathetic. By perseverance, however, progress has been made ; the building purchased from the Methodists has been gradually converted into something like a church ; it is floored and ceiled, and has rough benches. The congregation are very steady, and though the day was very unfavourable more than one hundred were assembled. I confirmed eight. On the 23rd we drove to Londonderry, a settlement eighteen miles distant, among the hills which are crossed on the new road to Albert County from St. John. The little chapel was now consecrated by the name of St. Paul. It was crowded to its utmost capacity by a most attentive body of worshippers and hearers, who drank in every word, though I spoke for nearly an hour; and I am sure I felt as happy as they appeared to be. Some curious proofs were related to me of the readiness of some of these rough soldiers of the Cross, to defend the Bishop, not only by word of mouth, but if necessary by more powerful weapons. On the 25th, I confirmed nine at the little hamlet of South Stream, and on Sunday I confirmed eighteen at the Upham Parish Church, and preached morning and evening. Among the numerous congregation in the morning was an aged woman of eighty, who forty years since was an inmate of His Excellency General Smythe's family, and who, though living in the bush, had remained steadfast in the communion of the Church. She had walked three miles to church this summer, and now the missionary went ten miles to fetch her, and brought her back full of a trembling joy, to receive the rite of confirmation. This is one of the most laborious missions in the Province; too much so indeed for any one man, or I may say for any one horse, but it is well served and the fruits are apparent. And though this mission always gives me a laborious round of work, yet I never leave it without comfort and satisfaction. Mr. DeVeber kindly drove me to Springfield on 22nd July, and though by miscalculation I arrived a day before my time, yet the people cheerfully left their work and came to the church in considerable numbers; twenty-four were confirmed.   .   .   .   .   .

September 22nd I left Fredericton with Rev. J. B. Medley for Prince William, where I confirmed seventeen, and the next day forty-two at Magundy, among the rest an aged man of eighty-nine, with his two children, daughters-in-law and five grandchildren. The present rector has been most kindly received, and is indefatigably engaged in the good work. His accession to our little band lays us under a second obligation to St. Augustine's College, Canterbury, of which my dear and valued friend, Bishop Coleridge, was the first warden. From Prince William we proceeded to Woodstock, where, on Sunday, the 27th, I confirmed thirty-five, and administered the Lord's Supper, assisted by Mr. Street and my son, and I preached again in the evening. In this thriving and populous neighbourhood there is quite work enough for a third clergyman.

The clergy who have hitherto assisted Mr. Street, though very kindly treated by himself and his parishioners, are not ambitious to end their days as curates of Woodstock, being very hardly worked and very poorly paid. The parishioners presented their rector with a new wagon the morning after my arrival.

October the 24th I visited Kingston, and on the following day confirmed in the church at the Reach (the Parish Church being under repairs) one hundred and seven persons, being the largest number ever presented to me for confirmation at any one place in the Diocese. I am still more gratified to find that this confirmation has added largely to the communicants, *one hundred and thirty-five*, all parishioners having communicated on Christmas Day, at Kingston, when the Parish Church was re-opened for divine service, having been almost rebuilt. It is much improved by a central passage, a small chancel, and by the removal of two most unsightly desks; and the whole expense being, I believe, more than £900, is met without any application for aid to the Diocesan Church Society, though I am afraid an undue proportion will fall on the rector. Kingston is an instance of what indefatigable parochial visiting will do to keep together a flock long united to the Church by loyal and hereditary affection. May its worthy rector long be spared to carry on the work which his father and grandfather so happily began.

On the 27th October I returned to Fredericton, having, by the blessing of God, travelled twelve hundred and fifty-five miles, confirmed eight hundred and ninety-six persons, and having had abundant evidence that our Church is, on the whole, at least, holding her ground, laying her foundations deeper, and that whilst her clergy can claim no exemption from the infirmities and imperfections common to their brethren, they are, as a body, striving to do their duty in the responsible office to which God has called them.

The mission of our Church in this Province appears to me to be a most important one, both as regards the laity and the clergy.

We have to prove ourselves the worthy successors of those noble and consistent men who sacrificed all their worldly prospects to what they believed to be their duty to their king and country, and brought with them an invariably strong attachment to the British Constitution in Church and State.

We have to prove ourselves the worthy descendants of those still nobler spirits who bequeathed to us the Reformation, whose efforts guaranteed to us freedom from persecution, from doctrinal corruption, and from the Roman yoke, and whose judgment and sagacity, aided by the assistance of wisdom from above, designed to reject only the evil and to retain only the good.

We have to prove ourselves worthy of the Church which numbers among its members a Ridley, a Leighton, a Hooker, a Taylor, a Pearson, a Kerr, a Wilberforce, and a Howard. We have to prove ourselves worthy of a Church which rejoices in the circulation of the Scriptures, because it acknowledges the Bible as its rule of faith ; which clings to the decisions of primitive antiquity as the surest bulwark against ancient and modern heresy; which has nothing to fear but everything to hope for from the progress of science and the spread of learning, and which desires nothing better than that its doctrines should be known, examined and sifted.

Some idea of the course of events during the next few years may be gathered from the following extracts from the Annals of the Diocese :

1860, August 4, Saturday.— His Royal Highness the Prince of Wales, accompanied by the Duke of Newcastle, Earl St. Germains, General Bruce, etc., arrived at Fredericton. On Sunday they attended the Cathedral at eleven o'clock. . . . The Cathedral was crowded to overflowing, but the congregation, though a very mixed assembly, were very orderly.

The Bishop went to the west door to receive the Prince, the whole congregation rising, and God Save the Queen was played by Mr. Hayter, who ably presided at the organ.

.   .   .   .

The Bishop dined at Government House on Monday, and presented an address in the name of the clergy at the levee.

September 2. The new organ, presented by the Bishop to the Cathedral, was used for the first time.

.   .   .   .

December 25. Observed as usual, and a midnight service, well attended, in the Cathedral on New Year's Eve. Three hundred and fifty-two persons communicated between Christmas Day and the Epiphany inclusive.

Confirmed this year, eight hundred and twenty-two; travelled fourteen hundred and fifty-one miles; consecrated two churches, one burial ground, one rural cemetery; ordained two priests. All praise be to God.

. . . .

1861, May 31. His Royal Highness Prince Alfred arrived in Fredericton, and stayed till Thursday, June 6th. He attended divine service in the Cathedral on Sunday morning, June 2nd.

. . . On Monday he inspected the Cathedral, the clock, bells, etc. His visit was without state.

In the year's summary it is stated that the Bishop travelled two thousand nine hundred and fourteen miles.

1862, January 18. The Bishop went to St. John and stayed two Sundays, preaching to some of the troops sent from England in consequence of the difficulty respecting the "Trent" with the American government. The soldiers assembled in the Mechanics' Institute. . . . .

On the 28th he returned to Fredericton. Five thousand troops, with artillery, passed through the Province on their way to Quebec and other places in Canada. . . . Some were landed at St. Andrews, and went by the railway to Canterbury, and thence to Woodstock. The travelling was very good, the troops were well provided with warm clothing, and they travelled on sleds holding eight men besides the driver, by stages of about thirty miles a day, in companies of one hundred men, and later of one hundred and sixty.

The inhabitants of St. John provided a series of entertainments for the troops, where they were most plenteously feasted. They were extremely pleased at their reception.

The records in the Annals for the next few years are mostly of a routine character. Every year speaks of an increased amount of work. Most touching notices are given in the case of the death of any one of the clergy, and sad expressions of deepest sorrow, in the happily rare instances of misconduct.

In the year 1872 the summary states :

Confirmed eight hundred and one; ordained deacons, two; priest, one; consecrated churches, five; burial grounds, four; travelled three thousand four hundred and ninety-nine miles, during which the Bishop enjoyed almost uninterrupted health. All praise be to God.

CHAPTER XIII.

Diocesan and Provincial Synods—The Bishop Chosen
Metropolitan—Extracts from Addresses to the Provincial Synod—Presentation of Crozier—Address
and Reply.

AS early as the year 1856, the question with regard to
the formation of a Diocesan Synod was agitated.
The work undertaken by the Diocesan Church Society, which embraced the clergy and representatives of the
laity, in some respect supplied the place of a Synod. In
nearly all the other Canadian Dioceses they had their Diocesan Synods, in connection with which the home missions
were maintained. At the time referred to, Fredericton and
Nova Scotia alone stood aloof from the synodical system
which had been adopted elsewhere in the Dominion of
Canada.

In his charge to the clergy, delivered in 1856, the Bishop
alludes to this subject. "Our Church," he says, "though
amply supplied with standards of doctrine, is ill-furnished
with discipline, and this is sometimes exercised in an infor-
mal manner. . . . The power left in the Bishop's hands
to enforce discipline is encumbered with many legal difficulties. . . . The establishment of a code of Church
laws would be one use of a Synod legally constituted."

When we look back to that time, it seems strange and
unaccountable to notice the warm opposition to the measure
of which we are speaking. This was the case with regard
to several of the largest and most influential parishes in the
Diocese. By a church newspaper of the day this opposition was encouraged. It was contended that undue power

(142)

would be given to the Bishop, and the rights of rectors of parishes might be infringed.

" The best answer however," the Bishop said, " to these objections, is, that in the Church Society, no freedom of discussion, no independence of opinion has ever been checked by the presence and veto of the Bishop, and that no measures adverse to the liberties of the clergy or laity have ever been carried by his influence. If, therefore, the constitution of the Synod should resemble that which is already in operation, what is there to fear? Or, why should this unworthy suspicion be entertained? Synodical assemblies would also be found useful in regulating the temporal affairs of the Church, and in devising such prudent measures as may promote its enlargement and prosperity."

It was not, however, till the lapse of six years after the charge, from which we have quoted, was delivered, that a Synod was constituted. During these years the rough edges of party spirit were being worn off. Time works wonders in this way, when there is really no ground for distrust or suspicion. A meeting called for the especial purpose decided *unanimously* in favour of a Diocesan Synod. The efforts of the best and most capable among the clergy and laity were engaged in the preparation of a Declaration of Principles, a Constitution and Canons. Proper and due authority was assigned to the Bishop. A charter of incorporation was obtained from the legislature, with authority to act in all matters relating to the well-being of the Church. Still later an act of the legislature was obtained, codifying all the laws relating to the Church of England in the Diocese, with the enactment of other provisions agreed to by the Synod. The organization of the Diocesan Synod, it must be admitted, has benefitted the Church in many ways. As in the deliberations of the Church Society, so without exception it has been in the Synod; in no instance has any conflict arisen with the Bishop. As chairman at all meetings, he presided with uniform impartiality and patience. Among the laymen attending the meetings of the Synod have generally been included the foremost men in the Province. They may have held decided opinions, differing in some cases from those of the Bishop, and perhaps from a majority of the members of the Synod; but- in no one instance has there been party strife, or a party vote in the Synod of the Diocese of Fredericton.

In this respect a striking contrast is presented in some of the other Dioceses of Canada. There you will find a marked line, a decided party vote, especially in the election of delegates to the Provincial Synod.

From various circumstances affecting the Dioceses in Ontario, and from the fact of many important livings having been filled by clergymen from Ireland, there was at one time a strong majority in the Provincial Synod, opposed to anything that might be called High Church views. There was danger, it was thought, lest measures might be adopted which might be deeply regretted throughout the Church in the Dominion, something allied to the line taken by the Church of Ireland.

Not a shadow of party feeling was manifested in the election of the first delegates to the Provincial Synod. The Synod itself was impartially represented. For the most part, however, the delegates were ready to act in concord. On their admission to the Provincial Synod, together with the delegates from Nova Scotia, many of whom were of a like type, the state of things there underwent a change. Dangers, which had been previously anticipated, were no longer dreaded. A prominent member of the Synod, as the proceedings went on, and questions of importance were discussed, was heard to say: " We greatly rejoice in the presence of your people from the Maritime Provinces; you are the very salt of the earth."

Of more importance still was the presence of the Bishop of Fredericton in the upper house. His wise counsel, his deep learning and theological attainments, were of the greatest value. Later on additional strength was added to that body by the attendance of the Bishop Coadjutor of Fredericton, with his bright scholarship and high intellectual culture.

In the Annals the Bishop wrote with regard to the first attendance at the Provincial Synod: "The delegates were received with great enthusiasm." He alludes to the presence of the Bishop of Lichfield (Dr. Selwyn), and his address at a great missionary meeting.

It is added: "October 3rd, the Bishop of Lichfield, with his chaplain and secretary, arrived at Fredericton, having travelled from Nebraska, one thousand five hundred miles, to show his friendship. He preached twice in the Cathedral, and dwelt most earnestly on the missionary work, especially on the life and labours of Bishop Patteson, of Melanesia. Great numbers attended. . . . He left us, much to our sorrow, on Monday, the 5th, to attend the General Convention in New York."

Upon the resignation of Bishop Oxenden, the Bishop of Fredericton was chosen to fill the office of Metropolitan. At first the Bishop's position was somewhat unsatisfactory, but not from any personal objection. It was claimed, that in point of law, the office pertained to the See of Montreal. The subject was discussed at length in the Synod, without any animosity, and the question was finally settled in favour of an election on the part of the House of Bishops. A canon was passed to that effect. By all parties, the manner in which the duties of the Metropolitan were performed by Bishop Medley met with full approval.

The first meeting of the Provincial Synod, under the Bishop of Fredericton as Metropolitan, was held at Montreal,

K

September 8th, 1880. The Metropolitan, in his address to the Synod, alludes to his election as the choice of the bishops. He then speaks of the position of the Church in the colonies as wholly set free from the ties which were long supposed to connect us with the State in England. This freedom required great caution. "Our wisdom," he said, "lies in making a broad distinction between what may be fairly regarded as things alterable, and of no vital consequence, arising either out of necessary political changes or the usages and feelings of congregations and the fluctuating sentiments of the times, and those deep and solemn truths revealed to us in holy scripture, embedded firmly in our three ancient creeds, interpreted by the first General Councils of the Church, and secured to us by our own formularies, to which the ancient rule, *Quod semper, quod ubique, quod ab omnibus*, may be safely applied."

The Metropolitan urged the need of deeper learning on the part of the clergy, especially with reference to the works of the primitive fathers, and the records of Church history. He then alludes to the proposal before the legislature, which was subsequently carried, to legalize the marriage of a man with his deceased wife's sister. "I trust," the Bishop added, "that it will be deemed desirable by this Synod to express in a canon what has previously been expressed by resolution, and to guard, as far as possible, our clergy and our laity from participating in marriages contrary to the spirit of the Gospel, contrary to the mind of the Church in its purest ages, and contrary to the judgment of the Reformed Church of England.[1]

"And now to bring this address to a close, we pray that the same spirit of brotherly love and forbearance which characterized the last session may be shown on the present occasion. Let the awful words of the inspired apostle never

---

[1] The advice of the Metropolitan was acted upon by the Synod.

be absent from our minds, that the 'fire' of God's searching judgment shall 'try every man's work of what sort it is.' No man amongst us can devolve on the collective body the responsibility which God has imposed on himself alone, and no man, therefore, should forget that if he build 'the wood, hay and stubble' of faithless counsels and unworthy actions on the great foundation of God's Church, the last fire will both try and consume it; the scheme which he deemed most successful shall perish in the sight of all men, even as the leaves and trees of the forest are caught up in the blazing whirlwind, and their place is found no more."

Immediately after the first day's session of the Provincial Synod, the Prolocutor—the Venerable George Whittaker, Archdeacon of York—in the presence of a large number of clerical and lay delegates, and in their behalf, presented the Metropolitan with a very costly and most beautiful crozier, or Metropolitan's staff, accompanied with the following address:

The first assembling of the Synod of this Province, under your lordship's presidency, has been regarded by many of its members as a most fitting occasion for presenting you with a small token of the veneration and affection with which you have been long and justly regarded by the members of the Church in Canada.

Your prolonged episcopate, extending over a term of thirty-five years, has furnished abundant testimony to your unwearied devotion to the duties of your sacred calling, and has given repeated occasions for proving your unshaken fidelity to the holy doctrines and the godly discipline of Christ, while the words of counsel in which your lordship addressed us, at the opening of the present session, give us profound cause for thankfulness, that, in a time of peculiar danger, we enjoy the inestimable benefits of witnessing the example of your steadfastness and of being warned with all fidelity as to our own most solemn obligations.

Such are the grounds on which our reverence for your lordship rests, while those of us who have enjoyed the privilege of personal intercourse with you cannot but have learned to regard you with deep affection. Witnessing, as we do, in your instance, a rare blending of strength with gentleness, of the unyielding constancy which refuses to relinquish any truth, or to abandon any duty, with a genial, courteous spirit of Christian sympathy, which draws others to itself by cords of love.

We pray that your lordship may long continue to preside over this Ecclesiastical Province, and that, if it should be necessary that your Diocesan labours should be shared with another, there may be associated with you one in whom you may place the fullest confidence, who may serve with you as a son with a father, affording not only official relief, but also the solace of personal friendship and of cordial intercourse.

This offering of our reverence and of our love is the emblem of that pastoral office which you have so long and faithfully discharged, and as we present it to you we would direct our thoughts and hopes to the Great Day "when the Chief Shepherd shall appear," when all who, constrained by His love, have lovingly tended His sheep on earth, "shall receive a crown of glory which fadeth not away."

To this address the Metropolitan made the following reply :

My Dear and Honoured Brethren:

Your words of affection and reverence can hardly be received by me without feelings of deepest thankfulness, humility and fear — of thankfulness for so unexpected and too little deserved tokens of your esteem and love, of fear lest the Great Searcher of all hearts should find in me far more, and more glaring, imperfections than your too partial eyes discern.

Still it is no small consolation to me, amidst the trials and burdens of my holy office, to know that my exercise of that office for so long a period, has won for me the regard of so many whom I esteem and love, and it will be an additional incitement to labour on in our Great Master's work, and to beware that no unwise or faithless act of mine may rob me of that approval which I hold so precious.

What could be more appropriate, what more touching, than the symbol of the Shepherd's pastoral office, committed to me by Him who laid down His life for us all! This valuable token of true love will be dear to me as the remembrance of yourselves individually, and as the symbol of a hope which looks beyond the grave to a place of blessed reunion, where the Shepherd and the sheep shall find resting places, quietness and assurance forever.

I thank you for the interest you take in my desire for a Coadjutor. At the age of nearly seventy-six, I naturally desire not idleness but help, and the help, I trust, by God's blessing to obtain, and I ask your earnest prayers that all you have spoken may be fully realized. . . . So may the love of God be with you all.

To the account of the presentation given by the Bishop in the Annals of the Diocese the following note is added: "The crozier is to be the property of the Metropolitan and his successors in that office."

At the meeting of the Provincial Synod, July 12th, 1883, the Metropolitan delivered an address, in which he says:

As three years have passed quickly since we last met in Synod, and each year calls more loudly upon us to "work while it is day," and that day short, so uncertain, full of a terrible responsibility, you will pardon me, I trust, for setting before you this urgent question, What is to be the future of the Ecclesiastical Province of the Canadian Church?

I call it the Canadian Church, not for a moment forgetting that dear Church of England, in whose sheltering arms the earliest years of many of us were spent; but chiefly to call to your remembrance that no love for the old country, no union and communion with the Church of England in the Catholic faith, can absolve us from a sacred and solemn trust for the good of Canada, for which we must give an account when our privileges, our duties, and our works shall be weighed in the balance of God's merciful, but even-handed justice. . . . .

Our position in Canada is a trying one. We live in the very midst of a very whirlpool of diversities of beliefs, of bodies all vehemently asserting their position in the Church of Christ; one large and important section claiming to be the only representatives of the Catholic Church on earth, others denying this claim, but divided into various sects and parties, yet full of energy, proving the strength of their convictions by the fire of their zeal, honourably desirous to raise and maintain their position by institutions of learning, and by all the other appliances which modern enterprise and ingenuity uses to increase its members and make itself a power felt and recognized in the body politic. We should do ill to overlook, we should do worse if we attempt to despise such efforts of Christian sentiment and earnestness. Even when we deem it misdirected, it is important for us to remember the peculiarity of our position. On some points we closely touch our neighbours, even while we seem most to differ from them. In others, while we seem to agree, we are forced to admit essential differences. For example, we entirely agree with our Roman Catholic brethren in all the fundamental doctrines of Christianity, as set forth in the three great creeds, and asserted by the four (Bishop Jewel says the six) first general councils. We have no difference with them as to infant baptism, or the primitive origin of liturgies; many of our collects unaltered, or only slightly altered, are taken from sources which they honour alike with ourselves; had they been content to add no new articles of faith, and above all, not to insert a new and impassable wall of partition between us, we might have dwelt at unity in one house; but, as long as their additions to the primitive faith remain, union is impossible.

.   .   .   .

Turning to the other side, we might suppose that those who believe in the fundamentals of the Christian faith, and have no fellow-feeling for Roman doctrine, would have little to find fault with in the Church of England. But here we are met by very considerable differences both in doctrine and discipline.

.   .   .   .

I cast no reflection on the personal piety of a single member of these vast communions. God forbid that I should presume to undervalue true piety, wherever it is to be found, or refuse to recognize—thankfully to recognize—the glorious fruits of the Holy Spirit of God. Amidst the melancholy spectacle of a disunited Christendom, it is good never to forget this truth, that Elijah's ministry was sent to the ten revolted tribes, and that God had seven thousand chosen ones, where His prophet knew not one.

The Bishop goes on at some length to speak of the proposed measure with reference to unity among the various Christian bodies. He points out the uselessness of any attempt to force the subject of union on any of the religious bodies which surround us, and that we must not surrender any truths committed to our trust which serve as a connecting link with the primitive ages of the Church. He then proceeds :

We have all the elements of strength in our Church if we wisely use them—an ancient foundation, primitive usage, brilliant examples, sanctified learning, capacity for progress, missionary zeal, a providential awakening from sloth and indifference, a wonderful eagerness for the right interpretation of Scripture, an unquenchable thirst for knowledge, we may stretch out our branches to the sea and our boughs unto the river, and make our Church known, respected, beloved, progressive, wherever our language is spoken or our empire bears sway.

The Bishop then alludes to the recent consecration of Dr. Sullivan as the second Bishop of Algoma, the Missionary Diocese of the Canadian Church, and he urges most strongly continued and generous support, not only in the missionary work, but in making a provision for the endowment of the Diocese. He speaks of the mighty prospects opening up in the great Dioceses in the West, and of one of the Bishops there, once a pupil and then a teacher in his Sunday school in England more than forty years ago.

The Bishop concludes in the following words :

What brotherly greetings we have ever met with from our dear sister Church in the United States is well known to us all. No

differences in civil government can ever part us. We belong to
the same lineage, we are heirs of the same promises, we cherish the
same truths, we maintain the same Church government. We are
numbered with them in faith, in worship, and in love. We joy in
their presence among us, and in the words of truth and soberness
that flow from their lips, and our hope is to be numbered with them
in joy everlasting.

But bear in mind that we are on our trial; keen eyes are watch-
ing our success or failure. "Canada expects every man to do his
duty."

At the meeting of the Provincial Synod, in 1886, the
Metropolitan made a brief address, referring chiefly to matters of a practical character. At the close of the proceedings he gave utterance to the following words, his last words
to the Provincial Synod:

I earnestly pray that both in what we have done, and even in
what we have left undone, a higher wisdom than our own may have
guided our deliberations, and that God may pardon whatever has
been done amiss.

The Bishop was unable to attend the meeting in 1889.
Acting in his place, at the opening of the Synod, the Bishop
of Montreal said: "He was sure they all regretted the
absence of the Most Reverend the Metropolitan, and still
more the cause of his absence."

CHAPTER XIV

EXTRACTS FROM THE BISHOP'S TRIENNIAL CHARGES TO HIS CLERGY, 1871–1877 — CALAMITOUS FIRE IN ST. JOHN — BISHOP'S SERMON.

AT the triennial visitation of the clergy on the 4th July, 1871, the charge of the Bishop embraced subjects of peculiar interest to the Church. The following extracts will be highly valued :

You may expect me to say something on two important changes in which we are all deeply interested — the revision of the Lectionary, and the revision of the English version of the Bible. Bearing in mind the eminent scholars and divines who are engaged in these revisions, and the worthy motives by which they have been influenced, I shall nevertheless venture to express my own opinions freely, and leave you to form your own judgment, according to the best information you can obtain from myself or from others.

St. James informs us that "Moses of old time hath in every city them that preach him, being read in the synagogues every Sabbath day ;" in other words, that appointed portions of the Pentateuch (and as we learn from St. Paul's address in 13th chapter of the Acts), of the Prophets also, were read on the Jewish Sabbath-days before the people. The fourth chapter of St. Luke supplies us with such a reading by our Lord himself. Following this godly custom of the Jews, the Christian Church in like manner ordered to be read select portions of the Old and New Testament. In the time of Archbishop Parker, Tables of Proper Lessons were introduced, which were nearly identical with those in our present Prayer Book, and they were settled in their present form in 1661. The Cycle of Proper Lessons seems to have been formed on two very wise principles. First, it was desired to set before us the creation, the fall, and the consequences of that fall; the steps taken by God to procure our redemption ; the election of a peculiar people to preserve true

(153)

religion in the earth, and to prepare the way for the Incarnation; and the conduct of that people, their apostasy, and their punishment, as illustrations of God's dealings both with churches and with individuals in Christian times. A second object in the selection of lessons was to fix in the minds of the worshippers the chief truths of the Christian religion in due order, whether by prophecy, as during Advent and Epiphany, and on Whitsunday; or by type, as on Good Friday, Easter Sunday, and Trinity Sunday; or by history, as in the lessons in Holy Week. Further, it is provided that the Old Testament should be read once, and the New Testament three times in the daily course throughout the year.

All will agree in the wisdom of these general principles, and in the value of the continual instruction thus given to the people at large. The chief thing to be regretted is, that both clergy and laity have so little availed themselves of the inestimable privilege; the Bible being to the great mass of our congregations, a sealed book from Sunday to Sunday, and the priest teaching his flock by daily example, that the church is the only place where, during the week, prayer is never wont to be made; and this while we vainly boast of an open Bible and an incomparable Liturgy. If we loved either the one or the other as we think we do, we should undoubtedly make much more frequent use of both. In towns especially, there can be no sufficient reason why this should not be done. Now the very fact of a selection of passages from the Bible, proves that we consider the Church authorized to consider some portions of the Bible as more instructive to a mixed congregation than others. And even those who cling the most closely to the divine authority of every syllable can hardly refuse to admit that there are chapters which we would not willingly hear publicly read; and that there are others, mere lists of names (I do not refer to the two genealogies of our Lord, the public reading of which is defensible on other grounds), which could serve no good purpose in being publicly recited.

But if there be a selection at all, the Church has clearly a right to improve upon that selection, unless it can be shown to be incapable of amendment. The need of improvement rests, I believe, on the following grounds: Some lessons are read, especially in the daily service, which it is desirable to omit; not merely chapters, but whole Books of Scripture, are in the present Lectionary for no valid reason omitted. Among these is especially to be noted the Book of Revelation, which in its obscurest parts is no more obscure than some of the prophetical books, and can be no darker to us than their own prophecies were to the Jews. The selection of chapters to be read on Saints' Days is, on many occasions most unsuitable, there being no apparent reason why the chapters selected should be read rather than any other. Certain of the chapters selected from the Apocrypha are unwisely chosen; and lastly, the lessons are (in many instances) too long, and break in on the unity of a history, or a parable, or an exhortation, by various other matters which fail to leave a distinct impression on the mind. I feel compelled to admit the reasonableness of many if not all these objections, whilst at the same time one cannot help making the following (I think) not unimportant observations! The Bible is remarkable not only in the Old Testament but in the New, for its distinct mention and its plain condemnation of sins, the very name of which is painful. The spirit of the age leads men to hush up all such matters, but to act in secret the vile things which it is afraid to speak of, and to hear condemned. As in this respect the Bible and the world are clearly at variance, nothing can be more dangerous to public morality than to refuse to read what the sacred writer has evidently recorded for the general good, and which will be in all probability unheeded in private, when the lesson is considered unfit for public reading. A clergyman who would close the book or substitute another chapter, when the chastity of Joseph is recorded for instruction, if he would be consistent must cease to read the first chapter of the Epistle to the Romans; and where are we to stop? I should regard this closing of the Scriptures as trifling with the Word of God, a kind of Protestant concealment of which a Romanist might be ashamed. A remark may also be made on the Apocryphal lessons. Admitting that there are a few parts of the Apocryphal Books which many will gladly see removed from the Lectionary, a very large portion of the rest contains lessons of the deepest wisdom; and on comparing the

Apocrypha with the Books of the New Testament, it is very remarkable that the sacred writers often make direct quotations from the Apocrypha; or it seems that the description or exhortation given by the New Testament writer was first sketched out by the ancient Jewish authors. For instance, the conclusion of the eleventh chapter of the Epistle to the Romans is taken from the Book of Wisdom; the description of the heavenly city in the twenty-first chapter of the Revelation, from the thirteenth chapter of the Book of Tobit; and the very striking account of "the multitude that no man can number, clothed in white robes, with palms in their hands," is adapted from the second Book of Esdras. The lesson in St. James' Epistle, against God tempting us to evil, is taken from the fifteenth of Ecclesiasticus; and the "one day with the Lord is as a thousand years," the being "swift to hear," the "weeping with those that weep," the "revealing of mysteries to the meek," from the same Book, besides many turns of thought, and parts of sentences, which reappear in the New Testament; and I make no question, that had the second chapter of the Book of Wisdom been found in the Prophet Isaiah, it would have been considered as perfect a prophecy of the conduct of the Jews towards our blessed Lord, as the fifty-third chapter of Isaiah is justly considered at present. It may therefore be a question whether the new Lectionary will not be found to have removed too much, rather than too little of those venerable books, which, though they never formed part of the Canon of Scripture, were highly esteemed by the Jews, and largely quoted and adopted by the writers of the New Testament. In the new Lectionary, the change in the Sunday lessons is not so great as at first sight might be supposed, especially from Advent Sunday to Trinity Sunday; and the general principles to which I have before adverted are still strictly observed. After Trinity Sunday the greatest change in the lessons occurs. But we have obviously a great gain in the insertion of lessons from the Book of Revelation, the Book of Job, and the Books of Chronicles, hitherto kept almost out of sight in public reading. It may be an objection, and a reasonable one, that some of the lessons will be found too short. It seems to me, that if the object were to shorten the time of the services, that object would have

been much more profitably attained by abridging the great number
of State prayers by which our Prayer Book is burdened, or by a
fresh arrangement of the services, or by shortening the sermon,
than by lessening the number of verses of Holy Scripture which are
read. If the Lord's Prayer is repeated rather too frequently, much
more unnecessary is the continual repetition of State Prayers, one
of which would be amply sufficient for a single service, but which
now occur four or five times on a single morning. And considering
the very few opportunities which the poor, and indeed many others
who are not poor, have of reading or hearing the Word of God, I
think they will much miss their accustomed portion of the Sacred
Word. Probably in other particulars too little time has been given
to the subject, and the Church at large has been less consulted than
is desirable. However, if the bill becomes law, I fear we shall
have no choice but to submit, as the new Lectionary will be inserted
in all new Prayer Books, and it will soon become impossible to
procure the old. I should advise the clergy diligently to study the
new Lectionary on its first appearance, carefully to observe when a
discretion is given them of choosing new lessons, and when it is
withheld, and to be very particular in reading, that they begin and
end with the right verses, as in the new selection the lesson often
begins in the middle or end of one chapter and ends in the middle
of another. If this is not read very carefully, the sense of the lesson will be lost. This is the first of the changes made; I cannot
say it is the last that will be *attempted* in our Prayer Book, and the
prospect before us is a very serious one. We see too plainly that
all changes must pass through the ordeal of assemblies consisting
in some part of unbelievers, and in great part of men hostile or
indifferent to our services; and that a great number of legislators
defer rather to what is popular than what is right; and that we are
supposed to accept as much or as little, as they in their collective
wisdom think proper to leave us. If this yoke is to be made yet
more heavy, and their little fingers are to be thicker than our
fathers' loins; if the voice of the Church is not to be heard, and
the very foundations of the faith are to be tampered with, subscription to the Formularies and Articles of the Church will become a

matter for very serious consideration with every man who has hitherto believed in the connection of the Church of England with the past, and in her succession not only of holy orders, but of holy doctrine. "Sufficient, however, unto the day is the evil thereof;" when the trouble comes we must pray for Divine light to see the right course to take, and for courage to take it.

I may now call your attention to another equally important matter, the proposed revision of our English translation of the Bible. I suppose few persons who have long read and loved their Bible — as I trust we all have — and have made it the subject of their daily study, can think without serious misgivings of the necessity for revision, and of the probable or possible consequences of revision. Our English translation is a household god (so to speak) among us. Its idiomatic felicity of expression, its true ring of sterling Saxon English, its charming rhythm, its memories which recall our youthful lessons, and suggest our holiest prayers, and linger on our lips as the last words we utter to those dearest to us when we bid farewell to earth, have given it a standing in our minds which approaches the idolatry of the letter. We forget that these are not the very words which our Lord and the inspired authors uttered. They are only an attempt, in all good faith, but an imperfect attempt, to reproduce their glory in a foreign — and to the original writer — a barbarian tongue. God has indeed signally blessed that attempt, but He has not been pleased to exempt the authors of our translation from the infirmities to which all men are liable. The Holy Spirit (I doubt not) blessed and assisted our translators as we may suppose he blessed the authors of the Septuagint translation of the Old Testament; but he no more made our translators good Greek scholars than he gave to the Alexandrian Jews good Hebrew manuscripts. And as our blessed Lord and His Apostles read, and used, and quoted from a translation which, when compared with the Hebrew, is extremely imperfect, and yet it would be absurd to suppose that this translation was intended to preclude all further improvement; so we have done well to use our (in many respects) faithful translation; but the time may come when amendment is clearly practicable, and if practicable, is a positive duty. It is not generally recollected, or perhaps generally known, that the present translation is the fifth, not the first, of such attempts in the English tongue; and if we owe much to the idiomatic version of Tyndale, in some places we have departed from his rendering, to the injury rather than the improvement of the sense.   Be this as it may, let it be remembered that the history of English translations is a history of attempts to do well and to do better, rather than one sudden and permanent effort.   It is a history which rather points the way to future improvement than bars the road by an absolutely perfect success.   The very fact that our translators adopted alternative renderings, some of which are in the margin and some in the text of our Bibles, and the better rendering is often that which is not read to the people, would lead us to the conclusion that we may lawfully revise both, if a still more accurate rendering can be found. But our duty to God must manifestly supersede all other consider-ations.   The Bible, like the Christian religion, is a trust consigned to us for the benefit of mankind; and we are as much bound to fidelity in our version as to the extension of the Christian religion; and fidelity is rightly shown when we allow the light which God gives us to be reflected on the version and on the text of the Holy Scriptures.

There can be no doubt that many of our translators were accom-plished Hebrew scholars; and in difficult passages it is evident that they generally leaned to the opinions of learned Jews, as may be seen by any one who reads either the Commentary of Pococke or Rosonmüller.   But it would be affectation to deny that great light has been thrown on various texts by the researches of modern com-mentators; and that in the Books of Job, of Solomon's Song, and of the minor Prophets, our translation is capable of a much clearer sense.   In respect of the New Testament, not only is the Greek language more studied and more critically known than in the time of our translators, but much light has been thrown on the peculiar phraseology of the Macedonian Greek in which the Apostles spoke and wrote, and the niceties and turns of thought are now more distinctly apprehended.   Those who hold to the verbal inspiration of every syllable of the New Testament are bound to reproduce the same in English, as far as is possible: and those who think that such verbal inspiration was not the object aimed at by the control and assistance of the Holy Spirit, must be no less anxious not to lose a particle of what our Lord said and the Apostles wrote, but to reproduce it as correctly as a version in a different tongue can ever do; though be it remembered, a perfectly exact reproduction of the original in another language is not possible in the most faithful translation in all cases.

It is doubtless a great convenience, and it is considered a paramount advantage to have one English Bible for the whole English-speaking race; but it may be doubted whether this advantage, great as it is, has not been overrated. The unity of the volume has not preserved us in unity of faith and practice. We appeal to the same texts, and to the same version of them, to support our respective differences; and scholars in the several communions in their arguments with each other, are never satisfied to abide by the translation even while they commend it, but invariably appeal to the original as superior, and to their own version as the best; so that even if a revised version should lead to other like attempts, which is not certain, that which Time proves to be the best will supersede the others, and Aaron's rod will swallow up their rods. These, however, are only possible or probable consequences. Duty is the first point; and fidelity to the text and to the version demands that we should make both as perfect as we can. Should it be still objected, that on this principle the version of the Bible may always be changing to the end of time, it may be answered that this is the history of the Bible from the beginning, as soon as the languages in which it is written ceased to be spoken and generally understood. A dead language can only be understood in a version. The present square Hebrew letter, with its accompanying vowel points, is a sort of version of the original character, in order to retain as much as possible the ancient traditional pronunciation and the use of the words. The Septuagint version was an attempt in a wider direction to reproduce the original in a foreign language. The earliest known version of the New Testament was in Syriac, made as early as the second century probably; but this was succeeded by others in the same tongue. Both Greek, Syriac and Hebrew being dead languages to the Latin race, the Versio Itala was made, the origin of which is lost in antiquity; and it seems uncertain whether it was made in Rome or in the African provinces, as the first converts at Rome probably spoke Greek. Be this as it may, that version, though widely dispersed, popularly used, and considered by St. Augustine as the best, was not the only Latin version. There were, it would appear, several others, which have long since disappeared. The greatest step in advance, and in the way of wholesome progress, was made by St. Jerome, the most learned of the Fathers, when he undertook to produce a version of the entire Scriptures from Hebrew and Greek into the Latin tongue. It was expressly written in Latin in order that it might be more generally understood; the Latin language being in the fifth century more widely diffused (in Europe at least, for which he wrote) than any other. So successful was his attempt that this translation rapidly took the place of every other; and having at length received the sanction of two Popes was, with some emendations or alterations, adopted by the Roman Church as the one correct translation; and in consequence of the sway of the Papal power (being called the Vulgate originally from its popular character) was received and used, and is the present version of the whole Roman Church. No possessor of our English translation ought to forget the debt of gratitude he owes to St. Jerome for this version; for without it, it is probable that inferior materials would have produced an inferior English translation; and had no translation been made directly from the Hebrew, we might possibly have been still dependent on a translation from the Greek of the Septuagint. It is certainly very remarkable, and reassuring to those who are alarmed at the consequences of a revision, to find so great a mind as is that of St. Augustine — greater in depth and original power than any of the Fathers, but deficient in scholarship and entirely ignorant of Hebrew — thoroughly shaken by the prospect of a revised translation, and most strenuously opposed to it, so little did that eminent man understand the advantages which would flow to all posterity from having recourse to the fountain head of all sacred learning, the Hebrew verity. Strange indeed it seems to us,

L

that whilst he must have known the advantage of reading St. Paul's thoughts in the language in which the Apostle wrote them, he should not have applied the same test to the writings of Moses and the Prophets. We see, therefore, from this hasty and imperfect glance at the history of translations, that we have no cause to be alarmed at an improved English version. We are not now (as St. Jerome) proposing an entire new translation from the Hebrew; that has already been done. Nor is there any desire for an entirely new translation of any part of the Bible. The only purpose of the revisors is to correct those errors which all scholars must admit to be numerous and important; in the words of that able scholar, Canon Lightfoot, "to substitute an amended for a faulty text; to remove artificial distinctions which do not exist in the Greek; to restore real distinctions existing in the original, which were over-looked by our translators; to correct errors of grammar and errors of lexicography; to revise the treatment of proper names and technical terms; and to remove a few ambiguous or faulty expressions, besides inaccuracies of editorship in the English. All this may be done without altering the character of the version; and if the language of our English Bible is not the language of the age in which our translators lived, but in its grand simplicity stands out in contrast with the ornate and often affected diction of the literature of that time," (as we may see by comparing our Bible with the sermons of Bishop Andrews and Dr. Donne), "we may well believe that if a better model was possible in the seventeenth century, it is quite as possible in the nineteenth."

So much I have deemed it right to say, to allay needless alarm in the minds of any of yourselves or of your flocks, as to the future of our English version. Still I am bound to admit, that the project has been taken up with more haste, and pressed with less consideration for the feelings and interests of English-speaking people living out of England, than was desirable. Whether it be that all real scholarship is supposed to be centred in men nurtured in the English Universities, or that as the present translation was made by English divines, it is thought the duty of the world at large to accept without reluctance or hesitation, the decisions of

English scholars; or whatever be the real cause, it is certain in my opinion, that the excellent bishops and divines who originated this movement, have been somewhat inattentive to the circumstances and feelings of the times. It is impossible to overrate the differrence between the days of James the First, when our translation was made, and of Queen Victoria. In the first instance, great power was centred in the royal will, great power was exercised by the bishops; all the scholarship of England was united in a few minds easily directed to a common end; the England of those days was bounded by the circumference of the little island, and the rest of the world was occupied for the most part by the Roman Communion, to whom our tongue was as foreign as our religion. How is it now? The tongue of the islands is spread abroad through the whole earth, but their political institutions have (in vast regions) ceased to hold their sway, and the influence of England is moral, rather than politically dominant and exclusive.

I have made no allusion, as you must have perceived in this address, to some of the controversies of the day, of which, if a man does not know already enough, he must be both blind and deaf. In their legal aspects, I do not feel sure that they apply to us at all; and in other ways we are not much affected by them, our danger at present lying in another direction; and I do not feel inclined to take up stones to cast at brethren, who, whatever may be their errors of judgment, are remarkable examples of self-sacrifice and continual devotion to their holy work, and from whom many who rail at them might learn much if they would.

Whoever reads the past history of our Church with candour, must see that excessive carelessness rather than excessive ritualism, has been the prevailing error, and that a hundred instances of slovenly irreverence have been passed over without notice, whilst a vast outcry is made against a single extreme in an opposite direction. Inasmuch then as the difficulty has ever been even to bring men up to the plain, positive, undeniable directions of the Prayer Book, I deem it wholly superfluous to speak at length on ritualism. Ritual of some kind we must have, for no assembled congregation of worshippers ever met together without it. The only question is what Ritual is most conducive to life, reverence and devotion. But the absence of any specific directions on the subject in the New Testament, whilst the most minute ceremonial is laid down in the old, would seem to indicate that greater variety of practice would be allowed in a freer dispensation, and that each church would be left to frame its own directions on the subject, provided all be done decently and in order. The stringent rules of the Act of Uniformity have confessedly proved an entire failure; and whilst general directions are observed, some allowance, I think, must be given to individual priests, acting, as would be desirable, in harmony with their congregations. But I think we have far more to fear from the dead level of cold worldliness, which eschews all reverence, and sees no reality in the Church and its sacraments, and reduces the whole act of worship to a meagre performance by a minister, than we have from any excesses of ritualism. Mere outward show, for show's sake, is certainly to be avoided in divine worship; but our Lord reserves for his severest displeasure the lifeless church, which He will "spue out of his mouth," the cold lukewarmness of respectable and fashionable worldliness.

I desire also to call your attention to the necessity of making due annual returns to the Society for Propagation of the Gospel, on the state of your parishes. I am well aware, how difficult it is to make such reports interesting to others without entering into details which seem ridiculous when printed in the report and circulated among one's neighbours. The Society, however, complains that fuller accounts are constantly sent from other Dioceses, and the impression gains ground at home, that negligence and indolence prevent the reports being duly forwarded.

The general state of the Diocese is, I hope, progressive. Since we last met, twelve hundred and seventy-five persons have been confirmed, a considerable number of whom received holy communion at the time of confirmation. It is of the utmost importance to press upon all such persons the duty of steady and consistent membership. If these young people were all, as they should be, firm supporters of our Church, regular attendants, and devout and constant communicants, how great would be our gain! how valuable their assistance! During the same period, seven priests and four deacons have been ordained, and there is plainly an increasing desire that churches should be made more worthy of the service of God, and the sacraments administered with more reverence and devotion. One instance deserves special mention. In rebuilding the Church of St. Paul's, Portland, the parishioners have given at the offertory $9,073, besides $3,400 on the day when the church was consecrated, and $4,800 given by themselves and various friends towards the memorial windows in the church. No bazaars have been held to procure this sum. All has been offered to God. In my last confirmation tour I was everywhere encouraged by signs of increasing spiritual life and activity; and the manner in which churchmen throughout the Diocese have responded to the fresh calls made upon them by the Church Society, under the direction of the Schedule Committee, is very gratifying, and exceeds my expectations. We have no doubt a great trial to pass through for some years to come, but with increasing earnestness, and in dependence on the Divine blessing, I trust we shall surmount all our difficulties.

I would also call your attention to the desirableness of pressing on your parishioners the general observance of such days as Good Friday and Ascension Day, not merely that the day itself may be observed, but that the great truths of Christianity specially taught on those days may be fixed in the heart. There is, I fear, an increasing wish to make Good Friday a mere day of worldly festivity, and totally to disregard the Feast of the Ascension, which is a plain proof how low the faith of many Christians has fallen, and how cold is our love for a crucified but risen Lord. Imagine what even John Wesley would have said of keeping Good Friday as a feast, and of revellings and banquetings at the hour of our Lord's last agony. With a view to induce a better attendance during Lent, to interest men's minds in what otherwise has no special characteristic service to draw them together, I drew up a special service, taken either from Holy Scripture, our own Prayer Book, and similar sources, bearing especially on the sins for which we need forgiveness, and the graces we desire most to be imparted.

Wherever this service was used, it met with acceptance among the people, and appeared to be a help to reverence and devotion. In doing so I only pursued the plan universally adopted in all primitive churches, and partially and frequently pursued in our own Church in England, and amongst ourselves, that *on special occasions* the bishop of each church is authorized by his office to assist the devotions of the faithful by special prayers. This is a truly catholic principle, which I am not prepared to surrender. If it had not been recognized everywhere we should have had no Liturgy at all, and specially no Litany. On every occasion of general humiliation or general thanksgiving, I have drawn up similar forms of prayer, which have been used in all our churches without hesitation, though neither ratified by our Statutes nor found in our Prayer Book, and the objection comes too late. The practice has already grown into a usage, and that usage is universal; for in England every bishop draws up similar prayers on special occasions, and not only does every bishop use a form of consecration not recognized by the Act of Uniformity, nor found in the Book of Common Prayer, but every bishop uses his own special form by virtue of the Apostolic power inherent in his office. I am aware that a Statute of this Province has been appealed to, which inflicts the grave penalty of deprivation on all who use any other service than that found in the Prayer Book. But it is no disrespect to the framers of the Statute who adopted the clauses from the Act of Uniformity to say that it was made when no bishop had been consecrated here or was contemplated, and that it never could have been intended to deprive the Church of those privileges which the possession of a bishop confers upon the people at large.

In those very early days confirmations were hardly to be obtained, consecrations of churches were hardly known, church assemblies could not be expected, and the only notion that prevailed was to restrain men by severe penalties from falling into entire anarchy. Now that we have a regular order of Church government, the construction of such Statutes must not be pressed too closely. For there is not a church in the Province (and they are more than a hundred in number), nor in any of the other provinces, which has not been consecrated in the teeth of the Statute; the service used is not provided for by the Prayer Book; has proper Psalms, Lessons and Collects of its own; and as you have all taken part in such services, and some of you will be again calling for them, you ought all at this moment to have been deprived, and be as if you were dead. My wonder is, that intelligent persons who desire that all possible life and vigour should be imparted to the Church, consistently with an orderly manner of devotion, should not see that an occasional departure from the one fixed order, at a special time and *for a special purpose only,* and in harmony with the principles of our Prayer Book, and under the direction of the Chief Pastor of the Church, rather tends to increase our reverence for our usual form of prayer than to diminish it.

One more matter I may very briefly mention, and it alludes to the occasional offices, viz., that all the baptisms, burials and marriages in your parishes be regularly entered in a suitable register book, recognized as the property of the parish. There has been a custom into which some clergymen have fallen, of making such entries in a private book of their own, mixed up with private memorandums of their own affairs. Great public inconvenience and injury have resulted from such a practice, and as it is much to be blamed, I desire that you will all entirely and for ever abandon it. I trust also, that you will be very careful to institute inquiries of those who come to be married, in reference to their consanguinity and whatever else is needful to be inquired into, especially if they come from another parish or Diocese. I speak advisedly on this point, for not only have there been rumours of persons being married in our Church within the prohibited degrees, but two cases have occurred within my knowledge, in which I do not mean to throw the blame on the clergy, of open sin, one of which has brought ruin and misery on an innocent family. I cannot but think if due care were taken, and all persons were married as the Church directs, that such guilty people would shrink from the danger of public exposure in the Church.

And now, dear brethren, before I dismiss you, bear with me, if as briefly as the subject admits, I venture to give you some fatherly

advice, which in my judgment is profitable for your soul's health.
Many of you have met often in visitation. We have seen our
brethren, one by one, called to the dread presence of our God, and
the account of their life's labours on earth summed up and closed
for ever. We have a little longer to remain, but the lines of our
hand-breadth are visibly shortening; the things that are seen will
soon be the shadows that are past, and the things that are not seen
the lights of the eternal world.

Once more, then, I press upon you *Progress.*

Progress in your spiritual life. Not only be more earnest in
prayer and more frequent in prayer, but let the stamp on your
character be that of heavenly intercourse. As the face of Moses
shone with a heavenly radiance, when he came down from the
mount, so let it be seen that you have drawn nigh to God by the
increasing reverence, humility, sincerity and simplicity of your character, and by that tender devotion in sacred things, which it is
impossible for the worldly-minded pastor to imitate, and that
thoroughly single mind without which the most ostentatious piety is
but darkness; and "how great is that darkness?"

Progress in your Pastoral work. Let this be proved by the earnestness and life of your discourses; by your throwing yourselves into
the spirit and marrow of Scripture, rather than in making broad
your phylacteries by mere repetitions of the letter of Scripture; by
your faithful, affectionate, hearty, and painstaking intercourse with
your flocks; encouraging the weak, warning the unruly, teaching the
young children, stopping the mouths of the profane and dissolute,
and building up, not destroying, the foundations of the Faith for all.

Progress in your acquirements of learning, for the Gospel's sake.
That you may know what the difficulties of the times are, and may
be able to encounter them manfully and solidly; that you may gain
some new learning every year; giving attendance to reading, to
meditation, till the Lord come; remembering that you cannot be
innocently ignorant of what a layman need not know; and that if
your office binds you to explain the Scripture to others, your duty
is to master its sense, and to search it as for hid treasure, not to be
continually repeating truths of an elementary character.

Progress in your Parishes. That in the midst of all the irreligion which abounds, many may be seen clinging to your side, and with you, fearing not to believe the faith and practice it; that your churches may be more frequently, and in town parishes, daily open for prayer; the sacraments more frequently and more reverently administered, and your people not slumbering in the prejudices of the past; not longing for the shadows that have departed, but active to supply the present needs of the Church, and helping themselves and you by a faithful, honest, manly and energetic piety.

Once more, I exhort you to *reverence*, that grace the most want-ing in an age of real or fancied light. Reverence in all your sacred offices will never be lost sight of, when the pastor lives, and works, and prays, as in the presence of God; and without this constant sense of the Divine presence, the very handling of the Divine Mys-teries begets irreverence; and the intelligent and devout layman witnesses with disgust slovenly reading, careless manner, unpunc-tual attendance, and above all, the unworthy celebration of the Lord's Supper, as if anything were good enough for that blessed feast, and the more slovenly the manner, the more spiritual the action. If the rubrics of our Church are carefully observed, their spirit is so reverent, that irreverence in the priest would seem im-possible; but such neglect is by no means an unusual error. Thus children learn irreverence from their youth; their elders set them no example, and the offices of the Church are not done unto God as acts of worship, but are done unto man as ceremonies which lend dignity to those who condescend to patronize them. Remember the words which were once said over you, and to which time only adds a fuller, deeper meaning — "Receive the Holy Ghost, for the office and work of a priest in the Church of God, now committed unto thee by the imposition of our hands." These words are living truths, not dead formalities; and it were better for us never to have heard them than by the actions of our life and ministry to deny them; and there can be none who ought to pray to be delivered from the unpardonable sin more than the clergy, for of them to whom God has "committed so much," he will surely "ask the more."

Once more, I exhort you to unity and charity. I do not mean that you, more than any other body or men, can be absolutely united in judgment on every point; but a good deal may be done to promote this end by those who strive for unity, and who do not factiously separate from their brethren, or secretly cabal against them. "The same spirit," into which (as the Apostle says) "we were all baptized," is freely given to us all. We have the same Scriptures, the same Creeds; we were born within the same Church, and have declared that the whole Prayer Book we use is agreeable to the Word of God. If we were thoroughly taught by the Blessed Spirit of God, there is no doubt that we should all be, as the denizens of heaven are, in all things one. But as by the imperfection of our nature this cannot be at present, at least let us believe the best we can of each other; and not only practice the usual courtesies of life, but use no terms which imply that other clergy neither believe nor understand the Gospel, neither pray for, nor are taught by the Spirit of God. In the free discussion of our Synod, we shall have much need of charity. There will be of necessity, as there was in the first Council, "much disputing," but there need be no breach of unity. And let us learn wisdom from other quarters, to keep our discussions to ourselves, and not expose our weakness to the outside world. We are weak enough already; we do not need to excite the contemptuous pity of others, by taking the whole community into confession. Whenever we have mastered the principles and adopted the practice of the thirteenth chapter of St. Paul's First Epistle to the Corinthians, we shall be a strong Church; strong in our unselfish and forbearing love; strong in our untiring and spiritual devotion.

It has pleased God to allow me for more than twenty-six years to preside over you, and during that long period I have to bless His goodness for an unusual measure of health, and to thank you, and many of the laity, for cheerful and ready hospitality in my journeys, and for many other kind offices of love. Unlike the blessed Apostle, I have not gone from place to place knowing that "bonds and afflictions await me," but rather encouragement and respect, and though occasionally hard things have been said and unjust suspicions entertained of me, I have, I hope, outlived many of them, and I wish their authors no worse than a wider grasp of truth and a less contracted vision. I have also much reason to rejoice that I cannot recall a single act of discourtesy and unkindness from the members of any other religious body. On the contrary, I thankfully acknowledge from some, who do not belong to our communion, acts of sympathy and kindness, and general respect to my office from many more; and if a nearer, dearer fellowship is hardly to be expected on earth, may we at last meet where a true understanding will be given us of the points on which we have differed, and there will be "no room left among us either for error in religion, or for viciousness in life."

The Bishop addressed his clergy as follows in his charge delivered at the Cathedral in 1877:

I must ask your indulgence for too hurriedly setting before you some topics of counsel and encouragement, having had little leisure for writing, amidst the perplexity and distraction which the late terrible calamity has brought upon us.[1]

Some portion of the work in which I have been engaged, on behalf of the Church, has been as follows: In the year 1874, I confirmed one hundred and eighty-five persons, ordained five priests and two deacons, consecrated two churches and one burial ground, and travelled three thousand four hundred and fifty-eight miles. Many visits were made to different parts of the Diocese; and in September, in company with the clerical and lay delegates chosen by our Synod, I attended, for the first time, the Provincial Synod of the several Dioceses of Canada. We were received with the greatest cordiality; and I have reason to believe that our presence was considered of advantage to our Canadian brethren.

.   .   .   .

I ought not to omit that at the Provincial Synod, we were all cheered by the presence and animating words of my dear and honoured brother, the Bishop of Lichfield, who, after the Synod, travelled one thousand five hundred miles in order to fulfil a

---

[1] The calamitous fire in St. John.

promise that he would visit Fredericton; and on the 4th of October preached twice in our Cathedral, and addressed our Sunday scholars with such good effect, that of their own accord, they proposed to contribute to the education of one of the Melanesian scholars at Norfolk Island. Ten pounds sterling has been raised by them annually, for this good purpose.

The intercession services were held as usual this year, and a lively interest created in the Diocese of Algoma.

In the year 1875, I visited a large portion of the Diocese, and confirmed nine hundred persons, ordained one priest and three deacons, consecrated one church, and travelled two thousand three hundred and seventy-three miles. It is very satisfactory to find that in the confirmations, the number of those who communicate on the same day, or on the next Sunday, has largely increased; in many parishes nearly all communicating, in others the great majority; though I have still to deplore the existence of backward parishes, in which those who made promises failed to fulfil their engagements, and appeared to be totally ignorant of the spiritual loss they sustained. Parents are, I fear, greatly responsible for this neglect of duty, and seem to be much hindered by a foolish notion, to which the Church gives no sanction, that it is improper to have their children confirmed before they are fifteen or sixteen years of age. By their delay it often happens, that this duty is postponed till the young people are easily led away by wrong impressions; become independent and most difficult to be convinced; and are led to believe that they can receive no benefit from the ordinance, unless they can declare themselves converted, not after the manner of the Bible, but after the manner of human invention.

Having been taken suddenly unwell before the close of this visitation, I was thankful to avail myself of the services of my valued friend and brother, the Bishop of Maine, who promptly and most kindly confirmed in several country missions for me.

In the year 1876, I visited the North Shore and other parts of the Diocese, and confirmed four hundred and three persons, ordained four priests and three deacons, consecrated two churches and two burial grounds, and travelled three thousand two hundred and sixty-one miles.

Early in the summer I had the great satisfaction of receiving into our Church, through the kind assistance of Rev. L. A. Hoyt, the whole colony of Danish emigrants, two hundred in number; and of ordaining, after due examination, one of their number, who had been a school-teacher, the Rev. N. M. Hansen. As Mr. Hansen speaks both Danish and English, and read the Gospel in both languages in the Cathedral, he is well qualified to lead the devotions of the people in their own tongue, and to help those who are desirous to acquire the English language. I procured one hundred prayer books, for the use of the settlers, in the Danish language. They have already begun to build a small church, and I should feel greatly obliged, on their behalf, by any donations sent to me for that purpose, as assistance is much needed. Her Royal Highness, the Princess of Wales, has kindly sent a donation of twenty pounds sterling.

This year was to me a sorrowful one, being marked by the death of three old and valued friends. The first, my dear fellow-worker in the Vineyard, four years my senior, Bishop of the Diocese of Newfoundland. Few bishops have presided over a harder field of labour, or have worked more faithfully or successfully in it. He left fifty-two clergy, where he found only twelve; a college endowed with £7,500; two orphanages; a clergy widows' fund; churches doubled in number; and a Cathedral partly completed, which requires only a dignified chancel to make it a very noble and striking church. His was a mind of no common order. An accomplished scholar; a well-read theologian; exact and punctilious in his requirements of duty, if stern to others, sterner to himself; playful as a child, and full of genial humour; flinching from no difficulty, and ever ready to expose himself to the severest hardships; bountiful to the Church; a true friend in need and sickness, — he shortened his days by exposure to the storms of winter in assisting a sick clergyman. He died in a portion of his Diocese at present deprived of all Episcopal supervision, and left only one wish ungratified,— to be buried under the shadow of the Cathedral he had built, and in which he had so long ministered.

Another friend, if less distinguished, was no less dear to me,— the Rev. James Ford, a brother Prebendary of Exeter Cathedral;

a ripe and elegant scholar, translator of Dante, and versed in Spanish and Italian literature.   His practical commentary on Scripture is well known to the younger clergy of this Diocese by his liberal presents, and I was often enabled to give assistance in quarters where it was required, by his generosity.   He died in Christian faith and tranquillity, in his eightieth year, at Bath.

A third valued friend and benefactor to this Diocese, who assisted me in my first effort in church building, in the year 1841, has also been called away — W. Gibbs, Esq., of Tyntesfield, near Bristol. His name will long be remembered in England from his munificent charities; and in 1868, I had the happiness of consecrating, at the request of my former Diocesan, the late Bishop of Exeter, the noble church he built and endowed at an expense of £28,000, in the city of Exeter.   " Unto their assembly may my soul be united,"

" In the blest kingdoms meek of joy and love."

With regard to the financial position and prospects of the Diocese, though we may expect this year to be a year of considerable trial and difficulty, we have reason to be encouraged, looking at the matter from the course of several years.   I am informed by a churchman who has devoted much time and labour to the interests of the Church, that if we allow $9,000 as a fair estimate of contributions to the Church Society, and parish payments in aided parishes about the year 1868, that it is probable that under the Board of Home Missions, nearly $50,000 has been raised from that time to the present, over and above what might have been expected under the old system; and the Board have been enabled to raise the average stipend, about $100, besides maintaining several new posts. Our inability to raise the stipend of the missionaries to a more reasonable amount is only prevented by the backwardness of a few parishes, which hold back, and refuse to contribute with their brethren.   No equitable reason can be given to show that gentlemen, living in quiet country parishes, should refuse to contribute less in proportion to their means than their neighbours, or should call on those who live in town parishes to make up their deficiencies; and in many cases, the subscriptions to the Church Society ill accord with the known wealth of the donors.   Wealthy persons still receive aid contentedly, when they could afford to do without it, and should be ashamed to take it. The present visitation, which has consumed property by thousands, is doubtless intended to remind many that what has been irrecoverably lost might have been laid up in the book of God's remembrance, where none of it would have perished.

It must not, however, be forgotten that contributions which we see in print do not include the numerous instances in which improvements have been effected in our churches, and loving gifts have been bestowed on the poor and needy. It is pleasant also to see that whereas for many years no offerings were made for missions beyond the borders of our own Province, that during the last year more than $2,000 was contributed through various channels for this good purpose, independently of what has been given in clothing to the inmates of the Shingwauk Home, and the large contributions which have been sent from different parts of the Province to the sufferers by the fire.

Nor do I mention such gifts as the only or as the chief tokens of spiritual life. They are only proofs of faith and love within the soul. But where they are wholly absent, we fear that the love of God has never taken root.

The growth of sin, and the general deterioration of public morality in many important matters, is indeed an alarming feature of our times. We see indications of self-will in general dislike and contempt of authority, unbelief openly avowed, exceeding selfishness, enormous waste and needless luxury; a scarcely disavowed Universalism taints the faith of thousands; and flagrant dishonesty occurs in public and in private accounts; a general distrust is felt in large classes of the community; in great calamities, multitudes resort to plunder and robbery with an eagerness which betrays an entire absence of all moral principle, of all kind and humane feelings; a frantic desire is prevalent to hear the sensational, without regard to the seriousness of the speaker or the truth of what is said; so that what is misnamed charity is sometimes no more than unbelief in any distinctive Christian doctrine, under the pretence that all teaching is equally good, or alike indifferent. Such are some of the

terrible evils we have to encounter. But it would be unjust to
society at large, and to Providence, not to acknowledge with thankfulness the tokens we daily witness of holy, reverent fear of God,
humble self-denial, patient endurance of sickness and losses, daily
charitable efforts to do good, purity of life, constant sobriety,
honesty and uprightness in all the transactions of business, unswerving loyalty to our Church even under the most unfavourable
circumstances, and regular attendance at the ordinances of our
Church, with a perceptible increase of devout communicants. When
the tares and the wheat so plainly grow side by side in the same
field, we cannot fail to ask ourselves with fear and trembling, has
the enemy sowed those tares while we slept?

.   .   .   .

I am bound, indeed, more than any other person, to thank you
all for the courtesy, hospitality, and good feeling with which you
have welcomed my coming amongst you, and for the unvarying
support you have rendered me, both in the Church Society, and as
president of the Synod. The laity also have given as freely and
abundantly of their valuable time and experience, and have been as
brothers to us in every good work. And not only in financial
matters, but in giving form to the discipline of our Church, we owe
much to their patient and assiduous labour. The busiest among
them have often worked the hardest, and I hope the time will come
when there will not be a layman in the Diocese, who does not think
it an honour to spend and be spent in the work of the Church.

.   .   .   .

The other subject on which I desire to say a word, is the spiritual
result we should endeavour to draw from this calamitous fire, and
the means which may, under God, contribute to this result. Whilst
we ought to be especially thankful for the great charity which has
been shown in all quarters towards the sufferers, that is, after all,
only an alleviation of our temporal wants. The good effect must,
under the Divine blessing, come from within, not from without.
A general reformation, we can hardly, I fear, expect to witness. It
seems as hopeless, as to "force the course of a river." But no doubt,
many will be led to own, that God has spiritual blessings in store

for them, under the guise of temporal evils, and will obtain from their sorrows lasting good.

We wish to see a deep humiliation of soul under the mighty hand of God. We wish men to acknowledge that it is a judgment, not a mere accident; in which the innocent indeed may suffer with the guilty, but in which we dare not fix on individuals as the cause of the evil, but must share with them in the effects. We pray that this suffering may not only lead them to rebuild their houses, but to improve their lives. We desire to see more plain living, and high thinking. We wish no longer to find young men and women indulging in expenses far exceeding their income, and in consequence, tempted to rush into wild speculations, or dishonest dealings with their employers; but incurring no debts which they cannot afford to pay, and free from the kindred vices of gambling, intemperance, fraud, and licentiousness. Above all, we would wish to see them such Christians as the Apostle describes, living temples of the Holy Ghost, pure in conversation, honest in business, full of undissembled love, "abhorring what is evil, cleaving to what is good, patient towards all men, not wise in their own conceits, of the same mind one toward another, and overcoming evil with good." And when we hear the wish uttered, that the City of St. John may rise from her ashes grander and richer than ever, we would proclaim in men's ears, Righteousness is the true riches, which never makes to itself wings and flies away.

It is for us, my brethren, to set an example of this Christian spirit; to take care that our families be models of purity, simplicity and prudence; to live in debt to no man; to aim at the highest standard of truth, that our example may shed lustre on our profession, and crown an humble and laborious life with a peaceful, Christian, and most blessed end.

In the foregoing extracts allusion is made to one of the greatest calamities by which the Province had ever been visited. On the 20th June, 1877, a fire broke out by which a large portion of the City of St. John was reduced to ashes. The loss to merchants and others engaged in business was enormous, amounting at a moderate estimate to $20,000,000.

M

Generous gifts and kind sympathy helped to allay, in some degree, the more immediate wants of the sufferers. The many years which have since elapsed, with all the energy and determination so largely displayed, have failed to make good many an irreparable loss. As always in seasons of trouble and distress, the Bishop was ready with substantial aid, warmest sympathy, and fatherly counsel. Soon after the fire he preached in the stricken city, at St. John's church. His text was taken from St. Luke xiii. 2, 3 : "And Jesus answering said unto them, Suppose ye that these Galilæans were sinners above all the Galilæans, because they suffered such things? I tell you nay: but, except ye repent, ye shall all likewise perish":

What are the lessons, my brethren, which God intends us to learn from the great and unexpected calamity which has befallen us? The text implies that all such evils are permitted by God, but it shows a clear distinction between the Providence of God and the agency of man. . . . Even when a special punishment was foretold by the prophets of old, for some special national sin, the righteous suffered with the wicked.

Jeremiah, Ezekiel and Daniel went into captivity, and lost all they possessed, together with the guilty Israelites, who had neglected and mocked at their predictions. Thus, the chief caution of the passage is a warning against self-righteousness; and we are reminded that our duty lies in doing all in our power to mitigate the evil under which others are suffering without attempting to penetrate into the counsels of the Almighty, or to pronounce judgment, individually, on our fellow-creatures.

. . . Our first lesson is one of deep humility. "We brought nothing into the world, and it is certain we can carry nothing out." Even if we admit that we cannot carry our possessions with us, we feel confident of being able to bequeath them. But God steps in and shows us, that not even this is always permitted. When the sense of possession is strongest; when the produce of our labour in our silver and gold is multiplied; when our houses are enriched with costly ornaments; when banks are laden with our accumulations; when private citizens and corporations spend as if there were no end to riches, and the world lay at their feet; when men cry "peace and safety," then "sudden destruction cometh upon them" and there is no escape. All is levelled to the ground. . . . .

What a terrible reflection comes home to us, that we shall have to give a strict account of all these riches which are gone, and which we are not now permitted to enjoy! A humble submission to the will of God will do much to mitigate the loss and soften the blow. There is much suffering, but the great hope remains. If we face this great sorrow manfully and resolutely, God may yet raise our city from the dust. Industry and perseverance will do much to restore our walls, but humility will do more; it will promote our moral and religious improvement; it will teach us lessons of good, which communities in general are too slow to learn. . . . . . Now is the time for plainer living and higher thinking; for contracting no debts we cannot in reason hope to pay. Till Christians come to understand that debts ill-contracted and undischarged are ill-disguised robbery, they have not learned the elements of the religion they profess. Their prayers, their alms, their communion, are of no value in the sight of God. . . . . . .

But to our comfort under this calamity, we may remember that punishment is always intended by God as a remedy. The sinful heart of man requires to be taught by pain. Unchecked prosperity corrupts and enfeebles the mind, as surely as a constantly hot climate enervates the body. Sin needs to be burned out, and grace to be burned into the soul, and we are braced and invigorated by chastisement. . . . .

Think of the readiness with which you have been assisted from all quarters; the spirit of Christian charity which has been called forth; the union of many hearts and hands in untiring and unselfish labour; the eager desire to benefit without hope of return; the happy forgetfulness of rivalries, all folded together in the embrace of a universal charity, and you will see that, probably, more zeal and substantial good may result, than if the evil had never been permitted.

Oh! the blessing of heavenly contentment in every station in which God has placed us; the blessing of imparting to the honest poor, what is in our power to give; of not hastening to be rich. Of being able to lie down in peace and safety!

Soon I shall have nothing but a shroud, my coverlet will be a narrow bed of earth; therefore, oh my God, make me satisfied with the portion Thou allottest me; give me a calm and thankful heart; religious and reasonable desires, honesty, prudence and simplicity; a guileless soul; a quiet, trusting spirit, that I may find all I need, desire and hope for, in Thee!

CHAPTER XV

INTERCOURSE WITH THE CHURCH IN THE UNITED STATES—
EXTRACTS FROM SERMONS—NOTES FROM THE ANNALS.

THE Diocese of Fredericton adjoins that of Maine, United States. Between the bishops and clergy of the sister Dioceses the warmest and most brotherly intercourse has always existed. These fraternal relations began in the days of the saintly Bishop Burgess, the first Bishop of Maine, for whom the Bishop of Fredericton entertained the highest regard.

It was the custom of Bishop Burgess, when he made his annual visitation to the eastern part of his Diocese, to pass over to the British Provinces, where he made the acquaintance of many of the English clergy. Referring to one of these visits, the Bishop of Fredericton penned the following communication :

I had the happiness of a short visit from my esteemed friend and brother in pastoral work, in June, 1863. I need say little on the personal pleasure we derived from that too brief sojourn with us. His conversation, always instructive and charming, was enlivened by racy anecdotes, and touches of genuine humour, which added to its cheerfulness without detracting from the solid sense which characterized all he said. To this was added a modesty and unaffected simplicity, which sat well on one whose learning and ability were unbounded. He kindly delivered an address at the anniversary of our Diocesan Church Society. In the simplest style, without any effort or desire to win applause; in weighty and well-chosen words, he urged upon us the duty of missionary work, and rebuked the unfaithfulness and coldness of heart with which such efforts were often met, and the excuses made for withholding what was justly due.

(181)

I may add that the Bishop spoke with the ease and fluency of a practised extemporaneous speaker: his sentences were uttered with as much deliberation as if he had been reading from a manuscript. Long will that brief visit be remembered, and great has been the sorrow of many among us, that we shall never on earth listen to his voice again.[1]

The regard and affection expressed for the first Bishop of Maine were fully extended to his successor, Bishop Neely. The Bishop of Fredericton was present, and took a prominent part in the services at the consecration of the Cathedral at Portland, Maine, in 1871. Along an extended border line the missionary work was, in many instances, greatly advanced by the services of the clergy from both Dioceses without regard to the boundary.

Bishop Medley, on several occasions, visited New York, and other principal cities in the United States, at the triennial meetings of the General Convention. It is quite safe to say that no Prelate from abroad was more cordially welcomed by the representatives of the American Church. This is, perhaps, the more remarkable, as, from his manner, habits, and early training, there was a strong contrast between the Bishop of Fredericton and his brother bishops and leading churchmen in the United States. His marked abilities, his plain, but impressive, sermons and addresses, his earnest teaching in accordance with the doctrines of the Church, were highly appreciated. American churchmen are very practical. They will not endure cant or pedantry. Among them, too, is wholly wanting that intolerance which so often, in former years, was arrayed in opposition to the Bishop in his own Diocese. They have, indeed, many varied bodies of professing Christians, of whom little is known in Canada. But they are free from that folly which

---

[1] Memoir of Bishop Burgess, page 356.

watches for the errors of Rome, under a cross on the altar, or a surpliced choir.

The principles and teaching of the Bishop were in accord with those which, in years past, have been set forth in those Dioceses in America which have made the greatest advance. Among the laity that represent the Church in their conventions will be found men well versed in the teaching of primitive times. Many such, by their very study, have been led from various religious bodies into the communion of the Church.

As early as the year 1851, the Bishop of Fredericton visited the City of Boston. At that time it was " the day of small things" with the Church of the Advent. Those who originated the movement connected with the establishing of that church had to contend with many difficulties and much opposition. Many of its supporters were far from being in favour with the ruling powers in the Diocese. The years that have passed have wrought a wonderful change. At the present day there is no church or parish in the Diocese of Massachusetts stronger or more influential than the Church of the Advent. The older members of that church to this day speak with grateful remembrance of the kindness and sympathy manifested towards them in their early struggles by the Bishop of Fredericton.

The following sermon was preached by the Bishop on the occasion referred to :

"So then after the Lord had spoken unto them, He was received up into heaven, and sat on the right hand of God."—St. Mark xvi. 19.

In these few and simple words does the Evangelist, after his manner, describe the greatest event which ever happened in the world,— the source of all blessings to the company of believers here and hereafter. What angelic hosts accompanied him as he went up, what songs of love and adoration met him in the air, and entered with him into heaven, the mind may imagine, but the record

is not preserved. Yet, as the angelic host were present when he
"emptied himself" to be born of a woman, and as two at least of
the number watched the place where the Lord lay, we may without
presumption gather, that they ascended with Him into glory, and
"awoke to joy" the spirits of the blest, who had long waited for the
great Deliverer's coming.

And even the disciples, by a miracle of mercy, cast all their
griefs and doubt away, and "returned to Jerusalem with great joy,
and were continually in the temple, praising and blessing God."
Now were the Scriptures opened to their minds. Their hearts were
full of wonder and of love. They were ready to preach the word
in season, and to suffer for the truth's sake, welcoming reproach and
shame, if, at the last, they might "shine as the sun in the kingdom
of their Father."

And should not some portion of their joy be felt by ourselves?
We are not "men of Galilee, gazing up into heaven," after our
ascended Saviour. But are we not, as they were, "fellow-citizens
with the saints, and of the household of God?" Are we not baptized Christians, the redeemed of the Lord? Are not the same
Scriptures before us? Are not the same truths our birthright? Is
not the same hope of salvation made known to us? What blessing
has the lapse of eighteen centuries quenched or diminished? Nay,
in one respect, we have more cause for joy than they; for surely
our Lord's second Advent is drawing nearer. Every Ascension
Day brings us nearer to that glorious era, when Ascension and Advent shall be one, when Christ shall be no longer "absent from us
in the body," but present as the Lord; when the new Jerusalem
shall be seen descending from above, Christ's redeemed celestial
bride, a blessed and a countless throng, containing in that vast and
ever-increasing multitude, some, at least, whom we have known
and loved on earth, and about to receive some (Oh! that it might
be all) of this present congregation.[1] But let us now pass on to
consider, in the explanation of this passage, what are the blessings
connected with our Lord's Ascension.

---

[1] How little did we anticipate that your blessed pastor would be the first to
follow in this train!

I. The Ascension of our Lord was the great witness to his innocence and righteousness. He alone had fulfilled the law, he alone could ascend to the Father. This our Lord had declared, when he said, "when the spirit of truth is come," that is of my righteousness, "He shall convince the world of righteousness, because I go to my Father, and ye see me no more." By this event, all the accusations of the wicked were proved to be false. "It is God that justifieth, who is he that condemneth?" The Father had accepted his sacrifice, had acknowledged his merit, and had placed in his hands as man, and as mediator, the kingdom of heaven and earth. This enables us to understand, why our Lord's ascension into glory is described as the reward of his sufferings. "He humbled himself unto death, even the death of the cross, therefore, also, hath God highly exalted him, and given him a name which is above every name," and this was done, "to the glory of God the Father." We are not to infer, that it was not done to the glory of God the Son also; for our Saviour says, "all things that the Father hath are mine;" he requires that "all men should honour the Son even as they honour the Father;" and they honour the Father with worship and adoration as the supreme God. Nay, St. John assures us, that Christ is "the true God," and St. Paul, that he is "God above all, blessed for evermore," and that he is "before all things, and that by him all things were made." But inasmuch as the Father, as Father, has a glory which the Son, as Son, has not; and as the Son, as man, is glorified and exalted by his Father, as God, therefore the exaltation of the risen body of Christ, is "to the glory of God the Father," who sent him into the world. For even the Son, as man, is to be "subject unto him that put all things under him, that God may be all in all."

II. Our Lord's ascension was the way to his glory, as King and Judge of all mankind; it is thus that the Apostle describes him as "sitting at the Father's right hand, far above all principality and power." He was seen by St. Stephen standing, which is the posture of a combatant; but is commonly described as sitting, which is the posture of a judge. In the Epistle to the Hebrews, the Apostle speaks of him as reigning; and the Psalmist says, "the Lord is

King, he sitteth between the cherubims," that is, on the seat of covenanted mercy; for the cherubims, in the Jewish temple, spread out their wings over the ark, and the mercy seat, the great emblems of our redemption.

All things in nature, providence and grace are subject to His will, are controlled by His power, are directed by His wisdom, are sustained by His love. Innumerable worlds, innumerable creatures in each world, gifted with various powers of life and intelligence, are all cared for by Him at the same instant. His mind comprehends, at a glance, the almost infinite proportions of the universe; and He is, virtually, and by control, present at once, in every part of it. The angels continually behold Him, "binding the sweet influences of Pleiades," and "clothing the grass of the field," "guiding Arcturus and his sons," and hearing the cry of the wild beast in the desert, and of the wailing infant at its birth, controlling the dark designs of the blaspheming legions of hell, and breathing comfort in the heart of the penitent, and giving strength to the walk of the believer. Yet the eternal Son sits on the throne of Heaven, clothed in human form, never forgetful of Bethlehem, of Mount Olivet, or of Calvary. Each separate saint in glory, each several pilgrim on earth, He knows by name. Their history, their difficulties, their fears, their sorrows, and their joys, are all His own. Oh, thought too great for utterance, too mighty almost for human contemplation!

III. But, further, our Lord's ascension into glory prepared the way for His intercession. The intercessory part of our Lord's priestly office is one of the most important parts of His mediatorial work. And it behoves us to have clear and distinct conceptions of it, as far as the Scriptures reveal it to us. He is represented, in the symbolic language of the Revelation, standing "as a lamb that had been slain," for His glorified body still bears the marks of His passion, and has an intercessory virtue in its very presence. For if, on earth, virtue went out from His body before He was glorified and healed all who had need of healing, much more do fresh springs of grace, and strength, and compassion, and pardon, issue from His body in heaven, of which His Church mystically forms a part.

When we reflect that we thus present our prayers and offerings through "the Lamb that was slain," to the Father, how joyfully do the Psalmist's words ring out in our ears, "Cast thy burden on the Lord, and he shall sustain thee;" "When my father and my mother forsake me, the Lord taketh me up;" "Though an host of men were set against me, yet shall not my heart be afraid;" "Thou hast ascended up on high, and hast received gifts for men!" We desire no better Intercessor — we ask for no more effectual pleader of our cause, than the great sacrifice for the sins of the world. He who laid down his own life to save ours, can want no stimulus from others to relieve and pity us. No name in earth or in heaven can compare with His in tenderness; no name in earth or in heaven can vie with His in wisdom; no name in earth or in heaven can compete with His in power. There was indeed one on earth whom he honoured above all her sex, by condescending to call her by the sacred name of Mother. But whence came this endearing, this most wondrous name? Was it not from His original love? Was He not, as the Eternal Word, the fountain of all her purest thoughts and holiest joys? And if she were both "highly favoured," and "full of grace," was not that very grace God's undeserved goodness to His servant? How, then, can we for one moment imagine that this most worthy creature, who owes everything to her Creator's love, should be necessary to infuse fresh sympathy and affection into the heart of the Creator himself? We might, with more reason, ask the dewdrop, that trembles on the little leaf, to swell the multitudinous sea, or bestow its plenteousness on the assembled clouds of heaven. Nay, let all the angels and saints in glory combine together, and let there be added thereto all the grace that dwells in the inhabitants of the countless stars of the firmament, and all is but as a single drop of goodness, flowing out of the vast encircling tide of Christ's unmeasured, unexhausted, everlasting love.

So that the words "Put not your trust in princes, nor in any child of man," apply universally, and have no exception, even in the mother of our Lord and God, "blessed" and honoured though she be, "above all women," throughout all generations. We do

not detract from her dignity, we rather preserve it, when we say,
"There is but one Mediator between God and men;" one Intercessor, "the man Christ Jesus."

But, if Christ ever live to intercede, should not we also ever live
to pray? Here, then, lies the practical use of daily public prayer.
It is the gathering together of the faithful, to remind each other of
Christ's intercession, to desire to reap the benefit of it, to enjoy the
assurance of it. It may be said that this can be done at home as
well as at church. But the same argument may be applied to the
observance of the Lord's day. It may be said, "I can read the
Bible at home as well as the clergyman can read it to me." Now,
as far as reading the letters and syllables of the Bible, this is very
true; but it is rarely found that those who absent themselves from
church on the Lord's day spend their time in reading the Bible.
Even so I question whether those who say that they do not require
the prayers of the Church to remind them of Christ's intercession,
spend their time in prayer at home. The truth is, they do not think
common prayer of importance enough to lay themselves out for it,
by using all practicable leisure times for its performance. If they
felt that it was a blessing to their own souls, they would use it
whenever their lawful business permitted. He who feels prayer to
be a blessing, has something within him which renders it as impossible wholly to abstain from it as to abstain altogether from bodily
food. There are times when food is not desired; but, in a healthy
state, we cannot live without it. In like manner the soul wants
daily food. This food is prayer; *private* prayer; *social*, or family
prayer; *public*, or common prayer. So far from either of these
duties clashing, they assist each other. They keep up the life of
God in the soul of man. They remind us of a daily, hourly walk
with God, and of the benefit of His presence, and watchful care
over us. They begin the work of heavenly praise on earth. They
put some check (alas! how faint and ineffectual a check) on the
vortex of Mammon and dissipation of heart which surrounds us.
They prepare the soul to take wing and fly away. Suppose we
were to be seized with a stroke of paralysis, or of any sudden
disease, where could we be found with so much comfort as on our

knees in public prayer? We might be suddenly smitten so as never to recover our speech or hearing. Would not the very strength and purity of prayer lend wings to our enfeebled body, so that it might be said of us, though speechless, or incapable of hearing the word, "Behold, he prayeth." [1]

IV. Christ's ascension was the means of procuring God's greatest gift to the Christian Church, the presence and indwelling of the Holy Ghost. Though the Holy Spirit was given to the saints in old time—for they spake by His inspiration, and all good things come from Him—yet we read that "the Holy Ghost was not yet given, because that Jesus was not yet glorified." Not only did the Holy Ghost descend on the Apostles at the day of Pentecost in a manner never known before, but his gifts were bestowed on all faithful Christians in greater fulness and abundance than on the Church after Christ's ascension. Great saints there were before the coming of Christ; but fewer, I suppose, than after His coming. And though the standard of perfection was higher, the number of those who approached it was greater. Few good men under the Old Testament dispensation seemed to have equalled Noah, Abraham, Job, or Daniel; but I imagine that St. Paul excelled them all, not only in the abundance, but in the perfection of his gifts.

What does the world owe, under God, to that one man? The greater part of the Christianity of Europe and America dates its commencement, in all probability, from the labours and writings of St. Paul. How precious a fruit was this of Christ's ascension! What joy must have run through the courts of heaven when the angels proclaimed that the relentless persecutor of the feeble Church in Judea was arrested, converted, baptized, and, by temporal blindness, had become the spiritual light of the world! But what angel in glory could have foreseen the whole illustrious result? Thus does the conquering king "ride meekly on," borne on the wings of righteousness and truth, while of successive generations of His willing captives the inspired poet sings, "with joy and gladness

---

[1] How blessed is the recollection that the summons to return found your loved pastor on his knees, in act to bless you, and to pray for a blessing! You will remember that the words are now printed, as they were preached.

shall they be brought, and shall enter into the king's palace; instead of thy fathers thou shalt have children whom thou mayest make princes in all lands." "The redeemed of the Lord shall return, and come with singing unto Sion, and sorrow and sighing shall flee away."

Finally, Christ's ascension is the proper proof of His present humanity, and the great pledge that He will return. Hence His Second Advent is called a "presence," a "manifestation," "an appearance," as of a body existing locally, and really to come amongst us again. Two facts are undeniable. First, that the time of His return must be nearer than when the promise was given; and, secondly, that the state of the world, in its main features, grows continually more and more like the time when we are taught to look for His coming. The witness of the Gospel is more generally proclaimed. Knowledge is more widely spread. The means of salvation are placed within the reach of a large part of the world. Yet dark and troubled are the waters and the skies. A general agitation pervades every branch of the Church Catholic. Men sigh for unity, but cannot find it, or seek it in error. The love of the world grows more and more intense in the hearts of men. Belief in any distinct system of truth grows weaker, and multitudes realize nothing, believe nothing, love nothing, fear nothing. Mammon is the measure of everything, and frequently takes the place of right and wrong. Concession is considered the standard of wisdom, and every truth revealed in the Bible is willingly surrendered in turn to conciliate the good will of mankind. Parental authority is becoming the exception, not the rule. Governments are weak, and exist in many countries because nothing better or stronger can take their place. These are tokens that the "Lord draweth nigh;" and, though to predict the absolute nearness of this event would be a foolish presumption, to watch the various signs of His approach, and to rejoice with trembling, is the part of the liegemen of the Cross, the followers of an ascended Lord. One thing we know, for He has told us. When the proud scoffer cries, "Where is the promise of His coming?" then will the King of Glory return. When the world is locked in sleep, and dreams of everlasting continuance, then will the bolt be launched. When the carcase lies prostrate at the feet of Mammon and unbelief, then spring the avenging eagles forth. When the fourth watch of the night is come, the form of the Great Watcher is seen "walking upon billows," and the ship draws nigh to the eternal shore.

Let us now draw one practical conclusion from what has been said. Those who would ascend to "meet the Lord in the air" must walk with the Lord on earth. Let us walk with Him, then, in our daily devotions, "lifting up holy hands, without wrath and doubting," hoping for His protection, trusting in His providence, and expecting His mercy. Let us walk with Him when the bell calls us to public prayer, "not forsaking the assembling of ourselves together," as the manner of too many is. Let us walk with Him in our leisure hours, lifting up secret ejaculations, in the open field, at the morning dawn, at even-tide, and in the silence of the night. Let us walk with Him in hours of business, when His awful presence seems out of sight, when lying and dishonesty stalk abroad, when temptation is pressing, and snares close round our path. Let us walk with Him in our recreation and mirth, never suffering our cheerfulness to sink into license, but remembering that it is "God who giveth us all things richly to enjoy," and that "every creature of God is to be received with thanksgiving." Let us walk with Him in time of trouble, when men accuse us falsely, when pains and losses come upon us as an armed man, when our eye is dim, and our memory gone, and our natural force abated. Then shall we walk with Him when death is nigh, and the awful tokens of our decay shall bring His presence more sensibly near, and our sick bed shall be the presence chamber of the King of Kings; and, as the cords give way that bind this mortal body to the earthly shore, the soul shall stretch out her hands to embrace the heavenly. Then shall we know that the ark of God bears us up, that the Lord himself hath shut us in, that His rod and staff comfort our steps, that our prayers are all answered, and our voyage past, and the long wished for land in sight; that the false tongues that assailed us have done their worst, and the devil that tempted us has lost his power. One short, decisive, bitter struggle more, and lo! heaven opens, and Christ, "with all His shining train," surrounds us, and we pass out of this gloomy valley into the calm and peaceful region of Eternal Day. Amen.

In October, 1853, the Bishop visited New York. He preached before the Houses of Convention and at the ordination of the Bishops of North and South Carolina. Thirty bishops were present. The sermon was printed at the request of the House of Bishops. The text was taken from 2 Timothy i. 6, 7. The following are extracts from this sermon:

We are apt to dwell so frequently on St. Paul's noble championship of justification by faith, that we forget the manifold graces which dwelt in this wonderful man. Yet it is good to point out each trait of nobleness; his burning love, his surprising wisdom, his unexampled tenderness, his ready self-sacrifice, his accuracy in the choice of words, his masterly arrangement of his subject, his judicious commendation, his no less weighty censures, his indifference to stripes, to imprisonment, and to death. Thus viewing his character on every side, let us exclaim with reverence and humility, "what hath God wrought!"

It seems to have been one part of St. Paul's peculiar trial, that he stood nearly alone, when he most required support. He entered the proud imperial city of Rome, a forlorn and aged man; in chains and needing sympathy; weak in body, worn with toil; borne down by clamorous injustice. . . . The trial was for life or death, and the judge was Nero. The spirit of fear seized some, the spirit of worldliness infected others. . . . Now one fancies that one sees through the veil of that fatherly kindness with which St. Paul addresses Timothy, an apprehension that this good and holy man might be a little timorous and yielding. He bids him to remember his ordination vows and graces. It is no disparagement to Timothy to suppose he might be less firm and courageous than St. Paul. Who is not? Perhaps we are not so courageous as Timothy.

All moral and religious qualities are the gift of God. Whether it be courage, love or wisdom, all is grace. From the corrupt fountain of the natural heart no good thing flows. "He prevents us, that we may have a good will." He works in us, when we have that will: pardoning, sanctifying, preserving grace, all is His; for His is the kingdom, the power and the glory. If this be so in the case of ordinary Christians, how much more forcibly must it apply to those who are appointed to teach others; to feed, to premonish the Lord's family, to seek out Christ's sheep out of this naughty world, to nurse, to govern and guide the Church. Every qualification of which they stand in need, is to be found out of themselves; it is to be sought as His gift, His special gift, who alone can qualify them for their work, and make them successful in it. The Apostle plainly declares that there is a special gift granted to faithful and believing clergymen at their ordination, and to be expected by them in answer to prayer.

.   .   .   .

The grand qualification named by the Apostle is equally needed — a loving, tender, affectionate spirit. What is more wonderful in the character of our Lord than the union of hatred of sin with love for the sinner? Now we find Him, with stern severity, scourging the merchandizers out of the Temple, denouncing the Scribes as whited sepulchres, "looking round about on them with anger — grieved for the hardness of their hearts"—even saying to St. Peter, "get thee behind me, satan, for thou art an offence unto me," and again we hear Him sweetly inviting weary sinners to their rest, drying the tears of the weeping penitent, praying for His murderers, and owning the repentant thief as His companion in Paradise.

.   .   .   Courage without love is harsh and forbidding. It loves to wound, rather than to heal. It speaks not only severely, but unkindly. It sees all the evil in men, and acknowledges none of the good. It is bold in denunciation of sin, but makes no allowance for the infirmities of the sinner. It might be a want of love that made St. Peter's boldness degenerate into cowardice. Therefore seek to unite boldness and affection. Sternly oppose sin; firmly uphold the spirit of the cross; but seek to win souls also. Learn to

N

distinguish between the ignorant and the vicious; the ill-instructed and the obstinate sinner. An unquenchable love for the immortal soul, "like a lively flame and burning torch, will force its way upwards, and securely carry you through all."[1]

.   .   .   .

And now, my dear and honoured brethren, whom I am permitted to address on this most solemn occasion, what can I, a feeble, sinful brother, say to you worthy of the dignity of the subject, worthy of the occasion which has called us together? My heart is full; full of sympathy and affection for you all; for you especially, brethren, who are this day to receive this most awful, this most blessed gift.

Oh! that the prayers here offered in godly unity and concord, may descend on both branches of the Anglican Church, in rich and abundant blessing! May the mass of ignorance, heathenism and crime which surrounds us, fall before the victorious banner of the Cross! May the blessed truths recovered at our Reformation penetrate every bosom, and reach other shores! May our Liturgy, preserved through many fiery trials, form a link for communion with churches of the East and Northern Europe! . . . May we become less bitter, suspicious and irritable; less vainglorious in our speech and action, esteeming the praise of men less, and the praise of God more.

And as for you, this day, to be called to the arduous work of the episcopate, may a double portion of the gifts mentioned in the text be poured upon you! May you be men of high unflinching courage! Never may you betray the interests of the Church you have sworn to defend! Never may you court popularity by the surrender of the truths entrusted to you! May unquenchable love for the souls for whom Christ died urge you on continually, nerve you with patience for the conflict, and bless you with increasing success! May a crucified Saviour be both your hope and pattern, the subject of your discourses, your " worship, and the lifter up of your heads," the joy of your hearts, and your exceeding great reward! As life wears silently away, as the hands now laid upon you grow feeble, and the tongues that now cheer you to your high course lie silent in the

[1] Thomas à Kempis.

tomb, may other eyes behold you with undiminished energy, and increasing love and wisdom, pressing firmly on; and may our arms be permitted to embrace you in the eternal kingdom of our Lord and Saviour Jesus Christ! Amen and Amen.

During his stay in New York, the Bishop was hospitably entertained by the Rev. Dr. Haight, at whose house he stayed. He attended daily at the Chapel of the Seminary, and once addressed the students. He was admitted to a place in the House of Bishops and in the Lower House at the sittings of the convention, and received every possible mark of kindness. He was also present at the solemn deposition of Bishop Ives, of North Carolina, for leaving his post of duty and abandoning us to join the Church of Rome.

Under date October 10th, 1877, the Bishop records in the Annals of the Diocese some facts connected with a later visit:

The Bishop, with Canon Medley, left Fredericton for Boston to attend the Convention of the American Church. They were most hospitably received by Mr. and Mrs. Rice, and the Bishop found a hearty welcome from the House of Bishops, and clerical and lay deputies. Fifty bishops were in session. It was a remarkably harmonious session. The Bishop met many old friends. He was present and took part in the service at the institution of the Rev. I. Allen, at the Church of the Messiah. Rev. Dr. Dix, of Trinity church, New York, preached an admirable sermon.

On Wednesday, the 17th October, after bidding farewell to the House of Bishops, the Bishop, with the Rev. Canon Medley, proceeded to Portland, Me. They were hospitably entertained by Bishop Neely, and on St. Luke's Day, the Bishop assisted in the service of the consecration of St. Luke's Cathedral, Canon Medley intoning the prayers with the Rev. Dr. Hodges, of Baltimore. Nine bishops and upwards of fifty clergy were present. The debt of $35,000 on the Cathedral had been entirely paid off this year. It was a joyful day.

CHAPTER XVI

SERMONS PREACHED IN ENGLAND — LAMBETH CONFERENCE —
EPISCOPAL RING — ADDRESS AND REPLY — NOTES FROM
THE ANNALS.

PREVIOUSLY to the Bishop's appointment to the See of Fredericton, or about that time, a volume of his sermons was published in England. This book has been very generally circulated in the Diocese. Those who have read it cannot fail to appreciate its value.

The Sunday after his consecration, the Bishop preached at Exeter Cathedral. The subject of his sermon is " Alone, yet not alone." The sermon itself is worthy of permanent record, and the following portions will be read with deep interest, especially the reference to the great work he had undertaken in connection with his episcopal office. The text was Psalm cxxxix. 9, 10:

No sentiment seems more profoundly true, or more deeply affecting, than that which was uttered by the great Pascal — "I shall die alone." This loneliness, which is peculiarly felt in the hour of death, when all human help is worthless, and even human sympathy is weak, is, in fact, a part, and a most important part, of man's moral nature.

We are born into the world alone — we live in many respects alone — we love in some degree alone — we rejoice and sorrow often alone. But live as we may, we must die alone.

Whatever station we may have occupied in society, by whatever ties we may have been surrounded, by whatever joys or sorrows encompassed, whatever of human sympathy may have been ministered to us, in that hour we must break off all, and, single-handed, surrender ourselves to the grasp of our last enemy.

But this sentiment of the great Pascal is applicable to many other states of human life, and is also connected with another great

(196)

truth, which I design to dwell upon at this time in connection with
the passage now before us. For the loneliness of man was foreseen
from the first, and provided for. "It is not good that the man
should be alone," said the Creator. The form of expression, *should
be alone*, if it be well considered, involves, as all words of God must
involve, great mysteries of our nature. But if considered without
reference to any other truth, the loneliness of man would be most
appalling to our minds, and would lead us to despair. For the
thought of dying alone may well shake the stoutest heart. . . .

What I design, then, to show at this time is, the fact of man's
being a creature made in some sense *alone;* what evils flow from
this part of his nature, if not balanced by any other truth; and
how God has provided for us under all the trying circumstances of
our lives, this very compensation which, when united with the
former principle, enables us to live happily here, and unites us
with all the faithful in a world where separation and anguish are
no more.

This loneliness of man seems the principle uppermost in the
Psalmist's mind, when he thus begins the Psalm: "O Lord, thou
hast searched me and known me; thou knowest my down sitting
and mine uprising; thou understandest my thought afar off. Thou
compassest my path and my lying down, and art acquainted with
all my ways. Whither shall I go from Thy Spirit? or whither
shall I flee from Thy presence? If I ascend up into heaven, Thou
art there; if I make my bed in hell, Thou art there." How deep
and mysterious is the hidden world of thought within the human
breast — only to be fathomed by its Maker — only to be compre-
hended by its God. Were it not so indeed, there could be no
separate virtue, and so no separate and enjoyable reward; but
that it is so, is as evident as that no two faces of mankind exactly
resemble each other. . . . .

And old age is proverbial for loneliness. The old man finds
his early companions gone or going, or taking a different course:
the busy work of life is somewhat past, but the love of life remains;
and even this makes him lonely, until in the closing hour he comes
to be alone with God.

Now though it is necessary to our separate trial, probation, and reward, and to our enjoyment of that reward, that we should be thus alone, yet we must feel that without some balancing principle it would be a fearful part of our moral nature; and, corrupt as we are, it becomes a most evil part—loneliness is of itself distressing. How severely do we all feel this, if we are called to part with valued friends, who have been staying with us, to whom we have imparted all our common thoughts, joys, and griefs! When they are gone, we turn back again to our house with a feeling of desolation: we are alone in the world. Much more is this the case if our separation be by death; for then our loneliness is more certain and more lasting; we turn to our accustomed home, but home it feels no longer; we visit our old haunts, but their former charm is gone: nature herself seems clothed in dreariness, and the busiest crowd presents the emptiest void.

And even in our studies and pursuits, in which we find a common interest, the solitary student feels a sadness creeping over him, which he seeks to dispel by contact with others, yet from thence returns again to loneliness.

One only Being then remains who knows us all, and all of us, and altogether; and yet is accessible to each one single heart—to search its inmost depths—to feel its utmost wants—to hear its separate prayer—to be to it, both now and at all times, its fountain of thought, and life, and hope, and peace—its fullness—its blessedness without end, all in one, and that one is God. In ourselves we are alone; in Him only have we full communion, or as our Lord expresses it—"ye shall leave me alone; and yet I am not alone, because the Father is with me." This principle, then, of divine incorporation is that which meets the wants of the human heart, and when we have learned our own part in it, we are then, and then only, truly useful, and truly happy. Then though "we take the wings of the morning, and dwell in the uttermost parts of the sea"—though we be carried to far distant shores, or separated from those we love, or tossed about by the opposing waves of conflict—even there also, where no friendly hand may aid us, where accustomed sympathy is denied us, when our heart would sink, and our strength fail us, there will our great Shepherd, master, and guardian dwell; there his supporting hand shall lead us, his strong right hand hold us up, till, as death's gates close upon us, the gates of paradise open before us, and we are admitted to the presence of our Redeemer and our God.

But we shall see this more clearly by endeavouring to point out the evils which arise from the loneliness of man in itself, apart from this blessed divine society, and then the happiness, and peace, and usefulness, which spring from the latter source.

Now, if man dwell upon the loneliness itself, he becomes a selfish being. Because he is alone, his hopes and wishes terminate in self — he sets up no other standard but that of worldly comfort. To obtain this he will sacrifice much; he will rise early, and late take rest, he will toil on the greater part of his short life; but he looks no higher than the world. He holds no communion with his God — he knows not the value of prayer — he esteems riches as the great good — yet, though he lives alone, he never loves to be alone, because then the sense of separation from God depresses him, and he finds how poor and miserable he is.   .   .   .   .

Such being the evils which flow from the consideration of man's lonely estate, apart from that gracious heavenly society to which God, his Maker, has called him; let us now see what blessings flow from this holy and divine incorporation.

First, then, as regards our own eternal welfare, when we are one with God our Father, by faith in his Son, our Lord Jesus Christ, and by the sanctifying grace of His Holy Spirit daily renewing us to a holy obedience; then, though we are alone, we are still always present with God. He is with us — He is in us — He is about us on every side. To Him we every day repair with child-like confidence, with humble submission, with meek faith. We ask His pardon, we obtain His strength, we commit all our ways to Him; whether we are still, or in a journey, in the chamber, or in the field — in the solitary place, or in the crowded street — in the Church, or in the haunts of men — we are His. He orders all our life — He sustains our going forth — He hears our prayers — He vouchsafes our answer — He directs, governs, chastises, or rewards us — He is our hope, our life, our morning star, our resurrection day. Though we "dwell in the uttermost parts of the sea," why should we fear? He who made the waves — He who walked on the waves — He who controls the waves — He who said, "peace be still," is here; we cannot see Him, yet we believe in His power; we know His goodness, we have tasted of His mercy, we will trust him to the end. Though we are weak and sinful, he will not leave us, for he hath said "I will never leave thee nor forsake thee." So that we may boldly say, "The Lord is my helper, I will not fear what man shall do unto me."

.   .   .   .

To part from all that England has of historic recollection, of ancient fame, of noble architecture, of Christian sympathy, of the great and glorious past; to be severed from this Cathedral Church, this holy, peaceful, common home, with other nearer ties, is indeed painful, but what then? What is apparent separation if we be verily members incorporate in the mystical body of Christ? What is a wide rolling sea, a far-off shore, a new and stranger land? The morning hour of prayer shall find us together, not in bodily society, but in true Christian fellowship. The sunlight of our Saviour's countenance shines full on us together in the duties and pursuits of life; the evening stars look out on us assembling at the common hour of prayer; the Sabbath bell still cheers our accustomed hearts; the same Liturgy, unaltered and uninjured, strengthens our union; and, above all, the Holy Eucharist, that most sweet and heavenly food, sustains, cheers, and renovates our hearts. One conscious spirit of fellowship pervades us all. Though our bodies are disunited, though the strains of earthly music be not equally harmonious, it is the Lord's song that we sing, and that song may be sung in every land, by every tongue.

Let us go forth, then, full of hope, and on the wings of prayer let us implore you who remain behind to send your prayers after us, and to continue praying, and as far as your ability lies to assist us in our labours. There are many difficulties, and many adversaries, though "an effectual door is open." There is need of a strong heart and mind, faith and patience.

But if His right hand hold us who sends us forth, and has given us our authority, and our work, we shall do well. Come what will —opposition, affliction, a life prolonged or shortened—all will be well if He be ours and we are His. Brethren in the Lord, members of one common Head, members of this Cathedral Church, we bless you in the name of the Lord.

Twenty-three years had passed. The same preacher stood in the same pulpit at Exeter Cathedral. He was somewhat worn and aged by these years of constant devotion to his Master's service. He had passed through many trials with unabated zeal and trust. It was the anniversary celebration of those great societies, both of which had extended fostering care for many years towards the Colonial Church. We give the concluding portion of the Bishop's sermon from Philippians ii. 4:

The Church has been, therefore, constantly "looking on the things of others" by educating her members. She has brought the unconscious babe to the Lord's feet, mindful of His precept not to forbid them. She has provided schools for orphans, and for little outcast wanderers; schools of instruction on the Lord's Day to supply the defects of parents; schools for their training in all the great walks of life; schools for the poorer, the middle, and the richer classes; schools of science and art; and our two famous universities, where so many of England's sons have received their highest inspirations, and have won their first great honours in the world. And when I say the Church is educating, I gladly recognize the efforts of all Christians in this holy work. For our controversies and our convictions must not blind our eyes to the fact that there are other Christians equally sincere with ourselves, many in the field before us, many who have come in after us, and all eager to fulfil the Apostle's precept, though some not in so excellent a way as, according to our judgment, might be desired. Secondly, all Church restoration and Church building, when it is attempted on sound principles, is a fulfilment of the same duty. We have lived to see a great work achieved by the Church in our own days.

The noble temples built by the piety of our ancestors have been rescued from the decay and degradation into which they had fallen. The spirit of catholicity has arisen, like that of the man whose lifeless form started into vigour when he touched the bones of Elisha. It has been seen and felt, and everywhere proclaimed, that Christ's Church, both material and spiritual, is not for bishops only, and peers of parliament, and learned judges, and wealthy commoners, and escutcheoned squires, but for all; for the meanest, and the feeblest, and the richest, and the wisest, and for the dregs of poverty; and that there should kneel in one temple, yea, often side by side together, the beggar and the rich man, the learned and the fool, and that in God's most holy shrine we should "forbear to judge" according to the judgment of men, "for we are sinners all." And our merchant princes in these days rejoice not to look only to the monuments of their own industry and skill, but to raise many a lofty spire heavenwards, where the blind may receive inward light, the lame may walk, and the mourners may be comforted, and where many a poor fatherless child, who knows no words but "mother" and "home," may learn dearer words than those in "Father" and "Heaven." And the Church has learned another lesson from Him who went about healing all that were "oppressed of the devil, and attending on all manner of sickness and disease among the people." She has taught the dwellers in the free homes of her Western sons that it is not woman's mission upon earth to grow up in a refined and idolizing selfishness, surrounded with every luxury that money can purchase, and surveying, as from a queenly throne, with half-averted eyes, the squalid sufferings of the poor; doling out crumbs of comfort to needy supplicants without sympathy, without personal interest, without house-to-house visitation, and ready succour of their woes. We have, blessed be God, heard, we have seen those sisters of mercy and charity — whether they be clothed in one garb or another can signify little in His sight, to whom all hearts are naked and open, and to whose favour not the clothing, but the heart of the visitor gains access — scorn them not, speak not ill of any of them, my brethren, however they may differ from your own mode of action, whose purpose is real, and whose charity is full to overflowing. Rather rejoice to see the well-born and well-nurtured daughters of our land prompt to every call of woe, entering the haunts of darkness and misery, where filth and fever lurk in ambush for the lives of men, passing even into the dwellings of sin and shame, without fear, with the Cross of Christ before them, and the love of Christ, like a lamp, gilding the dark passages, and illuminating the squalid rooms. Who does not recognize in that figure kneeling beside the fever-stricken couch the fulfilment of these calm and glorious words, "Look not every man on his own things, but every man also on the things of others?"

And the Church has learned a yet harder lesson for the benefit of fallen women — sisters, we must still call them, in spite of their most wretched and degraded fall; children they still remain of one all-pitying Father, members, if they knew it, though decayed members, of the Lord of Glory — heirs, if not in hope, yet once in gift, and still not altogether barred of hope, of the bright realms of purity and peace. To recall such hearts, "where wounds of deadly hate have pierced so deep," to lasting, life-long penitence, must needs be one of the hardest tasks we can perform: yet not an altogether hopeless task. For where was one such woman found, but at the feet of Him, whose precious blood was shed for every sinner and for every sin? If you have happily walked in the path of virtue, turn not away with scorn from such a sight as a fallen woman weeping for mercy. Recognize, loathe, and repent of the like sin in your own bosoms in its seed, which has blossomed and borne apples of Sodom in their bitter fruit. And if there be those who have played with vice, and have put the world's mean gilding upon loathsome crimes, how fearfully does the curse of broken hearts rest upon them! Surely, if Zacchæus could say, "If I have done wrong to any man, I restore four-fold," then not four, nor forty, nor four hundred-fold would be too great a restitution for him who has robbed a soul of its eternal peace, and has sent out into the world a false light which has lured many more to their never-ending ruin. Well, then, may we look pityingly on the sins of others, "pulling them out of the fire," and repeating the noble intercessor's prayer, "Behold, now, I have taken upon me to speak unto the Lord, which am but dust and ashes; peradventure ten should be found there." You know the answer. Imitate the loving importunity! Enrich yourselves by the glorious example!

Amidst so many tasks of love and duty, the rivers of mercy that fertilize and bless our land, I am asked to remind you particularly, that the Church has not forgotten her "banished ones." "Other sheep she has, which are not of this fold: them also she must bring, and they must hear her voice"—dwellers in the plains of India, and the forests of Borneo, in the vast continent of Australia, and the many-peopled isles of the Pacific, under burning suns, and by frozen rivers. Her mission is a grand one, if her children would acknowledge it to be such, and practically act up to their duty.

You live, my brethren, in the ancient and luxurious homes of religion. You have not wisdom to seek; it is brought home to your doors; it knocks daily at your gates; you cannot enter a city, you cannot ascend a hill, you cannot go through a village or street, where the "City of God" is not built, where the Word of God is not preached and maintained; maintained, not always by your own voluntary efforts, but often by the piety and liberality of past ages, of those who built the fanes in which you worship, whose bread you eat, whose sacred songs you hear, whose benefactions you do not scruple to appropriate, though it may be that you scorn their religion. And you are all enriched by the produce of those lands to which England has sent her colonists. Your children make their homes and their fortunes there: the commerce that girdles the world brings home daily to your shores a plentiful abundance of all God's good gifts. Think it not hard, then, if you are asked, and often asked, to help the two great handmaids of the Church in their efforts to maintain and to extend true religion in the regions beyond you. Remember that these societies (with some others) are the only expressions of the love of the Church of England towards her colonists, and towards the heathen. The State teaches no religion in her colonial possessions, and exercises no principle but that of impartial justice. But without a higher principle even than justice between man and man, great and godlike as that principle is, what State can long endure?

In these days of rapid communication and wide-spread intelligence, God calls us loudly by the material gifts he so prodigally bestows. As on the narrow wire, where the little birds sit securely, unconscious that the lightnings play beneath their feet, but fed by the same hand that gives the lightning power, one may listen to a sound of music, flinging its wild notes abroad, and showing that the harmony of God's voice is everywhere; so as we hurry along the great pathway of life, on land or on ocean, by railway or by steam, God still calls to us, sweetly, powerfully calls, Remember for all these gifts you must give account. Remember you are in like manner hurrying to your end. Your gifts are many, your privileges various and great, your opportunities of good are daily becoming fewer, your time has been often misspent, your talents often wasted. Sow, then, the seeds of good, which will spring up when you are dead; sow them plentifully, scatter them widely, sow them beside all waters; say not, "I have much goods laid up for many years," my skill, my industry, my might, has gotten me my wealth. None is thine own, all is God's; thy very soul is God's; thine only enduring wealth is the good thou leavest behind thee for mankind.

I must not enlarge on the whole field of Missions which these two Societies occupy, one by its Missionaries, and the other by its versions of the Scriptures, and its religious books. It will be more convenient as to your time, and more suitable to my powers of observation, that I should speak of the narrower field of duty which I occupy; for a narrower view, if it be the view of one who speaks from experience, is often felt to be more convincing, than the fuller tale of one who has never been an eye-witness. I speak, then, with only four years' less experience than the prelate who last year addressed you. I can tell you from twenty-three years' eye-witness, that the life and soul of the Church in North America is owing to God's blessing on these two Societies; that the one has fostered and assisted every mission in the whole country, till we have learned (and in all the towns we have already learned) to sustain our own Church by our own unaided exertions; and that the other Society has assisted with small sums of money most of the churches built in the infancy of the colony, thereby calling forth contributions to a much larger amount from churchmen in their several parishes, those contributions being often ten, and even twenty times the amount contributed by the Society for Promoting . Christian Knowledge.

You have, then, before you to-day the experience of twenty-three years on the part of one Bishop, who has been concerned in the planting or supporting of every mission in his Diocese; who has visited and confirmed in nearly every church; who has been consulted about every new mission, and every new building; who has lived to see his clergy doubled, and his churches or stations more than doubled; who has the happiness of seeing the laity of his Church contribute four-fold what they once did; and whose Cathedral Church, consecrated fifteen years since, is maintained entirely by its own resources. That this is matter of boasting, God forbid we should say or think. That this is owing to the exertions of the Bishop only, he would be the last to affirm. That this is matter of blessing, why should we deny? That there are no drawbacks, no dross mingled with the gold, no divisions, no tokens of man's infirmity or sin — Alas, my brethren, are you free from these evils yourselves? Would you have God's precious gifts withholden from *you*, because you have not always used them all aright? Then withhold them not from us.

One admonition more, and I have done. I return, after twenty-three years, to the accustomed place where, in due course, I once occupied this pulpit, but the whole is changed. The venerable Bishop is not here. The Dean and Chapter are numbered with the dead. I listen in vain for one clear, silvery voice which rang out the accustomed tones, or mingled in the harmony. I ask for the faithful, who once listened to my instructions, but many of them are "gone into the world of light, and I alone sit lingering here." And while I muse on these things, a sad voice is wafted over the waves of the Atlantic that another son of Devon, another prelate, is no more. Only a few months since he was among you, rejoicing in the memories of his youth, and full of that grace and strength which distinguished him above his fellows. And is not this a hand let down from heaven, a sure and manifest token to warn you, " Whatsoever thy hand findeth to do, do it with thy might, for there is no work, nor device, nor knowlodge, nor wisdom, in the grave whither thou goest?" Did you ever regret that you had done too much, given too much, suffered too much, for the Lord Jesus? So now give to Him. Give in the spirit which St. Paul recommends, " with simplicity," with a single eye, and a generous heart; "with cheerfulness," not in a hard, ungracious way, as if you grasped the gift tightly while you gave it; not as if you were doing a favour to the recipient of your bounty; but in the gracious spirit of that mercy which is "twice blessed," after the pattern of that love which gave Itself for us all. Ask Him to bless your gifts, and you cannot give meanly, unlovingly, unfaithfully.

Now may God bless you all. Amen.

It was ten years after the period referred to. The Bishop was in England in attendance at the Lambeth Conference. Again, at the anniversaries of the two great Societies, he preached at the Cathedral, at Exeter. His sermon was published and widely circulated at the time, under the title "Other Little Ships." The text was from St. Mark iv. 36.

Passing by the introductory portion of the sermon, the Bishop continues as follows:

The physical sleep of the Lord's body is not a symbol of His indifference. It is a lesson to us not to imagine that He is careless of our danger, because for the moment He takes no notice of it. How small and contracted is the view which poor sufferers have of their temptations and their trials, of the motive which prompts their Master to permit them, of the wise and tender love which every moment cares for them whilst they suffer, and because they suffer! And if He seems to sleep, it is to make them more vigilant, that they may cry aloud for succour, and may learn, as fresh troubles arise in the Church, or in their own life, not to be "so fearful," and to have more faith in Him.

And is our own vessel the only ship for which He cares? Are there not with Him also "other little ships?" Are there not many

souls of whom the world takes no account, unnamed in history,
uncounted in the chronicles of fame—poor, suffering, tempted
souls, for whom few human beings care, who live in toil, and want,
and penury, and suffer unknown agonies of dreary doubt, and fear
of what may happen, and their little boat is always tossing, no
sooner mounted on the crest of a wave than it sweeps wildly down
into the trough of the sea, and every one is too busy about his own
dangers to attend to the solitary craft? But does the Master forget
that in the "little ships" there are lives and souls as precious as
those of the Apostles themselves? Cares He not for those little
ships? Will not they also hear the consoling word, "Why are ye
so fearful?" Will they not share in the rebuke of the tempest,
and in the "great calm?"

Surely this is a lesson to all classes of minds, and all ranks of
society. It is not for the poor to think, Christ careth not for me.
It is not for the rich to imagine, I am one of the great pillars of the
Church, or of the State—one of the few who deserve consideration.
It is not for the laity to say, it is well for you, the bishops and
clergy, to possess the saintly character; we do not dream of ascend-
ing to such heights. The saintly character belongs to the Christian
man and woman everywhere, not to the clergy as a class. For
when they receive the Holy Ghost at their ordination, it is in
fulfilment of their Master's promise, to sanctify the word they
preach, to make valid the sacraments they minister, to render their
whole office valuable to the flock, and effectual for the purposes for
which it was designed, not to stamp them as the greatest saints
before the world. It is to strengthen them and comfort them by
the belief that this is not a sham of man's devising, but a real truth
of God's ordaining, which, rightly interpreted, and modestly and
reasonably set forth, is the strength and comfort both of the shepherd and of the flock: of the shepherd when he knows that not
only high and glorious intellects, profoundly learned masters in
Israel, are the Redeemer's care, but the "little ships" also, plain
ordinary men, whose hope lies not in brilliancy, but in rugged perseverance; in that simplicity and godly sincerity which an Apostle
gloried in, and which they may share with that great Apostle.

And so it is our comfort, brethren beloved in the Lord, when we come to England for a little season, we gaze on the magnificent shrines which ancient piety reared, and which your reverence and liberality have restored, but only restored (remember), for your hands built not these walls, your genius did not originate this mighty plan, your souls were not first inspired with these lofty thoughts; but when our joyful eyes behold it, we thank God and you for the sight, and see everything to admire in it, and nothing to find fault with. We know that in our colonial Sees we are but "little ships." Yet, whatsoever we are, we are in the great Master's fleet. It was His voice that called us to embark; it is His hand that beckons us to the shore; it is His arm on which we lean in the midst of the tempest; it is His compass by which we steer; it is His great salvation which we hope to share with you. You worship (it is true) in a church of more than common stateliness and beauty, and you have a history on which the mind loves to dwell. You can look back to the days when these ancient towers were built by Norman hands, when daring and successful builders pierced their mighty walls, when the great designer of the choir first opened out the vista, and the still mightier Grandison completed the o'er-arching nave and aisles, and when the whole structure assumed somewhat of its present form and comeliness. Beneath the shadow of these walls generations of illustrious dead repose, the echoes of the Civil War have here died away, the trump of God has sounded to awake a sleeping church, and through all changes of the State or of the Church the glorious walls remain, as if built for eternity, and scarce to be destroyed by time; and in a thousand churches England recalls the struggles and glories of the past. We have no history but that which we make ourselves. But we will never despair. Sons of the Church, we will build with the sword of the Spirit in one hand, and the trowel in the 6ther, bent upon reproducing in such ways as God shall lead us, and as the varying conditions of our life permit, England's Church, and England's faith, and England's loyalty, and above all the truth of God's most Holy Word committed to our charge. We are a body Catholic, because not merely Roman, separated, but not by our own desire; ever praying to be

o

reunited on primitive and Apostolic foundations, in true, substantial, visible union with the several parts of our Church in many lands, but holding to "one Lord, one baptism, one God and Father of us all," and "contending earnestly for the faith once delivered to the Saints." And when we have met together in conference, all in communion with each other, surely it is not too much to say, that while there has been free and friendly discussion, there has been substantial unity. No article of the faith has been denied, no venerable creed has been surrendered, no word of the living God has been thrust aside. Every Bishop has desired to build up the old primitive foundations of the Catholic and undivided Church. Surely this conference, if it did no more, would be a sufficient answer to those who unworthily represent us as one of many discordant sects, as a body rent by endless divisions, without foundation, without coherence, without orders, without sacraments, without unity in itself. Whereas by our marvellous increase throughout the world, and our union in all the verities of the Christian faith, we are "compacted by that which every joint supplieth, according to the effectual working in the measure of every part," and, we are (we trust) "growing unto a holy temple in the Lord."

"*Growing.*" Not till one hundred and fifty years after the Reformation did England begin to realize the blessing of growth. The "plantations" (so called) were feeble, struggling communities, without a native episcopacy, divided in religious belief, and unconscious of their destiny. Now we behold a church, vast in extent, considerable in numbers, with sixty Bishops, some of them missionary Bishops, with more than four thousand clergy, with multitudes of highly educated men who have passed into her fold, converts from all sides, a church thoroughly organized and synodically compacted. Rent from us by a political revolution, in all the great foundations of the faith, in all man's highest interest and hopes, in love for England's Church, the Episcopal Church of the United States is entirely one with our own in Great Britain and her colonies.

"*Growing.*" Once in India Christianity made its appearance as an alien, feebly halting on forbidden ground. Yet such has been

God's blessing that ten thousand native converts came to welcome the arrival of our Sovereign's son; and now, under the care of Bishops lately consecrated, eighteen thousand natives have requested to be enrolled in the Church by Holy Baptism.

"*Growing.*" About a century since, one Bishop was authorized as a state official to have nominal rule over the whole of the provinces of Canada, Newfoundland, Bermuda, and the Bahamas. So little notion had the statesmen of that day of the spiritual needs of churchmen and the duties of a Bishop. Now we have two Church Provinces, and fourteen Bishops in those vast and populous regions, presiding over their several Synods, who have each as much work to do as any man can reasonably desire. The same remarkable growth has been shown in Australia and in Southern Africa.

And what need to speak of New Zealand, when the memory of two loved and honoured names is fresh in your hearts, and placed before your eyes? Surely the love we bear them should stir us, as their best memorial, to greater energy and self-sacrifice, and nobler gifts. And as we have wept together for the father, let our prayers now ascend together for the son. Oh, that the fire of suffering through which he has passed may be to him the fire of strength, of patience, and of love. In the love of the convert, in the steadfastness of the native pastor, in the deepening convictions of the island race, that he, the old Bishop's son, is their true and lasting friend, may he find his rich reward. So may he land in safety where the meek Patteson fell, and the fronds of the palm branch, once the tokens of a wild and savage justice, become the peaceful heralds of the kingdom of the Prince of Peace. Thus from those five blest wounds there shall stream forth fountains of salvation, and the fair and the dark races shall kneel before one altar, and become as one in the love of that Redeemer who has bought them with His precious blood.

"*Growing.*" In the island of Madagascar, one whom I remember as a boy, the worthy son of a most worthy father, prebendary with myself of this cathedral, was lately confirming seventy-four native converts, and ordaining a native pastor, on the same Whitsun-day that I was ordaining the son of the old Pitcairn missionary to the children of the mutineers in the *Bounty*, and likewise was ordaining a Danish teacher to minister to a body of emigrants from Copenhagen. Truly the Gospel of Christ supplies a gracious Nemesis. The memory of old deeds of hate is repaid by new deeds of love. Mutiny is changed to bounty; and ravages of fire and sword are repaid by sending to the descendants of the Danes the tokens of a fresh and lasting peace. For when in that emigrant room in the wilderness, adorned with boughs, and fresh flowers gathered from the forest, I confirmed the children of the Danes, the first names announced to me were Canute, Eric, and Olaf. We sang the old Danish hymns; we offered our Litany in the Danish, and responded in the English tongue; and the little band, now members of our own Church of England, knelt around one altar, over which the cross of the Danish flag formed its simple but appropriate ornament. "For He has made us one by the blood of His cross." The history of missions is indeed a mingled record of toil and journeyings, peril and constant service, of disappointments, of contentions, of shortcomings and fallings away, of many prayers and many tears; but sum them all up, gather them from every age and every land, and they are not so precious as one drop of the blood of our Lord Jesus, the Prophet who teaches us, the Priest who offers for us, the King who dwells in us, the Intercessor and the Saviour of us all.

But, turning back for a moment to human agency, we may say, without any exaggeration, that much of the growth and extension of our Church is, under God, owing to the two handmaids of the Church, whose anniversary we celebrate to-day; and to whose strength and increase it is the duty of every churchman, of every class, to contribute according to his ability. Make their cause, my brethren, your own. Throw yourselves heartily into this work, as if you believed in it and loved it. We want from you the same kind of work which you very reasonably require of us; strong, hearty, continued work, not the work of *dilettanti* bishops and halting Christians, but the work of men; of those who know that there is dignity in labour, and that honest labour goes on till sundown, and does not cease when the sun is high. Let every Bishop speak for himself. I come here to-day to bear my testimony, that my Diocese owes a debt, which we can never repay, to those two venerable institutions; and that our greatest obligation is that of having called forth our own exertions, and enabled us to make some sacrifices for our religion. Certainly I hold it to be an *Articulus stantis vel cadentis ecclesiæ*, that we not only believe, but that we do the will of God. And where is the Apostle who, travelling in a foreign land, found, as I have found, two noble and liberal institutions ready to his hand; helping to support his missionaries, and to build his churches, and never failing him in time of need? Then are we Apostles, when we toil in rowing: when we toil all the night, even if we have caught nothing, hoping to find when the blest morning comes.

And if my voice could be heard, and were of any worth without these walls, it would be raised on behalf of our never undertaking Colonial work which we were not prepared to live and die for. If the greatness of England is not an insular but a maritime greatness; if her fleets go forth, not only to protect her harbours, but to extend her commerce; if her power is felt in the little flag of the fisher-boat, as well as in the mightiest of her ironclads; if her sons carry with them to all lands the proud trophy of her laws and of her freedom, much more may Christian Bishops glory in continuing to "sow beside all waters," and in holding the land where they have sown and laboured as their own.

Permit me, in conclusion, to remind you all of your own duty to the Church, which is your mother, and to those institutions which are the handmaids of the Church. That you are known at all as Christians, beyond the shores of England, is, in great part, the work of these two institutions. Your eternal glory will not be that you restored cathedrals, or that you made treaties, or that you abounded in riches, or that you conquered nations, but that you conquered sin. The living stones of the Redeemer's temple will be your coronet; the gathering in your own half heathen masses, the seeking out the lost, the strengthening the weak, the raising the fallen in this and in every land. Look you at this glorious Church, and fancy that your work is done. These dead stones, instinct with life, tell in your ears what living stones should be. The harmonies that daily wake within these walls are but the prelude to the nobler anthem of souls won to the love of Christ by your own efforts. Not to the clergy only, but to the Church at large, is committed this divine, this difficult, this unceasing care. Never for one moment is the cry unheard amidst the storm, Christian, "carest thou not that we perish?"

Unholy soul, what hast thou done for Christ? Selfish, indolent, careless, self-satisfied soul, what hast thou done for Christ? Bitter, vindictive, harsh-judging soul, biting and devouring thy brethren, what art thou doing for Christ? And as the last word I may, perhaps, be ever permitted to speak within these dear and holy walls, I say to you all, Work more for Christ.

Work on, work humbly, and the truth will dawn upon you. Work on, and peace will return to you. Work on, and sorrow and sighing will not burden you. Work on, and the tempter will flee from you. Work on, for this is life's business, this is death's happiness, this is eternity's reward: "I have finished the work which Thou gavest me to do." Amen.

We come now to the last visit to England in 1888. The duties connected with the Lambeth Conference, attendance at public meetings, and other calls upon his time and attention, were somewhat of a strain upon the Bishop's strength, now in his advancing years. Before his return to his Diocese he was taking a few days rest in the quiet and retirement of the home of his son, Rev. John B. Medley.

We have been favoured with a copy of his sermon on that occasion. Taking for his text the words from the Apostles' Creed, "And the life of the world to come," his lordship said:

This, my brethren, is the conclusion of one of the most solemn parts of our service, when, in the presence of God, we set forth those things which are to be believed and acted upon. What is this life of the world to come which we all look for? Some persons, from a misapprehension of the passage in the Book of Revelation, think we shall have nothing to do in the next world but to praise God unceasingly as we sing His praises here. That seems to be a great mistake. But what is the life of the world to come; and of what does it consist? It is life; that life of the world to come is the only true life, and in what does its happiness consist? In the resurrection of the body? We all know how imperfect our bodies are in the flesh; how often they get wearied; how often they become clogs to the spirits in worshipping God. But we read in St. Paul's Epistle to the Philippians that Christ will raise our vile bodies — the bodies of our humiliation, our humble bodies — that they may be made like unto His Glorious Body. What a marvellous thing is this! That these poor bodies — the slaves to evil feelings, evil thoughts and words, shall be made like Christ's Glorious Body. This is an important part of the life of the world to come. We know nothing of the new life when the soul shall cling to this new found partner — the body freed from all stain of sin. Made like Christ's Glorious Body! We almost tremble when we hear of such a thing. That resurrection of the body, when our bodies shall no longer be the weak and imperfect things they are here but like Christ's Glorious Body, if we are found true and faithful to Him in this world. The life of the world to come is increased and made blessed by the perfect unity which exists amongst all true followers of Christ. You know how difficult it is here to be absolutely one with people; what crooked tempers there are; what distempered views of things are taken; what difficulties there are in the way of making ourselves one. The Psalmist says, what a blessed thing it is to dwell together in unity. Yet what terrible divisions, what deplorable dissensions one with another there are now. So when we are made like Christ's Glorious Body all will be as one. You and I may hear of such things, we may speak of them, and try to realize them, but after all it is but little we know. The life of the world to come consists in work as well as in praise. When we look at the multitude of children who are called away, and think that far more children than adults depart this life, what becomes of those dear little babes? They must have something to do. In the world to come there must be a kind of growth. We know not. Do the Angels teach them

what we might have taught them.   There will be work to do, but
we know not what it is.   God is always working; never idle; never
at rest.   So the life of the world to come must consist, in some
way, of wonderful work which God has for us to do.   It is rest from
sin and sinful pleasures, but such a rest which consists of perpetual
and unceasing work, of great and glorious work of what we know
not.   How earnestly we should strive after this life; strive to be
one with Christ; one with each other; strive against sin; so that
the life of the world to come may be working in us, for when God
sends affliction and distress, God is perfecting us for that life.
There is one thing which I may notice—that when people think of
the life of the world to come they think of it as rest.   They know
it is a troublesome and a toilsome life here, and so they think
that the life of the world to come is rest; to sit down, as it were,
and do nothing.   That is not exactly the view that I wish you to
take; it is perfect rest, joy, pleasure, happiness, oneness, and unity
one with another in that life.   Oh that you and I, separated by
great oceans, separated but united in the Church and in Christ, may
seek to know more and more of the life of the world to come; that
God may work in us all that is necessary to fit us for it—whether
we have few years, or whether God spares us, whether our children
are taken away or grow up; however God deals with us that this
glorious life, that world which shall bear true fruit in itself and in
us, shall be begun, continued and ended in Him.   Knowing the
uncertainty of all life, and the difficulty of saying we will do this or
that, I can only say that I hope to again speak to you from this
place before I leave England, but now I entreat you as members of
the Catholic Church of Christ to seek more and more, by God's
grace, to become perfect for the life of the world to come.

The Bishop did not attend the meeting of the first Lambeth Conference in 1868.   To this matter he makes the
following allusion in his charge to the clergy, delivered on
the 30th June of that year:

You may, naturally, expect something from me on the subject of
the Lambeth Conference, and on the reasons which prevented my
attendance at that great assembly.   I may say, therefore, first, that

had His Grace the Archbishop required my presence as a matter of dutiful obedience, I should, without delay, have complied with his command. The matter coming before me, however, through his kindness and consideration, in another form, it was left to me to judge whether I deemed it desirable to attend or not. At the time fixed for the Conference, I had issued notices for many confirmations, and the clergy had prepared their candidates; and I was unwilling, without very strong reasons, to postpone such confirmations, as I must have done, for a whole year. Further, with the utmost deference to the wiser judgment of the Bishops who urged His Grace to summon that assembly, it appeared to me that in consideration of the vast distance from England of many of the Colonial Dioceses, and the grave importance of the step contemplated, a longer time should have been allowed to give the matters selected for deliberation full consideration, and to obtain, if possible, the judgment of the Colonial Bishops generally, and of their clergy (and indeed of the laity also, if the decrees of that council were intended to carry with them the force of general consent) on the subjects calling for the judgment of so august an assembly.

Looking back to the first great council of the Church, I see it stated in the Inspired Word, that in a time of great anxiety and much discussion on points partly ceremonial, and partly doctrinal, not the Apostles only, but "the apostles and elders came together to consider of this matter;" so that the second order in the ministry was not excluded from the deliberation. What part the laity took in the matter is not clear; but it is certain that the final decree was adopted with their consent, being issued in the name of the "apostles, elders, and brethren," and that "the whole multitude" were listeners to the addresses of the Apostles. I am well aware that what was perfectly practicable at that early period, when the members of the Church were few, may at the present time be practically impossible. But I see no insuperable difficulty in collecting within a reasonable time the judgments of the Colonial Dioceses on any given subject, before proceeding to a more full discussion of it by the general assembly. Above all, it appeared to me unwise to gather together from the ends of the earth Bishops of the Anglican communion, some belonging to an established church, some to a church partially connected with the State, or in a very anomalous position, and some to a church wholly unconnected with the State, without distinctly stating the purpose for which we were called together, and the subjects to be considered. Grave reasons, the force of which I do not presume to impugn, may have prevented this course from being adopted; but I am obliged frankly to confess to you (with the possibility that some of you may think me mistaken) that when no subject whatever was named for discussion, and when only three days were allotted for deliberation, according to the notice first given, I deemed it impossible that in so short a time a large body could come to a satisfactory conclusion on points with regard to which the members of our Church throughout the world might well look for wise counsel from the whole assembled episcopate.

The Bishop lived to see the difficulties and dangers he anticipated overruled, and at a later day he readily admitted the vast advantage to the whole Anglican communion arising from the deliberations at Lambeth.

The second meeting of the Lambeth Conference was held in 1878. On this occasion the Bishop was present. No prelate from afar was received with more respect and regard at that great assemblage. It was the first occasion of the Bishop's absence at the annual meetings of the Diocesan Church Society and Synod. In his letter addressed to the Synod, he said:

I greatly regret to be absent from the meeting of the Synod, where I have so often enjoyed your kind co-operation and support. Having been requested by His Grace the Archbishop of Canterbury to be present at the Lambeth Conference, which is to be held early in July, my absence is unavoidable. I shall, however, be very thankful to return to my work as soon as circumstances permit.

An interesting incident occurred on the eve of the Bishop's departure. Some time previously, the clergy had most gladly and readily contributed towards the purchase of an episcopal seal ring, as a mark of their affection and respect. There was no want of funds. The work was admirably done in Boston, under the direction of a kind and valued friend of the writer. It was completed just in time for presentation before the Bishop left for England. He was greatly pleased, more by the affectionate love of the clergy than by the beauty and value of the gift. On his return, he spoke of the ring as being greatly admired by his friends in England for its beauty and workmanship.

FROM THE ANNALS.

May 3rd, 1878. The Bishop received an address from the clergy and lay delegates of the Synod on his approaching visit to England and attendance at the Lambeth Conference, and the Rev. Canon DeVeber, in the name of the clergy of the Diocese, presented him with a handsome episcopal ring—an amethyst, with arms of the See, and the Bishop's arms engraved on it, and the mitre.

In his reply the Bishop says:

. . . I have found among you a home which is very dear to me, and warm and faithful friends. And as long as my Heavenly Father is pleased to spare my life and strength, I hope to labour with you in the good cause of Christ's Holy Catholic Church, and to prove myself not wholly undeserving of the confidence you repose in me.

. . . As unity must necessarily be of slow growth, and absolute uniformity is not to be expected, perhaps not to be desired, we must not be disappointed if less should be done at the approaching Conference than we expect. But we should put forth all our strength in the education of our members in the principles of our faith, and in those practical measures which will enable us to contend with present difficulties and dangers; and will afford the best guarantee that the Church in this Province will live after us, undiminished in power and efficacy, and fruitful in every good work which our Heavenly Master has commanded us to do.

It is my earnest wish and determination to spend my remaining days, so long as God shall give me strength to be of any use at all, among you, and the happiest day of my journey will be when I set my foot on board the steamer which will bring me back to your shores.

The Bishop left Quebec in the *Sarmatian* on the 11th May, accompanied by the Rev. Canon DeVeber, and landed at Liverpool on the 21st.

. . . On the 1st July he went to London, when the Bishop of Chichester (Dr. Dunford) kindly invited him to take up his abode at the Lollard's Tower, to which place Bishop Selwyn had given him an invitation. The Bishop was lodged in Bishop Selwyn's rooms. There he remained during the sitting of the Lambeth Conference.

The Conference met on Tuesday, the 2nd of July, and all the Bishops present received holy communion together in Lambeth chapel. The sittings were held in the Archbishop's library.

The Bishop was appointed to serve on the committee on union, and was invited with the other members to stay at Furnham Castle by the Bishop of Winchester. The meetings were singularly pleasant and harmonious.

The Bishop, after visiting many dear friends, on Friday, the 22nd July, returned to Lambeth. This week, until 26th, was occupied with receiving the reports of the committees, and on Friday evening, the Conference broke up. Thursday being St. James' day, all the Bishops received holy communion in the Archbishop's chapel.

. . . On the 11th August, the Bishop preached twice at Ottery, St. Mary, while staying beneath the roof where he had often visited his honoured friend, Sir J. T. Coleridge. Monday he stayed with Lord Devon, and on Tuesday, the 13th, he preached at the Cathedral, Exeter, now happily restored.[1]

Shortly before the time of the assembling of the Lambeth Conference in 1878, the Church in England had been deeply moved by the prosecutions instituted under the provisions of what was known as the Public Worship Act, against

[1] See Sermon, "Other Little Ships."

certain of the clergy and laity of the Church, who desired services of an ornate character with advanced ritual. The majority of the English Bishops were strongly disposed to uphold the law as laid down in the Act referred to, but as the question was a burning one, and one in which the entire Anglican communion was interested, the Archbishop, at one of the meetings of the Conference, invited discussion on the part of the American and Colonial Bishops, and indicated that as one of the seniors, he would like to have the opinion of the venerable Bishop of Fredericton.

Bishop Medley, being thus unexpectedly called upon, arose, and said in his quiet and dignified way:

I had not thought that my opinion in this matter was likely to have very much weight, but since your Grace has requested it, I freely give it. My opinion is that the Church of England will never enjoy any real peace until the Public Worship Act is *repealed!*

The utterance of these words immediately aroused a perfect storm of disapprobation on the part of the friends of the Public Worship Act. Cries of "Chair! chair!" were heard on either hand.

The attempt to call the Bishop down, however, failed, as all who are familiar with his courage and determination will readily imagine. He simply stood and quietly waited until the confusion had subsided, and then, stimulated by the opposition, proceeded to express his views with wonderful force and ability. The speech created a profound impression at the Conference. The American Bishops and the majority of the Colonial Bishops strongly supported the position assumed by Bishop Medley, and although they were in a minority in the Lambeth Conference at the time referred to, the memorable debate attracted marked attention on the part of the religious and secular press, and was not without its effect in bringing about that spirit of mutual toleration which now so happily prevails.

The Bishop left Liverpool on the 29th August, accompanied by Canon DeVeber, and reached Quebec on the 8th September. On his arrival at St. John, on Wednesday, the 11th, he was presented with a most kind and affectionate address, and a similar welcome was extended to him at Fredericton, on Thursday, 12th September.

Notwithstanding all the fatigue of his extended visit, and frequent sermons and addresses, we find in the Annals notes of an extended confirmation tour in the autumn, with the following note at the close of the year:

Confirmed three hundred and seventy-five; consecrated three churches; ordained two priests and one deacon; travelled about ten thousand three hundred and thirty-five miles. All praise be to God.

At the meeting of the Synod in 1879, the following address was presented to the Bishop:

We, the clergy and lay delegates of the Diocese of Fredericton, in Synod assembled, take this the earliest opportunity to express our warmest welcome to your lordship on your return from attendance at the late meeting of the Bishops of the Anglican communion in the Lambeth Conference.

We feel assured that the high attainments of your lordship in theology, as well as your long experience in the work of the Colonial Church, aided much in the deliberations and beneficial results of that important meeting.

It is also our wish to congratulate your lordship, most sincerely, on your recent appointment to the high office of Metropolitan of the Church of England in the Dominion of Canada—an appointment which we believe is justly appreciated by the Church throughout this Dominion.

That your lordship may long be spared to us under the well-remembered title of Bishop of Fredericton, and that your wise rule and counsels may ever be blessed as Metropolitan of Canada, is our earnest wish and prayer.   G. M. ARMSTRONG, *Chairman.*

FRANCIS PARTRIDGE, *Secretary.*

REPLY.

Your unanimous and most kind address is as gratifying as it is unexpected. I most heartily thank you for it, as an evidence of the warm feeling and affection which you entertain towards your Bishop, and which, I humbly trust, will continue to cheer me in my efforts to serve you, as long as it pleases God to spare my life.

In regard to the Lambeth Conference, I can claim no distinction beyond that of a peace-maker, and of an earnest endeavour to extend toleration to all who honestly subscribe to the Formularies, and endeavour to carry into effect what they deem to be the plain rules of our Church.

I thank you for your congratulations on my election by the House of Bishops to be the Metropolitan of Canada. I shall do all in my power to show myself not undeserving of so high an honour, and of your good opinion of me. But honourable as that title is, the name of the Bishop of Fredericton is dearer to me. It reminds me of many a trial, of constant labour in your service, of willing support, and faithful affection; of many a beloved fellow-labourer, now called to his rest; of a Cathedral Church, where, for many years, the faithful have offered a daily sacrifice, and where a body of earnest young men have received the grace of Holy Orders; of "psalms and hymns and spiritual songs" wafted to the throne of God, and chanted, as we hope, with fresh purity by those who have "washed their robes, and made them white in the blood of the Lamb."

My tongue must indeed "cleave to the roof of my mouth," if I forget the title which I never sought, but which continually reminds me, amidst the "troubles and adversities which God has shewed me," that He was pleased to "bring me to great honour, and to comfort me on every side."

I remain, my dear brethren,

Your affectionate friend and Bishop,

JOHN FREDERICTON, *Metropolitan.*

CHAPTER XVII.

NOMINATION, ELECTION AND CONSECRATION OF THE BISHOP COADJUTOR.

THE Bishop made a most important announcement at the meeting of the Synod in 1879. He said that, though still blessed with health and strength, his advanced years rendered it difficult to reach all the work required of him in the Diocese. After giving the matter careful consideration, he was minded to obtain assistance through a Coadjutor. He would still willingly devote the ability which might be given in his remaining years to the benefit of the Church under his charge. The Bishop expressed his willingness to provide the stipend of the Coadjutor out of his own income. He asked that the nomination of the candidate should be left to himself.

The existing canon, in case of a vacancy in the See, left the entire choice in the Synod. A canon was therefore submitted and passed in accordance with the wishes of the Bishop. It may here be stated that with several members of the Synod there was a feeling adverse to the principle of the canon. Only out of regard and respect for the Bishop was this feeling overruled. At the close of the proceedings the following resolution was proposed:

' Resolved, That this Synod, before which matters of so grave and delicate a nature have been brought, bear witness of our high appreciation of the dignity, the candour, the patience, and the impartiality which have characterized his lordship's bearing and utterances in presiding; our renewed love and respect for his lordship; our wish and prayer that he may long be spared to us; and our earnest thanks to Almighty God that the deliberations of this Synod have been so eminently free from the spirit of bitterness and

(224)

party strife, happily issuing in that harmony which comes from acting "in the unity of the Spirit and in the bond of peace."

The Bishop made a most cordial and happy reply.

When the Synod met the following year, the Bishop stated that he was not yet prepared to submit any name or names for the office of a Coadjutor. It was, he said, a matter requiring the deepest consideration.

A resolution was adopted by the Synod approving of the course taken by the Bishop, and expressing a desire to leave the matter in his hands.

At a special meeting of the Synod, held in St. John on the 12th January, 1881, the Bishop submitted his nomination of a Bishop Coadjutor in accordance with the terms of the canon lately adopted.

He addressed the Synod, and read certain letters and testimonials received by him with reference to the Reverend H. Tully Kingdon, Vicar of Good Easter, Essex, and he nominated him to the office of Bishop Coadjutor. The Honorable the Chief Justice was called to the chair upon the retirement of the Bishop from the meeting. On the first ballot there was a large majority in favour of the nomination. The motion was afterwards unanimously adopted by a standing vote. It may be added that the whole debate on this important question displayed the best of feeling, and a total absence of all party spirit.

The consecration of the Rev. Dr. Kingdon took place at the Cathedral, Fredericton, N. B., on Sunday, July 10th, 1881. The Metropolitan was assisted in the consecration by the Bishops of Nova Scotia, Quebec, Maine, and Albany. The sermon was preached by the last named prelate. In an account of the proceedings published at the time it is said:

Thus closed the interesting, solemn, and important services in connection with the consecration of the Bishop Coadjutor of the

P

Diocese of Fredericton. It was the first instance of the consecration of a Bishop of the Anglican communion in the Maritime Provinces. Few of those present had witnessed before the consecration of an Anglican Bishop. Few of the present generation can reasonably hope soon to behold such a ceremony. Notwithstanding the vast assembly, which crowded every part of the Cathedral, the utmost decorum prevailed from the beginning to the end of the solemnities. The spirit of the occasion was felt by all. The music was appropriate and admirably rendered. The responses came back from the assembly of clergy and laity with impressive distinctness.

All must have felt that it was indeed good to be present on such an occasion, and in such company, imbued with the spirit of brotherly love and Christian unity.

All must have come away impressed to some extent with the solemnity of the services in which they had engaged, thanking God for His past mercies to the Church in this Diocese, and prayerfully looking forward to the future.

Allusion has already been made to the great boon conferred on this Diocese by the endowment of the See to the amount of £1,000 sterling per annum for all coming years. The Bishop made over one-half of this income to his Coadjutor. For several years the Diocese has had the advantage of extra Episcopal supervision. The Bishop retained full management until within a few months of his last illness, presided over the meetings of the Synod and Church Society, and held confirmation in places easy of access. The most distant and fatiguing duty was assigned to the Coadjutor, who also rendered most efficient service as assistant chairman at the meetings referred to.

CHAPTER XVIII

PARISH OF ST. PAUL AND THE MISSION CHAPEL—FORTIETH
YEAR OF THE BISHOP'S EPISCOPATE—ATTENDANCE AT THE
THIRD LAMBETH CONFERENCE.

AT the meeting of the Synod in 1882, a memorial was
presented by the Rector of St. Paul's Church, Portland, St. John, with reference to a proprietary
chapel, erected within the bounds of his parish, contrary to
his wishes and assent.

The circumstances of the case were of peculiar interest,
and of a character to cause excited feeling. A lady, formerly a parishioner of the Parish of St. Paul, had given
a considerable sum for the establishment of the Mission
Chapel, and it was well understood that the services therein
were to be conducted with an advanced ritual. Whatever,
on this point, were the views and wishes of the Bishop, he
evidently felt that much wrong had been done to a class of
men in the Church desirous of more ornate services, and at
the same time most devoted to their Master's service, while
great latitude was permitted to those who came short of the
requirements laid down in the rubrics. Intolerance was his
great aversion.

The Parish of St. Paul, in the City of St. John, was one
of the most important in the Diocese. The congregations
were large, and most generous in their offerings. The rector
was singularly well fitted for his position. He was in closest
terms of intimacy and friendship with the Bishop, and
greatly beloved by his people. He had accompanied the
Bishop on his visit to England in 1878. A beautiful church
had lately been erected, and the services were earnest and

(227)

reverent.   The parish was almost wholly dependent on the free-will offerings of the congregation.

A few of the parishioners, earnest and devout, prominent members of the Church, found that they could not, in the Parish Church, have such a ritual as they desired. They applied to the Bishop and to the rector of the parish, for permission to erect, within the borders of the parish, the Mission Chapel referred to. They were allowed to proceed, and the chapel was completed. A clergyman from England was appointed to the charge. He was a man of good ability, high culture, possessed of considerable private means, and of unquestioned piety. Strange to say, there was no falling off in the attendance at the Parish Church, apart from those who originated the movement. The services went on in the Mission Chapel. Many from outside were drawn to them. The work of the Mission was carried on zealously, and no doubt much good was done in many ways.

All the while, the feeling with regard to the matter, both in the City of St. John and in the Diocese at large, was very deep, suppressed indeed, but not less trying. It was sad to notice estrangement on the part of many who had hitherto regarded the Bishop with reverence and affection. Probably no one felt this more keenly than the Bishop himself. Without doubt, he had acted in this case, as he ever did, from a sense of duty.

There was no public controversy, no writing in the newspapers. Discussions on the subject in the Synod were marked by the greatest forbearance. The rector of St. Paul's would not allow an appeal to the civil courts. Time, by the grace of God, was helping, all the while, to heal old sores. At length, under the wise management of the committee of the Synod, to whom the matter was referred for consideration, both parties were induced to come together. It was agreed to apply to the legislature for an act to legalize the position

of the Mission Chapel. To this the parish authorities of
St. Paul assented. In this way, what appeared at one time
a source of endless division in the Diocese, was amicably
arranged. This was the more especially rejoiced in, as it
removed what must have been a great trouble to the Bishop
in his declining years.

Since the arrangement of this difficulty, it may be said
there has set in a period of mutual toleration. Less objection is now made to what is called a high ritual, when it is
evidently accompanied by deep reverence and heartfelt
worship. From the Mission Church large offerings have
been given in aid of the missionary work of the Diocese.
It is said that teaching of the young is well cared for, and
kind attention given to the poor.

Controversy and strife on the matter referred to are now
to a great degree laid aside. It is felt that a united stand
must be taken against attacks by which the very foundations of the faith are assailed. People look back with
wonder, as they recall the desperate energy of leading partizans disputing on the subject of gown and surplice, coloured
stoles, or surpliced choirs.

Even in the case of those who considered that the Bishop
had made a mistake in the origin of the Mission Chapel,
they knew he acted from a desire to do what was for his
Master's service. To his firmness, to his tolerant spirit, the
Church in this Diocese is indebted for its comparative freedom from party strife.

The year 1885 completed the fortieth year of the Bishop's
episcopate. It was alike considered by the clergy and laity
that such a marked period should not be allowed to pass
without especial notice. They desired to present to the
Bishop a fitting testimonial, and much consideration was
given as to what it should be. It was well known that no
gift of a merely personal character would be acceptable.
Many plans were suggested.

There was a pressing want in the Diocese, which for many years had been in part generously supplied by the Society for the Propagation of the Gospel, and this aid had lately been withdrawn. We refer to assistance in their college course to candidates for the ministry. Without such timely help the admirable services of many of the most useful of the clergy would probably have been lost to the Church. In the Diocesan Church Society there was only a partial endowment. It was finally determined to raise an additional fund for this object, as a loving testimonial to the Bishop on the fortieth year of his episcopate, to be called the "Bishop Medley Scholarship Fund." Nothing could have been more satisfactory to the Bishop. A much larger sum than was at first suggested was gladly contributed, amounting to about $6,000.

The following is an extract from the Journal of the Synod in 1886:

Resolved, That the annual proceeds of the Bishop Medley Scholarship Fund should be placed under the control of his lordship the Bishop of the Diocese, to be appropriated, during his incumbency, as he in his discretion may deem in the interest of the Church, in aid of Divinity Students.

And that the Synod be requested to accept and deal with the said funds, and all other amounts contributed thereto, in trust, subject to the provisions aforesaid, under the name of The Bishop Medley Scholarship Fund.

Moved by the Right Reverend Bishop Coadjutor, seconded by Hon. Chief Justice Allen,

That the Synod has with pleasure learned of the formation of the Bishop Medley Scholarship Fund, as a slight token of appreciation of the work of our revered Bishop for the past forty years; and having heard the resolution requesting the Synod to accept the trust of the said fund,

Therefore Resolved, That this Synod do accept the said trust as requested.

During the summer of the next year the Bishop had a providential escape. The following note, from the Annals of the Diocese, August 18th, 1887, gives the particulars:

The Bishop left home with Mrs. Medley. At Zionville, seventeen miles from Fredericton, the cars ran off the track, and they were mercifully delivered from a sudden and violent death—the space between the cars and the edge of a precipitous bank above the river Nashwaak being only about a foot. After some delay they proceeded on their journey.

In the autumn of this year, October 15th, the Bishop was greatly cheered by a visit from his son, Rev. J. B. Medley, who remained at Bishopscote until Wednesday, November 2nd.

In the usual summary at the close of this year it is stated:

The Bishop ordained at Halifax, N. S., three deacons and two priests, and confirmed eight. Miles travelled, eight thousand six hundred and ninety-five. Confirmed in the Diocese by Coadjutor, one hundred and ninety-two; by the Bishop, four hundred and fifty-nine; ordained three deacons and one priest; consecrated one church; received one young woman from the Church of Rome. All praise be to God.

The third Lambeth Conference was summoned to meet in July, 1888. The Bishop, Metropolitan of Canada, was now in the eighty-fourth year of his age. Though wonderfully strong and vigorous, much anxiety was felt at his undertaking such an extended journey. Necessarily there would be much fatigue in connection with the various meetings, by which a life, regarded of such value, might be endangered.

He left home early in the summer, accompanied by his son, Rev. Charles Medley. The Bishop Coadjutor had preceded him. In the absence of both Bishops, the Rev. Canon Brigstocke, D. D., rector of Trinity church, St. John, was appointed commissary.

At the meeting of the Synod, July 4th, 1888, the chairman
read the following communication from the Metropolitan:

To THE CLERGY AND LAITY OF THE DIOCESE OF FREDERICTON,
IN SYNOD ASSEMBLED.

Reverend and Dear Brethren:

I have been requested by His Grace the Archbishop of Canterbury, to attend a Conference of Bishops to be holden at Lambeth,
in the month of July next, to consider several matters of importance
to the Church, which will be laid before us by the Archbishop.
The resolutions which may be adopted at the Conference of so many
of our Fathers in God, presiding over Dioceses in our own Church,
and in the sister Church of America, though not binding upon us as
canons, will, no doubt, receive the most respectful and attentive
consideration; and I have felt that I could not with propriety decline to be present at this Conference. On no other ground should
I be willing to be absent from you at a time, when the presence
and counsel of your Bishop seem to be especially required, both at
the annual meeting of the Diocesan Church Society and at the
meeting of the Synod. I rely, however, on the wise and zealous
co-operation of the clergy and laity of the Diocese to adopt such
resolutions as are calculated to promote its extension and prosperity.
And I take this opportunity of expressing a hope that it will not be
necessary to abandon any of the work which the Church has undertaken, and that by united and harmonious action this great evil
may be prevented.

I have appointed the Rev. Canon Brigstocke to be my commissary to transact such business as it may be necessary to do during
my absence, and the absence of the Bishop Coadjutor.

When the Synod is duly organized, I should think it desirable, if
there be a quorum, that the reports of the committees should be presented and the committees re-appointed; but I should not deem it
advisable that any business be transacted which involves a change
in the constitution of the Synod. Notice must be given of the time
and place of the next meeting of the Synod.

I hope to return by the *Vancouver* steamer, on September 6th, and I earnestly ask your prayers, that I may have a safe and prosperous voyage, and that I and my house may be preserved from harm.

Commending you all to the loving care of our Heavenly Father,
I remain, my dear Brethren,
Your faithful Friend and Bishop,
JOHN FREDERICTON.

In the Annals for 1888 is the following note :

April 21st.   The Bishop left Fredericton for Halifax, and on the Festival of St. Mark, at St. Luke's church, Halifax, the Rev. F. Courtney, late rector of St. Paul's church, Boston, was consecrated Bishop of Nova Scotia, he having been unanimously elected by the Synod.   There were present, and assisting with the laying on of hands, the Metropolitan, the Bishops of Ontario, Maine, Quebec, and the Coadjutor of Fredericton ; also about sixty of the clergy of the Diocese, several from the Diocese of Fredericton, and a deputation from the Diocese of Massachusetts, U. S.

The new Bishop was received with great enthusiasm, being the first Bishop consecrated in Halifax since the revolution, that is, in one hundred and one years.   Crowds of laymen filled the Church of St. Luke.   The service was most reverently performed, and in the evening the Bishop was formally installed.

Nothing but necessary business was taken up by the Synod in the Bishop's absence.   On the second day of the session the chairman was requested to send to the Most Reverend the Metropolitan, by cable message, an expression of most respectful and affectionate greeting.   It was also resolved that an address of welcome be presented to the Lord Bishop on his return to his Diocese, and that a committee be appointed by the chairman to prepare such an address.

The Bishop's long experience, deep learning, and high theological attainments, fitted him to take a prominent part in the important deliberations of the Conference.   He was greeted with respectful feelings of reverence and regard on his visits at Cambridge and Durham, where he received the highest honours at the universities. He also took a leading part in the anniversary celebration at St. Augustine's College.

The following extract is taken from a memorial article in the London *Church Guardian*, republished from the *Canadian Gazette:*

At the last Lambeth Conference the words and counsels of the Metropolitan of Canada were held in honour, while no one who was present at the S. P. G. meeting that year will forget how the simple pathos with which, at the close of his speech, he spoke of returning to his Diocese to die at his post, touched the large audience that filled St. James's Hall. When degrees were conferred at Cambridge on the leading Colonial and American Bishops, at no name — with the exception, perhaps, of Bishop Whipple's — did the crowd in the Senate-house so "rise" as at that of Bishop Medley.

The following extracts from the Annals enable us to follow the Bishop in his journey:

On the 14th June, 1888, the Bishop and Canon Medley embarked on board the steamer *Vancouver.* . . . They landed on the 23rd June at Liverpool. The Bishop and his son proceeded to Windesham, Surrey, and remained at Mrs. Robinson-Owen's till the 26th. They then went to London. . . . They proceeded on the 28th to Canterbury, and on the following day (St. Peter's) the Bishop preached in the chapel of St. Augustine's College, and after a public entertainment, in company with a large number of Bishops, he went to the Cathedral, where the Archbishop delivered an address from his throne in the sanctuary. . . . The Bishop received the holy communion on the 2nd July, with the Bishops, in all one hundred and forty-five, in Lambeth chapel. On the same day the Conference began, and the committees were appointed.

The Conference met daily at 10.30 a. m. and 2 p. m., allowing for an interval of a few days, when the committees were holding their meetings, until July 28th, when there was a general meeting of the Bishops at St. Paul's Cathedral, and the Archbishop of York preached.

July 7th, the Bishop and Canon Medley went to Salisbury by invitation of Bishop Wordsworth. On Sunday, the 8th, the Bishop celebrated at 8 a. m. in the Cathedral, and read one of the lessons in the afternoon.

An American candidate for the ministry was ordained deacon, with the Bishop of Salisbury's permission, in the domestic chapel.

At the morning service, the Bishop of Minnesota preached in the Cathedral, and in the afternoon the Metropolitan of India preached. A large number of laity called after the afternoon service. Prayers were said at 10 p. m., in the Bishop's chapel.

Mrs. Wordsworth, the next day, kindly took us to see the site of old Sarum.

July 10, a public meeting was held in St. James's Hall, on behalf of the S. P. G. The Bishop and other bishops delivered addresses.

We went to Lullington, and on the 15th (Sunday) I celebrated holy communion with my three sons, and preached in the evening.[1] In the afternoon John and Charles walked to Orchardleigh, and Charles preached. July 16th, a missionary meeting was held in the school room. July 17th, John, Charles, H. Lancaster (the Bishop's son-in-law), his wife and daughter, drove to Bath to see Mrs. Ford, who entertained us hospitably. We also went to see the chapel and the memorial window in memory of my dear daughter, Christiana. . . . The Bishop then proceeded to London, and thence to Cambridge. On the 18th, an honorary degree of LL. D. was conferred on me by the University of Cambridge in the Senate House. On the following day we went to Norwich, and we remained over Sunday, the 22nd July, when I preached twice.

From July 23rd to 27th, I attended the Conference. The last meeting was held on the 27th. The following day there was a grand service at St. Paul's. I did not attend, but drove to see an old friend, ninety years of age, and confined to bed, with whom I prayed and read.

On the 30th July, we went to Durham, and on Tuesday, the 31st, the honour of a D. D. degree was conferred on me by the University

[1] See Sermon, page 214.

of Durham. On the same day, two magnificently rendered services were held in the Cathedral. More than one thousand nine hundred singers took part in them. The Cathedral was quite full, and a long procession of Bishops and other clergy took place in the sacrarium. Before we left Durham, the Bishops present subscribed to present the Bishop of Durham with service books for his chapel. . . . On the 7th August, John, Charles, Edward and his wife, went with the Bishop to Exeter. . . . The Bishop and his son were most hospitably entertained by the Misses Marrich, the Chan, Exeter. Numerous friends joined the party. All the family went to St. Thomas and Exwick. The Bishop stayed on the three following days with Canon Courtenay, and his dear friend, Mrs. Fox Strangways. . . . On the 18th, the Bishop and Canon Medley went to Southleigh, and on the 19th, both preached in the old church. . . . .

On the 6th September, the Bishop and his son went on board the steamer *Vancouver*, and arrived safely on Friday evening, 14th September, at Rimouski, and, travelling all night, reached Sussex rectory on the 15th, having been preserved by God's mercy from perils on land and sea, and from any serious illness.

On Monday, the 17th, the Bishop reached home with his dear son. The clergy and laity, and Sunday school children at Fredericton, all joined in hearty welcome. A thanksgiving service was held in the Cathedral on Thursday, the 20th September, and addresses of welcome were presented to the Bishop and to the Bishop Coadjutor, in the Cathedral.

It was on this occasion that the following address was presented by the committee on behalf of the Synod:

TO THE MOST REVEREND FATHER IN GOD, JOHN, BY DIVINE PERMISSION LORD BISHOP OF FREDERICTON AND METRO-POLITAN OF CANADA.

May it please Your Lordship:

We, the clergy and laity of the Diocese of Fredericton, as represented in Synod, approach your lordship with much respect and affection, to offer our hearty welcome on your return to the Diocese.

We feel deeply thankful to our Heavenly Father for the gracious care with which He has watched over you during your absence; for the kind protection He has afforded you in all your journeyings; and for the safety and health with which He has been pleased at all times to bless you.

While greatly missing your lordship's counsel during our late deliberations, we were not unmindful that at the Lambeth Conference your deep learning and ripe experience were largely contributing to the highest interests of the Church throughout the world, and aiding in the solution of many difficulties which now beset her in her high and holy mission.

We gladly avail ourselves of the opportunity of expressing our deep sense of the signal benefits which have accrued to this Diocese from your lordship's work and example during your long episcopate, and we earnestly pray that your remaining years may be productive of still further blessing.

Signed on behalf of the Synod.

O. S. NEWNHAM,   F. H. J. BRIGSTOCKE,
    Secretary.   *Chairman*.

St. John, N. B., September, 1888.

The Bishop replied as follows : .

TO THE CLERGY AND LAITY OF THE DIOCESE OF FREDERICTON.

Dear Brethren of the Clergy and Laity:

I thank you heartily for the welcome which you have given me on my return to my Diocese. It affords me unfeigned satisfaction to be once more among you, and to be assured by you that my presence and labour amongst you are conducive to the best interests of the Church. I have to thank our Heavenly Father not only for the preservation from danger which He has mercifully afforded, but the abundant measure of health and strength which have enabled me to continue my labours among you from year to year during my long episcopate.

The honours which the Universities of Cambridge and Durham were pleased to bestow upon me, and the esteem and veneration which our brethren at home showed to my office in the Church, are not gratifying to me alone, but must be felt in their measure by yourselves, for when one member be honoured, all the members rejoice with it.

If it please God to spare me, I hope as long as I live to be a co-worker with you, taking the oversight of the flock of God, not by constraint, but willingly; not for filthy lucre, but of a ready mind, through the gracious help of the Chief Shepherd, Jesus Christ our Lord.

CHAPTER XIX

ILLNESS AND DEATH OF REV. CANON MEDLEY — THE BISHOP
AND THE LATE REV. GEORGE M. ARMSTRONG.

ON the Bishop's arrival in the Province in 1845, his family consisted of four sons and one daughter; the latter a lovely woman, afterwards the wife of an officer in the army. Three of the sons took holy orders, two of whom are now engaged in ministerial work in England. Spencer, the third son, became an officer in the navy, and afterwards resided in New Zealand, where he died January 30th, 1893.

Charles, the second son, remained in New Brunswick. For a while he was sub-dean at the Cathedral, and, at the time of his decease, rector of the large and important parish of Sussex. He was a most devoted missionary, singularly attractive in his demeanour, zealous and untiring in the arduous work connected with his charge. As his father's chaplain, he was in attendance on all public occasions. For several years he was secretary of the Synod, and he performed his duties to the perfect satisfaction of both the clergy and laity.

As was mentioned above, he accompanied his father on his last visit to England. On his return he seemed in good health, ready to resume his work with renewed strength. Soon after this, came the terrible announcement that he was suffering from cancer of the throat. It was a case very similar to that of the late Emperor of Germany, and strange to say, there was a startling resemblance in the personal appearance of the sufferers.

A life of exceeding usefulness was brought to a close on the 25th of August, 1889, after a lengthened period of acute

(239)

suffering. The bright example of patient endurance and cheerful fortitude, has made up, in some degree, for such a loss to the Church in the Diocese, throughout which he was so deeply mourned.

To the Bishop this was a terrible blow, yet it was borne with complete submission to the Divine will.

We subjoin the notice "In Memoriam," written soon after the time referred to, by the Rev. Canon DeVeber, rector of the Parish of St. Paul, St. John :

It seems but yesterday that we stood by the grave of our dear brother, Canon Medley, "sorrowing most of all that we should see his face no more." Two months have passed away, and the sense of our great loss is as keen and fresh as ever ; our thankfulness for the enjoyment of his friendship ; our appreciation of his useful life ; our sorrow on account of his sufferings ; our hope of his blessed rest in Paradise daily grow deeper and stronger. It was good for us to be there. It is good now to cherish the thoughts forever associated with that day and place.

Some, very few indeed among us, may perchance be able to recall pleasant memories of his bright and sunny childhood in the dear land of his birth. Others learned to love the genial youth as he grew in wisdom and stature, and the warm-hearted friendship of early days waned not as the stream of life flowed swiftly onwards. Most of us knew him best, when, after a well-spent youth and diligent preparation of mind and heart, he received from the hands of his Bishop, his Father in God and his father after the flesh, authority to serve in the priestly office in the Church of the Living God. Happy father! Thrice happy son! Prayers answered, faith rewarded, hopes realized, blessings abundantly poured out on the longing soul, gratitude too deep for utterance welling up in both hearts alike. Nor were the expectations of those happy days doomed, as, alas! too often happens, to end in disappointment. Thirty years of faithful service, thirty years of devotion to his Divine Master and labour for his Church proved the fidelity of the son and rewarded the faith of the father. In the Parish of

Douglas, where he won the hearts of the country folk by his kindness and warm interest in all that concerned their welfare, temporal
and spiritual; in the City of Fredericton, where the services of
the noble Cathedral, erected by the untiring energy of his father,
afforded scope for the exercise of those musical gifts, with which
he was so largely endowed; in Newfoundland, where his self-sacrificing love for the souls of the poor of Christ's flock imperilled his
life and left him for awhile a wreck of his former self; in Sussex
and Studholm, where he spent the last twenty years of his life in
abundant labours for the good of the souls committed to his care;
in each of these several spheres of duty, to which he was called in
the good Providence of God, he proved himself "an able Minister
of the New Testament." a faithful son of the Church of England,
and a wise and loving Pastor of souls.   All his gifts, and they were
of no ordinary kind, were consecrated to Christ and His Church,
never employed for his own self-advancement.   Generous, affectionate, sympathetic, his ear was open to every tale of woe, and his
hand outstretched for the relief of the needy and distressed.   No
presence so welcome as his in time of rejoicing, no voice more consoling in the hour of sorrow and bereavement.   How well remembered will be his ministrations in the House of God.   How grave
and solemn his demeanour, how plain, earnest and forcible, how
interesting and instructive were his sermons, his rich melodious
voice lending a peculiar charm to all he said.   In the celebration
of the Divine Mysteries, and in all the offices of religion, the deepest
reverence marked his every action, as became a faithful Priest in
the Temple of the Most High God.   His refined taste in music and
architecture gave him a singular advantage in building churches
and in elevating the character of Divine worship, not only in his
own parish, but throughout the Deanery of Kingston.   That such
an one should be personally popular with the clergy of all schools
of thought, and that he should have received marks of his Diocesan's
favour, and his brethren's affection and confidence, cannot, surely,
awaken any surprise.   The unanimous choice of the clergy, he filled
the office of Rural Dean of Kingston for many years with no less
credit to himself than advantage to the Deanery.   Mainly owing

Q

to his wise and able administration the Deanery has attained a degree of efficiency which is not surpassed, if, indeed, it be equalled by any other. Selected from among the clergy by the unanimous voice of clergy and laity in synod assembled, he always discharged the duties of secretary with equal ability and courtesy. It is not easy to estimate the loss sustained by the Parish of Sussex and the Deanery of Kingston, by the Synod and the Church in the Diocese by his death.

Gone hence to be no more seen. Gone to his rest after long days and weary nights of pain and agony. Gone to the Master, whom he loved so well and served so faithfully, who visited with heavenly consolation his long tried soul, and enabled him to bear the heavy cross of affliction with meek submission like unto Himself in the day of His own unspeakable agony. Cut off in the midst of a life fruitful in good works; called to lay down the weapons of his warfare while still longing to fight manfully under the banner of his Heavenly King; summoned home from the field while the sun was yet high in the heavens, and so much work remained to be done and so few labourers to do it. Be it so. To no ignoble rest was he bidden. The faithful no doubt serve their Master in Paradise no less than on earth. Not theirs indeed the toil of slaves, but the loyal and loving service of freemen. Let such considerations as these comfort our souls touching him who has gone from us. He has been graciously called away to another portion of his Master's Vineyard. His works abide with us. The sower went forth sowing good seed, oftimes weeping as he went onwards. The seed grows though he is absent. The Great Husbandman will make it fruitful, watering it with the dew of His grace, and nourishing it with the sunshine of His love. Not only in church and cottage, by the side of sick beds, and in chambers of sorrow and mourning did our brother sow the seed of Divine instruction and heavenly consolation. Upon his own bed of agony he taught us all such lessons of humble resignation and undoubting trust, of courageous endurance and all embracing charity, as, we fervently pray, may be ever engraven upon our stricken hearts. Though his ear could no longer hear the voices of dear friends ever welcome, and the tongue had lost its power to give utterance to the feelings of the heart, the soul could still breathe its fervent supplications and its thankful praise into the ear of his Most Merciful Creator and Redeemer, to whom he committed his spirit in sure and certain hope of a blessed resurrection. And now he waits in Paradise for the coming of our Lord Jesus Christ. Amen.

On the 12th October following, the Rev. George M. Armstrong, rector of St. Mark, St. John, was called to his rest. His parish was among the most important in the Diocese. Mr. Armstrong was a man of much ability, earnest and constant in his Master's service, and of sincere piety. For many years he was regarded as the leader of what is known as the Low Church school; and he was certainly an excellent type of that evangelical party to which the Church, in days past, was so deeply indebted. At one time he was strongly opposed to the Bishop. From a stern sense of duty, as he deemed it, he felt called on to speak his mind plainly, though he was never known to encourage factious opposition in the Church Society or Synod.

The Bishop, on one occasion, had preached in St. John's church. After the service, in the vestry, Mr. Armstrong went so far as to say to the Bishop that "he had not preached Christ." This rebuke was received without anger or feeling of resentment. The Bishop explained the subject of his sermon with the greatest kindness and humility, and expressed a hope that the charge was unfounded. This incident, with what afterwards occurred, produced in Mr. Armstrong's mind a truer appreciation of the Bishop. With deep sadness of heart, he previously had been inclined to consider that all true and vital religion was confined to those who held his views. Now he was thankful to find out that he had been mistaken. In his own practice, and in his own theological opinions, he himself remained unchanged to the last; but he afterwards became one of the most steadfast

and devoted friends of the Bishop.   There was between the
two a mutual feeling of respect and regard.   The Bishop,
more than once, spoke of Mr. Armstrong as among the
most respectful and attentive of his clergy.   During his
absence in England, in 1878, he acted as the Bishop's
commissary.

While suffering from a long and trying illness, Mr. Armstrong received from the Bishop many tokens of sympathy
and affection.   On his death, the Bishop, though at a considerable · distance and in enfeebled health, attended the
funeral, and pronounced the benediction.

CHAPTER XX

SERMON ON MISSION OF THE COMFORTER—EXTRACTS FROM RECENT CHARGES TO THE CLERGY—LAST CHARGE.

BEFORE proceeding to give extracts from the Bishop's later charges to the clergy, we subjoin the following sermon on the "Mission of the Comforter," preached in the Cathedral at Fredericton on Trinity Sunday, 1867:

> "The wind bloweth where it listeth, and thou hearest the sound thereof, but canst not tell whence it cometh, and whither it goeth; so is every one that is born of the Spirit."—ST. JOHN iii. 8.

There is an important difference between the three first Gospels and the fourth. The three first speak of the facts relating to our Lord's Incarnation as historical truth: St. John deals with their mysterious and sacramental character. We may observe this difference in the very opening of the Gospels. St. Matthew, after connecting our Lord with the royal house of David, simply tells the story of his birth. St. Mark, omitting this as already told, enters almost at once on his ministry. St. Luke, after recounting more fully the history of St. John the Baptist, gives us the particulars which, possibly, he had received from the Blessed Virgin herself, of the Lord's Incarnation, and all the attendant circumstances. But St. John (as the fathers speak) lightens upon us at once like a flash from a thunder-cloud: "In the beginning was the Word." And without pausing to explain why he made use of that expression, he adds: "And the Word was with God, and the Word was God. The same was in the beginning with God. All things were made by Him, and without Him was not anything made that was made. And the Word was made flesh and dwelt among us, and we beheld His glory, the glory as of the only-begotten of the Father, full of grace and truth." What depths of eternal greatness and wisdom are here unfolded; what a mighty mysterious revelation of

(245)

the Eternal mind, in a few verses, in language transparently simple, in depth of meaning wholly unfathomable!

The same difference of treatment is apparent in St. John's account of the two Sacraments of Baptism and the Lord's Supper. The first three Evangelists (with very slight variations) furnish us with the same account of our Lord's baptism; St. Matthew and St. Mark record the general commission to baptize all nations. All three Evangelists record the institution of the Lord's Supper; St. Luke according perfectly with the account of St. Paul in the first epistle to the Corinthians. St. John does not record the institution of the Lord's Supper at all; but he dwells on the mysteries connected with both sacraments, and refers to their perpetual witness to Divine Truth in his first general epistle: "There are three that bear witness on earth, the spirit, and the water, and the blood: and these three agree in one."[1] In the third chapter of his Gospel he selects Nicodemus, one of the great council of the nation, as the person whose conversation with our Lord he deems it fittest to record; and he proves from that discourse "the great necessity of the Sacrament" of baptism,[2] of a new birth by water and the Spirit. None are excluded from this necessity. All, learned or unlearned, rich or poor, venerated rabbi or "simple folk," must stoop by this door; for none can enter into the kingdom of Jesus but such as are born of water and of the Spirit. Nicodemus avows himself astonished at the statement. He cannot understand the mystery. He asks in amazement, can the natural birth take place a second time? Our Lord does not condescend to explain His statement, but assists the clouded understanding of His disciple by the illustration in the text: "The wind bloweth where it listeth, and thou hearest the sound thereof, but canst not tell whence it cometh, and whither it goeth: so is every one that is born of the Spirit." It is important to have a distinct conception of the points of the comparison, and of its bearing on the whole conversation.

Our Lord had announced to the astonished rabbi a new and spiritual life connected with His kingdom. He showed him that all who enter His kingdom partake of a new birth, and that in this

---

[1] 1 St. John v. 8.   [2] Service for Baptism of Adults.

new birth there are two parts, the visible and the invisible; the water which cleanses the body, and the Spirit which purifies the soul. Water, in the old dispensation, had been used as an outward means of bodily restoration; it should now be made use of in the "mystical washing away of sin." Our Lord connects the earthly element with the spiritual grace by a link, the subtlety of which altogether escapes us, so that what is perceptible to our observation is inscrutable to our understanding. He leaves it to time, and to the gracious teaching of His Spirit, to make known to Nicodemus the practical working of this truth. For we do not know that our Lord baptized Nicodemus, nor do we know at whose hands he received baptism. The mystery of the Sacrament is what St. John sets forth, and loves to dwell upon. In his view, it exalts the dignity of His Master to raise the Sacrament in the eyes of men. In our days men speak of elevating Christ when they depreciate His Sacraments, as if Christ could possibly be magnified by undervaluing what Christ instituted for the benefit of the whole world. Surely such Christians take a very different view of truth from the inspired Apostle. One would suppose the true way to raise one's Master in men's thoughts was not to idolize the servant, but to magnify the Master's law, and to esteem the lightest word spoken by Him as more precious than gold; to think of Him as ordaining nothing in which He was not forever present, never moving in the sphere of form and ceremony, but in that of intense solemn reality. In short, to exalt Christ is to lower the man who is sent in the greatness of the God who sends him; to magnify the thing done, rather than the earthly doer thereof.

On a former occasion I set before you the gracious work of the Holy Spirit on the Church at large, invigorating it with new life; bestowing on it both miraculous powers and spiritual graces; endowing the Sacraments with the gift of His presence; and so making the one to become, when rightly received, the ordinary channel of our new Birth, and the other the means whereby we receive the Lord's Body and Blood; inspiring fallible men with the power to reveal new and Divine Truth; commissioning His servants to declare that Truth, and validly to perform spiritual functions. But beside this general gift to the Church at large, the Holy Ghost carries on in the hearts of the faithful a work leading to their personal sancti- fication and salvation.   On this work I now desire chiefly to speak. And I wish you all to observe distinctly that when I magnify the Sacrament which Christ appointed, I neither attribute to it a super- stitious charm, nor wish to exalt it above the dignity which the inspired writer ascribes to it, much less would I deny the necessity of that continual life-long work of grace in the soul, of which the Sacrament is both the sign and the seal.   Our Lord's illustration in the text is taken from the natural world.   This is His continual habit, to dwell on and to spiritualize what we call nature, but which is not a power apart from God, but God's own handiwork ; for not only is the God of Nature also the God of Grace, but His work in the one sphere is analogous to his work in the other.   A very simple elementary truth, one would suppose, yet how much forgotten, mis- understood, misrepresented.   How many false principles would have been avoided in ancient and modern times, if men had only believed (as Scripture teaches) that God works in grace as He works in nature, making allowance for the different subjects on which He works, and the different purposes He has in view.   When God works in Nature He works on Matter ; it has no power to resist His will ; it forms such combinations as He directs, and is subject to such laws as he imposes.   But when He works in Grace, He works on Mind, to which He has vouchsafed a likeness in immortal being and attributes to Himself; to which He has given a power denied to Matter — the power to reflect, to compare, to will, to love, to hate, nay to work with or to resist, for its own good, or its own un- doing, Omnipotence itself.   The destiny of Matter is made for it. The destiny of Mind, the mind makes for itself, though whenever it works for good it must be aided and moulded by the plastic power of a higher, wiser, nobler mind.   And yet some men would repre- sent God as acting more arbitrarily, capriciously, tyranically, and far less lovingly, on the world of Mind than on the world of Mat- ter ; as less full of goodwill to the soul that thinks than to the matter incapable of thought ; and as "passing by," with a lofty indifference, the necessities, and the woes, and the aspirations of the souls which He has permitted for ever to exist. Surely the Bible, soundly interpreted, teaches no such doctrine; and the common sense of mankind will for ever revolt against it.

"The wind bloweth where it listeth." The grace of the com- parison is wholly lost in English, because we use one word for the wind and another for the Holy Spirit, whereas both in the Greek and Hebrew tongues the same word expresses both ideas. So that some [1] have translated the text, "The Spirit bloweth where He listeth," yet we cannot doubt incorrectly, as thus the point of analogy is lost.

Again, there are two words in the Greek signifying wind, one applicable to the more violent motion of the atmosphere, and the other, which is here used, signifying rather the gentler breathing of the air, which is in constant motion. "The wind bloweth where it listeth:" not the hurricane with its impetuous violence; not the simoon with pestilential blast; but rather (as it has been well trans- lated) "the air breatheth where it listeth." Go forth into the woods at noon, on some warm summer's day, and note the deep silence that prevails. The song of birds is hushed; the lowing of the cattle is still; the very hum of insects is scarcely audible. Not a cloud crosses the sky; not a breath of wind is felt. Suddenly, without a note of preparation, without knowing "whence it comes, or whither it goes," a rustle is heard in the forest. Every leaf feels the sweet impulse; a breath passes over the water, a soft murmur is heard, and gently dies away. "So is every one that is born of the Spirit." The free motion of the air is one of the greatest mysteries in nature. It is perceptible to all our faculties. It is the susten- ance of life. It infuses into us new vigour and unspeakable delight. Yet it is inscrutable. The whence, the whither, the how, the why, what philosopher can tell us? The secret mystery of its coming and going no man knows. This vital air that breathes everywhere in constant, healthful, life-sustaining motion, sometimes fluttering as a whisper or heard as a "small still voice," sometimes rising like a "mighty wind" that fills and overawes and is then hushed into silence, is our Lord's beautiful illustration of the working of the Holy Spirit on the mind of man.

[1] As Luther.

We learn from the comparison that the influence of the Spirit is as wide-spread as the breath of air. It is confined to no class. It is limited to no age or nation. The love of the Spirit is the love of the human race. Yet it is as free as it is wide, independent of human laws and conditions, to be vouchsafed or withdrawn as God sees fit. We may not, indeed, say that the gift was the same before our Lord ascended into Heaven, as after He ascended ; nor can we say that the Spirit is vouchsafed to heathens as to Christians; but I think we should not err in saying, that wherever there is a tender, loving heart, a generous impulse, an honest mind, a reverent homage to God, a desire to "do justly and love mercy," a shrinking from injustice, cruelty, and impurity, whether in Jew, heathen, or Christian, there is the motion of the blessed Spirit for good, however far the heart may be from the perfect knowledge of God. And how various and manifold is this gift. As the air blows on the mountain-tops, or in the sultry plains, in the autumn evening, or in the clear frosty air of the winter morn, or is borne in upon the tide ever in healthful though various motion, so the Spirit variously works on the human heart. Now it whispers simple truths into the child's breast; now it nerves the enduring man for a great and hazardous enterprise; now it suggests the first thought of devotion, or strengthens the last act of faith ; it speaks comfort to the mourner, and fear to the headstrong youth ; it places in the hands of the preacher the "bow that is drawn at a venture," and that sends conviction to the heart; it aids the counsel of friends, and helps the weak to resist temptation, and brings before us the better way, and bids us walk therein, and be safe; it speaks of contentment and hope amidst suffering, and assures us, in dark and dreary hours, that a way will be opened before us, and that at evening-tide there shall be light. O, how gracious is this blessed Spirit, how winning, and how wise! He chooses means adapted to hearts which differ as widely as the faces of mankind. He does not force truth upon us, but presents it to the mind, so that it may be the heart's own choice, inviting, persuasive, yet not irresistible, for then there could be no grace in accepting it; and that the Holy Spirit is not irresistible it is important to show for several reasons.

Nothing can more clearly prove this than our Lord's impassioned, bitter cry, "O Jerusalem, Jerusalem, how often would I have gathered thy children together, as a hen gathereth her chickens under her wings, *and ye would not!*" Words full of the insult of the deepest mockery had there been anything withheld which the Grace of God could have given, consistently with man's own personal responsibility of accepting or rejecting the offered mercy. And St. Paul's earnest entreaty is of the same nature. "We, then, as workers together with God, beseech you also, that ye receive not the Grace of God in vain." Yet He entreats mockingly if no grace that might be resisted were vouchsafed. If the Holy Spirit could not be resisted, though all might be saved by compulsion, salvation would not be the glorious crown of the Christian's own life-long struggle. All the sympathy of Christ with His much-tried and faithful soldiers would be lost; all the sympathy of the redeemed in Heaven with each other would be destroyed. For what is sympathy but fellow-feeling with other sufferers in their endurance? The redeemed will love each other in Heaven because they have all "come out of great tribulation," and they love Christ in Heaven because the Spirit proceeded from the Father and the Son to help them in their struggles, not to force them into salvation. They know they would never have reached that blessed shore without His constant aid, and yet there is a humble, healthful consciousness within each heart of having not done violence to those gentle breathings of goodness, of having made a vigorous and continued effort, of having cherished a life-long desire, of having struck out with both hands earnestly to reach the wished-for shore.

We know that even in the lower things, in schools, or contests for earthly rewards, if prizes ten times more valuable were bestowed without an effort, they would be valueless in the eyes of those who received them. And what meaning would those noble words have to us, "Who for the joy set before Him endured the cross, despising the shame, and is set down at the right hand of the throne of God;" and again, "But we see Jesus for the sufferings of death, crowned with glory and honour;" if instead of bearing our cross after Him, we were landed in Heaven without an effort, and had no need to raise an arm, or maintain a struggle to take us thither? So that the doctrine of irresistible grace is founded on a misconception of the whole nature of man, and of the reward proper to man's nature, and on a misinterpretation of all the passages of Scripture which describe the struggle and the success of man.

So, then, as the grace of the Holy Spirit is resistible, as that blessed Person may be resisted, grieved, vexed, quenched, and His light kindled or put out within us, we should see that we put forth all the powers and desires of our minds to meet that gentle motion, and to fall in with its first suggestions. Nor are we to look for His operation commonly, in a way implying violence, or sudden fiery impulses, that take the heart by storm, and leave no room for resistance. When the Holy Ghost first came down from Heaven, it was indeed "like a mighty wind, that shook the house" where the Apostles were assembled; for He was sent to give evidence to unbelievers of a power that could not be resisted, and to support weak and persecuted believers in the discharge of their high mission. But the miracle was never exactly repeated, not even in the Apostolic times, and the gift of tongues has since been withdrawn. We know, from the history of Elijah, that not in the "great and strong wind which rent the mountains, and brake in pieces the rocks," nor in the "earthquake," nor in the "fire," but in the "still small voice" of love, the Lord's presence was manifested. So it is not for man to assemble his fellows, and prescribe the manner of the Spirit's operation. "Now it is to be seen and felt; in this way only; on these very benches, with these set expressions of feeling and with none other, ye must be born again; feel as I have felt, or ye cannot be born of the Spirit at all." This is the direct opposite of the text. It is not the gentle motion of the air, infinitely various in its operation; now waving on the tops of lofty pines, now whispering on the lowly flower, now stealing over the wide prairie, or visiting the retired valley, or lurking behind the summer cloud, or quivering on the aspen leaf, and then retiring into silence; it is rather the fiery furnace-blast, that pours forth fast and furious, scorches but not invigorates, and requires again and again to be kindled by the same spasmodic effort. We do not look for the gentle promptings of the Spirit in such ways as these, much less should we limit His grace to such means. We may admit that He can bless efforts the most irregular, but we may rather expect His blessing in the meek and humble ways of sobriety and trustfulness, such as his word records and prescribes. The greatest favour ever bestowed by the Holy Ghost upon one of the children of men was granted to a lowly Jewish maiden, who in few words of artless modesty and confiding faith, with no graphic description or sensation-speech, humbly submitted to the gracious will and words of the Most High. And the words of the Angel were as simple as her own. In no less reverent spirit does our Church train her children to ask for the gift of the Holy Ghost, and with no less trustfulness does she humbly expect that it will be bestowed in answer to our prayers.

It may possibly be objected to our Baptismal Service, " Why, if you deny the Holy Spirit's visible operation, do you assert so positively that the child is regenerate? " But there is a vast difference between what we may expect when we use the means which Christ has prescribed, and where means are used which men invent themselves, to which no Divine promise is annexed. The Sacrament of Baptism is a Divine institution, to which Christ has promised His presence; and wherever Christ is, His Spirit is present also to bless and sanctify. But let it be remembered that when we say the child is regenerate, we do not mean what is intended when people say the man is converted. Conversion supposes a change of mind, an actual turning from sin to holiness. We ascribe no such change to the infant. We say that by the grace of the Holy Spirit it is taken out of the state of nature in which it was born, and is placed in a state of grace; it is made a Christian; it is now God's child; it has the adoption and the privileges of sons; it is an heir of the kingdom; and that so much is implied in all the Scriptural accounts of baptism in the New Testament, and that St. Peter expressly makes such promises to our children. But we nowhere speak of converted children. In order to conversion, a person must have committed actual sin, which we are sure infants have not done. Further, we do not limit the grace of the Holy Spirit to any one time, nor do we say in what manner He will work on the heart of the child; but we say distinctly, that in order to eternal salvation, the child, if it live and grow up, must "crucify the old man and utterly abolish the whole body of sin," and that "all things belonging to the Spirit living and growing in him, having victory over the devil, the world, and the flesh, and being endued with heavenly virtues," he will thus, and thus only, be in the end "everlastingly rewarded."

This office, therefore, only thanks God for a present promised benefit, but neither prescribes the manner in which the Holy Ghost will at any future time work on the man's heart, nor does it in any way anticipate his future and eternal state, except according to the conditions which the Scripture prescribes as necessary for all Christians.

And now, my brethren, how shall we improve this passage of God's holy word to our own use and benefit? If the air that breathes in constant motion be our blessed Lord's own symbol of His Spirit's grace; if we daily breathe and enjoy, and are sustained by the air, how much more should we long for, how careful should we be to pray for the higher gift? Above all, how much should we strive not to provoke, resist, grieve, or quench the Spirit of Truth, of Order, of Decency, of Beauty, of Wisdom, of Fear, of Love, Charity, Purity, and Peace; provoke Him by opposition, vex Him by neglect, quench His rays by deeds of darkness and impurity, by deeds and words of violence, by stifling the convictions of our conscience, by wilful disorder, disunion, and disobedience to any good advice; for if, even under the old covenant, " when they rebelled and vexed His Holy Spirit, He turned to be their enemy, and fought against them," how much greater the sin, how much surer and more severe the punishment, when the nobler blessing is obstinately rejected; and remember that all non-improvement of ourselves is virtually rejection of the grace which helps us to improve.

The more common and ordinary our duties in life are, " the more necessary it is" (as has been well said) "to keep up the tone of our minds to that higher region of thought and feeling, in which every work seems dignified in proportion to the ends for which, and the spirit in which, it is done."[1]   "And what we achieve depends less on the amount of time we possess than on the improvement of our time."

I leave the subject with one word of *warning* suitable to a generation ever boasting of superior light, yet showing too many tokens of unreality and blindness to its faults : " If ye were blind, ye should have no sin ; but now ye say we see: therefore your sin remaineth." And with one word of inexpressible *comfort :* " The water that I shall give him shall be in him a fountain of water, springing up unto everlasting life." And with one word of *praise* and *trust,* fit to express our sense of God's great mercy : "All my fresh springs are in Thee ! "

The following extracts are taken from a charge delivered on the 30th June, 1880 :

Reverend and Dear Brethren:

It seems desirable that at certain periods of our life we should pause and look within us to see what proof we are making of our ministry, and how far the objects which daily engross our time are helping us in the work of our salvation and the salvation of others. At such periods our minds may be withdrawn from many of the passing excitements of the day, and our eyes may be more steadily fixed on great moral and religious questions which concern the well-being of the spiritual Body to which we belong. The holiness of our members, our unity in the principles and rules given us by the Church herself, and the true methods of progress and permanence in well-doing, together with some regard to our financial condition, may well occupy our thoughts ; and it will be my endeavour to lead your minds in this direction to-day.

Of all notes of a standing and progressive church, the holiness of its members is the most important. It is the one permanent and eternal condition of the Church of God, whether militant or triumphant; without this, all party organization, all worldly respectability, all attractions and excitements, all popularity, all increase in numbers, is of no avail. The more ample our endowments, the more

---

[1] J. S. Mill. Address to the Students of the University of St. Andrews.

abundant our individual wealth, the larger our numbers, the more conspicuous our stations, the worse we are if we are unholy. It must be admitted that the tendency of all things around us is to forget this truth. Holiness is no qualification for office, no passport to society. Wealth is the universal measure of good things. Wealth is the secret of power in the Church and in the State. To gain it appears to many to be the sum total of human happiness. To lose it seems to lose all that makes life worth having.

An immense responsibility, therefore, rests upon the clergy and laity of our Church, for there is but one gospel standard for both, to be a holy body. More dutiful, unostentatious, self-sacrificing piety is required in all of us, and a deeper study of Holy Scripture, because objections are commonly urged against its inspiration and authenticity, which formerly were never heard of; and a more dutiful obedience to the rules laid down in our Book of Common Prayer, for how can we expect our flocks to comply with our exhortations if we break the rules of the Church every day of our lives, and our whole tone and temper be adverse to its spirit? How can the loose morality and sinking faith of multitudes in every land be looked upon without a jealous fear for our own condition? When a notorious atheist and teacher of immorality, who would take an oath, regarding it as a farce, is elected to the British Parliament, and when legislators nearer home proclaim themselves absolved from all reference to Scripture rules in matters where the very basis of faith and morality rests on the word of God, we may well see what firmness and courage are required of us to stand sternly by the truth of Scripture, and to abide by its holy and prudent restraints upon our passions. Nor is there a more important source of strength in our efforts after holiness than *quietness*, properly understood. The mechanical inventions of modern religionism are so complicated, and its demands so incessant and imperious, that a clergyman in the full tide of popularity seems deprived of time for reflection, study and meditation. Hurried from platform to platform, incessantly framing motions and contriving constitutions, soliciting new speeches or delivering them himself, he is in danger of becoming a talking machine, suddenly set in motion, without control, direction, or profitable result. Holiness seems frittered away and broken into loose fragments by never-ending excitements of the mere intellect, forgetting that "the talk of the lips leadeth only to penury." What a transition from this endless talk must be the deep silence of Eternity!

Such thoughts may surely be deepened by the reflection that in the last three years, the hand of death has been heavy upon us, no less than seven of our small band having been called to their eternal home: Mr. Milner, at the great age of ninety-one; Mr. Wood, aged eighty-seven; Mr. Allan Coster, at the age of eighty, and Canon Harrison, all having preceded me in their laborious work in New Brunswick; and Mr. Carr, Mr. C. G. Coster and Mr. Woodman, ordained to the priesthood by me, and cut off in the midst of a career of usefulness and in the prime of life. Thus those who lived in the early days of the Province, when the greater part of Church of England missions to the heathen were unknown, and those who have witnessed great changes in all our relations, political and religious, have gone down to the grave together, leaving us to question ourselves, which of us shall go next, and what is our preparation for the eternal world?

I spoke of the progress of our Church. With a full sense of all that has been left undone or done amiss, I desire thankfully to acknowledge the loving zeal and earnestness with which both clergy and laity have prompted and seconded my imperfect efforts to serve them. In constant visitation of the Diocese, it is impossible not to rejoice in the earnestness of the clergy and their flocks; in a greater degree of reverence, without which no service of prayer and praise can be acceptable to God or beneficial to ourselves; in increased opportunities of spiritual privileges both on the Lord's Day and on other days; in a more systematic and faithful preparation for Confirmation; in a far larger proportion of the confirmed (in many cases the whole number) who become apparently sincere, outwardly reverent, and, I hope, habitual communicants; in the loving care bestowed on the material buildings themselves, in regard to which, the expense of maintenance of churches falls wholly on the parish-

R

ioners; in the number of persons who on week days and even in
the time of harvest crowd to country churches to welcome their
Bishop and communicate with him; in the unpaid and untiring
labour of many hardly worked men of business who never make
their labour an excuse for neglecting to give their most valuable
assistance; and in a great general increase (with a few exceptions)
both of subscriptions and donations to the maintenance of the
Church and the clergy. God grant that there may be as great an
increase of personal holiness, of temperance, sobriety and chastity,
of charity and unity amongst us, such as our holy religion requires.
It is also a subject of congratulation that more young men, natives
of the Province, are devoting themselves to the work of the ministry. Some of them, during their college career, have proved most
energetic and useful helpers to the Church in Sunday school and
occasional week-day services; and I hope the time may come when
the wealthier members of our Church will not withhold their sons
from the ministry because it is a profession poorly paid, but will
think themselves honoured by being able to bring into the service
of God some part of that wealth with which He has bountifully
endowed them.

I also rejoice that there has grown up among us gradually, in
the course of years, a better general understanding of each other's
intentions, a more hearty and fraternal concord, such as Christians
should do all in their power to cherish, and that the spirit of malev-
olent suspicion and perpetual insinuation of ignorance and faith-
lessness has been put down, and has received a severe check, as I
hope, by God's blessing it always will. Our Synod meetings, where
the freest discussion is allowed, have no doubt contributed to this
good end; and the alarming predictions respecting their result
have proved to be without foundation.

A few words of advice from me on some of the subjects first
spoken of will, I trust, not seem out of place.

And first, of Confirmation. Important as it is to make a faithful
preparation for the rite, it is sometimes forgotten that the real work
is after confirmation. It is then that the most dangerous time of a
young person's life begins; when the heart, susceptible of good or

bad influences, has been for a short time impressed by the earnestness of the pastor, but is sure to meet with counteracting influences, with ridicule, with temptation in one or more of its varied forms, with the unhealthy excitements or even heresies of the day, fostered by self-conceit and spiritual pride. How many have been lost to the Church and to God from the delusive notion that our work is done when we have seen them confirmed. Considering, therefore, the ignorance and instability of the young, communicants' classes may be found of advantage, that good habits may be formed and strengthened, and help may be given in the many difficulties which surround the young. The pastor will thus be looked upon not as a mere preacher, but as a guide and director, to assist the conscience in forming correct and godly determinations, and in bringing them into action. Among these good habits thus nourished will be the habit of daily prayer, of strict honesty, temperance and chastity, of constant communion, and, I believe, of early communion. For without laying down this as an indispensable rule, one's feeling of ordinary reverence would lead one to see how well it becomes a sinner who owes everything to God's pardoning mercy in Christ, to ask for spiritual pardon and strength, and receive his spiritual food before, and not after, he has been all day long enjoying God's temporal bounty, just as every Christian asks a blessing before he sits down to meat. Another good habit which should unquestionably be formed in the young is that of dedicating to God a tenth of their substance, small or large. Did our laity universally act on this rule we should now be in a very different position. Till they come up to this scriptural requisite they can hardly expect God's blessing on their profits and possessions.

.   .   .   .

In his charge in 1883, the Bishop addressed the clergy as follows:

Reverend and Dear Brethren:

In addressing you for, I believe, the thirteenth time at a Visitation of the Clergy, it is my duty, first, to give thanks to our Heavenly Father for the abundant measure of health and strength which He has been pleased to bestow on me during the last thirty-eight years, so that I have not been obliged to postpone my visitation from sickness once during that long period; and as, with the consent of the Synod, I have secured the assistance of a dear brother who is ever ready to assist me, I still hope to devote the rest of my life, with all my remaining powers, to the service of the Diocese.   I do not know where a Bishop can be so happy, as well as so useful, as in continuing to work with those who have been admitted by him to the ministry, and have been trained up under his own fostering care. They will certainly be the readiest to grant him all the aid in their power, and to make due and kindly allowance for those infirmities and mistakes into which he, in common with themselves, may fall.

At almost every Visitation some circumstance has arisen to make our meeting one of unusual interest.   One period witnessed what few of us can remember, the consolidation of the good work which the late Archdeacon Coster worthily began, in laying the foundation of our Church Society.   Another period witnessed the completion and consecration of our Cathedral.   At another the decease of several of the elder clergy struck the note of warning.   At another our hearts were gladdened by the noble benefactions of some of our deceased members.   At another we were roused from torpor by the announcement that the long delayed reduction of the Home Society's grant would become a stern reality, and a voice sounded in our ears —

> " Sleepers wake, a voice is calling;
> 'Tis the watchman on the walls.
> Arise, and take your lamps."

At another the important step was taken of the formation of a Synod for this Diocese, built on the strong foundations of the Holy Scriptures and the Book of Common Prayer, fully recognizing the respective rights of Bishop, priests and laity, and in full communion with the mother church at home, though not part of its establishment, or retaining legal connection with the English state.   At another period we joined in union with our brethren in the larger and wealthier Dioceses of Canada and formed part of one Provincial Synod.   At another your own Bishop was elected by the

Bishops of the Ecclesiastical Province of Canada to be their Metropolitan, agreeably to the provisions of the first canon of the Provincial Synod. At another period united and persistent efforts were made to bring home to the hearts of all our members the duty of not only supporting their own churches and pastors, but of extending liberal aid to all poor missions within the Diocese. At another the important step was taken of electing a Bishop Coadjutor, with power to succeed me after my decease. It would be unthankful to God not to acknowledge such manifest signs of progress, whilst we must sorrowfully admit that very much has been left undone. Here, as in England and elsewhere, the poor and not the rich, as a rule, set the example of gifts corresponding to their means, while great numbers of our communion give next to nothing. And, while the books of the Government Savings Banks bear witness to a ten-fold increase of personal property within a few years, and while luxury and extravagant show are ten-fold what they were, systematic charity on scriptural principles remains, it is sad to say, unpractised by too many professed churchmen.

It will, perhaps, be said that collections of money are not the sole test of vital religion in the heart. Admitting this to be true, it must be remembered, on the other hand, that faith is not the mere assertion of any formula, even of that which has been called *articulus stantis vel cadentis ecclesiæ*, and unquestionably, in the view both of St. Paul and St. James, a grateful, liberal heart is one of the surest evidences of that faith "which worketh by love," without which "it is impossible to please God."

After this reference to the past, I proceed to set before you some thoughts on duties specially incumbent on you at the present time. The words of St. Paul solemnly and clearly warns us, "O Timothy, keep the deposit," the treasure of undefiled faith committed to thee. With every desire to believe and hope the best of all, we can hardly fail to see a lamentable want of faith in Apostolic doctrine everywhere prevailing. There is a vague reception of one or two parts of Christianity, soothing to the ill-informed and half-awakened conscience; the rest of its teaching is denied or neglected, and the Divine order is entirely broken. By many the necessity and the

efficacy of Christ's sacraments are surrendered; by others the
promise made on the day of Pentecost to parents and children alike
is put aside; by some the Atonement and Deity of our Blessed
Lord are rejected, and amidst the Babel of discordant tongues, even
atheism lifts its horrid head on high and proclaims war against the
sacred incommunicable Name. How blest are we, that we are not
left in these dangerous days to form our own creed, but simply and
resolutely to teach and to maintain what we find plainly laid down
in the various offices of our Prayer Book, and which can be " concluded and proved by most certain warrants of Holy Scripture."
This faith under all circumstances, at all hazards, among all people,
you, my brethren, are bound to teach and to maintain. You are to
teach it at home, you are to teach it in your Sunday Schools, you
are to enforce and explain it in your discourses; you are, above all,
to express it in your lives ; everywhere and among all men you are
to be known as those who will never betray or surrender the faith
of the Church of which you are ministers.

I hope it is not necessary for me to say much to you on the necessity of a religious life; and yet mourning over some sad instances of
declension, I must remind you that the evil which an unfaithful
pastor works cannot be measured by the harm that is done to a
particular parish. Surely, if ever the saying were true, that "if
one member suffer all the members suffer with it," it is so in the
present time, when what "is said in the ear is proclaimed on the
house-tops," and when it seems as if when men lose their faith in
the man whom they trusted, they lose faith in the Church of God
itself. Never was there a time when the various graces of the
Gospel were more required of us in combination, when the priest
must "add to his faith courage, and to courage discrimination, and
to discrimination temperance, and to temperance patience, and to
patience devotion, and to devotion brotherly kindness, and to brotherly kindness the love that vaunteth not itself, is not puffed up, is
not easily provoked, thinketh no evil, beareth all things as a
Christian, believeth of others the best that is possible, and endureth
all troubles patiently to the very end." A conspicuous failure in
any one of these graces seems sometimes to risk the success of our
whole ministry.

Let me also say a few words on order and reverence in your ministrations. It seems to be thought by some well disposed persons that the sole duty of the minister of religion is to preach the Gospel of Christ. This witness borne, this truth set before the people, all else may be left to chance, and the service of the most High God may be performed with a carelessness which most men would not tolerate in their own houses. Such persons must have read the Bible to very little purpose, and in a very superficial manner. Of what kind was that Divine pattern given to Moses on the mount, and taught in after ages to David by the Spirit of God? What could be more minute and careful than the Divine rules respecting the forms of the tabernacle, the offerings of the worshippers, and the dress of the priests? Admitting that our great High Priest has not enjoined on us the ceremonies of the old law, we cannot suppose that the principles of Divine worship vitally differ from those which were given by the disposition of Angels at Mount Sinai. If "God is a spirit and they that worship Him must worship Him in spirit and in truth," spiritual worship is not on that account, careless, irreverent, slovenly worship. The seraphim in Isaiah's vision did not presume to look with bold and unaverted eyes upon the Lord of Hosts. St. John, when he saw the Son of Man in His glory, "fell at His feet as dead." The four and twenty elders, and the representatives of creaturely life fall down and worship. St. Paul, in his first Epistle to the Corinthians, tells them that sickness and death were the proper punishment for their irreverence in not "discerning the Lord's Body" when they came to communicate.

Whatever, therefore, plainly manifests to the people our carelessness in the handling of Divine things, our coarse behaviour in celebrating what our Church rightly calls "holy mysteries" is calculated to shock the devout, and to harden the irreligious mind. Why, men may ask, should we believe in a holier presence when our pastor appears unconscious of the gift? Why should we offer gifts to make God's holy board decent and comely, if not rich, when we see him contented with the meanest covering on the meanest table, with total disregard to the plain, undisputed rubrics of the Church? Is the Church of God a music-hall or a theatre? Nay,

my brethren, in music-halls the singing is well-rehearsed and carefully performed, after the pattern given by the composer and
conductor ; and in theatres, the dresses both of the actors and the
audience are the best, not the poorest, they can find. But thus it
has ever been that the world gives to God the meanest, not the best,
of what God has given us, and lavishes on self what the Lord bids
us to renounce if we would be His followers. Let us bear in mind
that the pattern for His ministers to follow is that of the Saviour —
not of the world. In regard, then, to the vessels for Holy Communion, even if plain, they should be of silver — which is no great
demand even for a poor parish — and in every Church there should
be a comely, decent font, so arranged that the water used for the
Sacrament may never be suffered to remain after baptism, and on
no account should a little common basin be placed within a com-
modious font.

These, however, are topics of inferior weight compared with those
which a Bishop in the Church of God should ever dwell upon himself, and should rejoice to inculcate on his clergy. I am glad,
therefore, to pass from these " elements of the world " to those enduring truths which the great festival of Saint John Baptist
(already ancient when Saint Augustine preached upon it) has in
the last month commended to our daily prayers and meditations.
The Collect for that day in St. Augustine's time has not been preserved, but our present Collect is the work of men full of the grace
and wisdom of the ancient prayers, and able to understand the evil
of gathering up the tares by violence, and of rooting up also the
wheat with them. This Collect, which bears a family likeness to
its glorious predecessors, found a place in the first liturgy of 1549.
We have asked in this prayer (and may our petition be mercifully
answered) that " we may constantly speak the truth, boldly rebuke
vice, and patiently suffer for the truth's sake." And what grace
more thoroughly displays the nobility of a man's character than
truthfulness ? Religious feelings may come and go, like the passions
which flit across the human countenance, strong and sincere, but
transitory ; they may be counterfeited by the scheming hypocrite or

exaggerated by the fanatic. Even benevolence may be duped or corrupted by want of simplicity, but truth is a fortress the enemy cannot enter, and against this rock the proud and passionate waves of mere opinion lash themselves in vain. The men who lived and died for truth are those whose reward has been glorious, and whose names are imperishable, their sun will shine out in the kingdom of their Father, when deceit and guile will sink down in the pit that they have made, detected, exposed, and everlastingly contemned. But it is not only the truth that must be spoken, but the patient endurance of our Master that we must especially imitate. "God is strong and patient, and God is provoked every day." Why then should we complain of our unrequited labour who have neither suffered "cruel mockings and scourgings, yea, moreover bonds and imprisonment," whose severest trials only expose us to unjust accusations, bitter and reproachful names, unworthy motives foolishly imputed, and incessant abuse of the conscientious practice of what we have vowed to perform. If better Christians than ourselves have borne worse hardships patiently, let us be patient and endure; hoping and daily praying for all who may unjustly assail us by word or deed, that they may come to a more reasonable mind, and having carefully studied a subject of which they know but little, may even preach the faith which they laboured to destroy.

In short, Patience, Time and Prayer (as every student of Church history ought to know) are greater solvents of difficulties than the force of tyranny, or the subtleties of law; Patience, which displays the Christian character in its highest exercise of forbearance and of love; Time, which works unexpected changes in the most stubborn minds, and in their way of looking at things, so that prejudices are dissolved and obstacles vanish, if not within our sight, yet as the result of our endeavours; Prayer, which brings to our aid the grace of an unseen Power, working in its noblest wisdom, providing better things for us than in our weakness we know how to compass, and crowning us with unexpected triumph when in the eyes of the world we were most unsuccessful.

Nor can I dismiss you without an earnest injunction to that holy love which is the "bond of perfectness." Differences of judgment, schools of thought, existed in Apostolic times, and even Inspiration itself did not prevent the writers of the New Testament from presenting the same truth in which they all agreed in a somewhat different aspect to their readers. Making this charitable allowance for one another, we ought to see that each one of us, who believes all the holy truths of the Christian religion, and has voluntarily subscribed to the same formularies, and is duly licensed by the Bishop, has as much right in the Church of our Communion as the other, and should have the right hand of fellowship extended to him. Subtleties of law in which the professors of the science differ quite as much as the clergy, may embitter, but will never compose the differences in the Church, especially where rubrics appear perfectly plain to those whose common sense and earnestness cannot agree to be tossed about by the contradictory decisions of the courts of law. Be these things as they may, the truly Catholic spirit, the truly fraternal and loving heart will desire that as much or if possible more good may be done by the Christian brother with whose methods of action he cannot entirely agree. I do not say let all differences disappear or be smoothed over, but I say let our love shine out pre-eminent over all. "Let all bitterness and wrath and anger and clamour be put away from you, with all malice, and be ye kind one to another, tender-hearted, forgiving one another, even as God, for Christ's sake, hath forgiven you." For this Christlike spirit let us all devoutly pray. Amen.

On the Festival of St. Peter, 1886, the Bishop delivered his last charge, from which not one word can properly be omitted :

Reverend and Dear Brethren:

Being permitted by the mercy of God to address you once more on a triennial visitation, it is my pleasure as well as my duty to speak to you as one who is "Saved by Hope." It would be idle to attempt to conceal from you our difficulties, but it is on every account desirable to take the most hopeful view of our position. If we were a very rich Church, in times of great worldly prosperity, I could not have the same hope. Or, if we were striving to make the

Church a clerical club, from which the laity were rigidly excluded, to the support of which they contributed neither money, nor influence, nor time, nor diligence, nor patience, nor prayer, I should have but little hope; or if we were so misguided as to throw all our weight into the upholding one political party, I should have less hope, for the Church was never founded by a party in the State. It never throve on politics, and it was never in a less hopeful condition than when its richest benefices were the ill-earned reward of active and unscrupulous political partizans. My hope for the Church in Canada, of which we are members and ministers, is not that we are so numerous as to control the State; nor that we are so rich as to dispense with the contributions of our members; but that, being (as without arrogance we may consider ourselves) a branch of that Church which came to us from the ages past, which no storms of persecution have destroyed, and none of the manifold changes of the world have shaken, we still hope to hand down to our children the truth of God which is indestructible; and though comparatively poor, we labour to make many rich, "content with such things as we have," and seeking the good will and the assistance of all our brethren. It is hopeful, therefore, to look back fifty years, and see what the resources of the Church were then and what they are now; what the number of our communicants was then and what they are now; what the contributions of the laity were then and what they are now; what the number of our clergy and the frequency of our services was then and what they are now; what the appearance of our Church was then and what it is now. It is pleasant to find that we are not despairing because the grant of £3,000 sterling, from home, has been reduced to £1,250, and will be reduced still further, and that we are bracing up our energies to meet and overcome the difficulty.

It is pleasant to find so much interest generally taken in the Sunday Schools, and in increasing the knowledge of the Bible and of the Church, among those who teach in Sunday Schools, though our returns from the clergy are not yet complete. Our examinations for holy orders are more strict, and our clergy have access to theological libraries in their several deaneries. Above all it is a

ground of hope when we find the clergy rising to a higher standard
of knowledge and of duty, recognizing the blessing of more constant
prayer, more frequent communion, and giving more opportunities
to their flocks to unite with them in the blessed and heavenly work
of prayer and praise.

It is delightful to find that this is done with the zealous and
active concurrence of their lay brethren, who seldom fail to respond
to the joyful invitation, and turn the feast days of the Church into
occasions of earnest intercessions, abundant alms giving, attentive
hearing, spiritual communion, and heartfelt thanksgiving to God.
In such services it has been my pleasure to mingle, and as long as I
have strength, my countenance and support will never be wanting
to them. Nor ought I to be backward to acknowledge the active
and energetic assistance which has been given by the Bishop Coadjutor to every object that I have named, many which would have
failed to receive due support by physical inability on my part to
perform all the increasing work of the Diocese. Such are some of
the grounds of my hope; but it would not be a true statement were
I to disguise the magnitude of the task which lies before us.

The financial prosperity of our Church is owing in a great
measure to the active and unpaid support of our laity. To their
assistance we owe its present condition, and we look to them for
continued and increased care and diligence. But there is no reasonable doubt that our subscription-lists do not manifest any general
amount of self-denial. They might be doubled in many instances
without hardship. At the same time it is gratifying to see that
larger donations come from missions which have less ability to give
than they had many years ago, and that for the most part the
assessment which is imposed as a necessity is cheerfully and un-
grudgingly paid. We look forward with hope to the time when, by
the increased support given to our Diocesan Church Society, the
general interest taken by every layman in his own parish and mission, and the aid of moderate endowments, arising from benefactions
of the living, or the bequests of those who are called to give account
of their stewardship, we may become with unqualified satisfaction
to ourselves and to others an entirely self-sustaining Church.

But I gladly turn to that advice which it is my duty to give you as a body of clergy whom God has given into my care. We must thankfully acknowledge that we are spared the trials which fell upon the clergy in former times. But your Bishop is, I hope, the last man who would underrate or fail to sympathize with the trials of the clergy in our own day; yet perhaps the smallness and uncertainty of clerical incomes is not the greatest of the trials of a priest. From one serious trouble, the expense of outfit when he enters on the work of a mission, the missionary is to a certain extent released, or at all events he is greatly assisted, by the loan of $250 made by the Church Society without interest, to be repaid in moderate sums. With occasional donations granted by loving parishioners, and due care and forethought, a clergyman, if he be prudent, may keep out of debt. But only if he be prudent. Those who engage in early marriages before they have earned anything for their own support, and those who indulge in unnecessary expenses, cannot, on our limited incomes, keep out of debt. And debt is demoralizing as well as depressing. It is sure to lead to borrowing, and borrowing often supposes heavy interest, and interest supposes shifts and contrivances and all manner of uncomfortable practices, a doubtful morality and a heavy heart. To the younger clergy I unhesitatingly say, it is your duty not to marry until from your own income you have laid by something towards the maintenance of your household and the comfort of those who reasonably look to you for support. For the greater part of those who begin life in debt carry it on to the end, and harass their own minds and the minds of others by want of prudence at an early period. But after all, is not the greatest trial of a clergyman's life in himself? We who are called by the Church to the office and work of priests in the Church of God, who do not shrink from the awful responsibility of the message committed by our Lord to His Apostles, and through them conveyed to us, had need often to ponder in our hearts the words which no subtlety of reasoning can explain away: "Receive the Holy Ghost for the office and work of a priest in the Church of God." We know that they are the Lord's own words, which the Church uses because they are His, and because the promise is given us of His

presence with us " all days, even to the end of the world." We
know that not the Bishop, but the Bishop's Lord and Master, can
alone bestow this or any other spiritual gift. We know that this is
given by the channel of a human instrument, because it pleases Him
to work by Human means, and to employ "earthen vessels." We
know that the gift which the Lord bestows to render our ministry
valid, and His sacraments effectual means of grace, is not to be con-
founded with the personal sanctification of the priest, which must
be sought for by him as it is sought for by every Christian — by
humble and constant prayer and diligent use of all the means of
grace. But, on the other hand, he to whom the Church says,
" Receive," must believe that the Church has wherewithal to give.
And that this gift is the gift of the Holy Ghost for the effectual discharge of our ministrations is evident, for from the Spirit of God
" every good and perfect gift " proceeds, and surely that gift which
is bestowed on us " for the perfecting of the saints and the work of
the ministry." When we have ourselves desired this office, when
the Church, after due examination, has bestowed it upon us, when
the Church calls us priests and our order a priesthood, it were an
act of ingratitude and of cowardice to be ashamed of the name
when we use the office. None of us taketh this " honor unto himself
but he that was called of God, as was Aaron," and yet Aaron's
priesthood was disputed. Aaron himself was " compassed with infirmity." " The people made the calf, *which Aaron made.*" And,
in that great miracle, when water issued from the rock in Kadesh,
Aaron shared in the unbelief which led to the exclusion of both
Moses and Aaron from the promised land. If our priesthood be
not the sacrificing of bulls and of goats it is none the less a real
priesthood, because the Lord Jesus Christ confers it upon us.
Aaron's was a typical priesthood. Ours comes from the Great High
Priest in heaven, who says to us, " As my Father hath sent me, even
so I send you." But does this gift make us arrogant? Does it not
rather humble us in the dust? The more our priesthood is connected with the Word of Him who cannot lie, the higher it is above
the ancient sacrifices of the Mosaic rites, the more true and real and
awful it becomes, and the more holy we ought to be. If our office

be far nobler than the hire of the people for a morsel of bread; if we seek to please God rather than man; if we await the judgment of our Master, whose word " pierces us even to the dividing of soul and spirit, and discovering the thoughts and intents of the heart," what manner of persons ought we to be? What integrity, what diligence, what faithfulness, what serious study, what nobleness of purpose, what loyalty to the Church, what discretion, what deadness to the world, what weighing of the Scripture, what " ripeness and perfectness " of age in Christ, what watchfulness in prayer, what patience and humility, what courage and steadfastness, what care for every soul committed to our charge should we continually show. Surely the time of a Bishop's visitation should be a time of close reckoning with ourselves! How imperfectly have we fulfilled our ministry! What shortcomings are there in all our services! In the forty-second year of my Episcopate, no less than fifty of the clergy have been called to their account. As I cast my eye sorrowfully over this number, and wonder at God's sparing mercy to myself, I shudder at the thought that I may prove wanting in that zeal, steadfastness, courage and humility which make me an example to you who still remain amongst us.

" *The priest's lips should keep knowledge.*" Earnestness and integrity of purpose are great gifts, but the present critical age demands more of us. The knowledge which the priest's lips should dispense is of wider range, and of various kinds. In former days, poor and ignorant people took for granted all that their pastor said, and made no further inquiry. He must know what was right. They were simple and confiding. That was enough. But it is not so now. Everything is called in question, and the whole world is turned loose to inquire, to agitate, to debate, to applaud or to condemn. What chance has the simple minded clergyman who merely reads his chapter without thought, and performs his office without knowing the history of the Prayer Book and what is essential to a right understanding of it? The priests knowledge should above all be Bible knowledge, for this is the point in which so many of his hearers are deficient, and this involves constant labour and the most diligent inquiry. It is easy to select scraps of the English version

and quote them authoritatively on all occasions. But if we consider how the Bible is constructed, what knowledge is required of
history, of the gradual education of mankind, of successive eras of
progress, of the Levitical ritual, of the fulfilment of prophecy in
the birth and ministry of Jesus Christ, of the foundation, laws and
progress of the Christian Church, of the development of Christian
doctrine in the letters of the Apostles, of the history of the Jewish
nation since the destruction of the Temple, we must see that no
small task lies before us.

" *The priest's lips should keep knowledge!* " How careful should we
be that in answering the objections of the scoffer we do not insist on
unwise and traditional interpretations of Holy Scripture which the
text does not contain.   How sparing should we be of attempting to
lay down a scheme of future events instead of stating clearly the
fulfilment of the past.   What deep knowledge is required in explaining the history and unfolding the meaning of these ancient
creeds, whose root is in the Scripture, whose accuracy of definition
was obtained by men deeply learned in Bible truth, who were not
only defenders of the faith, but sufferers on account of their maintenance of it.   Nor is the knowledge of the foundation and progress
of the Church less necessary when our portion in the Catholic faith
is denied by some, and the continuance of the Church both before
and after the Reformation is set at nought by others.   Happily, the
greater the difficulty of acquiring such knowledge the more abundantly are we supplied with commentators of orthodox principles and
extensive learning.   And every year books multiply on us which
illustrate some separate portion of Holy Writ, and throw light on
its acknowledged difficulties.   Among our numerous benefactors of
this kind must be specially enshrined in our remembrance the
honored name of the late venerable Bishop of Lincoln, whose deep
and extensive knowledge of the Holy Scriptures and of the works
of the primitive fathers, and whose unswerving loyalty to the Church
is a safe guide to studious clergy ; whilst his unsparing liberality
has enabled us to enjoy the benefit of his labors at one-half the
price which we should otherwise have paid.   Such knowledge is indeed a possession forever, a treasure which in this new country we

could not otherwise secure, for which no gratitude of ours can be too great, no love can be too fervent.

I am very unwilling to detain you longer, but you will not think me tedious if I add a few words of advice on some important points. First, on the duty of those in whose hands the power of electing rectors to parishes is vested, and on the duty of the clergy in respect of testimonials which they give to persons who are desirous of obtaining a benefice. The law appears to impose checks on all the parties who are interested in this important matter. The laity have a large power entrusted to them, and the law very properly provides that it should not be autocratic and absolutely beyond control. The persons elected must be in priest's orders, without which they cannot, according to the rites of the Church of England, administer Holy Communion in the Church, or in the chamber of the sick and dying; and they must have the Bishop's license, which is a security to the laity that the Bishop has obtained proper and sufficient testimonials from those who are competent to give them, of soberness, piety, and honesty; and this during personal acquaintance for a period of three years. Similar testimonials are required by the heads of respectable firms before they will admit a young man into their employment. A check is likewise imposed on the clergy. For if they give careless testimonials out of mere good nature (as it is termed), they wilfully impose upon the Bishop, and testify to what they might know on inquiry to be untrue, and that by a most solemn attestation to which in writing they have voluntarily set their hands. A check is also imposed upon the Bishop. For if he institute and issue his mandate for induction without sufficient testimonials from the clergy, in respect of personal knowledge for the required time, and from the Bishop of another Diocese (if the person to be elected come from another), then he violates the order of the Church, injures the clergy and laity who are placed under his protection, and subjects himself to ecclesiastical censure. And the laity are equally wrong if they persist in electing a person who is not in priest's orders, or who has no testimonials or insufficient testimonials. And they are fighting against their own interests, for testimonials are required as their security against the intrusion of unfit persons.

S

And it is not unreasonable to suppose that the Bishop, who has familiar intercourse with the clergy, may have opportunities of knowing which the laity have not. And it is most desirable on all accounts that the laity and the Bishop should be satisfied as to the election.

Secondly—on Confirmation. It is no doubt a great benefit to parishes to have this holy rite administered frequently. But it should not be overlooked that there is as much if not more need for watchfulness after Confirmation is over than during the preparation for it. The minds of the young are open to every kind of impression, and when the first fit of earnestness has spent itself, if the priest be not watchful to strengthen the good impression which was made, there may be a speedy declension from the promise of early piety, or a disposition to seek assistance elsewhere. For this reason Bible classes or Communicants' classes are needed after confirmation ; and the clergy must not suppose that their work is ended when there are no more to be confirmed at that special time. The young require clear and definite teaching, lessons of reverence in regard to the service of Holy Communion, which, if they do not get from us, they will learn nowhere else. We must not take it for granted that they have all they ought to know on such matters. It is highly probable that no definite instruction has ever been given them by their parents on the fundamental doctrines of their religion.

Next, I would speak on the Marriage Service. I know of no more solemn rite in the whole Prayer Book than this. The symbolism of the rite taught us by St. Paul ; the solemn appeal to "the dreadful day of judgment, when the secrets of all hearts shall be revealed ; " the certainty that " those who are coupled together otherwise than God's Word doth allow are not joined together by God," and even if their matrimony be legal, it is not in God's sight lawful ; the solemn espousal " till death do us part ; " the three-fold blessing ; the prayer that they may " live together in holy love unto their lives' end "—these repeated cautions and warnings and blessings invest this rite with a significance and seriousness unsurpassed. And yet, where is there a rite more irreverently handled ? I do not speak of the baser sin that is sometimes committed before marriage, but of the frivolousness with which matrimony is undertaken. The absence of religious feeling, especially of religious unity; legality made the sole measure of lawfulness; the money-making business which often forms the chief desire for union; the hasty performing of the rite in a house, where the prayers seem unsuitable, the blessings unfit, where the whole wish is to make the service as short as possible ; or if it be fashionable to go to Church, the crowd of irreverent gazers, bent on nothing but criticism on the dress of those who are appealing to God for His sanction and His blessing—when all these signs of frivolity are manifest, who can wonder that the rules and prohibitions of the Church are trampled under foot? that bonds so lightly made are as lightly regarded, and that in a neighboring country (as stated on high authority) one in ten of every family is said to have had a divorce, and in some cases two or three divorces; so that mutual respect and family love have been broken up again and again. What kind of children must such disunions produce? A heathen poet who lived in a loose age will tell us—

> Ætas parentum, pejor avis, tulit
> Nos nequiores mox daturos
> Progeniem vitiosiorem.

I thank God we have not got so low as this. But we should fear lest one step further should lead us to a point from which we cannot go back.

The clergy, then, will do well to refuse to sanction unions prohibited by their own church laws, and to exhort and persuade their parishioners to have marriages celebrated in the most reverent way ; and further, which is probably the more difficult task, to persuade them not to contract marriages where there is no bond of religious union, more especially where it is almost certain that the validity of our orders and Holy Sacraments will be denied. Or, they will have to submit to being re-baptized, re-confirmed, and then deprived, as they most richly deserve, of one essential part of the Holy Sacrament of the Lord's body and blood. If you think highly of holy matrimony you will endeavor to counteract such evils as opportunity may be afforded you.

It only remains for me now to thank you for the many marks of your respect and confidence which have been shown to me on several occasions. A Bishop can only be useful when he acts, not as an autocrat over his clergy, but as their fellow-laborer, in concert with them in the duties of their common calling; and in the exercise of his ministry, the Church of God from the earliest days has committed to his care functions in which priests take a subordinate part. The clergy will readily acknowledge that these spiritual powers have been entrusted to him for the strength and protection of the whole body of the faithful, according to the wise rules which the Church herself imposes.

A Bishop is as much restrained as a priest in matters of the highest moment by the creeds which are the bulwarks of our faith, and by the definite and clear interpretation of Holy Scriptures, which our offices severally contain. As long as we abide by these landmarks there must be a substantial and visible union amongst us, greater than the mere opinions of any single member or officer of the Church. It were to be desired that we should see eye to eye in all things; and that there should be no division, even of opinion, but that we should be " perfectly joined together in the same mind and in the same judgment." But as this is not to be expected, and some points, either of ritual or of speculative theology, will probably always remain open to discussion, our best security is that charitable construction of the actions and motives of others which each man unquestionably desires to be practised towards himself. In these respects the Church of England occupies the peculiar position of being more tolerant and comprehensive than any other religious body with which we are acquainted; and while there is a considerable diversity as to the means by which reverence is promoted, the Church inflexibly holds fast to primitive doctrine, primitive order, and practical piety. So that whilst there has been in the last fifty years a peaceful revolution in matters not absolutely fundamental, and in the aspect in which certain theological opinions are presented to the mind, and multitudes see no evil whatever in what they formerly looked upon with distaste, or even with horror, the Church has not departed one iota from the fundamental doctrines of Christianity, and at the same time she has been everywhere stirred up to greater and more earnest efforts in reclaiming the fallen, in searching for the wandering, and in promoting every design which tends to the practice of reverence and love.

It has ever been my earnest desire and prayer to act on such principles; and if in the prosecution of these I have seemed to any of you to exceed the bounds of a sober judgment, I trust that you will understand that I have not acted without much weighing of the subject in all its parts. As Bishop of the Diocese I only claim what seems to me to be an essential part of the Episcopal office: to mediate between conflicting opinions and to give complete toleration and support to all that may fairly be considered as within the limits of the Church in the Province of New Brunswick. A narrower line than this does not commend itself to my judgment; and I am ready to bear patiently whatever amount of censure may be thrown upon me for having adopted it. More than this I need not say; less could hardly be said by one who has the courage of his convictions, and who desires to embrace in the circle of his charity and his prayers schools of thought which differ, and methods of action which vary, but which are consistent with the hearty love for the ark which contains us all. Brethren, the grace of God be with your spirit. Amen.

CHAPTER XXI.

Failing Strength—Instances of Kindness to those in Affliction—Last Attendance at the Synod—Last Sermon.

AT the triennial period in 1889 the Bishop felt unable to deliver a Charge to the clergy. His son Charles was then hopelessly ill, and had sent to the Synod his resignation of the office of secretary. In a brief address, the Bishop most feelingly alluded to his great affliction in words expressive of meek resignation. He seemed to appreciate very fully the deep sympathy on the part of the members of the Synod, and their kind and affectionate message sent to the sufferer.

The Bishop failed to recover from the effect of his son's death. Of this he spoke himself. It was noticed that his memory began to fail, though in other respects his health was good. In the winter of 1889 he slipped on a bit of ice at the steps of the post office. By the fall he injured his wrist and right hand, which induced for a time a good deal of suffering. With characteristic energy, he at once set to work to learn to write with the uninjured hand. He got so far on, that he sent this message to the present writer: "Tell him I can write more plainly now with my left hand than he does with his right." In the course of a few months he wholly recovered from the effects of this injury.

From the time now referred to, the Bishop felt unequal to extended journeys. He was able to administer the rite of confirmation occasionally. His time was mostly passed in his home at Bishopscote. He was constantly present at the daily services of the Cathedral, always reading at least one of the lessons. There was, at this time, something very attractive in his calm cheerfulness.

Allusion has been made before to the Bishop's kindness in visiting and caring for those who were in affliction or want. This continued as long as his strength permitted. Two instances here given will serve to illustrate his thoughtfulness. In Fredericton the Presbyterians were numerous. For many years the Rev. Dr. Brook was their pastor. He was on terms of intimate friendship with the Bishop. Among his own people Dr. Brook was greatly beloved, and he had justly won the respect and regard of the whole community. His wife, a most worthy helpmeet, had, after a period of great suffering, lost her eyesight. Soon after this occurrence Dr. Brook himself, by reason of a stroke of illness from which there was no hope of recovery, was obliged to resign his charge. The Bishop was most constant in acts of kindness and sympathy. His visits were frequent, and his ministrations most heartily appreciated. After the death of Dr. Brook the same kind attention was shown to his blind widow till her death.

Another instance, in another class of life. There lived a widow, advanced in years and of limited means, some distance from the Cathedral. She was a good woman and a constant communicant. No want of a temporal kind was left unsupplied from the Bishop's hand. At regular intervals he sent a conveyance to enable her to be at the Cathedral to receive the holy communion. The day was to be spent at Bishopscote, and then the poor widow was taken back to her home.

The Bishop was present for the last time at the meeting of the Synod and Church Society in St. John July 6th, 1892. The Coadjutor presided. At the opening of the Synod the Bishop read the prayers. His voice was quite distinct. During the session he came in now and then, and seemed to listen with attention to what was going on. At the anniversary service in Trinity church he was unable to join in the procession. He came in from the vestry and took his seat in the sanctuary, and he pronounced the benediction at the conclusion of the service. This was the final parting from his assembled clergy. From his seat in the chancel he was assisted by the Coadjutor to the vestry.

The Bishop remained in St. John the two Sundays following. He depended now, more than ever, upon the loving and untiring care of his devoted wife. She seldom left his side. With her he visited several old friends. He was, it was said, "so like his old self, only perhaps more cheerful."

The Bishop, on Sunday, the 10th, attended two of the churches in the city and took part in the services. In a sermon preached the Sunday after the Bishop's death, by the priest in charge of the Mission Chapel, he said: "Not many days ago, on a Sunday, and at evensong, an aged Prelate came up this aisle, stood in yonder chancel, spake the great words of absolving grace, gave us his blessing, and went on his way, to serve no more within these walls; and soon to exchange the life of wondrous labor for the life of rest and peace in the Paradise of God."

On the Sunday following, the 17th July, the Bishop was present in the morning at St. Paul's Church. He took little part in the service, and appeared very feeble. He was again present in the evening and was much stronger. On this occasion he preached a most touching and impressive sermon, and was heard distinctly in all parts of the church. The sermon is subjoined in full. Allusion has been made above to the comparatively brief interruption in the general feeling of affection and regard for the Bishop on the part of the members of St. Paul's Church. Only his long extended kindness and benevolence were remembered now. No feeling had a place but that of the greatest reverence and affection for one whose oft-repeated messages from the Blessed Master would be heard in that house of God no more.

Sermon at St. Paul's Church, July 17th, 1892.

"Quench not the spirit."—1 *Thess.* 5, *v.* 19.

Two things are spoken of in this text:

1st. The greatness of the gift itself. It is *the Spirit* which is given.

2nd. The possibility of losing the gift by negligence, indifference or positive sin. We may "quench the Spirit." To have lost the favour of a tyrant who never loved us, would not be a thousand-part so miserable as to have lost the presence of a loving, tender, ever-present friend, a wise counsellor, an unerring guide, who pleads within us that He may be allowed to save us.

The greatness of the gift of the Holy Spirit is seen, if we remember that the Spirit is God.

When Ananias lied to the Holy Ghost, he lied (we are told) "Not unto men, but unto God." And as the Holy Spirit is divine by nature, so is He equally divine by the personal relation He bears to the Father and to the Son. When God made man, He said, "Let *us* make man in *our* image." When God would make man *anew* the Son of God said to Nicodemus, "Man must be new-born of water and the Spirit," if he would become an heir of God's kingdom.

When our Lord before His ascension into heaven issued His first command, He bid His Apostles go everywhere and baptize in the one, yet three-fold name, of the Father, Son and Holy Spirit. Baptism in His name, signifies consecration to Him who is God, adoption into the service of God, a new birth into the family of God, a new gift to the presence of God.

When our Lord would instruct His Apostles on the deepest of fundamental articles of the Christian Faith, He dwelt especially on the divinity and personality of the Holy Spirit, who was to abide with us for ever. The gift of the Spirit was to be the fruit of Christ's going to the Father, and the answer to His prayers. He was to represent Christ on earth invisibly but most truly. He was to proceed from the Father and to be sent by the Son. He was to know the Son as the Son knew the Father. He was to take of what belongs to the Son, *i. e.*, of all that the Father had, His knowledge, His power, His love, and apply them to the good of man. As the Lord Jesus was directed by the Father what He should say and what He should do, so the Holy Spirit should represent to the world the thoughts and actions of the Divine Saviour. "Whatsoever He shall hear that shall He speak." He was to be the Comforter and the Advocate, the Friend and yet the Judge — the Spirit of Truth and Purity, of Wisdom and Consolation, of Unity and Love. As all the fulness of the Godhead dwelt in Christ bodily, so all the fulness of the Godhead dwells in the Spirit, the Father and the Son spiritually, truly and essentially. "For in this Trinity none is afore or after other" *in object* of time, "none is greater or less than another" in respect of *essence*, but the three persons in one Godhead are co-eternal and co-equal, and this is the Catholic Faith, which it is most perilous to our souls to deny, for it is proved by most certain warrants of Holy Scripture, and we are put in trust with it by God. This Holy and Divine Spirit is our Advocate, not as Christ is our Advocate, by presenting perpetually before the Father the merit of His passion and obedience unto death, but as coming into our hearts. He teaches us what to ask for, and how to ask; He puts the right meaning into our words. He sheds abroad the love of God in our hearts, causing unspeakable, silent yearnings after God, dove-like moanings of the heart pleading within us, warning, cheering, quickening, stirring the embers of spiritual life, supplying us with the oil of the anointing, the holy fire that burns within the breast. As parents teach their little children and pray with them, before the children can understand the meaning of the prayer, so the Holy Ghost is ever teaching us, His children, in prayers and holy hymns, in parables and summaries of belief, in inspired words and Christian exhortation, in holy sacraments and godly books, in everything that ministers to our spiritual strength and comfort and fruitfulness in good works, to our patience under suffering and resistance of sin, and perseverance in duty, and hope of the world to come. The two great means He is pleased to use are the Bible and the Church. The Church came before the Bible. Many ages before a word of Holy Scripture was committed to writing the Church of God existed on earth. Enoch was one of its prophets, and Noah too walked with God. "Then began men to call on the name of the Lord." Abraham had no Bible, no written revelation to guide him, yet he was the pattern of believers and the friend of God.

Thus the Holy Spirit strove with men of old and dwelt in them guiding them to the truth, though His grace was not given in the fulness which was manifested after our Lord ascended into Heaven. In process of time the book of the law was written by Moses and the writers of the History of Israel, and the Psalmists and the Prophets followed at great intervals after, adding by degrees to the inspired books of Holy Scripture, and last came the writings of the New Testament, not written all at once, but during a course of about fifty years, during which time the Church was growing every-where, built on the foundation of the Apostles and Prophets, " Jesus Christ himself being its chief corner stone."

The world was not converted to Christianity by scattering vast numbers of Bibles about the world. It was not a book that con-verted men, for the book, as a whole did not exist. It was not even written, much less printed. Men were converted by the living ministry of Apostolic teachers, guided by the power of the indwel-ling Spirit, proving their doctrine by miracles, and by the prophe-cies of the Old Testament to which they constantly referred and appealed. This appears plainly from St. Peter's first sermon on the day of Pentecost, and from the fact that St. Paul addresses his Epistle to the Romans, to Roman Christians " called to be saints," though they would have had very little, if any, of the New Testa-ment in their possession. Those who first brought to the Romans, the glad tidings of salvation through Christ were probably the strangers of Rome, whether Jews or proselytes, of whom mention is made in the Second Chapter of the Acts, as moved by the Holy Ghost to declare " in their own tongue the wonderful works of God."

Our great privilege is to have the whole Bible and the Church together. The Holy Bible is now complete. As it is the inspired

word of God we can neither take from it, nor add to it. It is closed
to the end of time. But the truth that comes to us in the Bible is
given to us by the living voice of the Church. We learn Spiritual
truth in the same way that we learn Natural Science. We are
taught it as children, we learn it as young men, not by picking and
choosing little bits of religion out of the Bible as our fancy please,
but by the ordinary teaching of the Church, *i. e.*, of those commis-
sioned to instruct us whether they be our natural parents, or our
appointed ministers, or the Church at large by her daily course of
instruction, her sacraments, her creeds, her large extracts from
Holy Scripture, her whole body of Truth.

Neither of these two gifts supersedes the other. The Church cannot teach us, as necessary to salvation, anything which cannot be
proved and concluded from the Bible, and the Bible sends us for a
sound interpretation of its words to the testimony of the Church in
all ages, received and professed by the general voice of all Christians, recorded in her Creeds, quoted in her Liturgies, and proclaimed
in her public assemblies.

Both those high and noble gifts are the work of one and the
same Spirit of God. We are not to receive one and reject the
other, our duty is to receive and be thankful for both, and to use
each of them in the order, and in the way that the Holy Spirit has
provided, humbly receiving, as children, mysteries beyond our
knowledge, advancing in the unity of the faith towards perfect
manhood, and to our dying day learning more and more, both from
the Bible and the Church, of what is the *Way*, the *Truth*, and the
Life which leads to everlasting salvation. Such is the gift of the
Spirit for which we thankfully bless God.

But the text also conveys a solemn warning to which every one
should give heed: *Quench* NOT *the Spirit.* This direction is a witness to the great and awful truth of our trial and probation. The
Holy Spirit is not given to us (as some teach) irresistibly — in such
a manner that when we have once received it we can never lose it.
Our Lord's parables point in the contrary direction. The ten Vir-
gins all had lamps given them, and oil to feed their lamps and keep
the light burning. In the parable of the pounds and the talents

the receiver was to trade with them and render the gift more valuable. Those who had the good seed were to receive it in an honest and good heart that it might bring forth abundant fruit. So the Apostle's words imply that we have it in our power to *quench the Spirit*, to put out the light, by unbelief and disobedience.

Fire was the symbol of the Holy Spirit's descent at Pentecost and it stood upon each of them. Even Judas Iscariot had his commission to heal miraculously like the rest, but he threw the gift away and became the traitor.

Observe them now, all the attributes of the Holy Spirit seem to give point and significance to the warning.

1st. He is the Spirit of *Truth*. Therefore hypocritical ways, false witness, the habit of lying and equivocation, the wilful denial of of Truth, the being ashamed of it, and refusing to own it, in order to gain popularity, the listening to sceptical objections without honest searching after Truth, the habit of slothful indifference to Truth, the mockery of jesting over the Bible, as if it were only half true and half false, the irreverence which listens to the Bible with a sneer, and never prays for the guidance of the Holy Spirit to make it profitable to the soul. All these come of evil and lead to evil. Therefore " *Quench not the Spirit.*"

2nd. He is the Spirit of *Purity*. Therefore the indulgence of uncleanness in thought, word, or deed, the telling of filthy stories, the reading obscene books, making a hero of the adulterer and the fornicator, the making light of unchastity before marriage, and generally speaking the words and deeds of an impure and corrupt life, these are of evil and lead to worse. Therefore " *Quench not the Spirit.*"

3rd. He is the Spirit of obedience. Disobedient children grow up to be wilful, headstrong, unruly, self-conceited young men and young women, and disobedient habits grow into hardness of heart, so that the Holy Scripture is a snare and a stumbling block rather than a guide, and the disobedient temper disdains humility, but loves pride and scorning, extravagance and dissipation and self-indulgence, and hates lowly self-denying ways which are well pleasing to God. Therefore " *Quench not the Spirit.*"

4th. He is the Spirit of Unity and Love. Therefore shun the quarrelsome, litigious temper, masterful, easily offended when no offence is meant, vindictive, thinking evil of others, rejoicing when harm happens to them, too independent to submit to the rules of the Church and to follow the pattern of the Saints, following after many teachers with itching ears and frivolous hearts, striving for wars and not for peace, "puffed up and behaving itself unseemly," and arrogantly boasting of knowledge but really ignorant of all saving Truth. This too cometh of evil and leads to evil. Therefore " *Quench not the Spirit.*"

5th. He is also the Spirit of Consolation, known by this gracious title, and so named by the Lord Jesus Himself. Seek not comfort then in avaricious ways, in ostentatious display of riches or of dress, for these things are a mockery of joy. They breed discomfort in the hour of sickness and extremity of pain, in sudden and unexpected losses, when the wealth of the world cannot buy an hour's respite, when sight is dim and memory failing and friends are helpless to assist us. Seek comfort in the light that shines brightest in adversity, in the support and strength ever given to the weak and friendless and desponding, in the hope that looks to the shining ones beyond the river, in the pure stream that makes glad the city of God, on the treasured promises that are "an anchor sure and steadfast" in the last extremity. All these blessings you may need sooner than you expect. It is the Spirit of God that seals them and makes them sure to the day of your redemption. Therefore " *Quench not the Spirit*"—the Spirit of *Truth,* of *Purity,* of *Obedience,* of *Love,* and of *Eternal Consolation.* Amen.

CHAPTER XXII

PRIVATE LETTERS—LAST EXTRACT FROM THE ANNALS—
PASTORAL LETTER—NOTES BY MRS. MEDLEY—ILLNESS
AND DEATH.

T HE following letters, written by the Bishop to a dear
relative in England, have been placed at the disposal of the author.   They exhibit another phase
of his life and character.   Some of the letters were written
at an early period.   The date of the last comes nearly to
the close of his life:

My Dear ——:   FREDERICTON, March 30, 1871.

H—— was so kind as to write to me a long letter, which I value
very much, containing many particulars of your dear husband's
death, and of the gratifying tokens of esteem and affection, which
were shown by his parishioners.

I need not assure you of our grief at the loss of one so dear to us.
His departure recalls many of the happiest and the saddest memories of my life,—the happiest and the saddest reminding me alike
of him, who was always a friend, and for so long a time, a brother.
Our last visit to you is as fresh in our remembrance, as if it had
occurred yesterday, and we constantly picture him to our minds, as
he sat at the table, and was the life and joy of the whole party.

I was spared what has proved so dreadful a trial to you—the
sight of his sufferings for so long a time, but I have not been permitted to witness his faith and resignation.   Accept, however, our
truest love and sympathy, and believe that we shall always think
of you, with the heartiest affection.

I was rejoiced to hear of H——'s plan, and trust it will be a great
help to you to share and promote his usefulness.   .   .   .   .

If you have any photo which you could spare, taken since we
were in England, we should value it very much indeed.

I am delighted with the idea of restoring the old cross.   I have
written to H——, but could not let the mail go without a few lines
to yourself assuring you of our sympathy.

(287)

FREDERICTON, Nov. 12, 1879.

My Dear——— :

It is always a great pleasure to get a letter from you, even when it is less quizzical than usual. I am glad you approve of the outward appearance of " Job," and I think you will agree with me that the printing is very clear and creditable to a Colonial establishment.

I hope also that you may like the matter as well as the manner, and find some instruction therein. It cost me a great deal of labour and my recompense will be to find some people, at all events, profited by it. The bookseller undertook the expense at his own risk. I sent H—— a copy.

I do not know whether Mr. —— told you that our Synod determined, by an immense majority of 102 to 20, to let me nominate a Coadjutor, when I desired it, who is to have the right of succession. As I shall be 75 December 19th (if I live) it begins to be time to get a little help, as well as to look out for the future.

It is astonishing how many of my contemporaries I have outlived, and how many juniors to myself are gathered to their rest. Every year adds to the number.

I had a long and laborious visitation this year, driving one day in a pitiless storm of rain 46 miles to keep an appointment, but I . stood it pretty well, except that on my return I had a lame knee (I believe from fatigue), which has kept me rather lame for a month. It is now much better, and I hope will soon be well. . .

We were very much interested in the visit of the Governor General and the Princess Louise. She went to the Cathedral. M—— and I showed her everything that was to be seen, and she took a most intelligent and appreciative interest in everything, even to our various beautiful altar-cloths, which she admired very much, and was quite knowing as to the different kinds of work. She was highly complimentary, so I hear, to M——, which, of course, I think was deserved.

Since her visit we have put in two new windows, by Clayton & Bell, and very charming they are — quite enriching the west end of each aisle — three-light windows.

I have to thank you very much for your very clear and pleasant group in a photo, which arrived uninjured. The photo of yourself is very good, but hardly looks as amiable as when I saw you last. M—— looks much older than I fancied him, but I think I saw him last in 1865—a prodigious interval, during which his hair has fallen off greatly. He looks less fierce than some of the others. I thought the boy looked as if he were just going to learn a hard lesson in Virgil or the Greek Delectus. But it is pleasant to think that no photo can prevent his smiles and pleasant looks over a plum pudding or gooseberry pie, or still more over a Christmas present from grandmamma.

We have been new-shingling our house this summer, i. e., covering the roof with wooden tiles, as is the universal custom here, as slates are seldom used. M—— superintended all the work, while I was on a visitation.

I forgot to say that we were especially delighted with the extreme simplicity, as well as with the gracious manner of the Princess. M——, who is a good deal of a radical, was quite won over, and I have not heard her talk radicalism since.

FREDERICTON, Dec. 9th, 1887.

My Dear—— :

I was hoping that you would kindly remember my birth-day, the 18th of this month, when you anticipated the day, and sent us both some mementos of the time. I ought to, be and I hope am, thankful for God's wonderful mercies to me, for I have enjoyed excellent health since my last birth-day, when I was 82, and now I have only nine days more to be thankful for 83.

I think every day of my life, of our old life at Truro—of your coming to see us, when our life was unbroken—when we all sat down on the green sward overlooking the long Ship's Lighthouse at the Land's End—of our going to St. Just four miles from Sennen, and going down the mine, and hearing the roll of the waves over our heads—of our trip to Falmouth harbour—of your temporary sojourn at Probus—of the great re-union at Kenwyn in 1836, of uncle S——'s sudden appearance and the text he preached from at

T

Kenwyn church, "She was a Widow," and then, the breaking up
of the family party,—last, but not least, of the ~~Vicarage~~ *Rectory* at ~~Sax-~~ *Way-*
mundham. . . . The world seems to roll on faster and faster
than ever.

It is a great pleasure to hear from you, of your son's well being
and well doing.

When one remembers the entrance into the next world, and of
what is going on there everything that is past seems invested with
a peculiar awe. I recollect what you cannot—my life at Southleigh, where the first days of my ministry were spent. How vividly
is that picture before me, as if it were only yesterday,—names and
doings as if they were just being done, and of how many I can say,
"They are all gone into the world of light and I alone left lingering
here,"—surely "Man walketh in a vain Shadow."

I *dream* of coming home next summer to the Lambeth Conference, but I do not know whether I shall accomplish it. I long to
see the dear faces again of such as are left, but most are gone.

I need not say what pleasure we had in J——'s too brief visit.
He was in high spirits, and was very stout and very rosy. I accompanied him and C— to Sussex Rectory and we spent three happy days
there, and then the parting came.   .   .   .   .   .   .

Dear M——t is much better. She had a long and very painful
illness,—prostration of the nervous system, with feverish nights,
which reduced her strength; but she now walks briskly about as
usual.

I was much amused with M—'s poetry.

What a state Ireland is in! Will it ever end?

The following letter refers to one of the greatest sorrows
the Bishop experienced in his entire life, and which we
have already referred to; viz., the death of his beloved son,
Canon Medley:

FREDERICTON, Aug. 24th, 1889.

My Dear——:

It is, as you said in your letter to M————, just a year
since our most happy meeting, and our uncertain parting, but not
then clouded over by "one being taken and the other left," and

saddest of all the one left is the oldest, the one taken one of the youngest of the party. How truly awful is the uncertainty of life, of sickness and of death! He whose health seemed so needful to be a prop and solace to the aged now called away and his assistance gone. His disease too, just what we should not have chosen; so very painful, yet on that account calculated to show forth his Christian faith, courage, patience and humility; but to those who stand by him, most certain to try their faith and to wonder why God hath done this?

The work of purification is no trifling sorrow: It is to us who witness it, "the spirit of judgment and the spirit of burning."

Dear C—! I saw him last Monday struggling for breath, and scarcely able to swallow, next Monday (the 26th) I know not whether I shall find him living. Many prayers are offered for him and all are needed.

I thank you very much for your kind and loving sympathy. . . .

I think the end cannot be far off. May God pardon and strengthen us and grant us His peace.

The Annals of the Diocese from which the extracts in this volume have been taken, with the exception of the first four pages, are in the Bishop's own writing.

At the close of the year 1889 we find the following notes in a tremulous hand:

This year passed amidst much sickness and sorrow, upheld by the Divine Helper and brought safely through.

For which all praise be to God. Amen.

The year following he again writes:

This year, 1890, sickness continued, and the Bishop was obliged to delegate a good deal of the hard work of the Diocese to the Coadjutor, who took it up willingly and kindly. The Bishop continued to preach in the Cathedral on Sunday evenings, and took part in all the festival services and daily prayers.

During the year the Bishop's strength was in some measure restored. He administered the rite of confirmation to a large number in the Cathedral on the 31st March, and in the month following confirmed at several of the churches in St. John, and preached on several occasions.

He was again in St. John in June. On the festival of St. Barnabas he writes in the Annals:

The Bishop consecrated the church of the Good Shepherd at Fairville. . . . In the evening the Bishop attended a meeting of the Board of Home Missions. This day 45 years ago the Bishop was installed in the Cathedral at Fredericton.

From St. John he went to Sussex on the 18th June and attended a service connected with the Choral Union of the Deanery of Kingston. The Bishop remarks:

It was well and reverently performed. On Friday he went to the grave of his dear son.

In the following August the Bishop left Fredericton for Chatham. He remained a few days at Bushville, the residence of the Honourable Judge Wilkinson. There he administered the rite of confirmation at the parish church, and consecrated a church. On his return he confirmed four persons at Moncton, on the 17th August, and preached in the evening.

The record continues:

Sept. 9th. The Bishop left home for Woodstock and Grand Falls. On Thursday he visited New Denmark, where he confirmed twenty. Holy Communion was celebrated and ninety-eight communicated. The congregation amounted to about two hundred, — all Danes. Canon Neales, who had accompanied the Bishop, assisted at Holy Communion, with the Rev. Mr. Hansen, who hospitably entertained us. Afterwards on Friday, the 12th, the Bishop and Canon Neales returned to Woodstock, after an Evening Service had been held at Grand Falls.

On Sunday, the 14th, the Bishop confirmed twenty-seven persons at Woodstock and preached in the evening. . . . . On Saturday, the 13th, the sad tidings reached Canon Neales of the death of his brother, the Rev. W. S. Neales, who had several years since been obliged to leave New Brunswick, on account of ill health. He resided in California, officiating for some years in San Francisco, where he was universally esteemed and beloved. He held the benefice of St. Paul's there, and was Secretary to the Synod in California. .   .   .   .

1891, July 21. On Tuesday, the Bishop left home for St. Andrews. He confirmed on the 5th August, twenty-four in All Saints Church.

On the 25th August, he left home intending to go to Sussex and Dorchester. He was laid up a week at Sussex, and was obliged to return to Fredericton on Saturday, the 29th.

The foregoing notes were made in the Bishop's own hand, and the following is his last record in the Annals of the Diocese :   •

1892. The Bishop issued a short Pastoral referring to his inability to continue the hard work of the Diocese.

PASTORAL.

BISHOPSCOTE, Feb. 23rd, 1892.

My Dear Brethren :

You are aware that some years since I thought it prudent, in view of a possible failure of health and strength on my part, to obtain the assistance of a Coadjutor, in order that the work of the Diocese might not be impeded. It has pleased God to take from me some portion of the strength which then remained, and I feel no longer able to undertake the laborious journeys which, up to a later period, God gave me strength to perform. Painful as it is for me to abridge any part of my former duty, I am obliged at the age of eighty-seven, to ask you to consult with the Coadjutor as to any confirmations for the coming year, and as to the administrative work of the Diocese in general, reserving to myself such work as is practicable for a man in my present condition. You will, I feel assured, not set this down to any want of affection or earnestness on my part, and will help me with your kind words and earnest prayers, that what remains of my life may be spent to the glory of God and the good of the Church over which the Lord hath made me an overseer.

Praying for a blessing on what has been done, and what remains to be done, I remain

Your faithful and affectionate friend,

JOHN FREDERICTON.

THE CLERGY OF THE DIOCESE OF FREDERICTON.

For the following account of the closing scenes in the Bishop's life, we are indebted to Mrs. Medley:

The Bishop's health and strength never recovered the blow of his dear son Canon Medley's painful death.

The heart's action became weak, and he was subject to attacks of faintness.

During the winter of 1891-2, he suffered much from neuralgic pain in the hand injured by a fall, but was able to take part in the daily service at the Cathedral, and to preach almost every Sunday evening. He appeared so well in July that he attended the meeting of the Synod in St. John. He opened it in person and was cheered by the clergy and lay delegates on taking his accustomed seat: they were so heartily glad to see him, and, as one remarked, "thought it so plucky of the old Bishop to be present."

He attended all the services in connection with the session, and specially enjoyed the Choral Evensong at Trinity, saying "he had never expected to witness three surpliced choirs taking part in a service in St. John!"

During his stay amongst them, the city clergy showed him much kind attention, of which he spoke most gratefully. On Sunday, July 17, he preached for his dear old friend, Canon DeVeber, at St. Paul's, and this was the last sermon.

During the week he went to Sussex, to visit once more his son's beautiful churches, and his grave.

Kneeling at the foot of it, "his white head bowed and bare," he had a short service. The 86th Psalm, 1 Thess. iv., collects from the Burial office and for "All Saints Day," and Hymn 428 — "The Saints of God." He then went to the Church, but seemed unusually feeble and depressed, scarcely speaking all the evening.

Next day he drove to Studholm Church, and to see the " Medley Memorial Hall," recently built, with which he was much pleased, and in the evening went back to St. John.

On his return to Fredericton the weather was extremely hot, and quickly prostrated him. It fell on the heart, still further lowering its action, and on the nervous system. He had sleepless nights and faint, feeble days, and in six weeks was worn out, and calmly and peacefully entered into rest—" The rest that remaineth for the people of God."

During his illness the Psalms, especially the Penitential ones, were his constant solace and support. On the Sunday before his death he asked for the xxvii. of St. Matt., the chapter which Bishop Juxon relates gave such strength and comfort to King Charles I. on the morning of his martyrdom. It was read to him at intervals through the day. The crucifixion made his tears flow, he said, " I never knew what *He* suffered for me till now."

He left messages to all his friends and to the clergy, repeating again and again, " Tell them my heart was full of love to them all." His dear Clergy for whom he felt such ample sympathy in their laborious work, and for whom his prayers were daily offered, were much on his mind, he often broke out with, " Oh my beloved Diocese, my dear Clergy!" The Cathedral bells chiming for Even-song always brought him back to consciousness, " Why there are my bells! yes, they are my bells!" he would say, and a gleam of pleasure would light up his face. The last connected words he uttered were from the Liturgy, " O Lamb of God, that takest away the sins of the world, grant me Thy peace."

On Tuesday morning he became unconscious and remained so till the calm and peaceful end on Friday, Sept. 9, at 8.30 a. m.

The tribute of respect to the Bishop's memory was universal and spontaneous, and only a very small selection can be made in these pages of all that has been written.

One of the clergy of the Diocese said :

As we recall the wise and true-hearted shepherd who has gone to the bright pastures and still waters of Paradise, of all he has been, and of all that he has done for the priests and the people in this Diocese, we may take up the Psalmist's words and say of him with grateful love, "so he fed them with a faithful and true heart, and ruled them prudently with all his power." The Bishop's last illness, his death, the carrying of his body into his beloved Cathedral by his Clergy, the watch all through the night, the crowded church, the thronged eucharists on the day of his burial, all told of a great burst of love, and respect and veneration, which his life in its truth, its simplicity, its unfailing courage, its deep and loving humility, called forth from all who knew him as a great Bishop of the Church of God.

Another wrote:

It is not easy at once to throw back our thoughts over the space of forty-seven years to that first summer and winter when the young Bishop began his journeyings in this region, and thence on to the later years, when he was called to "endure hardness" in the charge of this Diocese.

How feebly can we recognize what it meant and what it cost. In this, as in so much else, he was "an example of the believers," a true Missionary of the Cross, in toils, in perils, in travels, in exposure and hardship, in the persistent effort to gather the scattered members of the household of faith, to secure the funds, to find the priests, to found and strengthen the missions and parishes, to build the churches, to overcome prejudice, to bear the conflicts with ignorance, and still as the work grew to feel the burden heavier, and all the trials none the lighter, as misunderstanding and distrust so slowly retreated. One is amazed at what the grace of God did in that soul, and at the thought of how the spirit of ghostly strength dwelt richly in that ripening character.

The funeral services were held at the Cathedral on Sept. 18. They were most solemn, impressive and well arranged. Towards evening on Monday there was a short service at Bishopscote.

· A procession was then formed, consisting of the Clergy and choir. The body was reverently borne by six of the younger Clergy to the Cathedral. It was placed in the chancel at the entrance of the choir. The well-remembered face was scarcely changed at all. He appeared as if in a calm sleep. In his robes, with pectoral cross and ring, it seemed as if he must rise and join in the holy services he loved so well. The Cathedral was well filled at even-song. From 6 to 9 o'clock there was a continued throng to pass by the body and take a last look. All was so quiet, orderly and reverent! At 9 p. m. the coffin was removed to the sanctuary. It was watched over all through the night by relays of Clergy and laymen.

On Tuesday there was a celebration of the Holy Communion at 8 a. m. and afterwards at 11. Very large numbers attended. At 12 o'clock the crowd in and around the Cathedral was very great. Large numbers had come from the City of St. John and more distant parts, amongst whom were to be found representatives of the church corporations of very many parishes, and the St. George's Society of St. John. After the service in the church, including hymns 401 and 428, A. and M., the coffin was carried out by the six Canons, preceded by the band of the Infantry school, the Bishops and Clergy, and followed by a lengthened procession to the grave at the east end of the Cathedral, just beneath the chancel window. The spot is well chosen. There, in accordance with the oft expressed wish of the Bishop, his body rests in Christ under the shadow of the building which he so loved.

After the the benediction, hymn 140 A. and M. was sung. The whole service was most deeply impressive throughout.

On the return of the Clergy to the vestry the following minute was adopted:

"We the clergy, met together after having paid the last tribute of regard to our late dearly-beloved Bishop, desire to give expression to our feelings of deep mourning and sorrow.

" We call to mind his lengthened, constant, unwearied work in our blessed Master's service, his deep learning, his knowledge of the Word of God, his wise teaching in accordance with the doctrines of the Church of Christ.

" We shall cherish in our memories his frequent, generous gifts, his zeal and steadfast purpose in everything that related to the well-being of the Church in this Diocese.

" We regard his saintly life and high attainments as having been eminently fitted for the high and holy office which he filled for nearly fifty years."

The Lord Bishop was requested to forward a copy of the minute to Mrs. Medley, with an expression of the deepest sympathy and loving regard.

It was also proposed by the Clergy to erect a memorial cross at the grave.

Subsequently, a general meeting of the Clergy and Laity was held in the Church Hall, with the Lieutenant Governor, Sir Leonard Tilley, in the chair. A large representative committee was appointed to carry out the wishes of the meeting with reference to a memorial, the form of which to be decided upon at a later day.

The meeting of the Provincial Synod, on September 14, hindered the attendance at the funeral of the Bishops from the northern Dioceses. The Bishop of Nova Scotia was present, Archdeacon Gilpin and several other clergymen from that Diocese. Father Benson was also present. A telegram was sent by the Presiding Bishop of the American Church, expressive of his deep sympathy and affectionate regard and of regret at his inability to be present. The following was the inscription on the coffin :

"The most Reverend Father in God, John Medley, D. D., Lord Bishop of Fredericton and Metropolitan of Canada. Died, September 9, 1892. Aged eighty-eight years."

CHAPTER XXIII

Extracts from Letters to Mrs. Medley—Notices in the Press—Resolutions—Letters from Rev. Canon Brigstocke, D. D., and from Rev. Canon Neales, M. A.—Extracts from Memorial Sermons.

THE universal esteem with which the late Bishop was regarded found fitting expression in the letters of sympathy received by his bereaved widow, from which we are permitted to take the following extracts.

A dignitary of the Canadian Church writes:

The work which your great and noble-hearted Bishop did for the Church not only in his own Diocese, but in the whole of Canada, will only now be fully appreciated when it is set forth, as no doubt it will be, in some worthy form by those who know it best.

For myself I was greatly attracted to the dear Bishop when I first met him, now nearly thirty years ago, and felt even in one evening's intercourse how much of sympathy and help and *stimulus* his Clergy must have in him in their studies as well as in their work.

I felt too at once the charm of his preaching—so simple and yet so eloquent and profound, so penetrating—and all beautified and perfected by the savor of piety which ever encompassed him as an *atmosphere*. I do not know that I ever heard preaching that moved me so deeply in the best sense. If his influence was thus felt by one who saw him so rarely what must it have been to those to whom he was for years and years their Father in God!

A clergyman, ordained by the Bishop, but who has been working in the States for many years, thus writes of him:

I was confirmed and ordained Deacon and Priest by the Bishop, and have always had the highest admiration for his ability and learning. There is nothing in his death to regret; it was a full

(299)

life, full of days and of honours ; he accomplished a great work and
did it well. I well remember the opposition and difficulty he encountered in the earlier part of his episcopate, and how bravely he
carried the banner of true and loyal churchmanship through it all.
I shall remember him in every celebration as among the faithful
departed.

This voices the feeling of many other clergymen working
in the United States and in other parts of the Dominion.
A layman writes :

I cannot, even at the Bishop's advanced age, hear of his demise
without a keen pang of sorrow and a deep sense of irreparable loss.
And if this be so to me, how much more to you, the privileged
partner of all his labours, cares and joys ; how much more to the
bereaved Diocese, which was almost his own creation, and of which
he was in the fullest sense a Father in God. Among his many high
and noble qualities there seemed to be *two* especially godlike : First,
his great patience and silence under attack and injury, of which in
the earlier years of his episcopate he had so much to bear. He
lived down all attacks, and so far as I can remember he answered
none, at least in the public prints. Second, his great and unceasing
benevolence : receiving nothing from the Diocese, he gave it everything, even to the half of his income, and much more. But while
we mourn so great a loss, for him we can only rejoice, for, like a
ripened ear of corn, full of years, full of honours, and laden with
the loving prayers of thousands of his children, he dropped gently
into the garner of his Lord. *R. I. P.*

Another layman says :

At length the long struggle is over, and our dear Bishop is in the
rest of Paradise ! How blessed a rest for him after the weary days
and nights of the last few years. How often he must have longed
to lay aside his armour ; yet how patiently he waited his Master's
time. And now the earthly tie is severed that for so long a time
has bound the Diocese of Fredericton to its first Bishop, its most
generous benefactor and truest friend. It is hard to realize, but we

must all thank God for the noble life and bright example. Grant him, Lord, eternal rest.

Another friend writes :

The lesson of the Bishop's whole life seemed "patient continuance in well-doing." "For My sake thou hast laboured and hast not fainted." His devotional habits reveal the secret of his influence more than anything. Would that in this which seems the imitable part of his example one could in any way resemble him. He might have said, though he was too humble to do it, "Lord, how I love Thy law, all the day long is my study in it."

An old friend, Canon Townshend, now living in England, says :

When the dear Bishop was last in England he did me the honour to come down to see me ; as we stood by the grave of our old Rector we read the following lines on his tomb :

"Solo in cœlo quies
Et sine nube dies."

In that cloudless light our beloved Bishop now joins the song of the Redeemed, adoring with the holy Angels the Lord God omnipotent ! How blessed a thought is this, it is yours, and it is mine. Thanks be to God !

The Colonel of one of the regiments at one time stationed in Fredericton says :

Shall I ever forget his bright, hearty services and his trenchant sermons in that beautiful Cathedral which he had raised and adorned in every possible way, neither shall I ever forget his kindness and geniality to my wife and myself.

Lord Chief Justice Coleridge says :

It gave me a pang to hear of the death of my dear, old, honoured friend who has for fifty years been by me most truly and deeply honoured and beloved. . . . . He has been so intensely taken up with the duties that lay around his feet that he has not been known in England so well or so widely as he deserved, but Mr. Gladstone once said to me he thought " his was the wisest head that wore a mitre." His goodness, his accomplishments, his noble simplicity, I have seldom known approached in the experience of what is now a long life.[1]

Another correspondent in England writes :

How many delightful memories you have to sustain you amidst the daily trial? Every spot, every spiritual theme, even every cross will recall him in some way to you. How you must miss his melodious voice at the Cathedral,[2] his gentle, thoughtful, reverent manner, and the look of absorption in the worship, his hands folded in prayer, as they now are "in peace," his face radiant with delight, so quiet and intense in the Psalms and music, his manly, clear utterance, so full of faith in Divine truths and so pregnant with learning, and clothed in simple, terse, comprehensive English, his quiet tread along the aisle, or by the altar, with such an absence of self-consciousness, and the unexaggerated reading of Holy Scripture, devout, yet marked with true and subtle perception of the inner meaning and spirit of it all. "Truly a Prince, and a great man is fallen in Israel."

_Sa. J. J._

[1] In his life of Keble, Lord Coleridge gives a letter dated at Hursley Vicarage, 6th October, 1853, in which Keble writes: "I do wish to know whether you have any objection to appropriating the proceeds of the next edition of the 'Lyra' to Fredericton, for I very much wish to do something for dear Medley, and hardly know how to do it any other way."

Commenting on this, Lord Coleridge remarks: "I am unable to say what answer I returned as to the 'Lyra,' nor is it material; but I would not omit the question, because it is a testimony to a dear friend, one of the most sound, and zealous, and able of our Colonial Bishops, which it will give him a pleasure he well deserves to see recorded."

[2] The Bishop had a very melodious voice, and his reading was simply perfect. The late Principal of Education frequently said it was the greatest treat to hear the Metropolitan read the 15th of 1 Corinthians—the Burial chapter. It was a perfect piece of eloquence, every accent, every tone giving the full sense and beauty of that wonderful chapter. His reading of the daily lessons was looked forward to by many as a commentary on the chapter, and throwing new light on every verse.

Rev. H. W. Tucker, Secretary of the S. P. G. writes:

I heard of the death of the great and famous first Bishop of Fredericton with much sorrow. The Bishop's life and work has been familiar to me from my boyhood, and I shall always honour his memory as I honoured his life.

In conveying a resolution of sympathy from the Standing Committee of the Society for Promoting Christian Knowledge the Rev. W. Osborn Allen, Secretary, says:

The Bishop of Fredericton had been a member of the Society since 1828 and one of the Vice-Presidents since his consecration in 1845. We have therefore to mourn the death of one, who was not only a standard-bearer in the Church in Canada, but also one of our oldest members, and honoured Vice-Presidents. I find that in the ten years between 1880 and 1890, we helped him to build no less than twenty-eight Churches in his Diocese, our correspondence with him was always a pleasure, and we received from him many expressions of his gratitude. You alone can estimate the depth of your own loss, but it may be a comfort to you to know that the Metropolitan of Canada was honoured in England as a great figure, and a truly good man.

The Bishop of Bloemfontein writes from South Africa:

I feel I have lost a dear and revered friend, yet we cannot grudge him his rest after such a long, devoted and honoured life, and after passing through so many trials, so bravely borne. I would fain hope that in his place of rest he still remembers us who are struggling here, as we are permitted to remember him, and all other faithful departed, in our prayers.

Extracts could be made from more than five hundred letters received within the first three months of his death, and from the public addresses, but the above will suffice to show the universal love and veneration with which he was regarded.

It was remarked that on no previous occasion on the death
of any public man was the press in the province so unanimous in notices of regret, and in expressions of regard.

The following is an extract from the letter of a correspondent in the *Church Times:*

It may be well said of Bishop Medley what Dr. Maclear has
embodied in his able monograph on St. Augustine's college, viz.,
that he brought home to himself and to his clergy the great fact
of the spiritual and catholic character of the English Church, that
it holds entire and uncorrupt the inspired Word of God; it retains
and uses the three creeds which it has inherited from the earliest
times; it has in the works of its own famous teachers a rich store
of accurate and philosophical divinity; and it has ever been the
foremost in its witness to the cardinal truths of the incarnation and
sacrifice of the Son of God.

It would take volumes to tell of our dear Bishop's goodness to
"all sorts and conditions of men." By the poor around his home,
whether in England or in Fredericton, he can never be forgotten;
the sacredness of his personal share of sorrow and pain cannot be
more than named here; to his great generosity to his clergy their
churches, their homes, and, most of all, their libraries, bear abundant witness; to his full knowledge and great skill in administration,
to his strong and definite church principles, his diocese and every
parish and mission within it afford plentiful testimony.

His last illness, his death, the carrying of his body into his beloved
cathedral by his clergy, the watch all through the night, the
crowded church, the thronged Eucharists on the day of his burial;
all told of a great burst of love and respect and veneration which
his life in its truth, its simplicity, its unfailing courage, its deep
and loving humility, has called forth from all who knew him as a
great Bishop of the Church of God.

This short remembrance would indeed be incomplete if it did not
contain some tribute to our dear Bishop's wife. She, as his unfailing
companion and help-meet, has done more than can ever be known
here for the Church and for our Bishop; as she is still here, as all
hope and pray for years to come, more cannot be said than this, that

the Diocese turns to her with an expression of sympathy deep and true, because its love for the Bishop was deep and true.

The following notice is from another English paper:

In after years the good Bishop often related some of the amusing memories of his first experiences in the colony. From the first he set a fine example of simplicity and domestic life, so needful above all in a land where wealth confers the chief distinction, and where ostentation too often passes for the hall-mark of social pre-eminence. He was enabled to lay broadly and deeply the foundations of the Anglican Church in the Province to which he was appointed. Many spots in New Brunswick which were spiritually "waste places" on his arrival are now centres of spiritual enlightenment. As a preacher Dr. Medley's style was never wearisome or diffuse. He was a master of English, and he never talked over the heads of his people, but used pure strong Saxon that went straight to the head and heart. His services in the cause of church music, church architecture, and the better and more reverential performance of public worship are well known. In every sphere of life throughout New Brunswick his name will long be held in hallowed remembrance, while many in more distant places will bear witness to his piety, his singleness of aim, and his personal worth.

At the meeting of the Provincial Synod, held at Montreal, the following resolution was adopted by a standing vote:

That the Lower House of the Synod of the Province of Canada do place on record their grateful sense of the treasure possessed by the Church in Canada in the life and labours of the venerable and venerated Metropolitan, the Most Rev. J. Medley, Bishop of Fredericton, from the creation of that Diocese in 1845 down to this year of grace 1892. Forty-seven years' service in the sacred and laborious office of a Bishop of the Church of God marked by such unceasing and devoted labours and distinguished by such soundness of judgment and ripeness of learning cannot be summed up in any brief statement. The history of this ecclesiastical Province and of the Church in the Diocese of Fredericton is the memorial of the most reverend Father in God, for whose entrance into rest we bless God while we mourn our own loss.

That the Prolocutor be requested to convey a copy of this resolution to the Synod of the Diocese of Fredericton and to Mrs. Medley, with the earnest assurance of the heartfelt sympathy of the Lower House of the Provincial Synod.

Letter from the Rector of Trinity church, St. John:

ST. JOHN, January 10, 1893.

My Dear Canon Ketchum:

In complying with your kind request, that I should furnish some personal reminiscences of our late beloved Bishop, I must confess that I naturally feel a good deal of difficulty in making a selection from those that crowd on the memory, through the lengthened period of nearly twenty years, that it was my privilege to work under and with him.

From my first introduction to the Bishop in October, 1873, when I arrived from England to undertake my present duties, to the last time he was with me in Trinity Church in July, 1892, I received from him nothing but the greatest consideration and much personal kindness. As I was frequently associated with him in Diocesan work, it is almost needless to say that much occurred that called out diversity of opinion, and sometimes constrained me to take a line to which he did not altogether agree, but I never heard a reproving or unkind word. In one matter it was my painful duty to differ from him so much as even to record my vote in the Synod against a work which he had approved, but his charity did not fail, and no disturbance of his uniform kindness ever took place.

The first special mark of his favour I received in 1876, when the Bishop appointed me one of the honorary Canons of the Cathedral, and asked me at the same time to be one of the trustees of the building and its furniture. In 1888 he still further honored me by asking me to be his commissary during a lengthened absence from the Diocese, while he went to attend the conference of Bishops at Lambeth.

In thinking over his life and work, no one, I should say, could fail to admire his attachment to his clergy and devotion to his

Diocese generally. To the younger clergy especially he was indeed a father in God, and felt for them the warmest sympathy in their endeavour to grapple with the difficulties of their often widely extended and arduous missions. His frequent gifts of money and books, as well as his kind hospitality so freely bestowed on them all, leave no doubt that he bore with them the burden of ministerial labor, and held them in remembrance in his thoughts and prayers. The Bishop's attachment to his Diocese is the more worthy of notice, as the history of the Colonial Episcopate furnishes, alas! so many instances of Episcopal resignations, and return to the mother land. I do not believe that our dear Bishop ever entertained such an idea. It is well known that when he went to England for a visit, I think it was the last one, he stated that the happiest day he spent away was the one on which he put his foot on the steamer to return.   *O si sic omnes!* The Church would then have a chance of taking far deeper root in the land, and growing and expanding as we desire.

I must further say that in nothing did the Bishop's saintliness of life appear to me more conspicuous than in his simple habits and unaffected piety. The fashion of this world was not his guide, and it was easy to see how much he disliked ostentatious display. He even doubted the use of public meetings, because as he once said to me, people so often say on platforms such nonsense and speak so insincerely. Very closely did he follow the steps of the Master who came not to be ministered unto, but to minister, and whose voice was not heard in the streets.

I have mentioned above the time when I first met Bishop Medley; I must tell of the last scene. It was my privilege to be in Fredericton during his closing hours. The day before he died, as he lay quite unconscious of what was going on around him, I knelt with several others around his bed in supplication for Divine blessing and help in the parting strife. The next morning I was in his room at any early hour to know how he was. Apparently he was much the same. I knelt by his bedside and said the "Nunc Dimittis," and then took a farewell look. That was the closing scene. In less than an hour, the dear Bishop had entered into rest. The life of eighty-seven years, and the episcopate of forty-seven were ended.   It was a calm sunset after a life of long and glorious work.

I shall trespass no more on valuable space.   I feel it a privilege to have been allowed to make this brief contribution to the memoir.

Yours very sincerely,

F. H. J. BRIGSTOCKE,

Rector of Trinity Church.

P. S.—I herewith enclose a copy of the resolution passed by the Vestry of Trinity Church in memory of our late Bishop.

"We, the Rector, Church Wardens, and Vestry of Trinity Church, place on record our deep sense of the loss which the Church, in this Diocese has sustained by the death of its Bishop, the Right Reverend John Medley, D. D., which took place on September 9th, 1892, and the expression of our high esteem for his life and work.

We regard with much veneration his long episcopate of forty-seven years, and admire his abundant labours, his single-mindedness, and untiring devotion to the work of his Diocese.

By his great attainments, and high standard of Christian living, we readily recognize his eminent fitness for the office of a Bishop, and how richly he adorned it by his saintly life.   As comparatively few have attained his years in the Episcopal office, so we believe that few will be found who have more faithfully performed the sacred duties attached to it.

We offer our respectful sympathy to Mrs. Medley in her bereavement.

Further Resolved, That the Vestry Clerk transmit a copy of the above resolution to Mrs. Medley."

Letter from the Rural Dean of Woodstock :

WOODSTOCK, Feb. 14, 1893.

The last visit of our dear Bishop to our Deanery was made early in September, 1890.   On Tuesday, the 9th, he came by train to Woodstock to start the next day for New Denmark, but in the night he was taken so ill that Dr. Smith was called in under whose skilful treatment the Bishop soon rallied and recovered so rapidly that by noon he determined to proceed on his journey.   He would not if possible disappoint the Danes who were expecting him, and in whom he had always felt the very deepest interest.

I accompanied him by train to Grand Falls, whence we drove to New Denmark a distance of eight miles, the next day. The service at New Denmark was of a most interesting character, twenty persons were confirmed, and ninety-eight received the Holy Communion out of a congregation of about two hundred. It was pleasing to see the deep affection and respect of the Danes for the Bishop, as they gathered around him after the service to have him shake hands with them, and to speak a word of kind encouragement to them.

Service was held that evening at Grand Falls and the next day the Bishop returned to Woodstock, still feeling the effects of his late sharp attack of illness. On Sunday, September 14th, he administered Confirmation at St. Luke's Church, Woodstock, and in the evening preached. The next day he returned to Fredericton. This visit of our dear Bishop was a cause of great joy to us all though we were forced to feel that it was likely to be, as it proved, the last visit that he was to make us.

To express in few words the view which his life and character present to our minds, and the place he ever held in our hearts, would be impossible. As for me personally, the earliest recollections of my childhood are associated with him as friend and Bishop, and through all the years of my life and ministry his wise and loving character has ever been a deep and powerfully inspiring influence.

In our Parish he always seemed to take an especial interest,—as was shown by his ever kind intercourse, his wise guidance, his constant gifts in aid of the Church, and his fullest sympathy whenever any sorrow or trial befell us, either personally, or as a Parish.

And the Clergy of our Deanery have placed these few words on record. " To us his Clergy, he was at all times a wise, patient and loving Father in God, and the memory of his teaching and the example of his life will serve to encourage us in all our future labour in the Church of Christ."

THOMAS NEALES.

The following extracts are from sermons preached the Sunday after the funeral of the Bishop, in prominent churches in the City of St. John, by clergymen of different schools of thought.

From a sermon at the Mission Chapel of St. John Baptist, St. John, by the Rev. Pelham Williams, S. T. D., Priest in charge, from the text Psalm lxxviii. 73, the following passages are taken:

While there is a hush in the air and a shadow over the Diocese, men are saying to each other, "That was a great career which found its earthly close last Friday." That was a great heart, which beats no more; and a great brain, which has been bright, and clear, and busy for many a long year with the grandest themes and interests; and a great will-power, which pressed right on, right through, right over the most real hindrances and difficulties; and a great wisdom, which knew how to deal with knotty problems and perplexing facts; and a great courage, which never quailed or failed; and a great patience which could wait, and wait, until the storm should pass, and the turmoil should cease; and a great firmness which could not and would not yield one inch of holy ground, or Catholic truth, or lofty principle, or steadfast conviction; and a great perseverance, which could renew, in the fitting time and way, some hindered purpose, or baffled effort; and a great energy, which kept vigorous nerves in an old manhood, until its work was done.

One would gladly turn to those pictures in the long life-story, which would give us the sturdy boyhood; the diligent student at Oxford; the Curate serving in the rural life in Devon; the young Priest toiling in Cornwall; the Vicar and Prebendary under the strong Bishop of Exeter; then himself a Bishop, crossing the seas to serve and rule, in colonial life, a diocese not too ready to understand and appreciate, and uphold him; and then, at last, the Metropolitan, honored, trusted, revered, wielding all his power for the welfare of the Church; ruling with gentle and gracious dignity, enforcing respect, winning admiration; true to his work, true to his God, and true to the hope set before him.

Yet the sermon space is ever brief; and we may be content just here and now, to ask what gave to Bishop Medley, that vigorous, inflexible devotion to duty, at any and every cost, which made him the hero and the saint, and which fairly won for him, ere he fell asleep, the title of the Brave and Wise Bishop?

I. First, there was the clearest vision, in that strong and active mind, of the Catholic Church, as "the Church of the Living God, the pillar and ground of the truth." For him, who holds that verity, with an intense grasp, it is wonderful how much else is clear, in all the realms of faith and duty. Vagueness goes. Light comes, more and more. The Christ is not an absent Lord, but present with his priesthood, in His mysteries of the altar, under the veil of the written word, through His appointed means of grace, by His angels leading His people, and sending His Spirit of Truth into a world of ignorance, and darkness and error. The Church of God, militant here, guarding, defending, proclaiming, upholding the truth of God, cherishing that truth as her most sacred trust; living for it, glorying in it, and faithful to it above all things; it is just this when fully and fairly apprehended, which ennobles and intensifies a churchman's life. And it is this, my beloved, which is the prime element of power in the episcopate. There is the semblance of power indeed, which comes with some brilliant gifts, and exquisite culture, and charm of oratory, and skill in organizing, and perilous toleration; and with that so-called "breadth of view," which is only broad because it is neither deep nor high, and with that "charity," which at last gives away as much of the truth as it firmly retains.

Our Bishop, now at rest, was grandly restful while he wrought, because he held the Catholic Faith, which upheld him. In wearied and troubled moments there comes to us a "great calm," when we say the Creed very slowly. After a second or third repetition, very often the clouds vanish. When we have come to see again, with keen and patient glance, the Church, as the very ark of God, the sense of peace and security is renewed; and when we behold her, as the pillar and ground of the truth, then we know that all is safe and well, where that truth abides, which the Church keeps and maintains, for the saving of our souls.

II. If one word of St. Paul could be chosen, as symbolizing Bishop Medley's Episcopate, it might well be this,—" I magnify mine office." Never from that day when he first put on his robes to the day when last, with trembling hand, he took them off, did he ever seem to forget, or allow any one else to forget, that he was a Bishop in the Church of God. Whatever else he might be— courteous gentleman, ripe and accurate scholar, gracious host, skilful architect or musician, thoughtful counsellor, in all, but above all, the grandeur of his office lost nothing in his conscious estimate of its sacred dignity and its holy responsibilities. It is a cruel mistake, when men choose to think that this savors, in a devout servant of God, of aught, which destroys humility. Far from it. The humblest heart may recognize, with ever deeper lowliness, before God, the height of a great trust, which must not be imperilled, in our keeping. So, he magnified, that is, made great,—never him- self—but always that office, which had come to him, from the Shepherd and Bishop of our souls.

While his personal life was noteworthy for rare simplicity in all which pertained to fashion and style, he did not disdain, here and there, the symbols and tokens of his vocation, as the Bishop of a diocese, as the Metropolitan Bishop of a province, as the successor of the Apostles. Yet, it was never the outward claim as separated from the interior reality, but it was the harmonious recognition and exercise of power, which had come to him, and which must be made visible and forcible, for the sake of the highest ends and the very noblest results. Nor is it easy, at once, to measure the influence of such attitude and character upon the Episcopate of the whole pro- vince—upon the Episcopate of the future.

Extracts from a sermon by the Rev. J. deSoyres, M. A., rector of St. Mark's parish, St. John, from the text 2 Tim. iv. 7, " I have finished my course."

Many of you have heard that one whose life from any point of view was noble and memorable, has " finished his course." Already from the columns of the press words of generous acknowledgment —of merited recognition—have gone forth. Praise almost unmingled and yet truth ; for there are lives where the old and abused maxim, *nil nisi bonum mortuis,* can be exchanged for the better rendering, *nil nisi verum.*

But we can do more than echo the words of praise that are on the lips of all, irrespective of creed and party. At the end of a course so long and so eventful, we can judge — we can anticipate posterity itself, for many of us are the posterity of that generation which gave birth to John Medley, Bishop of Fredericton.

The preacher then alludes to what is called the " Oxford movement," with which it is well known the Bishop was in sympathy. He then proceeds :

But the people of his Diocese knew him in other respects than as a staunch upholder of one school of thought in the Church of England. They knew him, and I know that all respected and were proud of him as the manly-sided man — the man whose entrusted talents had not been few, and had been richly increased ; the man who in many, if not all intellectual qualities, stood above those who met him or opposed him.   .   .   .   .

But two gifts were especially his. Powers which, if not indispensable for a minister of God, are invaluable helps — the one for the work of rightly dividing the word of truth, the other as the means of making its teachings clear, intelligible, and felt by the heart. I mean scholarship and eloquence.

And another great gift he possessed was utterance, both by voice and writing. Not his the popular eloquence which is advertised and sent to market; not his the power, and far less the inclination, to startle or puzzle and excite to laughter in sacred places, or to the vulgar admiration which demands a coarse sustenance. But his was that true eloquence which depends upon accurate thought and exquisite fitness of language, pulsating with true feeling, like the gentle rise and fall of billows on a summer sea. And when that true eloquence is aided by the inflections of a voice like his, by an utterance simple, distinct, earnest and coming from the heart, it is a power for God.

Mr. deSoyres. illustrates what he has said by several

quotations from the volume of sermons the Bishop published in 1845, and concludes as follows:

With Christ his loved Master rests our good Bishop and Pastor. He has bequeathed an example to all of us, not in this opinion or that practice, but in the scheme of his whole life. He has left to Canada an example of a type which, whether in the mother country or the colonies, tends sadly to diminish — that of the gentleman who needs no lavish surroundings to prove his position and maintain his dignity, who is equal to himself in all circumstances. . . . . . He has left us the example of a citizen who was an honour to his adopted country, avoiding no duty, grudging no obligation, but knowing that it was in the due performance of his own work that he best proved his citizenship. Rarely he offered counsel; more often it was asked of him, and then he gave the ripe fruit of a keen intelligence and wide knowledge of the world, and a profound sense of what was due to a country's and a city's honour. And to us his subordinates, his spiritual children, especially, he has left an example most precious and yet most exacting. Though he never concealed his own firm and strong convictions, no one could have been, in his later days, as I knew him, more tolerant of legitimate difference, more courteous to adverse opinions within the limits of our Church.

What that example was in munificent generosity, in anxious care for his subordinates, in encouragement to young ministers, in scrupulous performance of duty, that is known to us all. May it be ours to follow in his footsteps! May his constant prayers for this, his beloved Diocese, be heard! May the good providence of God help us at the present time, assist the present Bishop, the successor of an historical episcopate, the inheritor of difficult responsibilities!"

In addition to what is here so impressively said, the following words of the preacher are subjoined, which were written during the Bishop's lifetime:

Let us think of the Cathedral placed by the river side forever afterwards his monument and his work. Of that moment when it seemed that it would never be finished, and how prayer was raised, and confidence survived, and then the generous and unknown contribution made all things possible once more.

What daring scribe will venture to dwell with needless emphasis on what all who read this journal know as the living and acted sermon of a life-time, that embodiment of the Christian and gentleman, blended so that each aspect is the necessary supplement of the other.

Who will dare to repeat the genial stories which the good Bishop (not seldom at his own expense) loves to relate, and relates so well, of amusing experiences in his travels, and of the records of intercourse with many minds, of which none left him unimproved or uncheered by courtesy or friendly word?

Who will speak of that perfect example of simplicity and domestic life, so needful above all in a land where wealth confers the chief distinction, and where ostentation too often passes for the hall-mark of social pre-eminence.

But of these things we need not write, because they are known. The people of this province know now, if they knew it not at first, and learned it but tardily, that they have among them one who in any century, and in any environment, could have stood in the foremost rank, not as a scholar, although his knowledge far outstrips many possessors of showy academical diplomas; not as an orator, though to listen to his preaching is the supremest luxury to a trained literary taste, and not one of his clergy even distantly approaches him; not even as an organizer, for the business faculty does not thrive perhaps in Devonshire; but in that mysterious result which men call character, which transcends all that men can *do* in what they *are*.

No figure at the recent Pan-Anglican Congress excited such attention as that of good Bishop Medley, who (had he wished it) might have preached in every Cathedral pulpit, and been spokesman at each banquet. Around him scholars of European reputation like Lightfoot and Stubbs, preachers like Magee and Boyd-Carpenter, yielded willing deference. And we believe that none can have read without emotion the notice of that service in the little village church of Lullington, where the Bishop and all his sons met together for a last meeting, perhaps.

CHAPTER XXIV

IN the course of his labours in the preparation of this work the author has received many letters of interest from those who had known Bishop Medley intimately. The presiding Bishop of the Church in the United States, the Right Reverend J. Williams, D. D., LL. D., Bishop of Connecticut, writes as follows:

MIDDLETON, Conn., Nov. 17th, 1892.

My Dear Canon Ketchum:

Absence from home and a great press of work since my return have prevented me from making earlier reply to your favour of last month.

I am very glad to know that you are preparing a life of your revered and beloved Metropolitan. It will be as heartily welcomed in the United States as in Canada or England, and I rejoice in knowing that it is in such good hands.

The first time we had the pleasure of seeing your late Bishop in the United States was at the General Convention of 1853, during the session of which he took part in the consecration of the Bishops of North and South Carolina, and preached the sermon on that occasion. I well remember that after that sermon, or, possibly, after one of the addresses which he made, the late Bishop Potter of Pennsylvania said to me, " What a full man he is."

He was with us again at the General Convention of 1883, and I think, at that of 1877. In this way as well as in others he became widely known among us; and for him to be known was also to be honoured and loved. When he "came to his grave in a full age, like as a shock of corn cometh in his season," there was sorrow and a sense of bereavement far beyond the limits of his own Diocese and Province.

It will always be one of my own cherished remembrances, that he honoured me with his friendship and regard.

(316)

Wishing you all success in your labour of love, I am, my dear Canon, Faithfully yours,

J. WILLIAMS,

Bishop of Connecticut.

P. S.—I hope the volume will be put on sale in our principal book stores.

From the Bishop of the adjoining Diocese of Maine, the Right Reverend H. A. Neely, D. D., the following letter was received:

My Dear Dr. Ketchum:

I feel that your request for some word from me to appear in your forthcoming biography of the late Bishop of Fredericton and Metropolitan of Canada should not be unheeded, and, indeed, I would gladly embrace any opportunity to express my appreciation of the excellence of the man, and of the value of his work. I could not, however, hope in anything I might say from personal knowledge of either to give any information additional to that which will elsewhere be furnished in your volume, and, therefore, in complying with your request, will restrict myself to a brief account of the impressions made upon me when brought into personal contact with my beloved friend, Bishop Medley. My interviews with him were not very frequent or prolonged; for though in charge of adjacent jurisdictions, home duties were very exacting. The first of those interviews was on the occasion of the consecration of your own Church in St. Andrews, twenty-five years ago, and I well remember both the kindness and cordiality of his greeting, and the warm terms of respect and regard with which he alluded to my venerated predecessor, the late Bishop George Burgess. He then struck me as being (according to the common American conception) a typical Englishman of the cultured class, who could, however, both conceive and recognize excellence in other lands, homes and institutions than those of England. A further acquaintance with him strongly developed this first impression, and did not thereby lessen my admiration of his character. Honesty, courage, firmness, resolute persistency in labours and under trials, without show or boasting, these seemed to me to be among his strongest natural traits, and with them may well have been conjoined a temper, which would be impatient, especially of any manifestations in others of cowardice and moral flimsiness. These are the distinguishing moral qualities of a good soldier and successful leader, and to them may doubtless be ascribed some measure of the success which crowned the life-work of this eminent man. But not less conspicuous in him were those spiritual endowments and the tokens of that inward discipline without which a real and worthy success in the work of the Christian ministry is unattainable. One could not fail to note that his eye was single to the service of his Divine Master, and that in that service he had subjected himself, his will and judgment to the methods and precepts of his Chief. He was ruled by no selfish ambition, he sought not his own glory or the praise of men; he was distrustful of his own wisdom. Whatever may have been the dominating natural traits of his character, the meekness and gentleness of Christ had attained in it a manifest supremacy. Strong and tenacious in his own convictions, and frank in the expression of them, he was neither narrow nor harsh in his judgment upon the views or acts, much less the motives, of others. In the exercise of his high office he had no disposition to assert for himself a lordship over God's heritage or demand an unquestioning submission to his personal authority. And how self-sacrificing he was in his labours, how abundant in deeds of kindness, how considerate of the wants of his whole flock, there are hundreds to testify. Of the thoroughness and sturdiness of his churchmanship and of his attainments as a scholar and theologian, I will say no more than that for these the name of no Bishop or Doctor of our sister Church is more honoured among us.

The brief estimate which I have presented of his characteristics as a man and an administrator is, I know, very inadequate, but I trust that it will not be regarded as wholly indiscriminating.

I had thought that I might send you one or two letters in evidence of my own indebtedness to his unfailing kindness and affection, but find that those which I have received should hardly be published.

The Bishop of the Diocese of Albany, the Right Reverend William Croswell Doane, D. D., LL. D., writes as follows:

ALBANY, N. Y., Nov. 9th, 1892.

My Dear Brother:

You put upon me a duty which is really a privilege in asking me to add a word to the life which you are proposing to publish of the venerable Metropolitan of Canada.

My personal association with him dates back to some of the earliest and most sacred memories of my life. He was my father's very true friend, and during the painful and trying days of my dear godfather, Dr. Croswell's difficulties in Massachusetts, he was his brave and loving supporter.

He is indelibly connected in my mind with the founding and supporting of the Church of the Advent in Boston during its troublous time; and I have the most vivid and grateful memories of his clear and courageous positions in the various Lambeth Conferences at which I had the honour of being present with him.

His bright and genial kindness to me when I had the pleasure of being his guest at Bishopscote, at the consecration of the Coadjutor, are lifelong and delightful recollections. And I feel that to no man on the continent of America more than to him is due the great advance in all things that tend to the upholding of the Catholic faith and order in America. He was Nestor and Patriarch really among us all, and was more closely identified, I think, with the Bishops and with the interests of the American Church than any English Colonial Bishop has ever been in America.

I venture to add the words which I have written for my own Convention in regard to his death, which perhaps you will think worthy of insertion in the volume which is to commemorate his long and most useful and distinguished episcopate:

"Almost one of our own Bishops, the beloved Metropolitan of Canada has been so identified with the growth and life of the Church on this continent, that we mourn his death as though one of our own number had been taken away. He was a power in the Catholic revival. He came to America exchanging the sacred shades of Oxford, the companionship of its great scholars and schools, and the serene sweetness of English pastoral life, for the bleak and barren loneliness of what New Brunswick was fifty years ago.   He was a scholar of rare ripeness; a born leader of men; strong as a lion in his maintenance of the faith; full of elegant accomplishments — architect as well as musician.   And he was a man of most holy, self-denying life, to whom " to live was Christ," to whom we humbly hope " to die" has been " gain," for all the grave and grievous loss to us."

An eminent layman of the Church in the United States, one of the delegates to the General Convention, Causten Browne, Esq., of Boston, writes:

My dear Canon Ketchum:

You have asked me.to set down in writing my recollections and my estimate of your late Metropolitan, the revered and beloved Bishop Medley.   My first feeling has been that of gratitude for the opportunity of contributing anything, however slight in value, to the memorial you are preparing of that truly great and good man ; but now that I set about it, all that I can say seems so inconsiderable and so inadequate that I would gladly be excused from the attempt.   We all know how near you were to him in his confidence and affection.   You can tell us all more about him than any of us can tell you.   And yet it may be well and acceptable to the readers of your memorial if a voice, and particularly a lay voice, comes from the sister Church to say how we too loved and honoured him, claimed our share in the pride of possessing him while he lived, and claim now the right to mingle with yours our grief that so noble and beautiful a life is ended.

It is the simple truth to say that wherever Bishop Medley went among American churchmen he inspired the warmest affection and the profoundest admiration and respect.   He was recognized everywhere as an absolutely first rate example of an Anglican bishop. We all knew him for a theologian and scholar of distinguished learning, a forceful preacher and writer, and in social life a most interesting and delightful companion.   I believe that no Anglican bishop that ever came among us was more admired and respected than he.   I am sure that none ever came nearer to our hearts.

It is delightful to me now to remember my own intercourse with him, if I may not even say the friendship that existed between us. For no man that did not come within the circle of personal friendship could know, or begin to know, the charm of his character and deportment. Never for a moment failing in the truest dignity, he enjoyed social life frankly and heartily, and while he made it radiant and delightful by his genial spirit, he elevated it always by the sweetness, gentleness and simplicity of his bearing. He was indeed a singularly charming gentleman. All the while he was "every inch" a bishop. One's warmest affection for the man never displaced or obscured the sentiment of veneration for his spiritual office.

If I should try to single out one aspect of the Metropolitan's character which was most impressive, it would be the union in him of personal meekness with a lofty conception of the dignity, authority and responsibility which belong to his order. He was utterly without personal pretension or self-assertion of any sort; but with respect to his office, its rights, its powers, its duties, he was as unyielding as the rock.

The last time I saw him he was visiting a very small and poor insular parish in your Diocese, and, manifestly for some good and peculiar reason in the circumstances of the parish, he preached upon the subject of peace, peace-making and peace-keeping. It was a noble sermon in its simple and earnest eloquence; the heartfelt talk of a father to his children. I shall never forget it. The exhortation to brotherly love and to the cultivation of peace among Christian men came from his lips with almost Apostolic authority, while it seemed at the same time to be the spontaneous pouring out of his own sweet and lovely spirit.

I know, my dear Canon, of how very little worth is what I have written; but you must take it as the expression, not only of my own affection and veneration, but of that which I can truly say was inspired by Bishop Medley wherever he went among our American churchmen. You may be perfectly sure of finding here sympathetic and interested listeners to all you will have to tell us of one whom we so loved and honoured.

Believe me, always sincerely yours,

V   CAUSTEN BROWNE.

One of the Canadian House of Bishops, the Right Reverend Charles Hamilton, D. D., LL. D., Lord Bishop of Niagara, writes:

Hamilton, 14th Oct., 1892.

My Dear Dr. Ketchum:

My veneration and affection for our Metropolitan prompt me to do all in my power to aid you in gathering up and preserving all that will be of interest in his life and acts and words. I wish that I felt myself in a position to furnish you with some points, which may be overlooked by others.

My first recollection of him is in the Cathedral of Quebec and its pulpit in 1850, when the North American Bishops assembled there in conference. I was too young to appreciate or remember his sermon, but the remarks of some of my seniors as to the clearness and force with which the Bishop presented the question of Apostolic Succession fastened themselves in my mind. He made many friends in Quebec in his several visits to our venerable Bishop (Mountain) and his son. His advent into our Provincial Synod brought to all a sense of additional power and confidence. You have the sermon which he preached at the opening of the session and his address which produced a strong impression upon all.

Bishop Nicholson, of Milwaukee, in his address to the recent Provincial Synod, as a member of the deputation sent by the American Church to greet us, gave us a very touching and attractive account of a sermon preached by the Metropolitan in Philadelphia on the words: "Speak the Truth in Love." His fatherly interest in me at the time of my consecration went down deep into my heart and bound me very fast to him. It was a relief to me in my troubles and in the hard questions that have beset me since to write freely to him as my Most Reverend Father, and I think that he valued my confidence and affection.

My opportunities of intercourse with him were, however, very few, so that I have no storehouse to draw from for acts and words which are not already and better known to you.

Believe me,
Yours very sincerely,
Charles Niagara.

Colonel George J. Maunsell, Deputy Adjutant General of New Brunswick, an old and valued friend of the late Bishop Medley, contributes the following interesting letter:

FREDERICTON, St. Andrew's Day, 1892.

Dear Dr. Ketchum:

You have most unexpectedly asked me to add a few biographical details to the already abundant stock of evidence you possess as to the place in the heart of his people occupied by our dear Metropolitan Bishop. In thus asking a layman, one, though, who has had the great privilege of "sitting under his preaching" for over twenty-five years, and one of the oldest living members of the choir, whose efficiency he had so much at heart, you may naturally expect a fitting reply, yet no words can adequately convey any idea of our sense of veneration, love, respect and esteem for him who has, without our being able to realize his absence from our midst, peacefully passed from a life of incalculable usefulness to the Paradise of God.

"No fading frail memorial" his! Neither the beautiful Cathedral, he laboured with a labour of love and with much faith and prayer to build, and in which he so often worshipped, nor the many spires pointing heavenward, which speak volumes for his valued active influence in this diocese of churches, include all that tends to "keep fond memory in her place and certify a brother's love." "His *unconscious influence* will endure treasured up in the eternal world, where nothing really great can be lost or pass away, to be revealed at that day when God's Book shall be opened, and the thoughts of all hearts be made known."

Yet one should not hesitate to add a word, however feebly, if it contained anything that may serve to bring to light any of the hidden treasures of a life full of lessons of good, of "duties well performed and days well spent." In the first place may be noted his desire for accuracy, his leaving nothing undone to master every detail. This was always apparent in the training of his choir.

In looking backward to days of Costers and Carters, Streets and Wards, Ewings and Roberts, all remarkable for musical taste and skill, no choir practice was considered complete until every anthem

and introit, every chant and hymn was perfect. ⟩ Happy memories
of the choir practices and genuine hospitalities at Bishopscote will
linger so long as life lasts.   I remember distinctly his asking a
member of the choir whether he considered a new piece of music
correct in some particular; on receiving in answer, " I take it for
granted," he administered a severe rebuke, speedily followed by a
kindly smile—and who can forget those well-known " kindly smiles "
of our good Bishop ?

A word about his own personal musical taste and skill, his rare
talent as a composer and lover of music, may not be out of place.

Those competent to offer an opinion have pronounced many of
his anthems, introits, chants and hymn tunes as worthy a place
amongst the best collections of such music.   Amongst others is the
opinion of Harvey, the great composer, and Major A. Ewing, his
dear friend and companion.   His anthem, "They shall hunger no
more, neither thirst any more," is undoubtedly one of his best,
though no Christmas anthem gives me more pleasure than that in
which he so beautifully gave prominence to hymn 62 A. & M.:
" While shepherds watched their flocks by night."

In all his compositions careful study of detail is plainly seen.
No inaccuracy, however slight, in seeking for effect, can be
discovered, while there is abundant harmony and proof of genius
throughout.   In all this is apparent the same principle that prevailed in all his literature, where the pure and undefiled Anglo-
Saxon type, in all its freshness and beauty, stamped its every line.
There is no straining effort for ornate wandering style or poetic
vagueness.   His conversation was full of " finesse " and humor,
while in condemnation of fraud he " hit from the shoulder."   His
stock of knowledge was varied and great.   Another characteristic
was his unfailing care to keep every appointment, to fulfil every
engagement, his earnest effort to overcome every difficulty.

" Memory dear " carries me back to a mid-winter appointment of
our Bishop to hold an evening week-day service at St. Peter's
church, Kingsclear, and to share the evening meal with a friend en
route, such appointments in the case of others are subject, at that
season, to the proviso, " weather permitting."   No such proviso in

his case. One of the most severe snow storms ever known in these parts prevailed on the day appointed. The host of the evening made no preparation for the now not-expected guest, the roads being quite impassable it was considered. Knowing, however, the Bishop's determination to overcome difficulties, the would-be host set off on snowshoes along the road, where no track was to be seen.

He had not gone far when, to his surprise, he found the Bishop, in sleigh with weary horses, plodding along through deep snow-drifts. On being remonstrated with for coming on such an evening when there could be no congregation, there was the well known smile as he replied: " No congregation! I fully expect to see *you* and the *sexton* in church," and such was almost the extent of the congregation, when after a never-to-be-forgotten drive, encountering heavy drifts and deep snow, though with fresh horses, the host brought the Bishop in safety to the church.

A brief anecdote may not be without interest in proof of the Bishop's desire to teach a practical lesson on every possible occasion, in every-day, common-place life — on this particular occasion the lesson of patience.

In days before the opening of the Intercolonial, Canada Eastern or Canada Pacific railways, a journey to our northern counties was not made so easy as it now is. An " extra " stage, wagon or sleigh, via Chatham, or the sea voyage, Shediac to Dalhousie, had to be resorted to. The Bishop had ample opportunity to test both of these weary means of locomotion. On one of these journeys by " extra " stage both Bishop and driver were long silent, the former, well knowing that the driver was an inveterate smoker, and that the Bishop's presence alone prevented him from smoking. The Bishop at last broke the silence by inquiring after the driver's health. The latter replied, saying he was quite well. "Something is wrong," said the Bishop, "and I know what it is; I only wished to try your patience. You are longing for a smoke; pray smoke to your heart's content." Joy and gladness took the place of dull despair in the heart of the driver. The Prelate's command was immediately obeyed, and the practical sermon on patience will never be forgotten.

As a classical scholar, a divinity student, and a "great Captain" of the Church Militant, Bishop Medley is well known and appreciated. I can speak of his love of military history, of his many valued proofs of being the "soldier's friend." As relaxation he would turn again and again to "Napier's Peninsular War." He had a thorough knowledge of every detail of the strategy and tactics connected with the battle of Waterloo and the Peninsular campaign generally. He was an ardent admirer of that great military captain the Duke of Wellington. On one occasion he came suddenly into the office of a military officer at Fredericton, and at once put the question to him, "Why did Wellington form *goups* (oblong form), not *squares*, at a certain point in the battle of Waterloo?"—a question that might have puzzled many a military student. On receiving an answer he was satisfied. He had, he considered, acquired knowledge not previously possessed by him.

On another occasion he came into the same office with Sullivan's tune for "Onward Christian Soldiers" on his lips, which he rightly said is a grand march tune, and as he hummed the tune and paced the floor to this quick-step he looked every inch a model British general officer, a "great Captain" indeed.

Whenever practicable, too, lover as he was of a military band, and cheering to him as it was to see the soldiers march to its strains to church, he brought the band into his Cathedral in connection with special services. In this he was, he well knew, but praising the Lord "with the sound of the trumpet," while he never ceased to urge upon his people, "Let everything that hath breath praise the Lord."

No mere outline of a biographical sketch could possibly be complete without a word of reference to his helpmate, the good Mrs. Medley, who has been his stay and comfort amid all the "changes and chances" of his well spent life. The value of her services as the Bishop's wife will never be fully known this side the grave.

To her the chiefest solace, greatest joy—"thoughts of good together done;"—"To us may grace be given to follow in their train."

Yours most faithfully,

G. J. MAUNSELL.

The following letter from Lieutenant Colonel A. Ewing, the composer of the well known hymn tune " Jerusalem the Golden," is particularly interesting in connection with the Bishop's great love of music :

THE LAWN, Taunton, December 28, 1892.

During my residence in Fredericton in the years from July, 1867, to September, 1869, I was much associated with my dear and revered friend, Bishop Medley, in the music of the Cathedral. He was his own precentor and choir-master. The Cathedral choir (which, of course, was a voluntary one) consisted of persons of both sexes and of all ages, of various social stations. Naturally its members were not exempt from the natural (and not unwholesome) rivalry which is so frequent in such circumstances. Musical amateurs are proverbially "kittle cattle," and it required much tact and constant watchfulness to maintain efficient co-operation on the part of all its members, inasmuch as those who considered that they were not allotted their due share of "solos," were sometimes disposed to be recalcitrant (a phenomenon by no means peculiar to the amateur choir of Fredericton Cathedral).

In this field the Bishop laboured with the unceasing energy and assiduity which he displayed in everything to which he set his hand. Besides superintending in person the practices of the choir (a duty in which he was good enough to allow me to assist him), he continually enriched its repertoire by anthems, services, hymn tunes, and chants of his own composing, which, even at the time I am speaking of, formed a large collection of important MS. works. I am, of course, unable to say whether he continued to write music after my departure ; but, at the time to which I refer, the music of the Cathedral was completely "up to date," the repertoire comprising everything of importance, both old and new, which one might have met with in any home cathedral.

The music of the church was always one of the Bishop's chief cares. If he went from home he would carefully plan out all the music for the calculated period of his absence, leaving it in my hands to carry out, during my residence there.

He was good enough to allow me to relieve him, to some extent, of his duties as choir-master, as well as to accept one or two compositions of mine, written on purpose for the Cathedral, which are probably in its repertoire now. I consider that it would have been difficult to meet with a better service out of England. I have heard many a worse in this country in places of considerable pretention.

I always remember with much delight my association with him in the Church music, and the fact that he himself took some pleasure in this association. One of my most valued possessions is a collection of Motetts, by Palestrina and other old Italian masters, which he presented to me, and which bears the following inscription in his handwriting: "Alexander Ewing, from his sincere friend John Fredericton, in remembrance of many happy hours spent in the service of the Church of God. Fredericton, April 8, 1869."

Yours faithfully,

ALEX. EWING.

The Rev. F. Alexander, Sub-Dean of the Cathedral at Fredericton, also makes the following fitting reference to the Bishop's musical ability:

A memoir of our late beloved and venerated Metropolitan would be incomplete without a short notice of his musical talent and ability. For the Bishop possessed an enthusiastic love of music and was no mean connoisseur of the art itself. He had studied carefully the famous work of Marx, and was in the habit of minutely examining the compositions of the great masters of church music.

It was in the days of the great Samuel Wesley, under whose care and direction the cathedral choir of Exeter had assumed an importance and efficiency second to none at that time in England, that the Bishop occupied his Prebendal stall, and we may feel assured that it was while thus connected with the Cathedral that he received the most valuable musical impressions of his life. Certain it is that he brought with him to New Brunswick a knowledge of music that enabled him to take his place, and, *nemine dissentiente*, for forty-five years to keep it, as musical conductor, as well as head and director of his Cathedral choir.

Those who had the privilege of belonging to that choir will retain vivid recollections of the pleasant weekly meetings, for practice, in the drawing-room of Bishopscote, and the kindly welcome extended at such times to each member. Next to his Cathedral, perhaps, the Bishop loved his choir, though, as he has often remarked, nothing, not excepting his Diocese, ever caused him so much trouble as the management of this small, but musically, refractory body of people. But it was a labour which the Bishop loved, and none will forget how, when met together, all cares of office put aside, the often harassed look upon his face would pass away and the features shine with a happiness beautiful to witness. Not less striking was the zeal and enthusiasm with which he would throw himself into his work ; the active mind alert to notice the smallest indecision or mistake, while a vigorous movement of hand or foot, oftentimes both, would testify to the importance he attached to *time*.

Of the Bishop's love of music, and his diligence in its study, his compositions, which are numerous, bear abundant testimony.

Among some twenty anthems he has written, in order of merit, that to the beautiful words, "They shall hunger no more, etc.," occupies, perhaps, the highest place. Remarkable for its religious feeling, its natural and effective progressions strongly impress the listeners with the spirit of the words. Of shorter compositions, "Turn Thee, O Lord," and "Show me Thy ways," characterized by a free and flowing melody and a grave and solemn treatment consistent with the subject he is treating, deservedly take a place among the best of those in anthem form. A very effective feature in the former of these two is introduced at the words "For in death no man remembereth Thee" by a change of key, and the form of harmonic treatment adopted is worthy of our best composers.

Of his "Services," all of which are pleasing, the "Te Deum" in B flat, and the "Deus Misereatur" in E flat, are certainly his best efforts in this form of composition. Often sung in his Cathedral in Fredericton, they are ever hailed with pleasure, indeed are among the compositions of which the congregation never tire.

In the various collections of chants and hymn-tunes which have been published from time to time, may be found several bearing the

Bishop's name, while a number of his anthems, published by Novello some years ago, have found a ready sale, and particularly at St. Augustine's College in Canterbury, and in his former cures are frequently performed and always enjoyed.

The Bishop's great interest in every benevolent enterprise is seen in the following letter from Lady Tilley:

CARLETON HOUSE, January 22nd, 1893.

Dear Canon Ketchum:

I am sure you will be interested in a letter which the dear Metropolitan once sent me in regard to the Victoria Hospital at Fredericton.

He felt that it was too great an undertaking for a woman to do alone, and advised me to call a public meeting or consult with the older heads of the town, as he would feel keenly should I fail in the attempt. It was all so kindly meant, and I thoroughly appreciated the good advice. But when I wrote and told him that I had laid the matter before God and asked for Divine guidance, and that under His direction I feared no failure, the answer came from him saying, if that was the spirit in which I intended doing my work, he would add a blessing with an enclosed check for $100. It was so like his dear kind way of doing everything, always ready to respond to an appeal for good. His memory will long live in our hearts, and our lives will be better for having felt the sweet influence of his friendship.

I remain,

Sincerely yours,

ALICE TILLEY.

The following tribute to the memory of Bishop Medley by Mr. George E. Fenety, of Fredericton, is of special interest and value as coming from a *layman*, whose personal intercourse with the Bishop was intimate and long continued:

If the Bishop was at home in his church so was he at home in the dwellings of the most humble of his flock. Instead of folding his episcopal robes about him and standing aloof upon the dignity of his order, he ever seemed to feel it his duty, no less than if he were the humblest curate in the land, to visit the poor and sick, the widow and the fatherless in their affliction, and minister to their spiritual comfort and not infrequently to their pecuniary necessities. Many instances might be cited in support of this statement; one or two will suffice.

In a humble dwelling a young man lies sick and near his last. The good Bishop is seen beneath that lonely roof and in the presence of death spends hours together in the dark hours of night, even up to 12 o'clock, and not until all is over does he retire from the scene and wend his way homeward, and this long after he had passed his eightieth birthday and at a season of the year when only the vigorous and strong among the clergy might be supposed to be abroad engaged in the works of mercy and benevolence. A young woman, a domestic, is suffering from an incurable complaint; day after day the good Bishop visits her, talks with her, encourages her as to her future hopes, and to soothe her sensitive mind in regard to her worldly indebtedness, which disturbs her not a little; he promises to assume all liabilities and tells her to make herself easy on that score. The poor girl dies and the Bishop's promises are fulfilled. The very last time he was out of his house was in paying a visit to an old colored woman residing near Government House. It was only a few weeks before his death that he engaged a coach for this express purpose as he had frequently done before.

In the Sunday school he was at home among the children; until recently he was a constant visitor, and the children, even the most infantile prattler, were delighted at his coming and taken up with his fatherly admonition and kindly ways, and his tact in winning them over to a consideration of their childish duties and responsibilities. He sang among the children as though he were a child himself, standing in the centre of the group. He was indeed the great lode of the Sunday school. The children will miss him sadly and the teachers feel they have met with a loss that can never be repaired.

I have (as a journalist) known Bishop Medley since the day he landed in St. John in 1845, most of the time personally and intimately, and perhaps no other person at the present day has a better knowledge than the writer of all his ways and actions, whether in or out of the church, and therefore in a position to testify without presumption to the great services he has rendered, not only to the Church but to the Province at large, by means of the work he himself had set out to perform at the beginning, and which he lived long enough to see so abundantly blessed. No one can duly estimate the loss of such a man to the Church at large, and it is to be hoped by all Churchmen that the work he so nobly commenced and ably carried on, will continue and prosper, under wholesome guidance, but the place of Bishop Medley is not easily filled.

The Bishop was a man of strong and resolute will in all matters ecclesiastical, due to religious convictions, and yet in asserting himself towards those who differed with him he was gentlemanly and suave. There were times long since gone by when his lordship and some of the churchmen of his Diocese could not see alike; in two cases particularly which led to considerable friction and some irritation, but after a time it was generally conceded by those who took an active part in the respective disagreements that it was for the good of the Church that the Bishop was actuated and so harmony was once more restored.

Since then there has not been a single ripple in the Church as regards the Bishop and his people.

In his habits the Bishop was simple, frugal and unostentatious and always approachable by the most humble. Nor had he any deep-rooted prejudices. While he was convinced that his Church was of Divine origin, and while he was exacting in the loyalty of his people towards her, he frequently bore testimony to the zeal and good works performed by Christian denominations outside the Church of England.

I was present on the delivery of his first and last sermons in this Province in 1845 and 1892. At the time of the Bishop's arrival the Rev. Dr. Gray, of Trinity church, St. John, was pre-eminent as a theologian, able scriptural expounder and pulpit orator. The Rev. Mr. Harrison, of St. Luke's, Portland, was also regarded as a very able man, and his curate, Rev. Harrison Tilley (son of our

Lieutenant Governor), gave promise of occupying at no distant day a very high place in the Church, but alas he was cut off prematurely in the midst of his usefulness and prospects. When Bishop Medley arrived in St. John great expectations awaited him, from the knowledge many of us had of his great popularity in England long precedent to his coming out to New Brunswick. His first sermon fulfilled and gratified the hopes entertained of a sure success as time should go on in his new field of labour. As a preacher Bishop Medley was plain, practical, forcible, learned, and easily followed and understood even by the most illiterate; and, after all, the command of attention is the true standard of eloquence. His sermons were masterly pieces of composition, without superfluity of words —rather, every word fitted into its place as in a mould, and there was no room for another in the same sentence; while his delivery was forcible and highly effective, so that his listeners were always firmly held and benefited.

As an instance of the good Bishop's thoughtful regard for the members of his flock, I might state that only a few months before his last illness I was confined to the house by an attack of rheumatism, and in consequence, for the time deprived of the privilege of attending the Cathedral services. The Bishop then called upon me on Monday mornings and read to me his sermon of the day before. This he doubtless did with others detained from the house of God by sickness. He was a "Father in God" in the truest sense of the word.

As a composer of church music Bishop Medley would have held rank among the Masters, had not the Church demanded his services. His Anthems, Te Deums, Introits, Chants and Hymns are among the most beautiful sung in the Cathedral at the present day. Indeed, what is called classic music has no such charms as the Bishop's to non-professional ears; and it is to be hoped that his memory will forever be kept green in the Cathedral by a continued performance, at the right seasons, of these beautiful compositions.

Mrs. Robinson-Owen, formerly of Campobello, N. B., an old and highly esteemed friend of the Bishop's, contributes the following letter:

BELFIELD, Tenby, S. Wales,
6th December, 1892.

Dear Dr. Ketchum :

Thank you much for your letter of 8th November, which I only received this morning and hasten to answer it.

I am afraid I have no incidents to record of our dear Bishop's long and valued friendship which could be of general interest. His friendship was steadfast and warm, as you know, and like all his sterling qualities, unfailing. I have a few of his letters written in our times of sorrow and bereavement, but unfortunately when we came here in June for a lengthened period, I left them with other possesions at Dindlesham.

I suppose you know that the first place in his Diocese upon which he landed was Campobello. My father, then Capt. W. F. W. Owen, R. N., in command of the survey of the Bay of Fundy, took H. M. S. "Columbia" to Halifax to await his lordship's arrival in 1845 and brought him and his family, etc., round in the ship, calling at Campobello (on account of the grave illness of one of my children) for a few hours on the way to St. John.

The dear Bishop's interest was shown by deeds in every parish in the Diocese, but Campobello seemed to benefit specially and ever found him a generous patron and most loving shepherd. The experience of many, if not all, must be like my own. In weal or woe he was a sure and tender friend, and the house of mourning always brought his ready presence when possible and his deepest sympathy. Every sorrow found in him a responsive chord as I can well record, and he certainly fulfilled the apostle's injunction to " Rejoice with them that do rejoice," as well as to " Weep with them that weep."

His intense truthfulness, too, made his friendship such a real thing. One knew he never could say a word that he did not mean. I think you will agree with me that wherever he touched the daily life of those committed to his charge, he influenced them for something better than they had thought of before. All this is simply truism and not a bit what you want, I know. No doubt you know the incident at the Pan-Anglican in 1878, at Lambeth Palace, when our dear Bishop spoke so nobly to the Archbishop about the P. W. R. act, for I suppose Canon DeVeber was there. Bishop Medley was so Catholic minded that I hope that incident may be contributed. I don't know whether it was in consequence of that, but I fancy it was, that Mr. Mackonochie presented our Bishop with a gold chalice.

I know Mr. John Medley has written to you, and perhaps has given you much valuable information about the Bishop's life in England. Believe me,

Yours very cordially,

C. ROBINSON-OWEN.

The labour of love, undertaken by the writer with much diffidence and a deep sense of inability, is now brought to a close. By very many instances of kind encouragement and valuable aid the work has been greatly lightened.

The endeavour has been to present the record of a life and work such as have not often blessed the Church of the Living God.

If in reading these pages any one is led more fully to follow him as he also followed Christ, the chief end proposed will have been attained. A marked, a saintly character is brought out, both by what he has said and by what he has taught.

The name of Bishop Medley may be included among those of whom it is said: "Their reward is worthy of them; their memorial shall never perish; the wide world is their sepulchre; their epitaphs are written in the hearts of mankind; wherever there is speech of noble deeds their names will be held in grateful, loving remembrance."

"HE BEING DEAD YET SPEAKETH."

www.ingramcontent.com/pod-product-compliance
Lightning Source LLC
Chambersburg PA
CBHW020942030726
47496CB00005B/1319